PREVALENT INSANITY

Patrick Gallagher

D1570427

Amazon Direct Publishing

Prevalent Insanity
By Patrick Gallagher

ISBN:

Amazon Direct Publishing

Technical support by Mia Paltrow-Murray

For Irene Bradley

Prologue

'In his diet the Irish peasant is remarkably frugal.... Tea is drunk in enormous quantities, and of formidable strength... The visitor...in Donegal will generally see a pot of tea simmering...summer or winter, night or day....Tea is often the only extravagance which the poorer classes in the north allow themselves....A good deal of the prevalent insanity is traced to excessive tea drinking.'

The Standard Library of Natural History, Vol. V, Living Races of Mankind, New York, 1908

Editors and Special Contributors:

Charles J. Cornish, F. C., Ernest Ingersoll,
Sir Harry Johnston, K.C.B., Sir Herbert Maxwell, F.R.S.,
H.N. Hutchinson, F.R.G.S, and many other eminent naturalists

CHAPTER ONE

For one or the two-hundredth time Kevin O'Donnell threaded the story through his mind: A cool April evening hovers lightly around the figure of his great uncle, Philip O'Donnell. Philip O'Donnell is standing on the sidewalk, in the middle of a block of white frame buildings. Dormant flower boxes and wooden shutters of dark colors delineate the nearby windows. In the street, the black shapes of horse drawn vehicles rattle past him. Riders unseen behind canvas curtains are likely jostled by unyielding springs, while the knock of the hooves balances the screech of wooden wheels. Hissing alive in glass housing, gas lamps extend their nearly perfect circles of influence. Philip has stopped walking in order to savor both the scene and the moment. He may have thought, I'll photograph this street some day. A sensation of joy had suddenly mushroomed through his chest, threatening to invade his head with vertigo. By coming to a halt he was able to avert the dizziness. He concentrated on the flush of happiness that billowed inside him like a silver-lined cloud.

It was a San Francisco street that flowed around Philip. However, it was not the street alone that affected him. The shook of good feeling that embraced him flowed from several sources. Like a mildly intoxicated gourmet quietly picking delicacies O'Donnell selected the reasons for his high spirits. He had finally arrived, he thought, he had found the right place. He could proudly claim membership in a profession and becoming a man of some means was within his scope. For the first time in his life he had equity in the world. Prior to this he had been a traveler, a seeker, a man in random motion. A latter-day Marco Polo, he had ventured out not from prosperous Venice, but out of an impoverished Irish countryside: beautiful Donegal, with craggy, turf-clad hills, peat smoke lounging eternally in doorways, and rock-fenced farms hugging the moist glens. A haunting vision of that setting shown likes a gilt-framed masterpiece in his mind. On a straight line drawn on a map, his journey was six thousand miles—half Atlantic Ocean, half United States. His migration had taken ten years. By his reckoning he had actually tracked ten thousand miles on the American continent and he had grasped a generous portion of life. Unlike Marco Polo, however, he had no intention of returning to his homeland and enthralling his countrymen with stories about unknown geography and exotic cultures. But wait, he thought, that's not completely true. There *were* the letters. In the middle of each month for the last ten years he had sent a letter about his travels to his parents in Glenties, County Donegal, Ireland. He tapped softly at the breast pocket holding this month's version, the envelope thicker than before because he could afford to send them ten dollars. This largesse pumped him up as if it were one hundred. He intended to mail it in the morning.

The font of Philip's economic well being and the structure of his workday were based on a contract to photograph San Francisco.

The people famous, colorful, and commonplace; the city from its precipitous vantage points; the cold, current-sliced bay, alternately fog-topped and glaringly sunlit. The mundane details of life seen on any sidewalk, but here, played out with a sense of excitement, possibly even danger, lurking nearby. O'Donnell's earlier work in the west had attracted for him limited attention and no general recognition. He would have scoffed at calling it *Work*. "I have these pictures of Indians and such," he told the editor, a bristling man in need of striking photographs of frontier cities and with an ability to pay half decently. A five-minute review of the photography, a one-ounce glass of brandy, and Philip was put to work.

He proceeded walking again, moving on a stretch of flaking slate paving into the April coolness. Philip was five feet, nine inches tall—a very respectable height for his generation—with short legs that emphasized the size of his trunk, making him appear heavier than he really was. As he ambled on he seemed to have no particular destination. That, however, was far from true and his mind worked with the abruptness of flash cards. A private magic lantern show of city scenes entertained him. These were photographs that he had recently taken or contemplated. Fishermen in green mackintoshes slapping tuna the size of church statues on the slick, weathered wharf. A large laughing seagull on a breezy morning, patient as a decoy, reminiscing atop a solitary piling. Laborers shoveling a small mountain of red earth in a Chinatown building site and the intricate cornice on a substantial new house on Pacific Heights. Five or six decades prior to this San Francisco wore a primitive, frightening face. But now progress and sophistication floats at you with a smile at every intersection. That very morning Philip had met and photographed the renowned tenor, Enrico Caruso. Development at such a delirious pace was both exciting and unsettling. The friction generated by the momentum of the new grinding away at the old was an intangible that Philip pursued.

Philip was wearing his newest and his best clothes. His suit was of finely woven black wool, the smooth texture of it pleasing to the touch of his left hand. He grasped a box of chocolate truffles in his right. To think that individual threads could meld together so evenly—well, give thanks for small miracles. The tailor had exclaimed in apparently honest delight at its quality. O'Donnell had never owned nor worn anything so fine and the tailor's excited whoops boosted his satisfaction with it. In a contrast of color and feeling, his shirt was bright white and correctly starched. A thin ribbon of black silk made a bow tie at his neck, and his head and his outfit were topped off by a stylish derby. All in all, Angela's love of finery should be deeply gratified by it.

He was at her front door now. Her home was a towering brownstone, three stories in height, with soft ivory light escaping from deeply recessed windows on the middle floor. The oak door had a stained glass panel, which was sectioned into octagonal shapes by thin lead piping. Philip rapped briskly, and, as the noise sank into the house, his resting fingers could feel a cool, damp glaze on the glass. He shivered, imperceptibly, and thought, ah, the best part of the night is still ahead. Angela herself opened the door for him. He knew that she was excited because her maroon linen coat was already on and she pulled at the buttons while clutching her gloves in one hand. Aunt Emily, tall, white-haired and elegant in a black brocade dress stood some distance behind her in the wide vestibule. The lamp above her head acted like a spotlight, reminding Philip of a character from an opera he had seen with Angela. In his lighthearted state he half-expected the old woman to leap into song—some shattering, tragic, unintelligible, Italian tale of woe. Instead, she nodded to Philip in a stately way and withdrew into the house. The candy Philip brought was for her and he left it on a console table by the door. For the first time he noticed that his formal photograph of the family had supplanted the reproduction Etruscan vase.

Their destination for dinner was the Palace Hotel, on Market Street. They rode there in the dark back seat of a hansom cab, resting on green velvet upholstery pulled taut over a hard bench, silent much of the way, but holding hands with supple fingers loosely entwined. Philip loved the Palace Hotel; to him it was a gigantic layer cake of gray stone, eight stories of substance and elegance. Imposing yet inviting to someone in his highly charged state. He had to restrain himself' from thrusting his head and shoulders out of the cab for a better look when it came into view. Angela was more than tolerant of his antics, more likely to laugh than protest, but Philip did not want to shatter his elevated mood. Tonight had a special feeling and he would act accordingly.

Inside the soaring hotel lobby, which was dressed up in marble tiles and suspended succulent palms, near the bustling, chatting cloak room, he got his first direct look at Angela that evening. He felt expansive enough to willingly share it with two portly men seated in wing chairs who were pretending to read the San Francisco *Chronicle*. The three of them admired a women of twenty-two (ten years Philip's junior) with thick black hair, wide-set brown eyes, soft, dark complexion, wearing a new lavender dress; the dress had sleeves delicately ruffled leading to white cuffs set softly against her pink fingernails. Perhaps he was deluding himself, but he sensed that her heart was racing slightly as he had removed her coat. But from three feet away she looked coolly composed. When Angela was in a new setting — this was her first visit to the Palace Hotel — or confronted with new circumstances, she met the situation with deliberate moves, holding her body erect, as if she had a sore rib cage. When Philip taught her to use his cameras, she initially handled the apparatus as if it might explode. The shutter release could have been a dynamite plunger. But within a month she handled the equipment with authority, snapping in a photographic plate like a blouse button. She would swing a wooden tripod under one arm, step over a low fence or a narrow stream, finding secure footing with a casual glance, talking the whole time, as effortlessly as if she were pouring cappuccino. In the Metropolitan Opera House, her beloved opera house, Angela fairly pranced. She waved to other patrons and sang along under her breath. Tonight, at the luxurious Palace Hotel, following the maître'd single file into the dining room, Philip ached to set off this kind of transformation in her.

"When will your father get back," Philip asked. They were finishing an appetizer of Dongeness crabmeat and muscles delicately soaked in

Napa Valley chardonay. "Papa and the boys won't be back for a few more days. What's today? Tuesday? Thursday, perhaps. Whenever they go to look at a new fishing boat they stay a few days. Papa likes to sail it out on the ocean and test it against the current and the wind."

"Won't you and Aunt Emily be afraid to be alone? I guess the dogs are good company."

Sometimes Angela talked to him as if for the first time. Her brown eyes would widen and look directly at him. She would speak very slowly and appeared greatly interested in the impact of her words. "The dogs are usually alert and protective," she was saying. But didn't I tell you? They've been acting so strange today. This afternoon we couldn't find them for a while. I was afraid they had jumped ever the fence or something, but Aunt Emily found them hiding under the porch in the back of the house. You could hardly see them under there, they melted into the shadows, and they were whimpering like puppies."

"Those two big hounds?" Philip's surprise was genuine.

"Yes. And they wouldn't eat. And when I was getting dressed this evening Lazarus let out a howl that could give you the shivers."

Both were silent for a while. Philip was unconcerned about the dogs; It might just be a reaction to the exotic eggplant dishes that Aunt Emily fed them. However, he was mildly worried that Angela would want to go home early on their account. "Speak about howling," Philip said, brightening, "I took some photos of Enrico Caruso today."

"You devil. I think he's performing Carmen at the opera house. I've never seen him. But why were you shooting him?"

"I've often taken portraits of the local big shots. They pay me directly sometimes. But an editor wanted Caruso's photo while they're out here. Yesterday, I did a series of shots on Sullivan. The fire department chief. Now there's a man to scare you."

"Why," Angela asked.

"Not him, exactly. His stories. He said that, since San Francisco is mostly wooden buildings and frame houses, we're especially susceptible to fire. And there's these mammoth underground cisterns that could hold an inland sea of water for firefighting. They are less vulnerable than pipes to the collapse of buildings. Or earthquakes. Except they're dry now. And the city won't bother to fill them."

"Well, San Francisco burning of falling down doesn't scare me," Angela said, smiling, "because I live in a stone house."

Their dinners were nearly finished: beef Wellington medium rare, scalloped potatoes encrusted in herbs and sautéed in light cream, string beans almandine. An expensive bottle of French burgundy, the best quality Philip had ever ordered. Philip's earlier exuberant mood had softened, but at a higher than normal plateau. The thought hit him that Angela was still a mystery to him, with much yet to be discovered. He had known her just six months. Her mother had died when she was ten, and Aunt Emily moved in with them. The loss, Philip believed, had nurtured two opposing characteristics: independence and vulnerability. Drawn closer to her two brothers, she still had a tomboyish streak. She had taught Philip to throw a base-ball like a native. On photo taking trips to Russian Hill, she had to be persuaded not to follow him as he clambered up fog-slicked balconies or trees in search of better vantage points. But she could be as excited as a child about ducks in a pond or marionettes dancing to a twinkling music box. She was a powerful, soft, fetching, delightful mystery.

Leaning over the table, speaking just above a whisper, Angela asked, "What ever happened Sunday when Papa and the boys took you out on the boat? Georgio and Papa kept looking at Julius and would roar laughing."

"I thought we would die on that boat. From laughing, not drowning. You know that I had an idea of taking pictures from a camera suspended on a kite. It's not original. I saw some fellow try it at the Grand Canyon. I doubt it has ever been done from the bay here. A carpenter down in the Mission District built me this great box kite and helped me rig up a camera on it. What a contraption it became, with braces and canvas and loops of wires. But it worked. I wanted six good exposures for a panorama. Julius was holding both the line to the kite and the cord to the shutter release. I had one eye on the kite, the other on the city. It was a devil of a time to get the camera facing the right way. The breeze kept twisting it these cockeyed angles. When it was in position I'd yell 'Pull the cord now.' Unknown to me, just before we took the last shot, a sudden gust of wind pulled poor skinny Julius like a sparrow right off the deck, and him still holding both lines to the kite. He was trawling up to his knees in the bay. But I yelled 'Pull it now, Julius,' and damned if he didn't. I look around and they're hauling him in like a load of abalone."

"Did the photo take?"

"Yes. It was too late in the day to try another one. I developed them that night. It was as good as the rest."

They savored the story as if for dessert. The bill for the evening was laid beside him on a silver plate. A glance at the total took Philip aback. It was six dollars more than he had estimated, a casualty of the expensive French wine. The green bottle of Chateau d'Lichon had an elegant golden label depicting poplar trees standing as if at attention, lining the gravel drive to a Renaissance manor house. The empty bottle, standing at ten o'clock against his dinner plate, mocked him silently. A sense of embarrassment gnawed at him because he would have to shortchange the superb waiter Eduardo on his tip, the very fellow touted in the *Chronicle* who had only recently learned English, overcome a slight stutter and the handicap of two fingers mashed in a freakish bocce accident. The solution came to him quickly—he had ten dollars in the letter to his parents. His mind worked as fast as flash cards again. Angela might recognize the overseas envelope if he pulled it out here. And with her prosperous father out testing a third fishing boat. Philip did not want her to know that he was sending money to his parents.

"Excuse me a moment, Angela. I've been meaning to speak with the hotel manager." He scurried to the lobby, feeling like a giddy, guilty schoolboy. Light beads of sweat emerged under his starched collar. First seating himself, he removed two five-dollar bills from the letter. He was in one of the wing chairs occupied earlier by the fat gentlemen. One of their newspapers was sprawled on a butler table, with an absorbing drawing on page one. A pen-and-ink drawing of Mt. Vesuvius erupting. The column said that the volcano had been stirring for several days. What photographs to take, Philip nearly said aloud. Volcanic ash drifted silently down as a deathly black snow, topping off terracotta flowerpots, roof drains, and public cisterns. Local citizens—even the farm animals—were hysterical. Cows would not milk; cats crouched on rooftops; dogs burrowed under sheds like badgers and sometimes howled like wolves.

Fresh, chilly air surrounded and followed them as they left the Palace Hotel. Angela clutched Philip's arm affectionately. Why waste time, he thought. I'll get things moving. "Angela, remember I told you I had a surprise in the works?"

"Y-yes."

"I've gone and rented me a little house." She had stopped walking and turned towards him, her left knee bent lightly against his wool pant leg. Again, her eyes were wide, alert and her words slow and distinct. "Have you left the boardinghouse and moved in yet. Is downtown here?"

"On Jessie Street. Not far from here. Come, have a nightcap there. Your father will never know you've been there."

It was a two-story brick house that crowded a 20-by-40 foot lot on Jessie Street. A gabled roof carved to resemble a sailing ship bow reached over the front of the building. Chips of dusty white paint curled up like pouting lips from the shutters, one of which was askew from a rusted hinge. Reaching the front steps, Philip threw his arms out dramatically and exclaimed, "My Fire Chief' Sullivan Special." On his insistence, Angela accepted a small glass of sherry but did not sip from it as she toured the first floor. The kitchen was sparsely furnished, but the dining room and parlor were still empty, except for tacked up photographs of Indian scenes above the mantelpiece, pine floorboards of random-width creaking in surprise at their trespass. One hand rested on Angela's hip; the other held up her sherry glass as if it were a lamp as she reviewed the photos intently, almost reverentially. At times she gave his efforts such respect it made him feel old. But right now he felt wonderful — excited, tense, adoring, lustful. And his thoughts were as clear as crystals: he knew now that for at least one day in your life everything comes together like a perfect focus. The happiness did not seem fleeting, or forever just over the horizon. The pleasures could be savored, and touched, and be just as real as this lovely young woman. He explained that the bedroom in the back of the house would become his darkroom. After the third match, he lit a lamp in the middle bedroom, illumination expanding in a ball tuned to the whisper of the gas, revealing stacked wooden boxes of photographic plates and chemicals, plus two cameras and the wigwam skeleton shape of collapsed tripods of various sizes. The master bedroom was crowded with furniture: a brass bed, two wardrobes, a teak desk. Philip nearly felt compelled to explain what a piece of groaning work it had been hauling this stuff in here, but cut himself short. He pulled Angela towards himself instead.

Now she made him feel veryyoung, being such an enthusiastic lover. Her uncoiffed hair cascaded ever her shoulders, over skin that was as tan as her face even though it had rarely seen the sun. He tended to be serious when he was in bed with a woman, but she opened up to him such a glistening, precious softness, kissed him as if to suck the air out of him, and, with the fresh, vital scent from her body cutting through the light mask of her perfume, Philip laughed aloud with surprise.

It seemed only moments later when he was aware of the dawn. Heavy gray light slowly receding to blue. Philip observed the eternal see-saw of the rising sun leveraging down the shadow line on the yellowing wallpaper, gradually unveiling a line of Grecian urns entwined with ivy. But why was it so silent? Were there no birds on Jessie Street? Blinking open an eye still sticky from sleep, his pocket watch read 5:17 a.m. Philips thoughts were nearly as dim as the light, but he calculated that they could get Angela home well before her aunt awoke. Aunt Emily was not in the habit of waiting up for her, and as Angela said, she slept like the dead. The expanding daylight continued to revive him in mind and body. The unexpected visits you everyday, he said to himself, nestling on his left side against Angela, a couple of cozy spoons, his face pressing her long hair and his right arm finding a soft pillow of her breasts. Often he had imagined that Angela initially would be a shy, reserved, even stiff-limbed lover, and not the graceful, flowing, passionate woman she had been in reality. He had hoped to be the teacher, but she made him the pupil.

"I see you moving. Why waste this opportunity," Angela whispered. Philip tossed aside the quilt and rolled upon her like a wave. Deafening sounds louder than a freight train, at a decibel level that was felt as well as heard, started coming in their direction from the bay—as if many, many freight trains were now right on Philips's block on Jessie Street. But there were no railroad tracks nearby. Angela may have had time to think, My God, it can make the earth move, but nothing more. Joists straining at every bolt, the gabled roof of the house stayed mostly intact and barely hesitated on its descent to ground level, looking like a sort of landlocked ship crashing through a breaker of noise. The plane of particles thrown skyward, with distinct dark eddies enveloped within larger cumulus billows, was, on this crisp and fogless morning visible to fishing boats several miles out on San Francisco Bay.

CHAPTER TWO

It may have happened that way. In any event, it was Kevin's favorite version of the story. His thoughts about his great uncle Philip O'Donnell and Angela faded like a movie ending, he almost expected to hear stirring music to embrace the scene. His modest state of tension ebbed along with it. It was early afternoon and Kevin O'Donnell was sitting in his office, alone. Today, Kevin would give his last lecture of the spring session, one of his "special lectures." He was an assistant professor in the American Civilization department. In the previous year, the university had awarded Kevin the Lucius MacRobbins award for teaching excellence. He was the first "Am Civ" professor to be so honored. Carefully encased in a custom-made gold leaf frame, with double matting in blue and tan, the coveted certificate hung on the wall just above the budding avalanche of paper on his desk.

Thirty-seven years old, Kevin had now taught at the university for four years. Few of his colleagues could hope for the MacRobbins salute in a thirty-year career. His special lectures were peak performances that brought students to their feet, cheering. They would talk about particular highpoints for months. There was a theatrical element to these class sessions, and he liked to sit quietly beforehand, soaking up concentration and energy. He hoped that he had not displayed an annoyed face when Mercedes came in and nearly fell into the chair beside his desk. Normally there was no person alive that he would delight to see more. In recent months she was the focus of much of his free time and most of his random thoughts. Kevin had browsed through Wanamaker's Department Store the day before, wandering around for an hour in the jewelry and sportswear departments, ascending and descending the long and venerable escalators on a half-dozen aimless journeys, thinking about a gift for Mercedes for a birthday that was two weeks off. Like a magician's secrets, his time before a special lecture was closely guarded. However, he decided that it was not completely bad that she did not know all of his quirks.

"I just dashed over from my university to catch this lecture," she said, breathlessly, and then laughed. It was a girlish laugh and a slightly nasal western Pennsylvania accent.

"I hope our standards will never get that low—you must be in training."

She laughed again in a rich way, full of confidence. "Kevin," Mercedes said then, in a serious tone, "Are things going to work out for you on that photography project?"

Even with the Lucius MacRobbins award, Kevin was under increasing pressure from the university to publish more research articles. Not that he hadn't tried. Two projects in which he had recently submerged himself had gone no farther than a secretary's typewriter. One subject was the Amish culture of Lancaster County, Pennsylvania, some fifty miles west of Philadelphia. The second topic was a barely known group, but one dear to his heart: a band of early nineteenth century German mystics who settled along the Wissahickon Creek in what is now Philadelphia to await the end of the world. Kevin's own home was less than a mile from where this pessimistic crew had decided to face the music. His spirited defense of these articles with a dozen magazine and journal editors had gotten him nothing but a swollen telephone bill. The editor at American Civilization Studies considered the Amish report as having only parochial interest. "But it's there old, set-in-their-ways uniqueness that makes them significant," Kevin had told her. "It's their contrast with the rest of our society. We're told that farming is the closest thing to pure competition in our economy. Yet many farmers all over the country sign contracts for federal subsidies for not growing certain crops. The Amish farmers would sign nothing— but they did what the government wanted. When the agriculture department sent them checks, they quickly got them back, uncashed. 'We don't sign government contracts and we don't take government money,' the Amish told them. Kevin's paper on the German mystics had received even less consideration. "The role of religious cults in American society is still an intriguing phenomenon," he told one editor. (We start out saying 'Da, Da', and end up talking like this, he thought). And with a wry smile, added, "I saw a mother and young son on Market Street today, literally in the shadow of the William Penn statue on City Hall, both dressed in sandals and identical orange and red saris. She was peddling incense and distributing inspirational leaflets called "*The White Path.*' Plus the son was wearing a cowboy hat and a toy pair of six-shooters."

Mercedes was looking at him with a curious expression. Her head was slightly tilted and her eyes searched his as if for clues. She slumped comfortably in the chair, her long legs resting on her heels. She had blue jeans closely sculpted to her and she appeared from Kevin's current perspective to be two-thirds legs. "This morning I got a call from an editor at Lee and Winslow," Kevin told her. "He gave me his promise that he would seriously consider a book proposal on the work of Philip O'Donnell. This editor's a young guy. Comes across as a smooth talker, but I think he's for real. But it's far from wrapped up."

"Won't you have enough material, or what?"

"I've got to do the job as completely as possible. I may get only one shot at getting a publisher's interest."

"Could that be your problem, Kevin. Don't get me wrong, but sometimes you take things very,...very personally. Is it good to be so close to your subject matter?"

Kevin's face was broad, open, and handsome. He looked at Mercedes pleasantly, and as if mildly confused, but inside he winced. His response was not to her advice, but to a memory. A lot of times he had declared that he was going to remember something for the rest of his life—and for once he knew it was true. What was worse, no one else who was there would probably ever forget it either.

It happened the previous December, before Christmas; it was the day Kevin and. Mercedes first met. A friend of his in the American

Civilization Department was a neighbor of Mercedes and her roommate. Kevin—and most of the American Civilization department—ended up at their party. He was enthralled at parties anytime, but this was particularly good timing. Final examinations had been marked and the grades calculated. Six work-free days were left to complete his Christmas shopping. Even the weather was cooperating: an early snowfall glazed the lawns, and the trees, and the rooftops. Christmas lights draped on trees and shrubbery had no difficulty melting small circles through the light coating of snow. Mercedes and her roommate, Jan, lived along Montgomery Avenue, one of the principal avenues leading out to Philadelphia's Main Line; the roadway was easily plowed, and Kevin was out in great spirits, singing snatches of Christmas songs along with the radio. The building that housed their apartment was an old home, at least one-hundred-twenty-five years old. Generations had made additions to the house haphazardly, matching the original gray stone closely, but it was insufficiently weathered to be an exact duplicate. This created for the building a slightly disheveled appearance, but Kevin appreciated its seasoned, lived-in feeling. Climbing the hardwood staircase to the second floor, he could sense rather than see the sculpturing effect countless feet had had on the steps. Their apartment door opened into the living room and a striking contrast. Lots of chrome and glass tables, Picasso and Braque prints in silver frames, a pair of white sofas on a brown and white rug. The coexistence of the venerable stone house and their modern decor pleased him immediately. An intelligent respect for the past without conceding anything from the present. It was one of his favorite contrasts.

Bob Goodall, his best (and only really good) friend in the department had invited him. A master at putting one at ease, Bob saw to it that Kevin was introduced to Jan, one of the two women throwing this party. She had black hair and large, serious brown eyes; she was wearing a full-length dress of green velveteen material. She took her hosting seriously. Kevin joined a young couple that he did not know for an impromptu tour of the apartment. Old houses chopped into apartments are usually full of oddly placed nooks and crannies, and these Jan filled with antique china closets and hutches that she collected. Even the one most out of the way was decorated with ceramic Christmas figurines and a thick red candle in a nest of natural holly leaves. Just off the kitchen was a small screened-in porch, apparently their favorite habitat in warmer weather. Now it lay quiet and desolate; a miniature drift of snow that barely mirrored the ivory moon light hugged one edge. Back in the living room, they admired the Christmas tree for its healthy branches and its intricate decorations. "I stayed up until two o'clock one morning stringing the popcorn that's on there. Mercedes—that's my roommate—thinks I'm crazy sometimes." They were charmed by the Victorian fireplace. It was brick lined and had an imported marble mantelpiece. A pyramid of logs burned serenely and over the years heat had carved an arch-shaped hollow into the carbon blackening the back wall. The other fellow in the group noticed a video cassette recorder sitting on top of a large television console. "Oh, Dad's an appliance distributor," Jan explained. "That's an early Christmas present for me. And today, I was able to get a special movie that Mercedes loves as an early present for her. She might say I'm crazy, but she'll probably stay up half the night watching it after everyone leaves. And the movie is recommended for viewers six years old and up."

Kevin had enjoyed the tour well enough. However, he never liked to get locked into any one group when he first came to a party. For the same reason, he would not accept a drink initially and thereby preserved for himself the freedom to later look for the bar. He removed himself to the spacious dining room and joined Bob Goodall, Bob's wife Elizabeth, and a half-dozen other guests. Everyone in that circle, except one older couple, he knew through the university. Kevin perched himself comfortably as a cat on a large windowsill and just listened. Among what he hoped was not a majority of his colleagues, Kevin's reputation was something less than golden. "Showboat" and "superficial" were two comments that had gotten back to him. The price he paid, he thought, for getting his students interested and even excited about the field of American Civilization. But his methods were unorthodox, even he had to admit, and that was bound to raise hackles. At times he would try to counter this negative image; temporarily, he would adopt a face, a manner that was serious to the point of being grim. This expression was like a Halloween mask on a chill: it soon gets uncomfortable and stuffy and impossible to keep on all night. But, situated on the windowsill, which he shared with a lush poinsettia plant, Kevin listened in on the group with what could be taken for an intelligent, serious look.

Conversation was in progress about their assorted children at Christmas time. The Goodall's five-year old had recently suggested a sort of plea-bargaining letter to Santa Claus to beg for some gifts based on future good behavior. It was the only scheme of personal accounting that offered her any hope. Suddenly, Kevin was attracted to a woman across the dining room from them. It was her laugh that he had noticed: rich, confident, enthusiastic. She was tall and striking in black stretch pants and a white blouse. Her hair was brown, full and long and she had a pretty face and vibrant eyes, even from a distance. Two men equally unknown to Kevin were talking to her. The taller one was obviously coming on to her. He had a drink in one hand. In the other he had a cigarette; he had that hand up against the wall, almost over her head, sort of boxing her in to a corner. Periodically, he puffed on the cigarette and then quickly shot the hand up high again. Either the guy had good lines or she was a patient audience. Already, Kevin was dying to break up that trio and talk to her. In his own group, the conversation had taken an odd shift. The older couple's son had recently purchased a house at an astronomically high mortgage rate. Sympathetic murmurs made the rounds. "The prime rate," Kevin said suddenly and a little too loudly, "The prime rate, interest rates, are all we talk about anymore. I can even imagine kids spending their time talking about them. Hey, Bob, what did we talk about as kids. Sports. Baseball. In our day we'd sit on big benches at the playground, cracking our knuckles, arguing over baseball statistics. Most of the fights I had were with my oldest friend Jackie about whether or not I was out at home plate."

Kevin hopped from his window seat and swaggered into the middle of the group. He was just under six feet, thin but athletically built, but just now Kevin looked positively boyish. "I can picture the arguments at the playgrounds these days," he continued. "Hey, Goodall, you big dope, I say the prime rates' gonna drop twenty-five basis points in da next quarter." Goodall flew to his feet and put his face three inches from Kevin's. Goodall was two inches taller than Kevin and his glare slanted downward as menacingly as possible. "So's your old man, O'Donnell," Bob said. "Don't you know how to read or nothin.' What about the Fed's tight money policies?" Fierce phony glowering from both of them.

"They're just a bunch of pansies, like you, turkey," Kevin answered.

"If you're so smart, O'Donnell, what's the money supply definition of M1"?

O'Donnell couldn't answer. "M1. M1, you punk," Kevin said, "that's easy. It's the name of your mother's motorcycle helmet. The one she got most of the grease off of. The one she wears to church on Sunday."

Finally attracted by the silliness, the woman deserted her two male companions and accosted Bob and Kevin. She laughed with the crowd and her face flashed crimson with pleasure. "Bob, I'd like to meet your friend," she said in a mildly nasal accent. "You know, before I call the police on the two of you." Up close, Kevin could see that her big, vibrant eyes were gray-green in color. Also, that she had large breasts on an otherwise slim body—another one of his favorite contrasts.

"Mercedes," Bob was saying," this is Kevin O'Donnell. I'm not sure how he got here. I think he just climbed in that window over there."

"And are you always like this?" she wondered.

"Only when I'm stone sober. Could you help me? I couldn't find any beer, only punch."

He followed her quick, forceful steps into the long galley kitchen where she swung open the refrigerator door. The top shelf was all ranks and files of green beer bottles.

"What a strange place to hide the beer," Kevin muttered loudly.

Mercedes seemed content to stay put in the narrow kitchen for a while. God bless Goodall for picking up on his goofy routine. Without planning it, now he had her sole attention. It turned out that, like her roommate Jan, she was studying for her Ph.D. in marketing at another Philadelphia university. And, yes, it was a western Pennsylvania accent. Until a few years ago, she had always lived near Pittsburgh. With a couple of questions about her academic progress, Kevin determined that Mercedes was about thirty years old.

The big guy who tried to monopolize her earlier entered the kitchen. The cigarette was now propped in his mouth, with the smoke making him squint in one eye. He spent an inordinate amount of time at the freezer selecting from a plastic container of identical ice cubes. Then he left without even a parting grunt and Kevin thought, eat your heart out Cyclops. Define M1.

"Oh," Mercedes said. "That's Hal Litchfield. He was saying that he's been pretty successful as a computer software salesman. He was very interested in my marketing program. Have you ever met him?"

"Well, sort of," Kevin said in a slow, measured voice, almost at a whisper level. "I had to identify a mugger once, and Hal was in the lineup."

After a quick, shocked laugh, Mercedes said, "What did they do? Let you out of the prison on a two-week pass."

"What? Me? A pass! After what I did to the warden's garden? Hell, no—I busted out."

Occasionally his routines grated on him. Kevin would to try to rein himself in. "Mercedes, I'd like to hear about that movie Jan got you. Is it something fairly new?"

"No, it's ancient. Older than me even. *Miracle on 34th Street*. I've got to watch it tonight."

Tonight he was King Midas. A sly idea crept into mind like a snake slowly unwinding. "I loved that movie as a kid." Actually, he had heard of it but never seen it. "Mercedes, you've got to let me watch it with you later."

She grabbed his elbows fiercely. "Wonderful," Mercedes said. "I needed one other person to say they wanted to see it at the party tonight. Come on, it's my party. Let's watch it now."

Ah, shit, he thought. Even gold prices fluctuate. Kevin thought he had wrangled himself a stay-late invitation. Instead, he ended up following Mercedes into the living room where he watched her swoop upon the videocassette recorder and the tape of the movie. In her excitement, she fumbled with the equipment. Jan quietly insisted that she set it up instead. Standing around for half a minute, feeling a little bit like a dumb ox, Kevin recovered just in time to beat out super salesman Litchfield in a game of musical chairs to see who sat beside Mercedes on a white sofa. He could scarcely believe that everyone in the place wanted to watch it, too.

A few lamps were turned off. The lights from the Christmas tree and the softly burning fireplace grew in importance. The scurrying behind him was the last minute rush to refresh drinks. *Miracle on 34th Street* was pleasant enough fare. The old fellow who does look like Saint Nicholas and who works as a department store Santa Claus implies that he believes that he's the real thing. With half a mind he could skewer most movies, but Kevin had trouble getting a handle on this one. His aside on the skittish marketing-types at the department store went unacknowledged by Mercedes. In the semi-darkness, he thought he could hear her breathing slowly and deeply; she clutched a side cushion in her arms like a teddy bear. It was obvious to him that the genial, mid-thirties lawyer and the somewhat younger, divorced mother (was that Maureen O'Sullivan?) would fall in love and marry in the end. Kevin had to admit that her kid sort of got to him. She was six or seven, had penetrating dark eyes, and was very loving. He had a niece something like her. The mother in the movie, having been hardened by her divorce, knew the limits of love and hope, and tried to steer her daughter accordingly. Forget that Santa Claus nonsense. Mommy buys the presents. Do you want to see the receipts? Why should the little girl try to fight her mother's sad experience? But that crazy Santa Claus guy—who even spends a short time in the psychiatric lockup for whacking the department store psychologist—pumps hope and belief at her with the persistence of a beating heart. (Kevin's sister sometimes reminds him of her favorite saying of his. 'There are worse things than to lose an arm, or your leg, or your life—you could lose hope). Why not make a Christmas wish, little girl, Santa says, and see what happens? Her wish is a challenge. Instead of the fashionable New York apartment shared just with her mother, she wants a particular little house out on Long Island, with shutters on the windows, a swing set out back, and her mother, and a father, and her, living happily inside. Santa cautions her that she's asking a lot. Oh, no, is he backing off? Kevin stirs in his seat uncomfortably. Sensations of anger and sadness arise in him nearly simultaneously. Jesus Christ, he thinks. The girl's not asking for so much. A lot of people have that kind of life. And it's not the material things she's after; the little girl doesn't want a hundred gaudy presents. She just wants to be made whole. It's only fair. Too much has been asked of her already. Wait. The crazy old guy says it can be done. But she must truly believe it and say it with all her heart. Despite her mother's earlier hardheaded advice, she starts in fervently:

I do believe, I do believe, I DO believe, I DO believe...In his own heart Kevin is saying it too, fiercely, and not just for himself: he's hoping to help her out a little. The living room was silent for a moment, except for the weak clicks from the dying fire, when Kevin O'Donnell burst into the loudest sobs of his life.

He was not at all used to crying. It shook his entire body. Mercedes, sitting on one side of him, and Hal Litchfield, sitting on the other, must have felt the vibrations through the sofa itself. Kevin put his fingers up against his eyes. However, he had no real expectations that he could staunch the flow of tears. It was like springing off a high diving board: too late to try to stop yourself from getting wet. For what seemed like a very long time and was actually thirty seconds Kevin's thoughts were barely coherent. Finally he was aware that the movie was still playing on, and that everyone else in the room was absolutely silent. He was regaining control, but still sucking in air like a noisy pump. Not a soul in the room knew what to do. Then he felt a hand on his shoulder for a few seconds. It was a heavy hand; thick masculine fingers. Hal Litchfield gave his shoulder a quick, sympathetic squeeze, a sort of gesture you night get from a teammate after you lose the championship on the last play. When Kevin finally looked, up blinking to clear the salty haze from his eyes, the little girl was happily romping through a house that had shutters on the windows and a nifty swing set in the back yard.

****

Kevin gave himself credit for having a certain irreducible amount of courage. He saw it as basic to his core, an asset that did not depreciate over time. (His father owned a consulting business, and, like a weekend handyman whose shelves are burdened with remnants of pipe and concrete mix, and stacks of vinyl floor tiles, Kevin possessed a selective, random vocabulary of business terms). Or perhaps it was foolhardiness that drove him this time, or, worse yet, a wave of desperation that imparts a fierce energy normally associated with brave acts. What difference did it really make? Her phone number was in the book. Kevin called Mercedes the very next morning, shortly before noon.

She answered the phone herself; in the single word "Hello" her voice was guarded, defensive, as if expecting bad news. His mind was sent racing on something as inconsequential as this. The spectacle that he had made of himself must have hit her squarely in the face. Party goers scattered an hour earlier than normal, leaving half-filled drinks cluttering the end tables and suddenly neglected hor d'oevres sprawling unappetizingly on paper plates. And the mess that he had created in front of her friends would not he so easily sweat up by a vacuum cleaner. Where did he get the brass, calling her us like this? But on he plunged, determined to charm her. It was about a month later when he would realize that Mercedes answered the phone this way every day of her life.

"I didn't get a chance to thank you for the party," Kevin was saying. "I like to limit the amount of my rudeness in any one week."

"Oh, no. I felt bad that I hadn't said goodnight. I even mentioned that when I was sitting up talking to Jan. And would you believe this. She likes to jump right in after a party and completely clean up the place."

"Get out," he said in mock horror. "Is she afraid the trash is going to go away on its own? Maybe burglars will break in, in the middle of the night, carrying big green trash bags and say, 'Forget the damn stereo. There's a nickel deposit on each of these beer bottles.' Maybe if they were ecology minded his partner'd say, 'Check to see if the soda cans can be recycled.'"

"And our renters' insurance doesn't cover that," Mercedes said, lauding uproariously. "How dreadful."

This was great: talking bullshit right off the bat. Nonsense pinged and ponged between them for a few more minutes. Then, Kevin went for the jugular.

"Mercedes, there's one a second reason why I called. I'd like the chance to play host to you. I can get tickets for Sinatra, or maybe the Temptations, down at one of the casinos. Atlantic City. Dinner and everything. And most importantly, I mean for New Year's Eve." Ah, the old thrusting O'Donnell style that had once gotten Kevin recruited straight out of gym class for the university fencing team.

"Oh, how sweet. How'd you think of that? I've never been to the casinos."

"Neither have I. But for some reason I feel I owe you," said the former NCAA foil champion. (Both junior and senior years).

"Oh, no, you don't. Not at all. But I can't go anyway. Just this morning I made some other plans for New Year's Eve. A concert at the Academy of Music. Dinner afterwards at Le Bec Fin. 'Champaigne and caviar and elegance.' Can you stand it? Maybe you remember the fellow who invited me. A big, tall guy: Hal Litchfield."

Back in his college days, Kevin's daring, attacking style and pinpoint accuracy with the slender foil weapon had never carried over to the heavier saber. He utilized finesse and cat-quick reactions and sophisticated variations of balance and tempo to drive home his point. But the saber was all muscle and upper body strength and ferocious slashing. He could not rebuff such pounding. For a few tremulous seconds, Kevin relived the unpleasant sensation of insistent metal crashing into his crazy bone. So he wasn't a torrent of power; he had long given up hope of becoming one. But he was a persistent stream of energy, and like a flow of water that plunges underground to carve out cathedrals of limestone and then resurfaces to sluice along slate ridges and bound around granite outcrops, he could always find his way to the sea, his ultimate goal. By February Mercedes and he had their first date. By mid-March they were lovers. Perhaps, at thirty-seven, Kevin had reached an age when the prospect of a long-time relationship, or even a love affair, must be examined with special attention. It was like a much-desired, expensive painting or rare book in the minutes before the auction at Sotheby's is to start. Timing is paramount: go for it now or possibly lose it forever. Watch someone else carry it away in triumph. He was still a young man, pre-middle age, but at the far end of the scale of youthfulness. Never did Kevin see himself settling down with a much, much younger woman. And he always assumed that he would get re-married some day, have a child or two. In his mid-twenties Kevin had been married for two years, a long forgotten mistake of a relationship. By his own predilections, his own standards, he had to get a move on to obtain his romantic goals.

It was no major surprise to him that within a few weeks of seeing her Kevin was wild about Mercedes. Lately, all the advice columns and popular psychology magazines were reporting that men—much more than women—fall in love with the suddenness and force of summer storms. In theory, the layers of toned muscle only hide a romantic male heart. But if Kevin was like a euphoric skydiver ready to fling himself from an airplane not ever sure if he had strapped on the damn parachute, Mercedes' response was like that of a rider on the boardwalk parachute jump that he had seen as a child. The same principles were operating, the same laws of nature governed, their bodies plummeting to earth and yet feeling weightless at the same time, but the most unadventurous, even myopic observer could have recognized the differing degree of risk, the differing sense of *abandon*, in each of their flights. Mercedes was tender, and considerate and warm while Kevin was burning hot. His friend Goodall kidded him that if the engineering school could develop a reliable lustometer and scan a few centimeters of his bare skin, the sensitive needle would be driven right off the scale. He thought of this comment when he was visiting Mercedes one Saturday afternoon in early April. It made him laugh to himself—at himself, more accurately. She was showing him her prized Hammond world atlas. Two feet high, an inch and a half thick, a high school graduation present from her grandparents. A third of the dining room table disappeared when she opened it out flat. Silently, almost solemnly, Mercedes pinched the edge of the page to turn the giant leaves, slowly fanning passed their eyes primary colored empires of the Holy Romans, the Hapsburgs, and the conquering Wehrmacht armies. Her fingers were supple and purposeful; from her neck Kevin could detect the mildest hint of cologne. Mercedes' face, and her gray-green eyes, particularly, could belong to a pretty but serious teacher who was molding the imagination of a ten-year old. She was utterly precious to him then. That stopped him from saying, "Screw this. These guys are all dead. Let's hop in the sack." He could contain himself if need be. He was not going to blow it at this point.

Under the flush of blazing emotion, like a feverish person playing ducks and drakes with hallucinations, Kevin could still try to capture some thought that was solid and illuminating. This usually hit him at the oldest moments. Just ready to shave one morning, Kevin realized that he was viewing Mercedes as a woman without any faults. The face in the mirror with the thick, prematurely white beard of lather kept tilting itself from side to side, like a mime imitating a slow metronome, as if this thought were three-dimensional and subject to observation from many angles. It was not that Mercedes didn't aggravate him; far from it. She would not commit herself to an exclusive relationship at this point but Kevin wanted only her. Few details were shared, yet he knew she had occasional dates with other men, Litchfield for one, maybe one or two more. Jan, answering the phone one day, mistook Kevin's voice for someone named Doug; Kevin's heart took a quick elevator ride south until Mercedes mentioned that Doug was a school colleague co-authoring a term paper. His annoyance—his jealousy—did not diminish his desire for her the slightest. If anything, it fed it. Fed it like a calibrated intake valve on a wood-burning stove. Independence, self-containment, on his scale of values, far outweighed the importance of graduate degrees, teaching awards, or old NCAA championship rings. Such kudos had settled on his shoulders as much from endurance as any distinctive skill that he exhibited. (Not that Kevin down played endurance: it was as central to his being as his skeletal structure). But obsession, addiction to work could also propel a man to such accomplishments. Self-possession, independence, were virtues that Kevin experienced intermittently. Mercedes seemed to come upon them like a child's instinct to breathe, a sort of reflex response that defined her very survival. For him to fault such a stance he might as well fault the automatic pumping of her heart or the blinking of her eyelids.

As he had shaved that morning with patient, studied strokes, examining each swath like a sculptor, Kevin pursued this conversation with himself. She was a human being, wasn't she? That guarantees imperfection, doesn't it: Was gauze laid across his eyes or was it wrapped around her blemishes? Was it a question of his not seeing or her not revealing? For a woman who laughed so spontaneously, she could be rather earnest at times—should that concern him? Not even counting the night at the Christmas party, it was miraculous in a way that they ever got together. He'd say the craziest things at first and she'll take them at face value. Mercedes had questioned him about his father's line of work. "Oh, Dad's a geologist," Kevin had said. "Yes, Dad's got a degree in geology." This was far from the truth. "And my father runs the only earthquake-predicting business in North America." "Oh," Mercedes had answered, softly, perhaps startled. Then, as if delicately shifting gears with a recalcitrant clutch, and engaging her professional interest, "Oh—what kind of demand is there for a service like that?" "Sluggish, admittedly sluggish for the last few years. But Dad says to expect a lot of movement in the next quarter." In the kitchen making a Caesar salad, slicing anchovies at such close millimeters they would disappear except for taste into the coated Romaine lettuce leaves, Mercedes was silent for two minutes. Then, at the doorway, she suddenly materialized, and laughingly yelled, "You lunatic," and launched a dishtowel that landed on his shoulder like a cat.

Well, there are worse traits that earnestness. Actually, he thought it rather charming in her. Come to think of it, Kevin had to admit to having a fair dose of it himself; in a way, his theatrics, his bizarre bantering provided an effective camouflage for a rich vein of seriousness that ran like a seam of coal through his own psyche. Mercedes might be seeing right through that mask right now, with her gray-green, penetrating eyes, as she sat in the Windsor chair beside his desk. "I've got to be close to my subject matter to do research," Kevin answered her. "I can't get very motivated otherwise. I'll go that extra mile to do the best possible review of Philip O'Donnell's life and work in part because

35

he is my great uncle. Remember that he's an unknown. I may have to scratch the earth with my fingernails to come up with enough dirt on him to make him even a minor figure."

"Please don't mind my concern. And I know that you know how to handle yourself. Hey, you seemed awfully preoccupied when I came in. Are you going to give one of those crazy lectures today?"

"Crazy lectures! 'Special lectures' I'll have you know. Who told you that anyway?" Kevin laughed.

"Bob Goodall. I saw him as he was getting into his car this morning."

"He should talk. His office is across the hall, right. I come in here this morning and he starts harassing me by doing his impersonation of Luciano Pavarotti—Bob's an opera buff, you know—his impersonation of 'Luciano Pavarotti Sings Everyone's Country And Western Favorites.' He swears he got the album by sending away to one of those television ads."

"Now I know why I shouldn't watch T.V. But I want to take a break for a while today. Can I come to this special class of yours?"

"Oh. That'd be a little different. Yeah, come along. I'm going to go over there right now. I like to be early for them."

A minute later they were in the corridor, where Kevin, carrying a fat, old leather briefcase, briskly jangled his keys as he locked his office. Probably that noise served as his cue because when they passed Goodall's office (the door was closed, but the dusty transom was open like an antique Victrola megaphone) they were treated to a passable Italian tenor soaring into song:

"You ditched me for the guy in the Ford Torino
And I reconned I had lost my Sweet—Bam-bino."

A master of timing, that Goodall fellow.

CHAPTER THREE

Kevin's classroom resembled a small auditorium. Rows of desks in a U-shape surrounded the teacher's platform. Each row was raised twelve inches above the proceeding one, giving every student in the room unimpeded vision. American Civilization courses used a lot of teaching aids: tape recordings, movies, slides, drawings, audio cassettes, records. This classroom was designed to use this equipment and it had rather good acoustics. Thirty students were enrolled in the class. Few would be expected to miss one of Kevin's "special lectures"—occasionally, students even brought along friends. Mercedes had to scramble to select a seat in the next to last row.

What Kevin called a special lecture was known to his class as a "dollar day." If everyone agreed, he would bet each student one dollar that he could get at least one hearty collective laugh or cheer from the group during the class. Individual laughs, cheers, clapping, no matter how exuberant, did not matter. He had to knock them all flat at the same time or he lost. Kevin never failed to arrange the wager once he told them that he had never lost the bet in four years. For one class he called his winnings his Atlantic City gambling money. Another class heard that he used the money to sponsor an orphaned grizzly bear in

Yellowstone Park. As consolation, at least they could choose the cub's name. Being such a good, democratic sport, O'Donnell permitted them to bring friends whom he had never taught, and they too could participate. Why he even insisted that they place their bets. No one ever caught on that these visitors—with no exposure and therefore no immunity to his style—were all but hysterical before he said his first word.

The teacher's platform was raised six inches above the floor level. On a large table sat a portable record player and an overhead projector. Kevin was fiddling with these as the room filled. As carefully as an airline pilot touching down, he laid the needle on the L.P. Rich violin sounds welled up around Kevin O'Donnell. The music had a rising, swelling, victorious feeling, an effect Kevin enhanced by slowly increasing the volume. He imagined a motorcyclist cresting a hill at the very peak of a personal triumph. Here and there in the room was whispered "Beethoven"; "Ninth Symphony"; "Second Movement." The orchestra played on for two more intense minutes. With a red plastic straw for a baton, cutting the air with decisive strokes, O'Donnell exhorted the lush strings to stirring heights. It was the kind of action that students labeled "spontaneous" and "exhilarating." He had practiced it the night before in a full length mirror. When with a quick, sure touch he plucked up the needle, Kevin was surrounded with faces that were happy, or quizzical, or at least eager to be entertained.

"'Why', you cleverly ask, 'is he playing some German guy's music in an American Civilization course," Kevin said. "'What's wrong,

39

Professor, have you run out of domestic material? Is this on the final exam? Hey, can I get a refund for this stupid class?' Calm, down, children, everything that I have here is for a reason.

"In this course this semester I've tried to give you an overview of the field of American Civilization. Today, if you will indulge me, my purpose is broader than that. Let's talk about civilization, and people, and problems of communication and understanding. More specifically, how do we send and receive important information.

"About a year ago a space probe was launched by the United States into deep space. Part of its purpose is to send information about the planet earth to anyone—or thing—who might be out there in the universe. Its a pretty egocentric kind of behavior; we presume the good people on Planet X would give a flying saucer. But it was all done with great seriousness, considering that we will all be long gone by the time it gets to wherever it is going. Think of the space probe as a type of a time capsule. Modern society is very much taken with time capsules of any kind: King Tut's tomb and his burial artifacts; Stonehenge; the cliff dwellings of the Anasazi Indians in the American southwest. Painstakingly we chip away the lava covering of ancient Pompeii, a cubic centimeter at a time. In recent years during the American bicentennial celebration we read a lot about people opening or constructing their own time capsules. In our lives we cherish private time capsules. We save the torn halves of tickets from theater or the World Series. Some of you have in your wallets pictures of prom dates you haven't seen in four years. What is it that we learn from this gossamer bric-a-brac from the past? What are we trying to accomplish when we deposit articles for a hundred years' safekeeping? In my opinion we are looking for some kind of personal statement. Something that touches our lives in a personal way. Not some kind of long term historical importance—I want something that means something to me.

"What do people accomplish when they preserve items in the form of a time capsule? In my opinion less than they think. For one thing, we select things that are familiar and easily recognizable. That makes sense. What good would it be to open a box full of one hundred year old objects and have no idea what anything was used for? Its like getting a wedding present of some contraption that you don't recognize—it has little value for you and makes a real challenge out of the thank-you note." Kevin flicked on the overhead projector. "So, say we unearth and open a crate full of goodies from a century ago and we discover: a toy locomotive, a carpenter's plane, a horse's bit, an oversized kerosene lamp, the local newspaper, a trainman's broken pocket watch, a list of everyone living in the town at that time. Opening the capsule can be done with great fanfare and create tremendous anticipation and fun for all. But what have we really discovered? Exclude the newspaper and the list of citizens, and we have a bunch of items we could find any fall weekend up in Bucks County. I say this from experience. I took this list of items—I had seen it in a newspaper account about a capsule opening—and spent most of a Saturday in antique shops and at country flea markets. Before dinnertime, I was able to see virtually every item on the list offered for sale. The items were so regular, so everyday, that they weren't special. That had no special or unique meaning, as far as I could see.

"Another problem with time capsules, whether they be of a public or private nature. Many American families have photo albums of some kind. Lots of families preserve home movies for years and years. If we brought in family albums and passed them around I can guarantee one thing: they would all be very similar to each other. There would be pictures of family gatherings and celebrations: Thanksgiving, Christmas, the Fourth of July. Religious ceremonies like baptisms, confirmations, weddings. Pictures in cap and gowns. Photos of folks in white hats fishing or sailing a boat. I'll guarantee another thing. Here's some shots we won't find: Mother and Dad's monthly argument over paying the household bills. The time your brother fell out of his tree house and broke his leg in two places—great to have a sound-recording movie camera handy for that. Or a shot captioned that we were sitting around bored on a rainy Sunday. And especially this kind of situation: a photograph of dear old generous-to-a-fault Aunt Julia (who for ten years was chief teller at the Savings and Loan) contemplating prison because the auditor wants to see her on Monday. You've noticed that the media doesn't share this attitude. Climb out on the ledge on the thirty-fifth floor of an office building in town, and you're talking front page coverage and before and after shots.

"What are the alternatives? I've claimed that our time capsules are too mundane, too similar, not special enough. And, like our family albums, we only want to include the good things. We want to create a nice positive image. It seems that we want to write an acceptable resume that we forward to our great grandchildren. What job are we hoping to get, you might wonder. Have we applied for sainthood and need them for references? But I read about one time capsule that you should hear about. Again, this was during the American bicentennial celebration. A small Massachusetts village had the care of a time capsule for one hundred years. They decided to open it on July 4, 1976. Opening the box was made the centerpiece of their bicentennial festivities. There had long been an active historical society in town, and they were pretty much in hog heaven, or so the news wire tells us. You can envision the classic New England town square, outlined in huge swags of red, white and blue bunting, and what seems like a million flags. The high school band has played the national anthem, then *America the Beautiful,* and something that resembled a John Phillips Sousa march. After the appropriate speech making the magic moment arrived. The time capsule was pried open, ancient dust creeping out in a light brown cloud around the Mayor's expansive hips. And what wondrous things did they find? One pair of men's long underwear. A pair of long johns! Nothing else. The historical society was momentarily nonplussed, but everyone else rocked the square in laughter. Someone must of said, "What is this? Some kind of a joke?" Maybe it was the world's longest played out practical joke. Do you think it was a lot of nonsense? I say it's not. I think that something significant happened there: a value was communicated to our contemporaries by some unknown persons living one hundred years ago. That value, of course, was humor. It's one of the most important currencies that we exchange. This particular time capsule really accomplished something. It reminded us that people generations older that ourselves were human beings too. Let us catch them with their pants down. We don't think it through. Let me give you an example of what I driving at. Last year, I had a student say to me, 'Dr. O'Donnell, I've only recently realized that the American Civil War and the First and Second World Wars were not fought in black-and-white. If you got shot, it wasn't some ambiguous dark stain spreading on your uniform, you were pumping out deep red blood.' He went on to explain to me that all of the photographs and motion picture clips of those wars that he had seen were in black-and-white. Those wars happened before he was born and seemed as remote as dinosaurs to him. I thought his point was well made—I've been guilty of the same kind of thoughtlessness myself. We forget or misunderstand that pictures are only a small representation of gigantic events and are not the events themselves. At times we should adopt the critical eye of the very young children you see with their parents at Valley Forge National Park. In and out of the station wagon they go, every half-mile. The kids soon tire of the memorials and the plaques, the old cannons, and the reconstructed wooden huts, wondering aloud what all the fuss is about and whether or not the ice cream stand is open.

"Which brings us, of course, to that guy who jumped off the Chestnut Street Bridge.

"'What? Sez who,' you say. Let's review for a second time what I've been talking about. We send data to and receive data from people and our environment. I've been complaining that we often don't do such a good job of interpreting it. Many of our time capsules are too mundane, too goody-two shoes. The century old long johns were exceptional because they hit us in the gut; they had some depth of feeling to them. And, on a lovely May afternoon we barbecue hamburgers and smuggle Budweisers past the Park Rangers and think we know all about roughing it at Valley Forge. What's the thread here? How do make sense of all these things I'm throwing at you. I think its a question of uniqueness. We fail to see or to even look for unique qualities. I'm calling them qualities but I'm speaking about the bad as well as the good here. Unique features are part of every situation we face, and yet, we settle for the familiar. Our worse offenses are against ourselves. We accept what's comfortable in what we think, our choice of words, careers, even lovers. A rainbow of colors is splashed before us but were wearing gray-tinted sunglasses. I'm driving on the Benjamin Franklin Parkway the other day, inching along in heavy traffic, fooling with the F.M. radio, and suddenly I notice the bumper sticker in front of me: Make Today Special. That's the logo of an organization that helps people suffering from terminal illness. Why is it that we need a death sentence, in effect, to appreciate what's around us? Shouldn't the healthy individual try to squeeze as much juice out of the orange as the sick fellow?

"A few years ago I noticed a peculiar story in the newspaper. It was about a would-be suicide. Some guy who jumped off the Chestnut Street Bridge that runs over the Schuykill River in downtown Philadelphia. Unfortunally It's usually an effective way to kill yourself. This was in late January, during the fiercest cold spell in recent history. I don't know why this person would want to do themselves in, but I found this enlightening in a way. The distraught man flung himself over the railing. He survived, however. He was rescued by a policeman using a wooden boat. Pretty commonplace so far, right? However, his injuries were a little out of the ordinary: two broken legs. What happened, did he strike a bridge abutment? No. He landed on a river covered by six inches of solid ice. He wouldn't have penetrated that ice if he were wearing lead shoes. His leap was like jumping out of a third story window. Guaranteed to hurt, but it probably won't kill you. In Helsinki, Finland people expect to drive cars on river ice in January. To them a river in liquid form is a temporary condition. But in Philadelphia, total river icing is an unusual event. It might not happen for twenty years at a time. On average, our suicidal friend's assumption was correct. Even in January, it was logical to expect the big splashdown. Wasn't this, though, the biggest decision in his life? Shouldn't he have reviewed all of the relevant facts to see things were in order? He could have developed a game plan, checked out the important details in advance. You can see that I'm asking rhetorical questions. He was in no condition to collect new information. He was cut off from life. From his environment. He had all the facts. His internal clouds were locked into place. His legs had to become shock absorbers before he would open *his* eyes.

The *Philadelphia Inquirer* must have been fond of this story because they apparently reprinted it the next day. For the second day in a row I find myself reading about a suicide attempt at the Chestnut Street Bridge. As we all know it was thwarted by the unusual ice cover. The policeman cleverly pushed a wooden row boat *across* the surface of the frozen Schuykill River to rescue the poor guy. But wait, there's a discrepancy here. It says he suffered a broken arm and a broken leg. Now I distinctly remembered two broken legs. I had even remembered the policeman's name—Keogh. Oh, my God, it was a completely different person rescued this day. Two days in a row two different people unknowingly crashed onto the ice and sustained injury. Both on Officer Keogh's shift, and both rescued by him and the wooden boat. Now this really drove home to me how isolated, how cut off, we can let ourselves become. A person planning to kill themselves doesn't read the newspaper or watch the news on T.V. They don't take into account a frozen river. However, I also thought that there was a unique opportunity here. I called the Streets Department and I called the Police Department to see if they know what happened to these two injured persons after their rescue. They both said that they hoped for the best for those people but they do not conduct those types of inquiry. In a similar vein the newspaper reporter was not charged with doing a follow up report since the people survived those events. There weren't any TV interviews afterwards. No lawsuits appeared. But we can hope that the terrible physical pain might lead to both physical and emotional healing.

"Earlier in the lecture I mentioned a unique space mission recently launched by the United States. This effort is a deep space probe that has two essential objectives. One is to seek radio signals that would signify intelligent life in other galaxies. The other is to deliver information in a physical form about this planet that could give these intelligent life forms a basic understanding of human beings and our level of cultural adaptation. To my mind we're talking the ultimate time capsule here. And totally different from any other model in history. Who will be the recipients? What will they be like? How do we successfully communicate with them? Other than our hope that they exist, we don't know if we share any aspect of life, any single characteristic with them. As you can imagine, word of this impending project had set my heart aflutter. Concern about the typical bland ineffectiveness of time capsules stabbed at me like a swarm of hungry mosquitoes. I sent a letter to the project directors, pouring out my deepest thoughts. Gratifyingly, I received a letter in response. A genuine response, not some mimeographed public relations fluff. Have you ever written to a politician. You head the Committee to Impeach Congressman Easybribe and send him a letter that casts aspersion on his mother. Back comes a mailgram that says, 'Dear Mr. Smith, your expression of support is deeply appreciated.' No. None of that here. Let me quote from the response from an assistant project director.

"'Professor O'Donnell. The mission directors were greatly interested—even moved—by your comments concerning our upcoming launch. They specifically asked that I write to you to thank you for sharing your thoughts.

"'Constructing our 'Time Capsule' as you so aptly named it has been an exciting and yet at times exasperating challenge. Advice and ideas have flowed in from many sectors. Many of the comments forwarded to us have been of the highest caliber. Some, as you could perhaps imagine, are cunningly self-serving, and others patently ridiculous.

But, all in all, the torrent of thoughts and requests have been a source of stimulation. We recognize, however, that our limited choice of items for this space flight will not satisfy everyone. We simply have to live with that. However, I can assure you that intelligent input like yours will not be ignored. The spirit, if not the letter of your suggestion, remains with us.

"'The project directors fully agree that the spirit of mankind is the spirit of struggle; the determination to overcome the obstacles that trip us up daily. We particularly liked your allusion to Jacob Bronoski's *The Ascent of Man*: how Early Man, faced with a burgeoning population that could not be supported solely on the African savannah, emigrated northward into central Europe at the very time the ice ages crept down from the polar cap and encased their new home in ice. It was hand to mouth for hundreds of centuries, but caveman endured. And as you point out, the continuing ability to adapt to an hostile environment is one of man's greatest skills. Eskimo hunters build shelters of ice and have fifty words to denote snow. Bedouins find water in rainless deserts. The Indian subcontinent radiates 130 F. as it awaits the monsoon. Thanks to you and like-minded people, our project has incorporated an appreciation of the unquenchable spirit of man. Indeed, it is with regret that we return the particular item that you felt best represented your ideas. Enclosed, please find one pair of men's long underwear, size forty regular.'

"Well," Kevin said, looking up from the letter, "at least I had the satisfaction of communicating with the project directors prior to launch. I got my two cents in and then got them back. The concept

49

of this space mission has continued to fascinate me. I've had my concerns about its ultimate success but on the whole I have resolved that in my own mind. For example, I found it galling to think that our capsule might travel trillions of miles over eons of time only to be viewed as a trinket by whomever finds it. I read where a Japanese fisherman stumbled upon an old wooden shield that he took a fancy to. But then he tossed it into his tool chest and forgot about it. Luckily, it was rediscovered and recognized to be a sixth century admiral's shield, a priceless national treasure in Japan. What if our spacecraft was melted down to make cufflinks or something?

"I think not. I take comfort from one of the most unusual stories to emerge from the American Civil War. The story tells us that the most ordinary of people can rise to the occasion in recognizing truly unusual and valuable data.

"Perhaps you know the story. The Battle of Antietam was fought in September, 1862, in the state of Maryland. This was the autumn before the Gettysburg invasion. Momentum was completely on the side of the Army of Northern Virginia and Robert E. Lee. Lee had entered Maryland to ignite southern sympathies, to scare up supplies, to impress the world with Southern might. Perhaps Pennsylvania could be invaded before the fall elections. The stakes—to put it mildly—were sky high. General Lee had kept scooting off Stonewall Jackson on end runs around the hapless Federals. Lee and Jackson were working this routine one more time when they lurched into a piece of rotten luck: a complete set of Lee's marching orders fell into the hands of the Union army.

"This copy of General Lee's plan came like a gift from God to the Union forces. Two Union privates, two ordinary infantrymen, trudging down a dusty Maryland byway discovered a copy of the Confederate battle plans wrapped around two fresh and highly aromatic cigars. These privates had the presence of mind to notify their regimental officers, and ultimately, the commanding Union general was alerted. The information emboldened the Union forces to checkmate Lee at Antietam Creek. The rebels retreated to Virginia with little additional support or supplies and with Pennsylvania as yet uninvaded. Lincoln issued the Emancipation Proclamation on the strength of this victory. As one absentminded Confederate courier once did, historians will long ponder two crucial questions with respect to the Antietam campaign. Would government of the people, by the people, and for the people have vanished from the earth if the Federals hadn't intercepted Lee's plans? And, who ended up smoking those two cigars, anyway?

"It is sheer speculation to predict the impact of this space capsule on an alien cosmos, and yet it is an effort not without merit. While the technological features of this expedition are based on the hard sciences, its conception is pure fantasy. To dream about its future is to be attuned to its very purpose. I have taken the liberty to design one possible—I think very highly plausible—scenario. Hopefully, it will serve as a metaphor for out time spent together today.

"Once upon a future time, our space probe will descend into an orbit around an inhabited planet located a fabulous distance from earth. The population of this planet, called Lugar, is highly advanced in science.

In fact, they track the incoming space capsule for several decades and millions of miles. They have ways to determine that it is not a hostile ship. The citizens of Lugar awaited our unmanned emissary with curiosity, even a degree of fascination, the way we anticipate Halley's Comet. When it advances within several hundred miles from their planet, they hauled it in for a closer look. A farsighted people— they were roughly humanoid in appearance, by the way—they already have committees in existence to study this remarkable visitor.

"A word about life on Lugar. At first glance it might appear as an almost utopian society, if a little on the frivolous side. There is a high and fairly uniform standard of living. Folks work hard and they love all kinds of games, competitions, contests. Every week the whole family hikes out to the local stadium to see whatever sport is in season. Now this is a little odd. Let's say the fans are watching the Lugar equivalent of football. A hometown player drops an easy pass and fails to score a touchdown as a result. The spectators immediately give him a rousing round of applause. I don't mean scattered clapping. The fans, as one, jump to their feet and give the hapless fellow a standing ovation. This is remarkable, you think. These sure aren't Philadelphia sports fans. This isn't me at the Eagles' games. How considerate and mature of them, you announce.

"Ah, my friends, appearances, as they say, can be deceiving. Someone takes you aside and explains their behavior. They are cheering widely not to buck up the poor guy but because any public display of failure on Luger means that you will be killed or exiled into deep space. The greatest joy to the people of Lugar is the suffering of others. They don't care if they win as long as you lose.

"Now enters the protagonist of our little fable, Lugnut. Lugnut heads the committee to study evidence of artistic accomplishment manifest in the objects of the earthling space capsule. I should mention that the probe does include a range of materials chosen to represent life on earth. For example, there are drawings of a man and a woman, and some mathematical method of explaining the physical size of human beings. There's a drawing to show the location of earth in relation to our sun. There's a golden record on board—literally a record made of gold—that's pressed with various sounds from earth. A diamond needle was included. The scientists on Lugar, or wherever, will have to provide their own sound amplification equipment.

"Various types of animal sounds, and music, including classical are carried on the golden record. Beethoven's Ninth Symphony is not reproduced there, but let's pretend it is. It is Beethoven's Ninth that Commissioner Lugnut has been diligently studying. To say the least, he's impressed. One of the finest examples of musical expression that he's ever heard, Lugerian or otherwise. It's one thing to think it, but he, silly, rash fellow has to say it. Now Lugnut is a friendly, expansive, absentminded sort of music lover that we would recognize anywhere. Sure, if you were the busboy who dropped a tray of dinner dishes he'd hoot along with everyone. But he wouldn't be mean about it. He'd still leave the waiter his tip. In any event, Lugnut was so enraptured by the Beethoven symphony that he invited the Lugar Ruling Council in to hear it. He promised to delight them with some of the finest music in the universe."

Kevin returned to the small record player. He turned the record over to side two and restarted the turntable. "Perhaps some of you are not familiar with this music," he said. "The last movement of the symphony sets Schiller's 'Ode to Joy' to music. It's a marvelous choral piece." Kevin tested the record at several spots until he found the libretto. "Oh, freunde," the booming German voice sang out. And, farther along, female voices sang, "Alle menchen werden bruder..." "Yes, all men will be brothers," Kevin O'Donnell said. "No wonder Lugnut's sensitive nature was attracted to this. Of course, like most of you, he didn't understand a word of the language. But he felt its spirit. But let me recreate just exactly how Lugnut presented it to the Lugar authorities. You won't be surprised that it created a sensation."

Within a few seconds Kevin had altered the lighting in this classroom. Throwing switches on the wall behind him he blackened every light in the room, except for one small spotlight. The spotlight was aimed directly at the waiting, spinning record. "In a brief, impassioned introduction," Kevin continued from the shadows, "Lugnut set the stage for his presentation to the Lugar council. He claimed that what they were about to hear proved that truly intelligent life existed elsewhere in the universe. The planet Lugar would soon rejoice in these alien sounds."

Only those students in the first row, and with the best of hearing, would have recognized the small clicking sound from the direction of the record player. Then, Kevin lifted the needle arm and dramatically lowered the diamond stylus to the record's surface. The change that he had affected was startling. For four seconds his classroom remained still. (Out on Lugar, Lugnut, as yet unconcerned, was grinning from antenna to antenna). Kevin had purposely nudged the speed control from thirty-three r.p.m.s to forty-five r.p.m.s. Out from the speakers poured the sound of two hundred chipmunk voices shrieking gibberish German. When Kevin's students sprang to their feet it was with drill team timing. Their howling response eerily mirrored that of the Lugar Ruling Council as they yelled and laughed and cheered poor, careless Lugnut into oblivion.

CHAPTER FOUR

Thirty-four one-dollar bills. Kevin had counted them and stacked them on the plastic tablecloth draped over an old dinette set on Mercedes' porch. They had returned to her apartment shortly after class. While Kevin drank a beer and played with the money, Mercedes rooted through her closets for something appropriate to wear. A couple of times Kevin heard her call to him from inside the apartment. "I really planned to study tonight," she said. "I wasn't planning to have to look respectable." But shortly she emerged through the kitchen door, looking to Kevin the essence of spring in a white cotton dress with a straw belt. The day had been very warm for late April, but the porch was on the shaded side of the building and the thick stone walls were remarkably cool to the touch. "It will get pretty cold at the seashore tonight," Mercedes said. "And the casinos can be overly cool if I remember. I think I'll bring both a jacket and a sweater." "When were you at the casinos," Kevin asked, immediately wishing he hadn't. Already in the house, Mercedes called back, "Let's see. This February, I guess," and they both just let it drop.

Since rush hour traffic had largely scattered, a three-quarter's hour drive put them on the Atlantic City Expressway in New Jersey. The roadway experienced the gentlest of curves and the barest of inclines as it cut its way through the vast south Jersey Pine Barrens. Once past the housing developments near Philadelphia, the view consisted of legions of scrub pines interspersed with a handful of shallow lakes and slateflat truck farms of indeterminate prosperity. Kevin may have been a city dweller but his own home backed up on a wooded section of Fairmount Park, giving him, in effect, a miniature hardwood forest for a backyard. The ebb and flow of nature, its cyclical retrenchment and resuscitation, could be observed there not just seasonally, but monthly. Through varying shades of green and then succulent reds, browns, and yellows, the trees turned as if on a rotating disk. But the sandy soil alongside the Atlantic City Expressway did not yield up such luxuriant growth; the scraggly bushes and scrub pines changed little in appearance from summer to winter. Even in the heaviest July traffic, this highway had for him a solitary flavor. However, Kevin was fond of it in a nonchalant kind of way because it led to the comfortable shore towns that he loved: Ocean City, Avalon, Sea Isle. He had the barest acquaintance with Atlantic City and none with the new casinos, but he was on a roll today and a gambling house was the perfect stage to test that string of luck until it snapped.

"Just what was going on today?" Mercedes asked, breaking a relaxed silence. "I know you better than anyone in that class and I can't swear I know exactly what you were driving at."

"Did you enjoy it?"

"Sure. And you son of a bitch. I didn't think you'd make me pay you a dollar." She laughed.

"Just for appearances. But I'll pay you back. For now you've got a one-thirty-fourth interest in that bankroll. I have big plans for that money."

"Oh, swell," she said. I've always dreamed I'd be rich. But in the meantime, Kevin, you could answer my original question."

At certain times, in certain moods, Mercedes had the concentration and directness of a heat—seeking missile. Correspondingly, Kevin, at times, would approach a situation along the broadest possible front, vaguely hoping to attack his target from every direction at once. It tickled him when their opposing tactics overlapped. Like the combatants in a newspaper cartoon, they would create a whirlwind of smoke and confusion, often obscuring the very question that launched them in the first place. But today he was like an engine only recently shut down; he was still warm. The lightest touch could restart him.

"The whole lecture was based on some personal experiences, but I think that only adds to its validity. Did I ever tell you about my sessions with the hypnotist?"

"Hypnotist? Are you kidding?"

"I didn't think we had talked about it. Well, are you familiar with that Bridey Murphy story?"

"There was something I saw in a magazine..." Mercedes face was a cross of skepticism and interest. There was a smile lurking there, too, but she held it in check as Kevin continued.

"The Bridey Murphy story was reported by an amateur hypnotist who these incredible sessions with a modern-day Colorado housewife. They were trying to bring back memories of her earliest childhood. But in doing so, they went right past childhood, whipped past that like a runaway train, and brought up evidence of an earlier life of hers as a nineteenth century Irishwoman. Sound familiar?"

"I read something or other about that."

"Sure you did," Kevin continued. "Even the Philadelphia *Bulletin* carried it. But I was intrigued by what I heard. I thought it offered some interesting possibilities for self-discovery. Probably cheaper than going to a shrink. And relatively painless—like getting a tooth out under sodium pentothal. Anyway, I went to visit this professional hypnotist. This guy's strictly legitimate, I swear to this day. Actually it was two hypnotists working together at that time—the second one was the biggest ass you ever met. Strangely enough their partnership dissolved over working with me. Now this might seem beside the point, but it's really critical to the situation. You see their findings are potentially a watershed in the development of modern professional hypnotism. This second moron totally disagreed with the findings of my hypnotist, Merl Charleton. Osmond was the disgruntled guy. Afterwards he wrote inflammatory articles in *Hypnotist Quarterly* and other magazines that were filled with bitter recriminations, wild accusations, pointless diatribes...and, and adjectives that aren't even invented yet, attacking Merl's work."

"Just *where* do you find these people?" Mercedes marveled.

"Ace Hypnology Associates. In the Yellow Pages. But Merl's a real blue chip guy. Wears suits custom-made on Bond Street in London, and has a tastefully appointed office on Walnut Street—the works. In his waiting room there's an antique case clock, a grandfather clock. You can check the part in your hair in the polished cherry wood cabinet. The gleaming brass pendulum sways back and forth and back and forth and back and forth. And back and forth. Every detail adds to the mood. Under Merl's guidance it took no time at all to bring me back. Way back. Before we got started I had mentioned to him that the Romantic poet Shelly used to ask street urchins in London and Leghorn, Italy to describe heaven as that had experienced it before birth. I was looking for the same thing. I went under like a rock or something and Merl hit the reverse button on my memory and he just wouldn't let up. I can't directly remember what I told him, but everything I said was recorded on tape. Old Shelly was apparently right. We do spend nine months in heaven before birth. I'd give anything to have conscious memory of that period, but Merl's tape recordings are pretty definitive."

Mercedes asked, "Spend your time soaring with angels and the like?" Incredulity ratcheted up the nasal sound in her voice a notch or two. The station playing low on the radio was fading out; Mercedes randomly played with the tuning knob, meanwhile giving Kevin a look of the keenest interest.

"It's amazing. Everybody asks me that. In many ways it's different than you'd think. I guess that helps prove it really happened. I described a scene that was absolutely mobbed with kids. Remember, this was just after World War Two: the baby boom. It seems they had us dormatoried off to the side. On the tapes I gave the impression it was kind of an annex. I even think it may have been rented. You'd hear this gorgeous music like the Mormon Tabernacle choir and glide towards the sound expecting to see some white clad heavenly host—it would be a record player. The accommodations were less than first class but we had the time of our lives. A thousand kids at a time playing stick tag, and tackle all-over, and kill-the-man-with-the-ball. The folks in charge didn't try so much to control us as to contain us. They'd get a memo from time to time reminding them to keep the 'To be borns' away from the main activity areas. Apparently St. Peter would be at the gate of heaven conducting a judgement on some poor sucker, and say he just got the printout on the sixth or ninth commandment that runs fifty yards long. St. Peter'd be really to lay into the guy but good when two of these little monsters would come tearing through like their pants were on fire. And the first kid yells over his shoulder, 'You'll never catch me, Rudi.' All sense of decorum is shattered. You can see they had to put a lid on something like that."

"Let me try to keep this straight," Mercedes said. "What reason was this to cause the two hypnotists to have a falling out?"

"Well you've really hit right on it. This second guy, Osmond, claims that Merl made some technical blunder and never really brought me back that far at all. I don't have a handle on their jargon, but essentially Osmond claims that my memory was fixated at some point between the age of eight and ten years. According to him, my alleged "prebirth" memories are actually the recollection of one particularly overheated fourth grade recess. Spring fever combined with a clunk on the back by a baseball playing running bases. I try not to get swept up in this controversy nor is there any need to. Merl himself has deflated these claims quite handsomely in chapter four of his recent book, *Life Before Life.*"

Mercedes' search of the FM band placed her on a station playing famous Motown hits. Smokey Robinson, then Martha and the Vandellas, boomed softly on the Camaro's four stereo speakers. Singing along in a whispery voice, Mercedes continued looking at Kevin with a sweet, sexy look. He knew she was trying to distract him; see if she could knock him off stride. It was a contest they played with a half-dozen variations: feeding each other straight lines to fan some outlandish dialogue, then whipping the bait back like a wallet on a string. But he was too far along this time, sheer momentum propelled him. Might as well try to brake a heavy truck on an ice-glazed roadbed.

"The descriptions of heaven were unique and startling," Kevin continued, "but that's not the part of the story that really affects me." The barest edge of a serious tone crept into his voice. In a way it was similar to the change he would make in the car's performance from time to time by applying an almost imperceptible amount of pressure to the accelerator. Extra fifty revolutions per minute would appear on the tachometer, pulling the Camaro a half-mile an hour faster. He continued, "On the tape recordings we discovered something that explains much about how people think and how they behave. I've always been flabbergasted that so many people are convinced they have the answer to everything in the world. Collecting facts is no concern; having any experience in the subject matter is irrelevant. Your family doctor, while pumping up the sphygmometer like he's filling a flat tire, expounds on politics or the economy. Your neighbor the stock analyst suggests landscaping that would cost you ten thousand bucks. Two older ladies at the next beach blanket trace the rise in marital dissatisfaction to the discovery of sexual positions—didn't need them in their day. Ah, a world filled with opinionated Einstein's cousins. Recall that I said most of the time before birth we simply ran amuck. There was one exception to this, towards the end of our stay. A group of us on a certain day were required to pile into one of the side rooms, a chapel or something. There we were to be told the one hundred most important things you had to know in life. I heard later that this data was crammed on to five mimeographed pages. Ever wonder why people react to strongly to the smell of mimeograph paper? Obviously it's very primal. Anyway, I get near the entrance to this chapel and it's already packed. The guys behind me are shoving, this little fat kid in front of me is crying, inside I see that a sort of paper airplane cottage industry has taken root—using the mimeographed pages, of course— and delta-winged aircraft are staging suicidal dogfights between the chandeliers: the whole thing's a madhouse. And you know how I hate to wait in line for anything. So I said 'Forget this.' and checked out. Figured I catch a later showing. The chance of a lifetime to get the answers to life and I take a rain check. But intending like all get out to go back the next day, attend the makeup session. But the Big Man in charge gets the last laugh, let me tell you. As so often happens, the penalty for procrastination is severe; you see, Mercedes, I was born later that same day, two weeks premature."

The Seahawk Hotel and Casino was the newest gaming house in Atlantic City. Already attracting a well-heeled, up-tempo clientele, the casino showcased celebrity performers and offered its customers five sumptuous restaurants and a glittering gambling room. At the better tables the drinks were free; the scotch sour or Gibson set down beside you by the attentive, blonde, slender-armed, mildly undressed waitress proves to be of a quality liquor. One of the accommodating credit managers, giving the merest appraising glance, and then smiling enigmatically, as if to say, hey, it's not my money, signals the cashier to advance you a line of one, two, maybe three thousand dollars. Unleash a sizable enough bankroll of your own and a hotel room is on the house. Perhaps a free call girl if you press hard enough. Pleasant little touches you'd never think of have been thought of. Every major sensual pleasure known to man—with the notable exception of dancing in the aisles—is lavished upon the valued patrons of the Seahawk Hotel and Casino.

An eight story building of black painted steel and deeply tinted glass, The Seahawk occupies a full block adjacent to the boardwalk. Sweeping out from the building on its north and south sides, up between the fourth and fifth floors, pointing expectantly towards the ocean, are aerodynamically shaped cantilevers. Stylized wings of a bird, Kevin wonders? Perhaps, if the wind could envelop it just right, the entire structure could be launched intact, like a gargantuan seabird, out over the pitch black Atlantic on an airborne cruise to nowhere. Gathering their bearings, he and Mercedes are standing on the sidewalk alongside a driveway that sweeps up to the building's west entrance. Two tuxedo-clad valet parking attendants had materialized beside the Camaro, one to open Mercedes' door, the other to drive the car off to an unseen parking location. Brighter than daytime, the immediate perimeter is soaked with illumination; floodlights are perched three stories up. The lamps are there to provide a measure of protection, or at least a sense of protection, from the ravages of the blighted neighborhoods of the decayed old resort. Under his left foot, absent-mindedly, Kevin is now crunching the cream-colored pebbles that serve for a lawn, a sure sign that he is annoyed. The cause of his annoyance is not absolutely clear to him. On one side of the casino he observed an abandoned, decrepit hotel. Apparently it is undergoing extensive renovation; any flimsy structure or forsaken patch of real estate in Atlantic City can become a treasure with the onslaught of the casinos. Not a light in this ancient hotel is burning, but Kevin can see a dozen windows with the panes smashed out and shards of glass littering the ground like piles of crystalline confetti. Partially concealed under plastic tarps, with their mechanical arms awkwardly angled and frozen in place, construction equipment awaits the morning. The machines are like beasts of burden, docile now, with enormous raw power lurking within. How do you start those things, Kevin muses, push a button or wave a red flag at them? On the other side of the Seahawk, the north side along the boardwalk, the land has been bulldozed flat. With his eyes Kevin tries to survey its depth: at least one entire city block, maybe more. A tall chain link fence protects and defines the flattened terrain. He figures a sparkling new casino complex is destined for that spot, assuming the financing hasn't collapsed. But Kevin O'Donnell never had any stake in Atlantic City, particularly not the old, faded, tumbling down Atlantic City, so what does he care how they carve it up or if they raze exhausted bath houses and rickety amusement piers. Turn of the century architecture, second and even third rate, rotted from within by a cancer of dampness and neglect was of no particular loss to him. Now silly as it might be, someone else driving his car always perturbed him. The parking attendant's manner was as unctuous as his attire, reminding Kevin of gangsters in movies who lambaste loansharks for their impoliteness and then kill them for it. That same car jockey was now probably timing the Camaro for zero to sixty. On his wrist, to get his attention, he gets a light squeeze from Mercedes. Wide-eyed and with slightly pouting lips, she is doing her flirtatious female act. Kevin knows she is saying, "Are we going to stand here all night, Buster?" At the instant of reaching the entrance, before they ascend through a series of carpeted landings and ten-foot high glass doors, an answer hits him, penetrates straight to his skin like a building's air conditioning in August humidity. He hasn't seen the ocean tonight. Kevin has no real sense of its proximity. Almost never has Kevin arrived at the shore, regardless of the hour or the weather, regardless of his condition, without an immediate stop at the beach. With his dock siders dangling in his hand, he liked to stand at the water's edge, gingerly testing the ocean temperature with one foot. So far, this casino might as well be in Las Vegas. In every direction, and for five hundred miles, might as well be a silent and unyielding desert.

The lighthearted master of ceremonies at the garden club dinner, or, perhaps at the Gierson Gasket Company western regional sales banquet, or even the invisible, authoritative game show announcer who declare, "And our next guest needs no introduction" come closest to the impression left upon Kevin O'Donnell by the appearance of Tony Connelli and Vic Kesson. But while they might not need an introduction, or more accurately, a description of who or what they were, they described themselves, individually and collectively, in the flow of the evening as: Displaced Persons; criminally insane; recovering alcoholics; captains of industry; bon vivants; defenders of the faith; victims of society; and, former high commissioners of that notorious drinking game, Zoom-Schwartz.

Connelli was the smaller of the two yet the most imposing in a physical way. When he asked a question or, more often, made a point, he would thrust his hand out, up about chin level, five fingers out thrust, as if he were holding a fine four-pound pineapple for public inspection. Kevin and Mercedes' table was on the edge of a small, crowded cocktail area and the plastic backs of their chairs were actually touching those of the Connelli-Kesson party, occasionally threatening to form a suction seal between them. About forty feet from them a live ten-piece band was puffing out a cloud of big-band music. Tony Connelli talked as though a ten-piece band continually shadowed him so for once his booming voice seemed acoustically appropriate. "Hey, Professor," he called to Kevin. "We need a man of your obvious talents to settle a dispute."

Kevin and Mercedes both studied Tony for a moment, trying to decide if they knew him, and this was all the green light Tony wanted. "I say me and Victor here just spent the smartest twenty-five hundred dollars of our lives. Vic, say hello to the nice people—okay, enough of that shit, Vic. We'll be able to recoup that investment in one night and get back at the casinos all in one neatly felled swoop. Now this dumb bunny partner of mine is having second thoughts. Do you catch my drift?"

Kevin answered, "Drifting is for wood. I'm counseling a direct approach. Cut out the middleman. Deal direct—no pun intended. Do you mind if we discuss my fee?"

"Oh, sure. Sure. Vic, where's those credit cards you found? Hm? Doc, here's the deal. A slick young operator's got a new scam to skim off the casinos. He was studying math at college when his widowed mother took sick (no, it was his grandmother, Vic argues) or so he tells me, and he needed to make some money real fast. Came up with a great new way to beat the casinos' odds and they don't even know it yet. Ha, they're so dense they don't know he can steal them blind: he's the world's first professional big-wheel counter. And he'll teach us to do it for a paltry twenty-five hundred bucks apiece. It'll teach us to memorize the last sixty-four turns of the big wheel. Just like card counting in blackjack. No more lining up like sheep to lose your chips to the wheel of fortune."

Vic added, "But I'm the kind of guy who forgets his social security number. I'm thinking I should have talked him down to thirty-two wheel turns for twelve-hundred fifty."

Catching Kevin by surprise, Mercedes burst right in, saying, "After you guys clean up house, I've got a bridge I've been thinking of selling..." For the first time Kevin took a good glance at the women sitting with Tony and Vic. Probably in their late forties, they looked a few years younger than the men. They were done up in a way Mercedes and her bunkie Jan might be for a Halloween party: hitting the party lights as a couple of brassy women. The blonde woman with Victor had wide curls and was partial to gold at her neck and on both wrists; the other had auburn hair and wore a heavy silver cross at the end of a necklace of tiny pearls. But marvel as he may, Kevin found himself involved in a little circle of people and he was not the man in control. As he vaguely pondered this Mercedes and Tony and Vic's dates swept to their feet to head as a group to the ladies' room.

"Well, chief," Tony said, "You look like a young fella who knows his way around these gambling dens. You've seen them all, have you?"

"No, no. Only this one. And only tonight. I've had a little luck already. I'm on kind of a hot streak today. Brought this little pile of winnings,

I'll call it—long story—won maybe sixty bucks extra already. Do you two belly up to the tables a lot?"

Tony and Vic pointed at each other with pretended anger and then dissolved into laughter. Gasping for air, Vic managed to say, "We would if he didn't get us thrown out of all the other casinos in town. Tony loses nine bucks at the three-dollar blackjack tables and leaves it yelling, 'I'm ruined. I've lost everything. And I pawned Ma's pearl necklace.' One thing we find consistent about the security people: they can't take a joke."

"We went back to that same casino a month later,"Tony Connelli said. "Friend of ours flew us into Atlantic City in his private Cessna. He demanded they send a limo to drive us to the casino—thought we were high rollers. We were halfway through the complementary dinner when the manager came and all but yanked the tablecloth off. But maybe it's for the better. Maybe we would be paupers if we ever got the run of the place. And seriously, a young man like you, you've got to try to control this yen to gamble. Lots of guys brag about their winnings until bankruptcy court puts a padlock on their business."

Before Kevin could counter this, Mercedes and the other women returned. Mercedes was dying to talk to him—her lovely eyes were fifty percent wider than usual—and she asked him to join her for a foray into the gambling area. She didn't just clutch Kevin's are, she all but dragged him away. An image of Tony and Vic in the arms of casino security pulsed in his mind. They stopped near a group of roulette tables; it would be easy to talk here. Croupier and bettors alike spoke softly or not at all. Kevin had seen Monopoly money change hands with more commotion.

Mercedes put her hands on both of his arms. She was bursting with stories. "Gloria and Maxine, that's Tony and Vic's dates, you'll never guess how they met them. They met them through a video dating service—but that's not the half of it."

Very, very casually, Kevin answered, "Oh, there's nothing wrong with that." In the past, he had been known to examine the personal advertisements in *Philadelphia Magazine* with more than scholarly interest.

"Of course," Mercedes continued. "This is where they are interviewers on video tape, and the tapes are reviewed by prospective dates. You know, they record your voice along with the video recording. But Tony and Vic didn't seem to understand that. You remember how people act on old fashioned home movies. There's no sound and people exaggerate their movements. Well that was them. They flapped around the chair like a couple of geese. Maxine said it was the most precious thing she had ever seen."

Kevin was pleased as a baby by this. He could already see himself recounting it to Goodall at the racquetball club. For emphasis Bob would slap closed any open lockers nearby, and the metal doors would clang like cymbals in support of their laughter. And just as quickly he thought, "Like Tony and Victor, I have a good friend. And I have dear Mercedes here. He felt wonderful. Instantly, they both seemed to want to go back and talk with their new friends. "Oh, and Gloria told me this," Mercedes added before they reached their table. "Don't even think that they are a couple of rubes or something. They own their own company and it does rather well. And they are used to sophisticated things. Years ago they were friends at South Philadelphia High School. Gloria says that they arranged that the Roseannadana Brothers were down from New York to perform at their senior prom."

Kevin, no slouch in this department (namely, snagging Lee Andrews and the Hearts for his post-prom gala) was markedly impressed. The live band at the cocktail area was playing "Tuxedo Junction" when they reclaimed their seats and the throbbing tempo seemed to pump up Kevin's enthusiasm another ten percent. He was intrigued about the Connelli-Kesson business and its reputed success. His father's monumental struggle to achieve the same goal had left an impression like the working of water on bedrock: slowly formed yet deeply felt. It was not idle chatter when Kevin asked, "Just what is it that you guys do?"

"You've never heard of us?" Tony asked.' "Where had you been, Siberia or something? We have a construction company, over in South Jersey. God knows how, but we still make a buck. And with a partner like Vic to boot, right? It helps when you make a pact with the devil."

"Listen to this bigshot," Vic said. "I'm carrying the place, as you might guess. Shit, in our hearts we'll always be a couple of bricklayers."

Ah, I like that concept, Kevin thought. That's my own real occupation: I am a bricklayer and I build the structure of my life one God damned brick at a time.

Tony Connelli asked, "And what are you going to take up when the last of Papa's Xerox stock is sold?"

"Oh, I wear the hat of a college teacher. And I have a book project I'm trying to get off the ground. I am trying to find old photographs a long-dead uncle took out west. I have a personal interest in it, of course, and it fits in with what I teach. This uncle never got the recognition he deserved. He died a young man in the San Francisco earthquake."

Kevin and Mercedes immediately discovered themselves sharing a look that said, "Gee, I didn't know earthquakes were so funny." This was because Tony and Victor erupted in whoops and howls of laughter. Composure regained, Victor said, "For years we've had a standing joke between us. Back in our navy days, out in San Diego, we had an exec who loved his collection of old photographs. We'd be in and out of his office a fair amount. At least every other time he'd ask us if we didn't find the pictures fascinating. Good thing we said we did: probably saved us from court marshall proceedings. Old Captain Bulwer backed us up like a trooper. Wasn't our fault, either. Anyone could have left that valve open and the destroyer was due to be decommissioned anyway. So lots of times, over a few beers, Tony and I kid that Bulwer should have left us a couple of those pictures in his will. Especially his pride and joy. Shots taken from the Bay a few days before San Francisco got hit by that earthquake."

THUNDERSTRUCK. Kevin barely drew a breath for thirty seconds, but he was in no danger because his metabolism slowed to a proportionate crawl. Once, years before, he had performed CPR on a stricken man on a downtown Philadelphia street, on 16th Street just south of Walnut, and his sensations then were similar to this. Time was experienced at about twenty-percent its actual rate. Vision was mildly distorted, with objects right in front of him larger than normal and walls at a slightly farther distance slanting a few degrees off true vertical. The effect exaggerated in part by the nearby optician's window that displayed sunglasses fifty percent bigger than their true retail size. The rescue squad's siren, coming at him at a seeming crawl, was alternately hopeful and menacing. Kevin was in the presence of sudden death for the first time and apparently it generates its own peculiar music.

"Describe those photographs. Tell me about the San Francisco photographs," Kevin found himself saying. He had one hand on Tony's shoulder, and Tony, unusual for him, had an apprehensive look, as though he would be pulled out of that chair like a yo-yo. "Okay, wait. I get the feeling they are important to you. It's been a few years, you know. I remember Captain Bulwer claimed that they were taken one or two days before that big earthquake. Christ, he repeated himself a lot. But I never looked at them that closely. We were kids and you don't appreciate these things."

"Listen up. I remember a thing or two more," Vic said. "They were a bunch of shots matched up in a row...the name's on the tip of my tongue — a panorama. And someone told Bulwer they were taken from an aerial balloon."

"Balloon, hell. It was from a huge kite." This was from Mercedes and with such conviction she could have been commanding the wheel of that long decayed fishing boat. Kevin was proud she knew the story so well. He loved her expression upon hearing something incredulous: her lips would part slightly and her eyes filled with laughter and shock. Victor was describing additional photos from old Bulwer's collection: Indian village scenes, wilderness studies, back alleys half lost in shade, half bleached with light, sailing vessels nestled in a dock like sleepy children on a small bed. Details poured like water from a high-pressure faucet; meanwhile, Tony's face imitated Mercedes astounded expression. Kevin sensed that this was quite a revelation to Tony. Something like seeing a ghost—no, just the opposite. Observing a side of Victor that was real but which didn't often aspire to daylight. They were like two grizzled prospectors, thirty years partners in panning for gold, knowing each other's moods and quirks like the trodden hillside and dusty mineshaft of an exhausted gold mine, and suddenly one reveals a fabulous nugget that he had secreted for decades. Their comfortable marriage was temporarily thrown off balance.

Kevin feels a soft hand on his own. A heavy ring band scrapes lightly across his knuckles. Maxine wants his attention. "Just what is going on," she asks.

"These pictures they're describing must be my uncle's," Kevin announces to everybody. "This is fantastic because they sound much better than any I have myself. By good luck, some old photographs of his were passed down through my family. None of the actual negatives, however. And there is a poor sampling of some of the more spectacular scenes he wrote about. From my grandfather I got a lot of the letters he wrote. Apparently his parents in Ireland never threw away a single one of them. One he wrote the very day before the earthquake...it describes a series of shots from a kite suspended off a fishing boat...ending up arriving in Donegal, Ireland, six months after the disaster. Whoever mailed it is unknown. Some money that was supposed to be in it was missing."

In her throaty voice Gloria said, "It would give me the creeps to get a letter like that. From the dead. And the money gone—like the devil took it." She made a start with her hand, as if to bless herself. For an intense moment Kevin remembered a train ride with five people in an old-fashioned compartment, from Coventry, England, bound for Edinburgh, Scotland, cold October night, raindrops quivering on the windows, everyone swamping ghost stories. Except, to the reincarnationist from Syracuse, New York, the stories were real. Twice that evening the electric bulbs had dimmed. This gave fresh meaning to the term "spine-tingling." Trained in psychology, the woman's graduate thesis hinged on the idea that homosexuality exists because some men come back as women, and women as men. She claimed that she was capable of giving details in depth of homes before she entered them. Three different years, on the exact anniversary of the death of her Springer spaniel, a strange dog had appeared at her patio window, scratched at the glass door as her pet had done, and then replicated the figure-eight pattern it used to walk on the smooth flagstones.

"How do I get in touch with this Captain Bulwer," Kevin asked.

"Well, it would have to be something in the order of what Gloria just said," Tony Connelli answered. "We understand that he's dead. He wasn't a young man when we last saw him years ago. He was married, but no children. His hobbies were his kids."

"Yeah. And who says the navy can't take a joke," Vic said. "We're invited to San Diego for the thirtieth anniversary of leaving the ship's crew. That's how we heard old Bulwer's gone."

"O'Donnell," Tony said, his hand. thrust out nearly in front of his face. "If I were you this is what I'd: haul my ass out to California when were out there and search for your heirlooms. We'll be out there over Memorial Day, into June. We'd take a few days and lend you a hand. Help you play detective."

My God, Kevin thought. He seems absolutely sincere about this. Well, maybe it's just the magic of the moment, with everything running my way. But what the hell. Kevin half leaped up from the table, grabbed each of them by a forearm, and said, "It's a deal" And then, to a waitress gingerly squeezing by their table, Kevin exuberantly commanded, "Champagne."

The champagne was a nice touch and a near disaster. Afterwards, Kevin remembered some of the more rambunctious episodes of the "Tonight Show" when Johnny Carson is moved to ask his sidekick, Ed McMahon, "Just when kid I lose control?" For the first two sparkling glasses his self-control was as marginal as the other fellows. He was a talking space heater. The champagne kerosene feeding a radiant circle of warmth. But as his own enthusiasm leveled off, as he settled into a softer, satisfied mood, much like entering a candlelit room at the onset of twilight, Tony and Victor were just taking off. It was as if a cluster of red-hot afterburners propelled them up to the stratosphere. Russian-style, an elbow crooked in reciprocal elbow, Tony and Vic toasted each other. To belt back the bubbly, they had to lean heavily across the small table, linked like furniture stacked together precariously, threatening to topple on Maxine sitting between them. In the middle of this tableside tango, with a mind that often sweeps like a radar scan, O'Donnell noticed that the band had changed. A young female singer backed up by a five-piece rock band. Powerful guitar amplifiers twanged in response to the twisting of a tuning knob. Coolly revving up, the drummer beat a soft tattoo on the snare drum, and then set the cymbals jangling. Registering the light touch at the keyboard, chords hovered briefly above the electric organ. In the crowded cave of the casino, O'Donnell rightly expected this to be a soft rock group. Their repertoire was mostly mellow, stylized versions of top-40 hits. But, as they launched into their first set, Kevin sensed an energy level, a toughness that would not be allowed scope at the Seahawk. Ensconce them in the right atmosphere, let them loose in a dance club, and they would really rip.

"Do you think this chickee takes requests," Tony asked.

"What specifically do you have in mind," Vic answered', grinning like a fifteen year old.

"Something musical. Something with a beat to it. Get our old toes tapping."

"Dance music, brother," Vic said.

"Let's find out," Tony suggested. "I live to dance."

For two men of decent bulk, they slipped away from the table with surprising agility. Kevin half reached after them: the exasperated parent. Take a picture of this, he thought, and it would be like a sports photo of the beleaguered defensive back, juked out of position, conceding the winning touchdown. Already they were in front of the bandstand. Hands were in their jacket pockets, and they were looking more innocent than sheep. When the singer leaned down to talk to them her honey blonde hair swayed almost in front of her eyes. With one hand she pulled some hair back. With the other microphone hand she shrugged a sure-why-not kind of gesture. Watching through the increasingly smoky cocktail lounge, Kevin was reminded of the late movies he sees on the old black-and-white television set in his bedroom. Apparently, developing the skills to play in a rock combo does not leave time to catch such informative fare. The innocent faces on Connelli and Kesson would be the harbinger of danger on the midnight movie. To a man and woman, the band members were like the trusting, Oregon-bound city folk whose wagon train is marked in Indian Territory luring the 1860's. Before settling in for the night someone cheerfully remarks on the Tasmanian sulfur-crested cockatoos that have been calling to one another on the immediate perimeter of their camp. That's strange: their Conestoga wagon just burst into flames...Meanwhile, back at the bandstand, the singer has turned to face her colleagues, a careless move, if not exactly a regrettable one. As Kevin had earlier sensed they were really going to let themselves boogie for this one. They launched themselves into it something like the way reconnaissance planes used to be catapulted from battleships. Once they were airborne getting back on that ship was something of a mystery. Into the music and each other, the band failed to notice a minor spectacle developing just east of their foot lights: Tony and Victor exuberantly dancing and singing to "The Girl Can't Help It" in the narrow aisle in the heart of the cocktail lounge.

Direct an electrical current through a magnet, pass it over a dune of metal shavings, and you are quick to draw a crowd. Dance without a license in a packed casino and you get to meet the security folks about as fast. Kevin, Mercedes, Gloria and Maxine arrived in the aisle simultaneously with several young security officials. All of them, Tony and Vic included, were mixed closely together like several parties entwined in an elevator. Perhaps it was this forced intimacy, or, perhaps it was the momentary confusion, but anyway Kevin felt he could take charge. "I'm Doctor O'Donnell," he said to a smooth faced young man in a blue suit, "and these gentlemen are with me."

With a sharp look, the security official dismissed his two colleagues. Then, considerably milder, talking to Kevin as though everyone else had vanished, "Well, we have a problem here. There's, uh, strict fire codes governing the premises, Doctor. It's critical that all avenues of escape are left open at all times. And it would be better if your patients would leave for the night. Does this, uh, happen to them often?"

Tony gave Kevin the high sign that they were indeed leaving the casino. In mere seconds the offenders and their dates melted away from the aisle. This security fellow was obviously inexperienced. In a month he would no longer offer such a sensitive face. "Thought I was making more progress," Kevin said, a trace of dejection in his voice. "But it's a somewhat intractable condition. Rare, extremely rare. They suffer from what, in clinical terms, is an inefficacious obsession to express primitive, unresolved emotional traumas in unrestrained motor schematics."

"Jesus," the security man said. "And I've got to write a report on this incident. Doctor, could you reduce what you just said to layman's terms?"

"Surely," Kevin said. He slipped an arm around Mercedes and very slowly they turned in the direction of their table. Again, his voice, a notch above a whisper, had a coloring of sad wisdom, of a man who had looked ugly realities in the face.

"In everyday terms it may even be more brutal," Kevin told him. "But don't hold back. On that report write it boldly, in big letters. They Live to Dance."

CHAPTER FIVE

"Who designed the shape of the football, anyway?"

"Sigmund Freud!"

(Question from Pat Summerall answered by Tom Brookshier,

former professional football players,

while announcing a televised game and watching a football bounce

crazily after a fumble).

The motivational speaker at the Gierson Gasket Company Western Regional breakfast meeting was a complete jerk and almost perfect at his job. Kevin O'Donnell found himself sitting at a table uncomfortably near this speaker's podium. Vic Kesson was at his left and Tony Connelli at his right. The breakfast meeting for one hundred people took place in Room C of the subdivided Gold Coast Auditorium at the Hotel El Dorado Conference Center in San Diego, California. There were two women at the table, identified by name tags in crisp 16-font print as Marion Devine of Crater Lake, Oregon and Katrina Butte of Logan, Utah. Instead of the pin-on variety, name tags hung from royal blue nylon cords that clipped to the top of a plastic sheaf, considerably avoiding the puncturing of delicate acrylic sport shirts and blouses. Old friends, or at least long time Gierson employees and acquaintances, the women were buzzing over an envelope of Katrina's Park City, Utah skiing photographs. In contrast to the women, the nametags laced around the necks of Kevin, Victor and Tony were handwritten in thick, black, felt-tip pen ink, hastily at that, with no mention of any operational site that they represented.

The other occupant at their table was man about fifty-five years old, with the muscular build of a lifelong athlete, and with a brindle pattern of graying hair, wearing one of the few suit coats in the casually dressed audience. A small centerpiece of yellow gladiolas in a tall ceramic vase obscured the fellow's nametag and title from Kevin, but he took this attire as a sign that he was a vice president or some other management stalwart. Kevin froze for a second when the man said, genially enough, "I'm not sure if I know who you three gentlemen are," but Tony responded with, "We're those new guys," then quickly looked back at the morning's speaker.

It was one of Bob Goodall's jokes that Kevin repeated off-handedly to Tony and Vic that maneuvered them into this situation. Kevin and Goodall had traipsed through a half dozen hotel conferences over the last four years, listening to profound discourse on topics such as "American Value Structure Influence on Emerging Third-World Economies," leading Bob to comment that he had found the solution to world hunger. Like a sort of linear, antiseptic corporate bazaar, mini-mountains of bagels and Danish pastries and miniature waterfalls of orange juice and apple juice bubbled on beckoning table after table in front of eight or ten separate seminar rooms in countless hotels. The seminar sponsors were anxious about turnout and welcomed every face picking through the continental breakfast. No one ever challenged the legitimacy of the person piling sweet rolls next to the sliced honeydew melon on paper plates. The immediate pressure of delivering a full house overriding the objective of compiling a reliable database of attendee names. Why not bring in poor hungry souls in here Bob said once, packing their tummy's with corn flakes as they happily packed the seminar room. Food for thought and their bodies. Tony and Victor didn't act like this was funny, but they veered towards the conference area anyway on the way to breakfast that morning. "Let's see if we *can* crash a meeting," Tony said, and brazenly marched into the first gathering they encountered. One might think that Kevin O'Donnell would have remembered his friends' behavior just the previous day flying to San Diego from Philadelphia before popping out with a comment like that. A little amazed he was at himself for agreeing to fly first class, paying for Mercedes ticket in the bargain. Captains of industry that they were, Tony and Vic would not travel any other way. But the first class expense was likely worth it, given the latitude apparently offered the occupants of those plush vinyl seats. They were not all that rambunctious, Kevin realized, actually he was the one making a spectacle of himself, Mercedes smacking him playfully on the right arm on two occasions to shush his laughter. Sitting immediately in front of Kevin and Mercedes, Victor commented that it surprised him that pilots always say, once the *Fasten Seatbelt* sign is disengaged, that passengers are free to walk around the airplane cabin. Exactly where are passengers supposed to go, Vic questioned. And more importantly, can everyone move around at once? Tony Connelli said he long shared the same concern, and had in fact once tested the limits of that largesse. He had wondered if he could get all 168 people in the coach section on a Denver to Philadelphia flight to pack into the last few rows of the aircraft following the captain's announcement.

Tony claimed that he went up to the flight attendant and in an excited stage whisper declared that he had lost an envelope with six thousand dollars in cash somewhere near the rear lavatory. Could he get volunteers to help him locate it? Tony swore that minutes later every coach passenger under the age of eighty was swarming over rows thirty-two to thirty-six at the tail of the craft (it was largely a Philadelphia crowd in the coach section). The pilots of that Boeing 757 had been cruising serenely over western Kansas, happy to be beyond the turbulent updrafts of the Colorado Rockies, their expert eyes barely lighting on a score of amber-glowing dials in the soft February evening, all readings hovering quietly within normal ranges. Suddenly they were clutching the wheels in a white-knuckled grip, struggling to maintain control something like bomber pilots scudding through flak-filled skies over nighttime 1944 Berlin. Kapow. Kapow. Boom! Tony had later heard from a reliable source that at least one set of pilots now routinely risks FAA and airline sanctions by requiring lengthy written requests from passengers to go even to the lavatory once the plane is wheels up.

Roland Brinkley, the motivational speaker, stood beside a high wooden podium positioned at center stage of Room C, sometimes radiating around it towards the audience in a wide semicircle as he addressed different topics. He paced almost furtively during the course of his presentation, now sweeping his left hand leisurely towards Kevin's right, now grandly sweeping his right hand past Kevin's left. Roland had thick black hair that was combed straight back, with no part in it, gangster-style Kevin thought, and was dressed in expensive but shapeless brown trousers, and a blue sports shirt layered under a brown sports coat. His outfit provided minimal contrast to the 20-foot oatmeal-colored drapes that cascaded from the ceiling behind him. To Kevin, Roland was rumpled and rugged at the same time, reflecting the fact as Roland later shared with the group that he had experienced and triumphed over rocky times. Roland was less polished in appearance than what Kevin O'Donnell envisioned in a "motivational speaker", assuming that businesses would rather ply the audience with the country club war stories of a tanned, avuncular professional golfer in a Gucci jacket and yardstick-straight creased pants. "Since Jack Nicholas was wedging out of a sand trap when Nick Faldo got set to drive on the eighteenth tee..." and all that. Yet Kevin took note that Mr. Brinkley was attired somewhere in the middle between the conservatively dressed Gierson Gasket Company managers and the polo-shirted rank and file attendees, a fortuitous coincidence no doubt.

"There are two main ideas that I want you to remember from my talk," Roland Brinkley was saying, "and they are so basic and simple that you can write them on an index card." Kevin O'Donnell nearly laughed aloud at this comment, wondering if Roland knew enough stuff even to fill up an index card or maybe the back of a first-class postage stamp. "In fact I want you to find the index cards we placed in your program manual," Roland continued. "You should find them paper-clipped on the top of the table of contents page. I have a story about index cards that I'm sure you'll find helpful. In my senior year in college I took an eighteenth century English literature course. The professor gave out index cards, everyone figuring they were for a list of other courses we had taken, that kind of thing. Instead, he informed us that he wanted us to be able to fill up at least one index card of what we learned in his course when the semester was over. Can you believe the gall of that guy? But then he said, "How many of you have taken courses at this school where you can't remember enough to fill out one little card?" There were at least twenty students there and lots were seniors like me. As the saying goes, you could have heard a pin drop after his comment. Now I am ashamed to admit that I couldn't today fill up one three-by-five inch card on eighteenth century English literature, but"—Roland paused for effect—"at least I remember the index card!"

A Gierson Gasket crowd may always be a sucker for a good punch line and the response might be anticipated. Kevin's table was no exception: Marion and Katrina were beside themselves laughing, Marion clasping her hands at her sternum to restrain herself, and even the manager-type was grinning and giving a thumbs up sign to a buddy at another table. But the Gierson folks were there for a reason other than entertainment. Throughout Room C people were flipping through the large three-ring binder left for each attendee in a pagoda-shaped stack beside the vase with the gladiolas. White index cards were being squeezed from under oversized blue plastic paperclips and momentarily held aloft in triumph. Kevin figured Tony and Vic would be rolling their eyes just like him. Instead they were still shaking their shoulders in enjoyment and peering at their blank index cards as if they encoded the meaning of life.

"You need to remember two basic ideas to be successful," Roland Brinkley said then. "In fact I recommend that you literally write them on your index cards. Some people like to print them in big block letters, and tape them up at home or in the office somewhere, or even on the dashboard of their car. I'm a little embarrassed to say that I have these messages taped all over my house to help keep me on track. They stare back at me from the medicine cabinet mirror as I reach for a razor. Come over for Christmas dinner and you might not see them anywhere, but I'll be sure to get them back up the next morning, Boxing Day as the British call it. And as basic as they are, these ideas are complicated, too—I've had folks argue that they are contradictory. Now you will decide that for yourself . Point number one, or idea number one is: Search for Commonality. Idea number two is: Discover the Uniqueness."

The audience in Room C in the Gold Coast Auditorium painstakingly printed out the words of Brinkley's wisdom on the small lined cards, as seriously and oddly tense as ambitious high school students filling in their names and testing location for the college boards. Place that middle initial in the wrong column and you can kiss Sarah Lawrence goodbye. Everyone had two index cards and that called for a major decision. Kevin noticed that Katrina Butte nearly filled all of the space of two cards, yet her friend Marion with a purple ink pen neatly compiled the sayings on the top half of one. There was minimal buzzing in isolated patches in the room as attendees wondered if they had gotten the exact wording. Finally Lester Lamont, the senior vice president at Kevin's table—-the guy reared back to raise his hand, enabling Kevin to read his nametag—-asked Roland in a deep voice to repeat the statements.

A large flip chart with white paper rested on a metal tripod on the other side of the speaker's podium from Roland Brinkley. Roland moved to it and counted off the first few sheets like a poker player counting dollars with his fingers. He then flipped the covering sheets to display his bold handwriting in red ink. 'Search for Commonality' was positioned in close approximation to an hour-glass shape on the page and 'Discover the Uniqueness' was similarly placed on the next.

"Six words in two sayings", Roland said. "Not too many to remember, yet they capture an awful lot. They certainly straightened out my life and they can help you, too. Every time—and I mean this—every time I make this presentation I find out new things about them. The "searching" process and the "discovering" process are never-ending, I guess, but that's not a problem at all. You'll always be dealing with new people and situations and you can keep these little mental tools handy."

Roland reflected for a short while on his next comments and then said, "At best I can give you an overview of the meaning of 'commonality' and 'uniqueness' as I see them. At most I can provide you with a front door key to this huge structure, this palatial estate that houses these powerful concepts. Once you pass through the cathedral-scale doors you are very much on your own in determining where you are and in interpreting what you see. Imagine being permitted to roam around in the middle of the night in the Metropolitan Museum of Art or the Prado museum in Madrid without even those confusing gallery maps for guidance. Five shadings of violet spanning the Venetian through the Flemish schools of art. The corridors are minimally lit, mimicking emergency lighting during a power outage, but the great halls of art works have piercing spot lights or shimmering chandeliers. No soft-voiced security guard materializes to tell you 'it's in the west wing.' Usually these are elderly fellows, slight of build, with thin or thick silver hair, working to supplement meager pension benefits, just what treasure are they are capable of protecting? And of course you are deep inside these monumental buildings, no windows in sight, and your supposed to recon east from west. But by inviting you to enter the estate, letting you meander around on your own, experiencing deep meaning that emerges from the lacquered canvases and the chiseled marbles, I think I am doing you a valuable service.

"'Commonality' in this context means the links that somehow make a group have the same drives or objectives. Of course all human kind has the need to breathe and eat and sleep and so on, but I'm thinking more in terms of an active linkage. As engineers, you would be interested in new advances that affect gaskets. Yet even your twin sister couldn't care less about that. By 'uniqueness' I mean that each of you would respond to that engineering advancement somewhat differently. Some might be pumped up about it, some might be threatened by it, thinking it will help a competitor leapfrog past Gierson, slice up your business like a stainless steel wheel churning through pizza."

Roland turned the flip chart to a blank sheet of paper, snapped up a blue ink marker pen and jammed its cap on to the end holder. Left handed, and with pressure heavy enough to slightly depress the chart Roland wrote 'Gierson Co.' in six-inch letters. "I want to give you folks an example of how I use these ideas. For example, when Mr. Lester Lamont, your senior VP over there, hired me for this meeting, I had to 'Search for the Commonality' connecting your group. Time was scarce since I was replacement speaker for a San Diego Padres' coach who banged up his Achilles tendon in an auto accident. Anyone could say you are all employees of the Gierson Gasket Company, but, we need something more deeply connecting than that. So I spent time speaking with Les Lamont and a few other managers and I determined the following major common traits." Roland proceeded to write out in his firm blocky style the words 'sales people', 'engineers', 'direct selling', and 'total product line.' "Everybody in this room can say that they know all of these things instinctively about the attendees at this Western Regional Conference." (While Katrina Butte subtly nodded in agreement this was not totally accurate. Kevin O'Donnell admitted privately that he had not for a second figured out the key characteristics of the people hugging the perimeter of the seventeen tables of Room C. Ninety percent males, the ages of late twenties to late forties captured most of them. They did not look unmotivated to begin with, bordering on overeager in fact in the rapt way they concentrated on Roland, sometimes jotting short notes in their meeting binder, and Kevin remained mystified for the moment for the need for Brinkley in the Gierson world). "The combination of these characteristics creates the commonality to a large part," Roland said. These items are not the unique aspect I have mentioned—we'll get to that shortly-because there are lots of sales people who don't work for Gierson, obviously most of the world's engineers are not employed by your firm, and so on. I have analyzed your group to find the links that bind individuals into a whole. And as quickly as that is accomplished, the differences between each and every one of you calls out to me like a song."

Roland moved away from the podium in a slow sweep that started from Kevin's right, steadily examining each table with a look partly calculating, partly quizzical, very intense and nearly mesmerizing. Kevin sensed an almost imperceptible reduction in people's eye movements as Brinkley's gaze settled on them. Old Roland had a theatrical flair, Kevin conceded, but another interpretation was possible, strange as is was to O'Donnell: Roland could not have begun to grasp the unique features of these people, having never interacted with them before. Couldn't he have made a stab at that prior to this moment, not leave himself so vulnerable to rejection in a public setting? Mr. Lamont's beaver-efficient executive assistant could have pulled resumes on many of them and Roland could have mingled pleasantly with attendees before his talk, scanning name tags, overhearing conversations, eavesdropping on their little stories. "Clayton, you must *love* living back in Scottsdale, now that the divorce is over." Instead he apparently chose to avoid close contact prior to the start of his presentation. What if audience members now refused to reveal themselves out of spite, or embarrassment, or a desire to fit in with everyone around their table? It could approximate trying to open cans of whole peeled tomatoes with just your fingers. And to make a difficult situation possibly more unmanageable, apparently they were a bunch of engineers, for God's sake.

Roland broke his silence by saying, "Possibly the most unique item about a person is his or her name. Yet most people fail to capitalize on the value of simply remembering the names of people they meet in certain business settings and social gatherings. Knowing the name of every person at a tense sales presentation might defuse your harshest critic in that board room. And once you start with their name you can build a whole repository of information important to people you interact with. I only met Mr. Lester Lamont today—he hired me over the phone—and this morning is the first time I have ever laid eyes on anyone here. I have read nothing personally about any one of you. Before we leave this breakfast meeting I will not only know your names perfectly, I will know your Social Security numbers and your addresses *better* than each one of you does. And I will start you on the road to learning how to do the same thing, and how to appreciate the uniqueness of individuals in ways to help enhance your own life."

Roland then asked that a person at each table volunteer to stand up for a demonstration. Compliance was slow in coming until Vic Kesson rose to his feet and stood behind his chair, looking like he had won a door prize for a trip to Hawaii. Within sixty seconds every table had a vertical representative in Roland's exercise. Roland then pointed at these seventeen people in random fashion throughout Room C, quickly getting each of them to call out their Social Security number and residential Zip Code, nine and five digit numbers shooting like feathered English darts towards the stage where Mr. Brinkley stood in deep and silent attention, taking notes only in his memory.

Roland had not heard the names of this select troupe so he simply pointed at a fellow standing at the right end of the room and said, "169-34-6756." The man laughed and said, "That's my Social Security number." Roland got the same result with another attendee on the left side of the gathering, a young guy hefting a wrist cast on his right arm. To a third man he said, "352-12-4081." Possibly the man was a skeptic, and possible, too, Roland knew it, but in any case the guy made a wry face and said emphatically, "That's not it, I've never heard that number in my life." "Oh," Roland said, "I apologize for giving you your Social Security number *backwards*."

This fellow hunched over his chair to write for a moment on a robin's egg blue five-by-eight inch Hotel El Dorado scratch pad, perhaps figuring just below the golden-colored hotel insignia of the sun cresting a treeless California mountain top, the room breathlessly quiet. Then the man held up the pad high overhead, like an eager buyer at an art auction, and said excitedly, "He got it right. He said it backwards!" Roland pulled the same stunt on the next person, a young saleswoman, who looked absolutely rueful when she reported to the crowd that five of the digits did not correspond to her Social Security number.

"Nobody's' perfect, people like to say," Roland announced calmly to the now quizzical crowd. "I forgot to tell you I was subtracting your Zip Code from the last five digits of your Social Security number before I reversed the numbers." The woman diligently ciphered away in her meeting binder for about forty-five seconds, and true to her Rensaleer Polytechnic Institute roots, or whatever her engineering school alma mater was, she had a colleague at the table review her calculations. Straitening up again she grinned hugely when she declared that Roland Brinkley's claim was exactly correct.

Gierson Gasket Company employees, including the sales people, did not in a highly charged state anyway mirror those frenzied Pamplona fellows two hundred meters into the running of the bulls or the pandemonium that reigns in the University of Pennsylvania Palestra when the La Salle or Villanova basketball team ties North Carolina with fifty-two seconds left in the second overtime period. The excitement that they felt could not be effectively captured on video tape that could then be exhibited on the 6:00 o'clock local newscast. One had to parallel the coordinates of their time and space—-you had to be there—-to detect the serious surge in energy that Roland Brinkley had extracted from this crowd. Kevin O'Donnell had engineering students in his American Civilization courses from time to time, sometimes they were there in begrudging fulfillment of graduation requirements, and he was always impressed with their sheer love of *precision*, let alone the application of some solution to a complex question. (He inadvertently drove them crazy by saying there was no one best answer to his non-quantitative test problems, they had to argue their point as best they could. But their well-researched term papers were always in on time and they were they only school major who never had typographical errors in their reports, one student admitting he proof read backwards, while fixing a ruler under each line of text). Roland Brinkley had likely elicited their love of the precise answer with his mnemonic nimbleness, but he had to carry this, in Kevin's opinion, move this in some direction and to some conclusion that did not disappoint the Gierson people, eager now as puppies to be fed. As if in response to this thought Roland stepped to the very edge of the stage and, with sharp eyes focused at the O'Donnell table called out the name of the first attendee who had volunteered for this exercise, but Kevin heard in surprise the statement, "Mr. Andre Bijou, please come up on the stage."

Kevin looked at Vic Kesson, expecting to hear him laugh or complain about Roland's error with his name, only then realizing that 'Andre Bijou' was proudly proclaimed on Vic's name tag in the black felt tip ink. Had Tony Connelli noticed this? But there was no 'Tony Connelli' name tag present. A certain 'Bradford Lippincott' occupied the chair on Kevin's right, Main Line scion no doubt, buffered by money older than the Appalachian Mountains and deeper than the Delaware Bay, 'Brad' perhaps to former Kappa Sigma fraternity brothers, maybe 'B-ford' to the upperclassmen there, nicknamed 'Buckboard' for some unrevealed reason by several nubile sorority sisters at Theta Psi and the inner sanctum six who shared the coveted third floor of the fraternity house during Bradford's senior year. Vic and Tony had not conferred on creating their nametags. They simply knew it was the wise thing to do. Kevin felt like a naive seven year old brother with his 'Kevin O'Donnell' as big as day in his scratchy handwriting, he had even considered putting 'Ph.D' at the end, but he hadn't left enough room for that, and the officious woman at the registration desk seemed annoyed enough as it was that they weren't pre-registered, so Kevin hadn't troubled her for a new blank tag.

'Andre Bijou' walked in heavy, steady steps towards the wooden staircase at the dark left corner of the stage, giving Roland Brinkley a brief spell for sharing some personal history with the hushed and focused audience. Roland shifted his voice to a softer octave, appropriate in the nearly silent room, almost whispering to himself, seemingly forgetting that he was ground zero for the rapt attention of one hundred motivationally-minded people. "Not always, not *always* was I the success story I find myself to be at this Gierson conclave," Roland said fervently. "I battled to regain my balance, I fought to overcome my torments, never giving up on the rainiest of days and in the deepest glooms. Yet this fine room could not accommodate my critics from that time, not if half of them stood on the other's shoulders, they were as numerous as starlings. That wrist laceration was misinterpreted; the caulking knife would have penetrated bone-deep if that was my intention. And that dirt-ball strip-mall developer from El Cajon wrestled away my wife and the IRS man cometh and took my money, but here I stand in a comeback that is hurtling me to the top. So living well will be my revenge and I invite all of you to share in this triumph."

Kevin observed that the erstwhile Andre Bijou was taking a preposterously long time to join Roland at center stage. Not sure perhaps in what he was enmeshed, Vic strode in a way that gave the impression of purposeful movement, yet he inched along at best. His leg thrusts were more sideward than forward, mimicking the rocking stutter steps of an experienced cha cha dancer in the moments before she propels herself towards her partner. Kevin could detect this most astutely because he had for years attended the awards dinner at the Philadelphia Cricket Club where his brother-in-law Timmy Gilbert was perennial club golfing champion (at the PGA-quality course in Flourtown no less, not the junior par-3 links nestled among the posh Wissahickon-schist stone homes on the west side of Chestnut Hill). Tim had devised a way of ascending to the awards podium in a seemingly hurried fashion, leaning forward in double-time cadence, as if in his modesty he desired to get the award ceremony over quickly, when in fact what looked like near-jogging speed was barely more than running in place, adding sixty seconds to his little trip, milking the applause crescendo to even more admiring heights. Kevin noticed, too, that another seat was vacant at their table since Lester Lamont had sidled over to the fellow to whom he had mirthfully signaled earlier that morning when Roland seemed right on the beam with his opening joke. Lester's colleague had pulled a manila file out of a black leather briefcase that was wedged like a truck tire chock against the fluted feet of the breakfast table, the two of them ominously devouring a memorandum that Lester squeezed at the edge with his tanned right hand, pointing to a name on a list that turned out to be 'R. Brinkley,' poised under a bold-faced heading big enough for Kevin to see that advised 'Prospective Speakers NOT Meeting the Quality Standards of Gierson Gasket Co.'

Kevin had no clear action in mind when he then pushed his chair back and walked briskly towards Roland Brinkley. He used the momentum he generated to help him catapult up on the stage. He employed a motion reminiscent of high jumpers in the pre-Fosbury Flop style of leaping face down over the aluminum bar, although he *was* aware of the fallout that was likely to thump Les Lamont and his cronies back at the home office if some dosage of sanity wasn't injected into the current proceedings, an unlikely outcome of Roland's pending collision with Andre Bijou. Upon later reflection Kevin realized that the sensation that he experienced literally jumping into this thing was not the common stimulus of plunging into a pool of cold, chlorinated water. That feeling of 'Is this real or what I anticipated it to feel like.' Instead it was a more rarified and frightening sense of climbing up the first steep ramp on a roller coaster, the thin-walled cars advancing in a slow, ka-ching, ka-ching "Nearer My God to Thee" type of cadence, gravity lurking at the top of the incline like a troll under a bridge, when one then notices a convoy of red and yellow fire rescue vehicles screaming their way into the amusement park (nearly flattening half of the sixth grade from Our Lady of Good Counsel school who are impatiently waiting in line for the Tunnel of Love) while the roller coaster attendants with names like Jennifer and Jim stitched on the pocket-opposite side of their olive- drab uniforms are looking skyward and frantically waving their arms in the direction of you and the other ascending thrill-seekers.

Roland's reaction to Kevin O'Donnell's intrusion was more gracious than Kevin expected. Roland extended his short, muscular arms (a slender gold bracelet clutching his right wrist) in a greeting than may have looked planned to the audience, giving him a sliver of hope that disaster would not crash like a searing comet into Conference Room C. Vic Kesson had progressed to center stage. Now he wears an expression like a concerned but relieved prospective juror dismissed from the sequestered panel for the tribunal for that spring water home delivery man who offered a flimsy explanation at best for the four hitchhikers and three formerly health-conscious Aqua Dale customers unearthed in his basement by the gas company. (Tragic that the Aqua Dale human resources people were not suspicious of the driver's chilling triple name: Gary Donald Nelson). His retinas squeezing to adjust to the stage lighting, Kevin experienced the audience as being larger and closer in than what he felt when seated at breakfast. Perhaps only an ocular affect, Lester Lamont presented the kind of strained smile common to emergency room patrons in the first few hours after the bars and nightclubs close.

"You will forgive me barging in like this, Roland," Kevin declared, "Given that your time this morning is just about up and Les Lamont needs to review the sales numbers with the troops here. Oh, I'm a consultant, yes, I'm a consultant to businesses, asked to comment on Gierson training programs and other things. And you have absolutely done an extraordinary job in merging philosophical and practical issues in a way that is beyond belief. I understand now why Thomas Edison was fascinated with his motion picture production work. Each little picture frame captures the essence of a moment, yet we must sequence and view these frames over time to capture the entire experience. He found both the commonality and the uniqueness. How appropriate for this engineering group. And as I have the honor escorting you and Mr. Bijou off stage, I'll take some Social Security numbers myself from these folks to see if I can concentrate as well as you."

Wearing a face and sharing a feeling known mostly to prison inmates strolling ever so casually out the steel-clad front gate while wearing a phony guard's uniform, Kevin hitched Roland and Vic at the elbow and moved towards stage exit left. He stopped at the last two tables and prompted Social Security numbers from six people. O'Donnell had no particular facility for remembering numbers. Each set of pro-offered figures knocked the proceeding ones out of his reach like maniacal railways cars pushing each other over a cliff. Nevertheless, with hands pumping at his respondents like bogus Smith and Wesson revolvers, he then ripped off a half dozen nine-digit numbers with as much authority as he could command. Audience members at other tables started clapping while the six participants uniformly looked at him askance, given that there was no conceivable mathematical connection between his response and their Social Security numbers this side of Cal Tech's math department. "I took the first possible square root, times six, before I reversed the middle numbers," Kevin said, getting even these skeptics to suspend their disbelief and join in the growing applause. Kevin threw his arms out in his final gesture and bellowed, "God Bless America," then hustled Roland and Vic down a metal spiral staircase backstage, the stomping applause ringing behind them in sympathetic tune with the quiver of the stairs as they exited into a bayside plaza of terracotta tiles, Royal palm trees, soft sunshine and indigo blue San Diego sky.

CHAPTER SIX

The swank hotel room that Mercedes and Kevin shared was on the second level directly overlooking one of the three swimming pools in the Hotel El Dorado complex. An oasis of palm trees, purple and red begonias, and bristling cacti, with canvas umbrellas angled like white berets over glass tables, the mint blue pool water in repose reflected a Roman tile mosaic skin. The pool area was protectively wrapped against sight lines and the motorized hum from the busy local highway by the curve of the four-story building. She had set the air conditioning pulsing on full power. This dropped the temperature ten degrees lower than the subdued corridor. Kevin was quicker than Mercedes to sense a chill in the air. It was not behind the front door and not above the king size bed where he vaguely noted two unfamiliar shopping bags lying on their side spilling out clouds of crinkly tissue paper. Finally, he found the tan plastic thermostat inside the walk-in closet and he cut the airflow back considerably. He found Mercedes in a fluffy pink terrycloth bathrobe reclining on a lounge chair on the shaded balcony.

The heavy but agile glass door slid open and closed easily at the touch of two fingers on a black metal handle. Mercedes had a yellow legal pad on her lap, some notes outlined on it with crisp bullet points or spidery brackets, and she was reading the survey research text that Kevin had virtually gone steady with in his own graduate school days. For reasons that Kevin could not fathom Mercedes had conscientiously stacked four or five bath and beach towels on a low table beside her lounge chair. How proud she had been back home in her apartment in leaf-lined Bryn Mawr of the just-bought beach towels before slipping them into the zippered crevasses of the lavender garment bag. Mercedes had held open a multi-hued towel with clusters of seaweed suspended on it and giant scallop shells with undulating edges that faintly rippled in tandem with her movements. A silver tea pot and fine china cups, a gold thread defining the circumference at the lip, delivered courtesy no doubt by a murmuring white-jacketed room service attendant, rested on a low table on her other side.

"Well, don't you look comfortable," Kevin said. "And being a scholar, too."

"Come on now. You go off to breakfast with your buddies and I think you've pulled a Judge Crater disappearing act. Did Tony and Vic try to throw you into the bay or what? I gave them that anchor to tie to your ankle and everything."

"Things would never be that easy with them," Kevin said with a chuckle. "See, don't ever pay them one hundred percent before the job is finished. You wouldn't even believe the story. This morning, either I made some interesting contacts or I'm going to be put away, sent to jail, sent to the Big House. I'll be 'away at school' as my home boy Goodall says. You did shopping with Gloria and Maxine already?"

"Oh, the shopping bags. Yes, right here at the El Dorado. It's called the Sunblast Beach Shoppe."

"The Sunblast Beach Shop", Kevin said. "What a crazy name."

Hey, is there an echo out here? Sunblast Beach Shoppe, just like it sounds. I didn't have much time to try things on. So, in a little while, I'm going to give you a terrific fashion show doing just that."

Kevin sat sideways in the matching cobalt blue lounge chair, his legs curling beneath the chair, and he pulled a folded sheet of paper from his back pocket. Normally he would have ricocheted a smirking comment about her promised fashion show against the balcony walls and lost focus on anything else for two vibrant minutes. Instead he took a deep breath, consciously. Pulling down from his diaphragm, the way his Hungarian-born fencing coach had taught him as he hovered in ecstatic tension on the brink of his first NCAA foil championship finals at the gym at Princeton. (So riddled with adrenaline, actually, that Kevin might have leapt into the stands of the ancient gilded gymnasium to skewer the wizened Tiger-loving hot dog vendor if he had dared squint at him cross-eyed). Now he was attempting to relax his reeling mind and feel more centered as to where he was. Events had been accelerating since he first agreed to visit California with Mercedes and this entourage. If the night at the Seahawk Casino four weeks before had been the first hundred yards of gradual descent along a mountain switchback, a light breeze barely twirling the ends of his generous black hair, the way a lightening-charged atmosphere had affected him once as he stood gawking on the South Rim of the Grand Canyon, frightening his summer girlfriend into backing away breathlessly, then the last twenty-four hours seemed like the frantic wind-blown finish of a bicycle race at the mountain's base. The chance of connecting with Captain Bulwer's family, if any of those people remained, was remote at best. Kevin knew he had simply ignored his bad odds in his flush of enthusiasm. He sensed, too, that he had been ignoring Mercedes since they arrived the night before. This was not intended: it was the byproduct of jet lag and distraction over his quest for Philip O'Donnell's photography. It was not by chance that she made herself look so soft and inviting in her pink robe, her brown hair thick and lightly brushed across her cheek and ear, the robe's belt reluctantly embracing the terrycloth across her waist and chest. The service tray beside her was likely for his benefit also.

"I've had breakfast but I would love some tea if there is some for me," he said.

"Of course I ordered for you, too," Mercedes answered. "There's whole milk, too, since you like it. You were born in a famine or something so I figure you're always hungry. What's on the piece of paper, anyway?"

"Thanks. I've got the name from Tony Connelli of a naval officer who might be a contact with Captain Bulwer's family members. Maybe they inherited Uncle Philip's photo collection. Who knows. A lot of the people attending the reunion are staying at this hotel, including this Commander Lapworth. I'm going to call him today. And I may have created a business opportunity for myself this morning. Never thought I would do that. Lester Lamont, a manager from a manufacturing firm based in the mid-west wants me to get in touch to discuss some consulting work for them. That's what my father does for a living. I don't know much about that kind of thing. This may seem weird, but this contact with Gierson Gasket Company may be of some value to you on your dissertation research."

"Well, hold the phone," Mercedes said. "You had an enterprising morning. Where is this Gierson guy located?."

I have his card. The guy scurried out on to the plaza during a coffee break to give it to me after we left this strange meeting that they had...I was leaning against an empathetic palm tree trying to make sense of a bizarre conversation taking place between a Mr. Andre Bijou and a Mr. Roland Brinkley, don't think you know them...Thought Lester might be reaching for a gun...Let's see...St. Joseph, Missouri, wherever the hell that is located in the Show Me State."

"Come on, mister American Civilization professor," Mercedes said. St. Joseph, Missouri, origin of the Oregon Trail. You know that, don't you? Up in the northwest corner of the state."

"How could I forget," Kevin said. "You have a much cherished atlas that you make love to. The rest of us have a life."

"Stuff it, Pal. I helped the little girl who lives down stairs with her mother do map research for a school project on pioneer history. As a favor to her mom, occasionally Jan and I let the kid hang with us if her mother has to work late. Sandy had to make her own colored maps with Magic Marker pens. It was really hilarious. Cartography taken to a new dimension. They probably had produced more accurate maps of the region in Europe by the year...1493. St. Joseph, if I remember, is in Buchanan County."

"Oh, sure, I'll fall for that. Just give it an Irish name, right? How about all-American names like Jackson or Johnson or something?"

Mercedes laughed. "Actually, Jackson is about two counties down. It's Kansas City. And Johnson or Johnston's nearby, too."

"Yeah, right. Didn't that little girl have to go to summer school for history that year? Do you mind if I make a call to Commander Lapworth?" Kevin slid open the glass door to the room, the temperature surprising him once more with coolness. The atmosphere virtually vibrating beads of sweat that had crept on to his forehead as he had sipped the Earl Grey English breakfast tea on the lounge chair. He figured he would have to sit awkwardly on the bed or perhaps on the undersized stuffed chair to orchestrate the call. However he discovered a speaker phone on a sleek desk near the balcony that was tethered to an unusually long cream-colored cord. By scraping the lounge chair closer by about one foot over the irregular, almost rococo skid-resistant flooring, generating a screech that was downright indecent in their balcony sanctuary, Kevin was able to recline and rest the telephone beside him. He absentmindedly stroked the parallel rows of gray and blue buttons on the phone console as he followed the ringing at Lapworth's hotel room. Waiting, he noticed that the balcony's wrought iron railing, laminated with shiny black paint, alternated rectangular and corkscrew-shaped bars at six-inch pacing.

"Hello, may I help you?" a male voice said in the telephone earpiece.

"Commander Lapworth? Kevin O'Donnell. I got your name from Tony Connelli, a navy veteran who is here for the reunion ceremony in a couple of days for the *U.S.S. Fidler*. He may have mentioned that I am looking for family heirloom photographs that a Captain Bulwer may have left to his family. This Captain died recently. The photographer was my great uncle who apparently died in the famous San Francisco earthquake. Does this sound familiar?" Kevin spilled all this out in one breath.

"Certainly, Kevin. In fact I just recently got some information that might interest you. In fact, I am sure it will interest you." The Commander's voice was friendlier, less officious than Kevin had anticipated.

"What's that?"

"The Navy has dug out an inventory that was compiled shortly after the *U.S.S. Fidler* was, shall I say, inadvertently sunk off shore thirty years ago." Now Lapworth's tone edged on conspiratorial, with O'Donnell a committed colleague worthy to be trusted with the deepest national security secrets. "An inventory that lists the personal items that crew members claimed to have on board and that went down with the ship in case they could get reimbursement. Or if the ship was ever salvaged or re-floated. Mostly there are odds and ends since the destroyer was coming back from a short Pacific cruise. Even though it was during the Korean War, that ship was only on a local patrol. But surprisingly, Captain Bulwer did claim to have lost a significant personal possession. He had on board with him a number of his best antique photographs because he was planning to re-catalogue them while at sea."

Kevin's attention was riveted to the point that he could sense the minute electrical hum that vibrated through the telephone. He sat as rigidly as he would have on the small stuffed chair in their hotel room. An image of Captain Bulwer as a real person emerged for Kevin for the first time, materialized like a portrait in a translucent dark-room tray, unshackled from Tony and Vic's wisecracks. With no basis more corporeal than the feel of the man's name, Kevin pictured a hefty, self-confident fellow in his mid-fifties dominating the warship's bridge, an unlit Camel cigarette clamped in his mouth, hoisting unsugared and uncreamed coffee in a blue and gold *U.S.S. Fidler* mug. (Sardonic mannerisms of John Wayne as a submarine commander in *Operation Pacific* crept in here, subtle as a shadow, but with no discernible harm done). High magnification German-crafted field glasses are suspended against his tan uniform blouse by a fraying brown leather strap. He imagined the Captain mothering his gray ship as it crisply furrowed the Gulf of Santa Catalina, splitting like an axe the distance between Santa Catalina and San Clemente Islands, the wooded and bouldered coast of Del Mar dead ahead through the fluid horizon. Powering to home port in busy San Diego harbor, the ship's wake as white, puffy and ephemeral as a skywriter's signature, approaching the coast line with its pirouetting pine trees and giant scoops of wet rocks, perhaps in a momentary indulgence he sought a binoculared look at sea lions grandstanding just beyond the thrall of the churning surf. "I don't know anything about his overall photography collection," Kevin said. "Is his list more specific than that?"

Lapworth continued, "Collecting was his major hobby, they tell me. Unfortunately the forms didn't leave a lot of room for detail. They were to provide something that was a basis for a monetary claim. And I'm working with a photocopy of a yellowed piece of paper. As best as I can make out it says, 'horizon shots,' 'fog series at the coast,' and 'San Francisco at dusk, panoramic.'

The list as it was proved nothing. There was no way to be sure that it reflected Philip O'Donnell's missing portfolio. Especially since Bulwer could have collected a score of different photographers' production. It had never occurred to Kevin that other people would be involved, other artists or aspiring camera artists. Nonetheless, Commander Lapworth's very words, the authoritative sound of his voice in relaying the information made the muscles and tendons on the sides of Kevin's neck momentarily tighten like tent ropes. A living demonstration from *Gray's Anatomy* as braided and fibrous tissue clenched, then relaxed. He looked to Mercedes' lounge chair intending to give her a synopsis of what he had just learned. However she had alighted from the chair and was carefully draping the huge beach and bath towels over the balcony railing. Coverage extended the complete span of the ironwork. It was like an incongruous wash day scene in an offbeat music video, her actions distracting and ultimately scattering two persistent finches that had been brushing up on quick-landing techniques there. Flying away, the birds playfully banked from left to right and then flipped near-summersaults before climbing out of view. As if resentful of being disturbed from their rest, the towels shrugged consecutively in the soft, slow-motion breeze. Rippling up and down the railing like a leisurely, limber chorus-line. Not evenly distributed the way a blanket sits under a horse saddle, about one-third of each towel hung on the pool-side of the wrought iron. The rest teased the balcony floor facing Mercedes and Kevin.

"Why was this list dredged up again," Kevin asked.

Lapworth responded, "There were a couple of reasons. One of the crew's daughters claimed that her dad had lost *his* father's gold wedding band on the ship and was wondering if it had ever been found. On the heels of that request, a local environmental group is challenging the Navy's plans to break up the ship with small explosives so the pieces can be towed to a better point to serve as a breakwater. The group claims it would harm current fishing patterns."

Kevin envisioned an underwater explosion punching up through the surface like a display at Disneyland, the chilly spray peppering the squealing families in the closest seats. (Oddly, as if on cue, two rambunctious children noisily burst upon the pool area below, blocked from sight by Mercedes' mildly flapping towels on the railing). Or like a hundred wartime documentary clips of depth charges scouring the dark, impenetrable North Atlantic Ocean for Nazi snorkel-breathing submarines, the TNT's shock waves rendered incarnate through the violent action of the sea. "Wouldn't that ignite the ammo magazine on board," Kevin wondered. He was hoping that sounded nautical and that the term "magazine" hadn't slipped into obsolescence with Admiral Nelson's wooden frigates. At least it had to approach more authenticity than 'Won't the whole damn destroyer blow up?'

"No, not really. The ship's magazine was salvaged by Navy divers shortly after it was lost."

"Do I have any options here," Kevin asked. He was trying to rank the different issues in a weighted order that would allow him to prioritize his next steps with a modicum of clear vision. However the onslaught of yet unmeasured outcomes triggered by Lapworth left Kevin feeling that he was hurtling down a shadowy tunnel, approaching targets tumbling like a kaleidoscope but deficient the beauty. Would the Navy help him or block his way, blasting his uncle's legacy to atoms? Had Bulwer left other O'Donnell photos to his family? Were these environmentalists going to help him?

Perhaps true believers planning to populate the destroyer's water-logged site with rubber dinghies and protest signs, grimly bobbing the swells in cut-off jeans or stretchy wet suits. With Jackson Browne earnestly wailing away on a boom box for inspiration. Or were they reserved individuals in khaki shorts and never-discounted polo shirts?

Diplomas in large Latin script from the best professional schools framed in tandem with Yosemite National Park retrospectives beaming prosperously from their office wall, and possible allies to Kevin? But of course they were all Californians, could he even tell the difference?

"Let's see," Lapworth said. "Today is May 29th and nothing will happen to the *U.S.S. Fidler* for at least another 30 days until the environmental impact study is released. My clerk is checking on information on Bulwer's surviving next of kin. That should surface within a week or so. This gives you about a month to try to pinpoint ground zero on the location of the photography collection. Seems like your first and foremost problem to me."

The Commander was off the line, on to other tasks. For moments Kevin reflectively cupped the hearing piece of the telephone against his chin, softly packing that minimal concave space, while appreciating the directness of Lapworth's summary statement. Naval thinking can be search beam direct when required, he thought. It was in the tradition of the U.S. Naval Intelligence scheme that put a U.S. 'Black Widow' warplane directly on the tail of Japanese Admiral Yomamoto's Betty class bomber as it vectored for Bougainville on an inspection tour one hot, fatal morning in April, 1943. Surprise, surprise. The vastness of the Pacific Ocean collapsed to a quarter-mile range. And closing. "Pardon me, Admiral Yamamoto," the ever-polite co-pilot might have ventured, "but seeing this U. S. plane ready to lunge at us does raise a question. Are those people still mad about that dust-up at Pearl Harbor?"

Wordlessly, Mercedes had slipped back into the hotel room, disappearing from view by pulling the drapes across the sliding glass doorway. The drapes were of a light blue cotton fabric, about as thick as a man's linen shirt. The drapes sashayed momentarily from her touch. Kevin was involved in switching his thinking from the conversation with Commander Lapworth to another telephone call; this he would make to Lester Lamont of Gierson Gasket. Mentally it was equivalent to the challenge of shifting one's footing between free-floating row boats in a mildly undulating sea. While you had to appreciate where you were going you could not yet disrespect the boat that you were exiting. In transit they both supported you but either could pitch you headlong into the light chop with a tentative step. He wanted to firm up Lamont's offer of visiting the Gierson home office in the very near future. Apprehensive he was about being a neophyte, but he wanted that consulting work. But when to go there and for how long? He had their return flight tickets to Philadelphia, with departure scheduled from San Diego. The travel documents were in nightstand drawer, tucked in the brand new leather-bound Gideon's Bible, by chance in the *Book of Revelations*. Kevin wanted to be in San Diego, California and St. Joseph, Missouri simultaneously, but he lacked a twin brother so that was impossible.

Kevin knew that he could sort the cards of the Gierson Company deck into appropriate suits only by taking a chair at the table. Irons not scalded in that fire could stir nothing up for his advantage. He dialed the number of the Gierson temporary business office in the hotel's conference wing. Passing it that morning, before barging into the breakfast meeting, Kevin had observed the studious bustle of salespeople on a small bank of telephones, returning messages. The junior fellows flipped through business cards slotted in plastic sleeves in identical maroon leather portfolios: Gierson company issue. Behind them at an angle that would have deftly caromed a racquet ball was a mobile cork bulletin board with notices for sales people posted in three different colors. The diligent energy of an overnight delivery service had transformed one corner of the office into a rectangular fortress of tan cardboard packages that climbed waist high. Or perhaps it was imagination that propelled the delivery guy, spacing apart the top row of boxes by three lengths of his hand to resemble castle battlements. Involved parents would have gushed over it in the kindergarten classroom of a fancy Montessori school. Hansel and Gretel portrayed by their little Douglas and Fiona. Kevin was half-expecting to leave a message for Lamont with some suspicious or bored clerk—'No, that's two 'n's and two l's' in O'Donnell (it's not Czechoslovakian, for Christ's sake')—and to be left pondering if Lester would even see the pink message sheet. His anticipation was in error. The secretary who took his call insisted he wait a few moments as she scooted down the corridor to collect Mr. Lamont. Apparently Les had exited the business office not twenty seconds earlier. I'll have him back in a jiffy she said, and as Kevin waited, feeling quite pleased, Mercedes re-opened the thin drapes and emerged from the hotel room.

He finally understood Mercedes' rationale for the beach towels and the voluptuous bath towels that hunkered like the side of a lightly swaying tent over the balcony railing.

Their upscale Bedouin oasis. She was holding the three new swimsuits. She had selected them that morning from the Sunblast Beach Shoppe. Perhaps one had adorned a boxum straw manikin under a recessed ceiling light on a glass display table. The crest of each stone in a graduated Majorca pearl necklace glinting a quarter-moon from the light and the torso impervious to the shivering air conditioned atmosphere. One garment a solid pink tank suit and two other two-piece suits that mixed up their floral and striped patterns as they dangled from her fingers. Cloth orchids and geraniums clutched at a red and blue cotton slat trellis like a climbing rose bush in a seductive arbor. Mercedes was sporting a grin that would have smartly matched the word 'vixen' emblazened across her tee shirt. But she wasn't wearing any tee shirt and she had shed the terry cloth bathrobe that had draped her minutes before. Kevin held the telephone in a soft fist against his cheek and soaked in the gorgeous picture of her totally naked good looks as she stood at the foot of his lounge chair.

"Well, HEL—LO there," Kevin said to Mercedes. But he also said it to Lester Lamont who had just returned to the Gierson business office and picked up the telephone, about to address Kevin. Lester seemed atypically tentative when he said, "Just *who* is this, now?."

"Oh, sorry, Les, my friends in the next hotel room are holding up that beautiful new baby of their's on the balcony and she's such a sweet thing. It's Kevin O'Donnell and I want to talk to you about that chance to consult with Gierson Gasket Company. You mentioned that this morning."

Mollified apparently, Les Lamont said, "Well, that's great. Your interest, that is, in working with us on some tricky problems that have bedeviled us for a few years. I appreciate a guy who shows some excitement about that kind of challenge."

"You don't even want to know how excited I am, Les."

"Gierson has been consistently profitable but we see profits eroding. We think that the problems are rooted in corporate cultural issues that have gotten us a black eye in some arenas. I think that for our image problems, our culture problems, you could be very helpful and sensitive."

Kevin answered, "Why I am feeling sensitive at this very moment." But he was not only aware of his pulsing feelings. Kevin detached a miniscule lens from his consciousness to consider the impact that Mercedes' body so frequently had on him. The breasts that he had noticed and appreciated from the night of her Christmas party hovered over him now as he sprawled on the lounge chair, just inches from his smiling face. Close encounters of the best kind. They looked enticing to him clothed or not. He admitted that he was glad that the spice rack over his kitchen range was inadvertently placed too high, needing clearance above the aluminum hood of the exhaust fan, making her stretch on her toes ballerina-style to get the marjoram or thyme for his marinara sauce. Her blue Oxford cloth blouse clasped firmly into her jeans by a belt with a silver Mexican buckle. Once or fourteen times he had asked her to grab a spice or two from that shelf, but more for the enjoyable sight of her outstretched figure than the taste of the dinner. "You really could use a little step ladder in here," she would say, and Kevin usually said, "I'm keeping my eye out."

"What I find kind of funny," Les Lamont was saying "is how off base some of our communications have been. Different units of Gierson are talking about some problem or another but they're talking right past each other. It cracks me up. Sometimes it's like two totally unconnected conversations taking place. It's like that cartoon of the two teams building a bridge from opposite shores and it doesn't come close to connecting in the middle of the river. Can you understand that, Kevin?"

"I've never understood that better in my life. And connecting is important, I mean really important in some situations." With Mercedes body weight pressing upon him it was difficult to keep his voice at his normal volume. Bouncing the bathing suit tops around his face wasn't helping either.

"We'll pay you $50.00 an hour for your time. Does that fit your thinking?"

Not quite. Kevin was going to ask for $40.00 an hour. "It's close enough, Les. The challenge alone is half the value to me anyway."

"So you want to get into it pretty soon? We are anxious to get started," Les said.

"I really want to get into it, and as soon as possible," Kevin answered. "We'll be in touch."

Those two finches were back on the railing, acrobatic and playful St. Helena Waxbills most likely, with their white crests and scarlet beaks, now clenching their little claws into the grass-like surface of a beach towel. Persistent creatures, indeed, and undoubtedly not the first time they had front-row seats on the hidden balcony shows at the Hotel El Dorado. Back and forth they looked from Kevin and Mercedes to each other. "What do you think," one bird might be saying with its quick swiveling head, "eight on a scale of ten?" "Yeah, yeah," the other perhaps responded, "but they're not too bright. As I tried to tell that lady earlier, that seagull who's been circling overhead's got the biggest damn mouth in San Diego."

CHAPTER SEVEN

Eugene Delacroix did the sky that morning. Under it Kevin and Mercedes, Tony Connelli, Victor, Maxine, and Gloria were standing on a dock next to a twenty-five foot sailboat. The boat's hull was thickly painted a royal blue and it had off-white decking. The Catalina sloop rocked slow motion at anchor at the West Harbor Island Marina in San Diego. West Harbor Island hovered above the bay water near the entrance to San Diego Bay. It resisted the invisible force of erosion close to where the water negotiated exchange with the Pacific Ocean. Rippling around it, much longer than it was wide, the huge bay carved a niche that looked like a stretchy potato sack found on the nautical maps in the marina's chandler's shop.

The marina was a bewitching, substantial place. Entry was gained through a locked metal gate. An elderly suntanned attendant in white Bermuda shorts and a polo shirt that displayed the marina's crest governed it. Vic tipped him five dollars since they lacked the boat owner's release form, a standard requirement of the marina. The attendant puffed on a Camel cigarette and said nothing. In a single motion he transformed the money into a key from his pocket. His bronze fingers worked the lock, the key a miniature medieval design.

Beyond that threshold, a resplendent pleasure fleet rested in long rows along a series of jetties, gently pulling against glistening mooring lines. Occasionally the bay would lightly surge. The estuary taking a deep breath. This would cause the speedboats to nose forward like thoroughbreds in a starting gate, ready for the race. Expectant, yet relaxed, occasional seabirds such as willets lingered on pilings, on cockpit hatches, near quiescent outboard engines. Less represented at that hour were boat owners hauling food or bait aboard or washing seaspray off of fiberglass decks with a communal hose. Where the group was standing the width of a single gray dock plank could encompass Kevin's boat shoes and creosote musk mingled with the slightly moist air.

It was the day after the Gierson Gasket conference and Kevin's telephonic discussion with Les Lamont about a consulting project. This morning the three fellows and Mercedes were wearing or carrying gear that was in the neighborhood of being nautical. Vic was hoisting a portable gray ice chest by its red metal handle. Gloria and Maxine presented a variety of pastel shorts and flowery tops and big straw hats and identical big aquamarine sunglasses. The mainsail and headsail on the boat were rolled up tight and lashed to the boom connected to the solitary mast. Therefore sails did not cast a shadow to deflect growing sunshine from lighting on the six figures on the wooden quay. Despite the thick sunglasses, Gloria held her hand in a kind of salute to further shield her pupils. She said that Maxine and her would be browsing the marina shops until the rest of them got back to dock.

Vic and Tony took first possession of the sailboat, bounding aboard with a heavy leap. Like a doorman greeting their arrival with a bow, the boat groaned against the pier bumpers. These happened to be one-third sections of light truck tires in semi-retirement. A retired wholesaler from the construction business lent them the craft for the day. The keys to the cabin and the auxiliary inboard motor were fastened to a key ring inside the zippered pocket of the windbreaker that Tony carried. Victor solicitously positioned himself to help Mercedes and Kevin step aboard. It was a short step down and unchallenging. Vic's gesture vaguely annoyed Kevin. Hadn't he talked about his Chesapeake Bay sailing school experience over steamed lobster the night before? But the annoyance vanished into the fog of good feeling that hugged him when he inspected the boat from the forward deck. It was a narrow and sloping perch. For balance he clutched the taut shroud line that angled up to the mast. He knew how to correctly unleash these sails once the boat would be underway. How to correctly crank the raspy winch to trim the sails and how to align with the prevailing wind the slender directional arrow atop the mast. This would maximize the air puffing out the mainsail. Lifting the boat like an aircraft wing. So few understood the aeronautical dynamics of sailing. He had been the only student at that Annapolis sailing school who had devoured the training diagrams before the weekend program had even begun.

Delacroix did the sky that morning. A softer Delacroix sky than usual, but the same swirling pattern of colors. Distinctive blues predominated, with purple and rose highlights, elsewhere small and isolated cotton candy clouds. The warrant of comfortable sailing conditions. From somewhere in the marina came the faint ratcheting sound of an anchor chain rising from the bay floor. The ratcheting arrived in uneven pulses: the anchor was ascending from muscle, not motor power. With the clouds largely dispersed and not forming an acoustic baffle, sounds were softened and hard to pinpoint; it was unlike a thickly overcast day when a ship's bell at a hundred yards seemed to reverberate beside one's head. Kevin observed that most of the marina slips were occupied, and with a confident fleet of seaworthy powerboats, sleek racing craft, houseboats, recreational trawlers, a catamaran, and two yachts over fifty foot in length. None of the group could maintain nonchalance about the larger yacht. It was a two-masted ketch, no less, with a spider web of rigging snaring the air around the boat and it sported a burnished teak deck. Chained to the divers' platform at the bow a dinghy slow danced in hesitant quarter-circles; the dinghy's outboard motor was angled out of the water like a big kitchen blender. Let alone the yacht, Kevin smiled when he realized that he could not imagine being able to afford the fragrant wood polish.

"Let's hit the high seas tomorrow morning," Tony Connelli had touted the night before at dinner. And with such exuberance that the restaurant staff from the maitre'd to the pastry chef might have appeared at the West Harbor Island Marina at crisp dawn, rigged out in docksiders, khaki pants, and blue-and-white striped collarless shirts, with a pack of smokes folded up in one sleeve.

Kevin and Mercedes had joined the two couples at Racine's Seafood Palace the previous night. Located in downtown San Diego, they

125

dined alfresco, right at bayside. When first seated, fading sunlight mustered a soft reflection on the water and the plastic green menus and the building's window glazing for twenty minutes. The glare from the rays leached out by the insensible rotation of the planet. Yet the woven cushion on the plastic seat was still a repository of the afternoon's residual warmth. A clamshell's toss away, an opportunistic duck family responded to the oyster cracker halves some children flicked off the dock. The mama crunched larger pieces in her bill for duckling finger food for her offspring. The heads of the baby ducks like sewing machine bobbins that blinked down to get the crumbs. It had taken driveway diplomacy to agree on two taxicabs instead of one for transit from the Hotel El Dorado to this restaurant. The drivers looked on impatiently, taking long drags on Newport cigarettes, but offered no advice or direct opposition to Tony's suggestion of piling into one vehicle. What a memorable lark that would have been for the five-mile trip. Automotive shock absorbers and struts taken to the perimeter of metal fatigue. As it was, Mercedes remarked that the straining cab with Tony, Vic and their lady friends resembled a teenager's car filled to overflow at a Philadelphia Flyers' victory rally.

Electric yellow lights in maritime lanterns on the railing now lit the restaurant's outdoor platform. Subdued for most of the afternoon, and not yet tasting her frozen Margarita, Gloria had become more talkative.

"I absolutely like to avoid the sun," Gloria said to Mercedes at one point during dinner that previous evening. "And Maxine gets seasick when Victor is too damn cheap to take her on a boat big as ocean liner, so there'd be plenty of room on the sailboat for you two."

Vic Kesson brought the auxiliary motor to life and set the sailboat in locomotion. Cognizant of the local speed ordnance, the boat maneuvered from the slip at just a few miles per hour. Yet Kevin sensed the crew's quiet exuberance that forever attaches to the escape of a boat from its dock. Unused for a few weeks, the motor's initial response was lackadaisical and mildly out of tune. It settled to a steadier and quieter chugging after fifty yards, fading from attention as the boat threw out gentle triangles of wash in the sleepy marina basin. All four passengers had some degree of sailing or boating skill. Victor and Tony claimed to have owned various seacraft in the past; Mercedes had spent undefined time with an unexplained friend on a ocean racing yacht, bumping into tidal rivers such as the Thames, the Medway, and the Swale on a passage from London to Dover in the English Channel. The launching this day was rather efficient for a pleasure cruise on an unfamiliar boat. No one in command and everyone being useful. Mooring lines were loosened quickly, a nautical chart fastened to a small table near the wheel, the ice chest of sodas and beer and sandwiches stowed out of tripping way. Mercedes noted the location of orange life vests in a side bench locker. In contrast, they got a good laugh at a gorgeous J-Boat nearby that was trying to navigate with a rookie crew. Making no discernable progress in apprehending some moveable air for the sailboat, the exasperated rented captain finally called out, "God damn it, Jason. I said four full turns of the wheel, not baby steps!"

Kevin often found vicarious enjoyment in pleasure boat names and this was no exception. Roaming through the marina that morning he randomly read off *'Dad's Toy,' 'Jonah's Belly,' 'Life's Lottery,' 'San Diego Dreamin,'* and *'Runabout Sue.'* This was no paltry skill. Kevin had never named a boat; he had once considered buying a vanity license plate for his Camaro but he could never settle on wording that not would have embarrassed him in a few days. In response to his question about the gold lettering, Tony said, "Our friend, who lent us this boat, he owned a lumber yard and a decorative stone supply company. So I figure that's why he calls the boat *'Sticks and Stones.'* That's what paid for the whole beautiful thing."

Abruptly then, Tony said, almost growled, "We need to unfurl the sail. Help me, will you, Professor?"

The sailboat was a quarter-mile beyond the marina's span now, continuing to move totally under propeller power. A decision loomed of heading northwest to the outlet to the ocean, or southeast to the heart of the San Diego Bay. They had not allotted enough time to traverse both in one daycruise. And in either case they wanted to transfer to sail. Vic had cut the engine to dead slow. A weekday morning, boating traffic was sparse, just a few isosceles triangles of white sail bobbing out at a safe distance. However, like a silent apparition out of the Pacific Ocean, a U.S. Navy submarine tender had entered the bay a mile from them. A quiet yet powerful gray mass compared to their 25-foot vessel. Volunteer lookout, Vic smartly called out identification of the boat's silhouette. It was wise to maintain some mobility at all times. Kevin joined Tony and Mercedes in surrounding the boom holding the mainsail and headsail in check. They nimbly undid the cords bunching the canvas material tight against the wood, unknotting in silence, finding a couple of troubling spots. Whenever he straightened Kevin sensed the breeze on his cheekbones. He always first detected a cool breeze just under his eyes. He would feel this when raking leaves in his front yard every October: the annual issue of a Bradford pear tree and two burgeoning sugar maples. A near-statue he would become to focus on the tickling sliver on his face. A big garden ornament with a bamboo rake in his hands, the rake's tines clutching autumnal grass like a football defensive lineman. His eyes were closed to the miniature tornado of leaves twirling near his workboots. Behind him two filled lawn bags resembled green plastic Buddhas. (Prior to Kevin's intervention, the fallen leafy canopy was always distributed with relentless fairness across the sloping lawn. Consistent with his neighbors on Walnut Lane, Kevin casually ignored this suggestion and swept the front yard clean). At this seaward moment on the *Sticks and Stones* the breeze sensation was augmented by the vortex of air planning in under his baseball-style cap and above his sunglasses, trying to lift the blue peak up his forehead. Kevin would be hard pressed to configure a more pleasant berth than the current one, a certain hotel balcony excepted.

"Let her rip," Tony called to Mercedes and Kevin, signally the time to unfurl the mainsail.

Within ten minutes both sails were stretched out and seeking the wind. The motor was shut off. At the wheel, Victor jockeyed the boat first left, then right to capture the breeze more effectively, generating a nice clip going toward the shore opposite. This was towards the Naval Air Station and Coronado, the slender holdout of land that demarked the bay from the ocean. Keep this approach indefinitely and the Catalina sailboat would splinter like a punchless torpedo against that green and brown headland. Therefore, to determine their route, all four conferenced over the chart held fast on the tiny table, the map's intention to fly away neatly frustrated by red and blue pushpins. Hundreds of depth sounding numbers displayed in miniature print, about the size of lucky numbers in a Chinese fortune cookie, were crowded into every twenty square inches of the chart. Kevin had assumed that they would eschew the bay and head right out to sea and cruise languorously a mile or two off the shore. As far north as Solana Beach they might go—what a lovely name—then amble back south to Imperial Beach, nuzzling Pepsi Colas and Coors Beer from their cooler. To pack that chiller Gloria and Tony had cheerfully looted the reservoirs of two ice machines at the hotel. Tony asked if he knew anything about the currents that his suggestion would entail. And had anyone sailed on the open water anytime recently? It was a loaned vessel after all. Kevin only had experience with bays and low sodium lakes and everyone else was in the same limited class when it came to sailboats. The San Diego Bay then would be it: down towards the center of San Diego and the Navy Yard the *Sticks and Stones* would tack, dodging the wake of powerful military vessels and the muscular commercial tugboats and the ponderous dredges.

The wheel of the vessel was placed well back, just in front of the narrow rear seat, upright and parallel with the single mast. The wheel was at least four feet in diameter. Six spokes radiated from the hub sprocket like a pie chart, allowing a scrupulously equal distribution of air to whisper through it. It looked newer than the rest of the boat; it had the silvery look and magnetic feel of a virgin baseball backstop dug into place some hopeful April weekend. Unobtrusively Kevin had tapped at the wheel while they prepared to launch. The safest way to pilot the boat called for standing, which Vic did as he continued to direct their cruise. He rested one hand on the rim and clutched a hand on a spoke. With his fingers positioned this way Vic's knuckles testified to his bricklaying past: every odd knuckle mashed out of alignment and spider veins tattooed like a purple river delta. Tony Connelli sat with one sneaker propped on the long bench on the starboard side. His green windbreaker was spread under him as a thin pillow. He was facing the front of the boat, aligned with the pointing foredeck with its aluminum pulpit frame, and staring straight ahead for minutes at a time. Kevin and Mercedes occupied the mirroring bench to port. Just visible under a blue cotton blouse, at the top unclasped buttons, Mercedes wore the pink tank suit that she never succeeded in modeling the previous morning at the Hotel El Dorado. Her knee lay cool against Kevin's. Maxine had kidded that they dressed a little like twins today. Both Mercedes and Kevin were in khaki shorts and blue shirts. (The difference was in their hats: Mercedes had a new, stiff, blue-and-red San Diego Padres cap. Her hair pulled above the strap in the back into a ponytail. Women in baseball hats and cowboy hats were to Kevin the sexiest picture in the world). While he increasingly favored their company, Kevin mused that it would have been crowded if Maxine and Gloria had joined them for this sailing.

When Tony seemed less distracted, less like a passenger on a Broad Street Subway express train impassive to the impending workday, Kevin called across the narrow beam of the boat to him. "So," Kevin wondered, "Gloria is very afraid of getting sunburned or sun poisoning, is that it, Tony?"

"Seems like it, doesn't it. But that's not the case at all," Tony said. The foghorn-deep voice so perfect in the whip of the breeze. "No," Tony continued, "it's more a case of her feeling it's disrespectful to purposely go in search of sunshine. And that's on a boat, a beach, anywhere. For Gloria, it's almost like a religious belief or feeling. You know how the Jews of old had the word 'Yahweh' instead of a word directly used for 'God'? And at least in this world they could never expect to look directly at God."

"I'm familiar with that but I'm not sure I can understand her beliefs on this," Kevin said. He did not think that Tony was kidding.

"Then let me ask you a question, Professor. When's the last time you looked directly at the sun?"

"Well, of course you can't", Kevin answered. "Burn your retinas if you did. But that doesn't make it religious to me."

Tony responded, "Gloria says that it is so basic to our survival that even children know not to look at the sun. Infants in a baby carriage on the boardwalk know not to do that. So it's a natural religion to her to respect or even fear the sun. She's kind of a creature of the night."

132

And what was *that* all about? But Kevin was anxious to get a turn at the pilot's wheel. Victor had already agreed that he was the next in line to steer. Carefully they traded places as the sailboat sliced about eight or nine knots through the lightly swelling bay. An awkward moment during the exchange of the wheel: Vic and Kevin looked like partners in the remedial dance class. Miscounting the time, one ready to fox trot, the other to waltz. Finally taking command, Kevin decided to hold a steady course, get the feel of the wheel in action. The metal felt cooler than he expected. The aluminum was light, a poor medium to store heat, and there was a patina of seaspray on it. Behind the *Sticks and Stones* the Navy submarine tender in silence had gobbled up half the distance between them. Presently eight hundreds yards of wrinkled water separated them. The prow of the sub tender came together at a sharp angle; it rhythmically kicked out white spray in two directions. But no need yet for Kevin to take evasive action from that ship. His boat would soon be cutting through the shadow painted by the Coronado Bridge, the narrowest pass of the bay. The bay resembled a wide river at this spot. About ten seagulls were lined across the lofty brow of the bridge, whose yawning clearance could accommodate the funnels and antennae of giant warships and commercial tankers, the seagulls spaced so regularly and being so motionless that they looked artificial. (Pigeons mimicked this on the peaked slate roof of an evangelical church that he viewed from his living room at home. Like little statues above the swelling ecclesiastical music and the purple-and-red stained glass windows. First Nazareth Something or Other. Turned at different angles, the stationary, dark gray birds resembled air vents drilled into an attic. Or oversized organ valves that could not be accommodated within the vault of the church. He had to see this three times before he would remember that the pigeons were real). At the same instant two of the seagulls came off of the bridge at them like a flight of interceptors sent to reconnoiter the boat's intention. Wing motion in perfect alignment, like a couple of whirling Rockettes, at least to the hopeful, lustful human eye. Actually the birds were just checking out the prospects for fishing scraps; they disdainfully floated back to their perch after a quick sweep. Kevin could relax after a thousand yards of progress under his control; it seemed so effortless with this boat. The mild up-and-down motion as they sailed through modest swells translated into a light tingle on his spine. Up through the soles of new docksider shoes the sensation climbed, unimpeded by gravity, eventually scaling his back vertebra by vertebra. Momentum pulled his arms forward in a rhythm similar to a seatless passenger on a trolley car, clinging to a pole.

"Drive it like a car they used to teach at sailing school," Kevin announced loudly, startling himself. "Drive that baby like a car. Turn the sailboat's wheel in the direction you want to go, just like in a car."

A shift of the wind came like a metal door had slammed shut. The mainsail's boom swung from right to left, rapidly dragging the sail like a giant fan across the boat, less than a foot over the startled heads of Tony, then Mercedes and Victor. Just a little more, too, than an arm's length in front of Kevin, who had crouched slightly the way people do from a lightning strike. The snap of the canvas trailed a quarter-second behind this movement like a starter pistol's report. Resembling off-tune sleigh bells, the pulleys holding the lines quivered and jangled for a while. And for a moment the boat pulled hard to port. Kevin had let the sail jibe, a potentially injurious event—concussion or worse written all over it.

Composure regained, Vic called to him, "Now, was that *tractor trailer* school down there in Annapolis, Professor? What'd you do, back that truck right off the dock into the Chesapeake Bay? Then they charged extra tuition, called it sailing school?"

Kevin had not totally ignored the threat of a boom and sail thrashing about with no warning and flailing in great force near the passengers. One of the top villains in fact illustrated in the "Accidents at Sea" chapter in his navigational textbook. (One cartoon panel showed a passenger knocked overboard, condition uncertain, the guy's fake captain's hat bobbing about like an inverted soufflé tin, while the surviving people look so impassive as to suggest that it was no accident). It's just that there were so many contingencies to consider. There are other, heedless boats about and the currents are deceptive. Foaming wake from a fat distant cruise ship arrives unannounced and there is clowning with your crew to distract you. Watch out for flotsam and jetsam floating in the ebbtide, and slime green ribbons of seaweed that can smother a propeller into an immobilized fajita. Then, rusting iron wrecks patient as sunken mines, or wait, catch this, submerged coral that punches through the hull—hey, keep this up and Kevin would become a nervous at-sea wreck. The sail injured no one after all; the jokes were cooking up at the usual rate from this crowd. Mercedes had fetched one of the orange life jackets from the locker, clutched it hard against her blouse with a desperate grip and was mouthing towards him, "Help, help!" Oh, *very* funny.

"Tony," Mercedes said shortly after that, "Can I ask you a personal question?" He nodded yes. "I've heard Vic say that he is divorced, but are you divorced or what?"

The *Sticks and Stones* had passed under the Coronado Bridge by then. The shadow from the bridge structure passed over them with slow grace, Kevin noticed, long enough to let them savor the cool air that hovered there. It was so different than the blink-of-the-eye rate of a car racing under a highway overpass. In a car the windshield and dashboard dim gray from shadow for a moment, but only teasing you with respite from the driving rain or piercing sun.

"Let me tell you my story," Tony said to Mercedes after a quick look to Victor. "If the Professor can hold the sail in check, I'd like to stretch my legs and stand up here by the mast and not have to shout in the breeze."

Kevin was breathlessly careful as Tony Connelli scrambled up to the foredeck and stood on the starboard side of the mast. Tony stood out of reach of harm if the sail launched a jibe to that side of the boat. From this unusual perspective, with Kevin standing on a lower level of the boat, he realized more clearly than before that Tony had short legs and a large and powerful trunk. Likely to produce good balance with

Tony's low center of gravity. They were heading away from looming downtown, towards the western edge of the bay, in the rough direction of a docked aircraft carrier undergoing repair, the black numbers on the side of which must have been three stories in height.

"My wife is dead," said Tony. "Died two and a half years ago from cancer. Victor talked me into one of those personal advertisements and I met Gloria a year ago or so. Good lady, Gloria. Terrific lady. But I miss my Rachel still."

The mainsail leaned outward in a gentle billow, describing an elliptical shape in front of Tony Connelli, on his right side. The white canvas sail formed an effective proscenium, shepherding and reflecting the sound of his words. This let Tony speak in a relaxed voice. His audience was attentive.

"She spent a few months at Doctors' and Nurses' Hospital in Philadelphia," Tony continued. "In Center City. We were living over in Medford Lakes, in New Jersey, where my house is now. I've never spent one overnight in the hospital since I was born, I guess—except with her. The doctors were great, the staff was great. But on that one long stay they were ready to give up. Her readings were so bad, white cells and things I can't remember. There were electronic monitors all around her, with gradations on the screen like a surveyor's tool. I studied those dark green screens everyday like my stockbroker follows Dow Jones. But a lot of that stuff I never really understood."

"What do you mean, 'Give up on her'", Mercedes asked. "Just let her die?" She had the bench to herself and had one foot up on it, arms wrapped around her tan knee. In her baseball cap, brown hair lustrous under the hat's border, expectant eyes riveted at Tony Connelli, Mercedes reminded Kevin of the goddess Philadelphia Phillies ball girls who effortlessly vacuumed foul balls near left field at Veterans Stadium.

"Exactly right, young lady, exactly right. And she was only forty-four. But what basis, what foundation did I have to argue with them? Rachel's horrible cell counts. Extremely low enzyme levels and what have you. Her Daily Numbers, I called them. And were all the high numbers in that building taken already? Can't we get another bingo game going? But I told Dr. Leopold 'No damn way we're giving up.' And on we fought...We fought for her life."

They had closed to about five hundred yards of the stationary aircraft carrier that was dotted with knots of workmen. Protective tarps, the yellow color of a school bus, flanked some of their workstations. The flashes from acetylene torches were like scattered campfires for frying bacon. Burdened forklifts and small trucks were visible driving short spurts along the cliff of the flight deck. Kevin started a gentle turn to the left, anxious not to disturb Tony. Two lengths of his fist he pulled the wheel to the left. From the tension in his wrist ligaments he monitored the otherwise imperceptible shift of their boat. Get just the correct arc and he should be able cautiously to swing by the vast carrier, heading deeper into the embrace of the blue bay.

"What can you really do for a person with that kind of problem," Kevin asked. "Sounds like even the doctors were confounded by it."

"You show up every day ready for battle," Tony said. "I used to walk through the hospital's main entrance looking like every eye on the place was on me. I'd pretend that the photo-electric eye that controlled the sliding glass doors was a television camera attached to Rachel's monitors. And every other one in the place. 'Whoosh' the doors would sound as I marched in. 'Whoosh' the next set of doors would go when they opened. Sometimes I thought it was like walking out on the stage at the Academy of Music. Up straight I would stand. Let everybody see that. Funny, too, because I'd walk up that block thinking about the dozen screw-ups on our projects—the cement subcontractor not showing up in Cinnaminson, the wrong color roof shingles delivered in Haddonfield—usual everyday stupid stuff. I couldn't help but check out the brick work on the hospital wall—Alveti's Masonry down in West Chester did it, Vic. Top notch work, too. Just what I needed, another Dago delivering good bricks. But I marched through those big doors like I owned the place."

"So, she survived that trip to the hospital," Mercedes asked.

"Yes, and she had some close calls. They needed to do emergency surgery early one morning, almost had to do it in the middle of the night. She wasn't conscious the day before. I drove to the hospital from home, took Route 73, heading for downtown. I left my pick-up truck in the driveway and took her Park Avenue. My only goal was to hear her voice once more. Real simple To Do list. Gets very basic at times like that. How many times have I driven that route in my life? Thousands and thousands, likely. And yet I found myself afraid to get to the bridge. Benjamin Franklin Bridge. Terrified. You'd think Godzilla was waiting there to gobble me. Because when I got to the bridge I'd have to cross and face what was coming. Did you notice that big bridge we just sailed under. Reminded me of it.

"Now this was pitch black early, no one on the road, many of the traffic lights were blinking on yellow at that hour. I'm up early in my line of work and I've seen that a lot but it seemed eerie that day. But some moron in a little car kept swerving in front of me, slowing down, not knowing where he was going. Stupid little Datsun or Nissan. Drove me to distraction. He's gone finally, like he disappeared and I looked around for him and there it was—the bridge. Lit up just for me, it seemed. A hundred bright lights pouring down on the black roadway. Not a sole blocking the tollbooth before me. Christ, when has that ever happened? So I got to the hospital and they let me up to her room in the surgical intensive care unit. She was awake. I watched the nurses in their green uniforms and their sneakers pouring over reports around a long table. Kind of looked and sounded like a library. You were glad to figure that crowd of nurses had gotten straight A's in school. But in its quiet way the atmosphere was as powerful as being on the command deck of a battleship. And Rachel surprised us all and pulled through the surgery."

"Even made it home again?" Kevin wondered.

"She did. Lived to make dinner that we had a couple more times in the dining room at home. Big picture window behind her, fat red roses tapping at the glass. But she slipped away from me later on."

"How do you pull yourself through something like that. That's so foreign to me?" Kevin asked. His plan of subtly whisking by the aircraft carrier seemed to be holding true. Only now could they hear the deep throbbing beat of the ship's repair work. Clanging tools seeming to fall down metal stairs, electric drills high-pitched and insistent, then heavy voices on bullhorns calling from invisible locations.

"I thought of my father a lot of times, Professor," Tony said. "How's this. He came over from Italy in his early twenties. Spoke not a proper word of English. Right away, moved upstate in Pennsylvania, got a brutal job working on the Pennsylvania Railroad, repairing track. The crew taught him to speak the language as best they could—weren't Harvard professors either. In fact Pop used to tease that at one time you could count his years of schooling on one hand, but later he got promoted to two hands—lost a finger to a wayward sledgehammer. After five years upstate he moved down to Philadelphia and got jobs in construction. Proud owner of two languages at that point."

"Was his English fairly good then," Mercedes asked.

"Not a bit. Polish and Italian were all he knew, made the Polish rail crew proud. But times were tough for him still in Philadelphia. On and off of jobs, struggling with English. Stayed a little while here and there with friends, had to sleep on park benches on occasion. A homeless person we'd call him now. Can you imagine surviving with your life stripped down to such basics. Once, though, over Chianti in Mr. Zaconeli's yard next door, Pop said he had been privileged more than most people. He knew what life was all about and didn't have to wait forever to find out. My God, old Mr. Zaconelli's backyard. The address was Dickenson Street, in South Philadelphia, but it was really a part of Tuscany. But of course Dad had hung in there. A house eventually, got married, had a son and two daughters. Grandkids from my sisters in his old age. Never a major complaint from him that I know of. Let me tell you something. His kind will never walk our way again."

"So thinking about him made things better," asked Kevin .

"Only a bit, though, after she died," Tony said. "It was pretty hard for me that first year alone. Strangely enough I saw a sign that really delivered a message to me."

In reaction to this Kevin nearly flung his arm up with the pilot's wheel, threatening to jostle them all or send the sail on another jangling fandango above their heads. He just caught himself. What's with the Sign, he wondered. First Gloria with her sun fears or lunar worship, whatever, and now Tony and the Sign. Kevin had the *Sticks and Stones* parallel now with the parked aircraft carrier, about two hundred yards off its port side, their sailboat moving southerly and away from it. A worker there lugging boxes off of a truck bed halted his activity, apparently to gaze in their direction. Kevin was no papal candidate but he wasn't a cocksure atheist either. He wanted to have everything balanced and crisp in the mainsail's efforts to pull the boat. And to keep the pounding of the sailboat over the surface at a respectful minimum. Quickly he thought: My unfettered reading at times is a curse. He recalled that Gnostic Jews of ancient times would mire themselves in their grief hoping to induce spiritual visions. He imagined them hungry and parched in the Negev Desert, initially despondent, then exultant, around the struggling campfire. To celebrate maybe they toasted fluffy cacti pieces on flimsy sticks. Snakes with poisonous sacs and poisonous intentions keeping a cool distance beyond the hovering light. Maybe Tony's sad loss had ignited an hallucination. Voices of the dead linger with living memory. Nevertheless, Kevin found himself looking skyward for a moment, perhaps curious or vaguely seeking a vision himself. The clouds in patches were now a thin high mist, light cream more than white, inexplicable otherwise. So ordinary a sky at this point; but didn't the alchemists envision glimmering gold in dingy lead? The sun slanting rays from their left had not taken to any noticeable psychedelic gyrations.

"What was this Sign like, Tony, can you even describe it?" By focusing Kevin kept his voice steady.

"Of course I can. It was as big as the day was clear. It was in West Palm Beach, Florida. Saw it the second I looked up."

Kevin had spent several months in sultry South Florida locales and had experienced the lightness of their skies. Colors soft as a delicate child's crayon touch. Twenty daily minutes of rain, apologetic for the intrusion, Royal Palms weeping astride the hot sidewalks. "How high up did you have to look," Kevin asked. "Did anyone else report seeing the same thing?"

"Huh, I guess they saw it. Who cares? And report it to who? Hard to miss it, though. It was on a sign right of front of a restaurant on Route 1 or Route 1A in West Palm Beach. There was heavy traffic on that road and it might have been in front of the Two Georges Restaurant. Vic knows that place. But I'll never forget that beautiful message, like it was placed there to benefit me, in black plastic letters stuck to a white board: it said, 'DAWN—-Had a Boy!'"

It took a few moments for his statement to make sense to Kevin. Then Mercedes said, "Oh, you mean a big old sign out by the roadway. I wasn't sure what you were getting at and Kevin's questions confused me. Did you know Dawn."

"A sign as big as day out at the end of the parking lot, at the entrance. Don't know who Dawn is to this second. Figure she had had a hard time somehow, and the baby's arrival was good news. Good news to her, to me, to everyone. You can pull from that treasure endlessly and it doesn't run out. Help yourself to it. And think of all the jerks you come across, then some assistant restaurant manager has the class to do this for her. Somebody loved that girl. I still think about that message on a rough day."

The *Sticks and Stones* had safely navigated beyond the area of the aircraft carrier and its banging and hauling and arc-welding workmen.

Tony quickly climbed down to the passenger deck and retook a seat beside Victor. The bay continued to produce gentle waves that at times lapped up against the hull with a light thumping sound. Kevin decided to begin a slow swing to his left to redirect the sailboat back towards the center of San Diego, near where they had dined the night previously. Like a distance runner on a cinder track changing lanes Kevin looked over his left shoulder and saw the Navy submarine tender nearly on top of them, at most seventy-five yards away, when the tender's klaxon roared "Uhhugah! Uhhugah! Mercedes, Tony and Vic howled out at once, "Hey, Professor, how'd you not see that coming? Didn't you hear the *bullhorn*?" There was no time to get the motor started, sail power would have to pull them to safety. "Hang on," Kevin shouted, turned the wheel more sharply to the left, and angled straight across the line in front of the sub tender's bow. After anxious seconds he cleared the ship finally, but with only fifty shrinking yards to spare.

They were happy enough to meander back to dock, everyone quiet most of the way, except that Vic pointed out how funny the seagulls looked on the Coronado Bridge as they closed on it a second time. "Reminds me of decoys when I used to go duck hunting with my son," he said. Before they made the marina, Mercedes and Vic caught the sails that Tony lowered with the winch, the sails tumbling down finally like blankets falling off of a packed closet shelf, the three then pulling and wrapping up the thick canvas with the rope ties. More responsive than the earlier ignition, the motor contentedly pushed them through the marina like a cocker spaniel in sight of home. Docking the boat was easier than Kevin expected, not taking much thought (however,

Tony did stand on the front deck, silent but very alert). Vic's feet hit the dock first and he caught and hooked up the mooring lines for the front and back of the boat. Like day trippers to the New Jersey seashore, and Apollo lunar astronauts hurtling back to the blue earth, or even vacationers returning from the Old World, the ride back always seems so fast.

Gloria and Maxine were not in the chandler's shop nor in any of the marina's three souvenir stores. "They are in here," Mercedes called out triumphantly. She was standing in front of the little bar and grille on the southern end of the marina. Her Pittsburgh resonance knocked about the rafters supporting a covered walkway. Kevin could see that she had burned a little bit about her neck and her forearms, despite her soft tan. Such a mild epidermal toasting that only an expert on her skin tones could detect it. He could feel a tingle of heat at the same locations on his body; not bad enough to blister but it would sting lightly in the shower. Gloria and Maxine had been standing inside near the front of the place, *Fishstories*. Apparently they were debating sitting down to lunch or waiting for the boating party. With one hand Tony held the windbreaker, and with the other he softly clasped Gloria's wrist. She gave Tony a fast kiss on the cheek, her blond hair quivering around her ears under her straw hat, and laughed when she said that his timing was always perfect. Gloria's sunglasses, like an elongated aquamarine brooch, were tucked into the collar of her shirt. Kevin plowed ahead to a big round table at the back of the bar, near mounted stuffed marlin and tuna dusty and faded on high shelves. Globes of green glass hung from thin netting, lightweight anchors were attached to hooks, and maritime knots sufficient to make a Boy Scout salivate clung to a wooden pillar. It was far enough back from the big windows and the streaming sun that you had to move the candleholder at that table to see the menu clearly. Kevin took the captain's chair to Mercedes left. He savored the cool, dark place, sinking softly into the seat with a refreshing glass of ice water that had a thick lemon slice floating on top like a two-color life preserver.

CHAPTER EIGHT

For almost ninety years the Gierson Company of St. Joseph, Missouri built gaskets to die for. Their boiler gaskets were like boutique ornaments that adorned the mahogany desks or bookshelves of manufacturing executives in both hemispheres. A range of rubberized seals, couplings, brushings, suction cups, o-rings both standardized and custom-molded, and rubber stoppers populated their bulging product manuals. Get one of the senior Gierson engineers rattling on about their grommets and then, grommet tubing designed to match client specifications, well pull up a chair—it's going to be a long, edifying afternoon.

The brothers Artemus and Alexander Gierson founded the company and directed it for three decades. They did so on a fiscal shoestring. One fierce as the rawhide-like cut that could lacerate one's leg from the virgin prairie grass that had once roamed to the horizon. The ownership of the company resided completely in family hands until post-World War Two. "Art" and "Alex" interchanged roles of president and controller until their respective kids ascended to upper management in the mid-1920's. The brothers lived comfortably but frugally as the company slowly expanded its marketing reach. Legend had it that Alex operated a Model-T Ford longer than any driver in Buchanan County. Gierson sales gradually leached across state lines and ultimately hurtled international boundaries. In a similar way, resembling the rippling of still water from the steady collision of plummeting weathered stones, the company's engineering repute radiated out into many of the best technical circles.

Their children spent more time than the founders at country club golf and short European sojourns. These cousins had custom-built houses on the bluffs overlooking the Missouri River. Over by the east bank. On some late mornings peaked shadows from the rooflines undulated dreamily on the slow-passing current. The homes were constructed close to the original factory. Also adjacent to the river, the factory was now a palisaded ruin of collapsing brick walls and rusted iron ventilator shafts. Ivy wove across the crumbling surface like a feasting garnish. At the homes Corinthian columns of stark white were like a proud skirmish line in advance of a red brick facade. A gazebo from Yorkshire, England, of cream-painted yew wood, held court in a quaint garden and rookery setting behind one of the dwellings. The gazebo was octagonal in shape; it was said that in August heat giant sunflowers towered like passive sentinels over one trellis wall while larks commandeered it as a clubhouse. However, even this younger set did not lose total touch with Kwanis meetings at Curley's Steakhouse. And Junior Achievement talks at the City of St. Joseph Senior High School. War economy business orders, followed by the post-war boom, prompted a public offering of stock in 1950. There was the need for huge buckets of cash to modernize. Plus competition from the rebuilding global economy. These were the levers that moved the reluctant manufacturer to the stock market. But what had not altered at Gierson over those vibrant years was a passion for quality products, and that, as they liked to say—forefinger and thumb parted the thickness of a sheet of excellent bond paper—down to the last excruciating millimeter. Moreover Art and Alex's individual oil portraits still solemnly oversaw things in the main lobby near the receptionist's desk.

"Mr. Lamont is just finishing up a meeting and will be down for you shortly," reported the Gierson Gasket Company receptionist to Kevin O'Donnell.

Kevin stood near her desk. He wondered if he could safely leave his wet umbrella in the coat closet nearby. Or should he carry it along with his new briefcase to the meeting with Lester Lamont? The oversized umbrella could not be collapsed into an unobtrusive size. He clutched it off to one side to avoid dampening a small block of parquet flooring. Beads of water clung to the fabric like quivering transparent domes. To look more official, more experienced at this kind of enterprise, Kevin had purchased the black leather briefcase back at the Sunblast Beach Shoppe. In the hotel lobby in San Diego. Merchandise well beyond beach gear was carried there: expensive wheeled suitcases, travel alarm clocks, imported wine corkscrews in suede satchels. Mercedes had insisted he get the leather article and not the cheaper naugahyde offering. Absentmindedly, before leaving the West Coast, like flattened frisbees he had tossed in a few manila file folders and yellow legal pads of Mercedes' into the briefcase. As a matter of Gierson security, the receptionist, a Ms. Lillian Cardiff asserted the copper nameplate, had requested a peek inside the briefcase. A bulwark against industrial espionage. He guessed her to be a woman of sixty, with soft features and blonde hair. She presented the contented look of a long-term employee with pension benefits to burn, able to buy Kevin and sell him and buy him back again. Lillian's eyes were a shade of chocolate that might nestle in a Whitman's Sampler box; even the whites resembled a confectionery filling. She squinted a bit as she inspected the briefcase. The paucity of items there seemed suspicious to her, as if Kevin lugged an array of infrared cameras or voice-activated recording devices.

The manager of their hotel in St. Joseph offered the brown plaid umbrella to Kevin that morning. A bit gaudy for a fellow not trekking in a caravan across a deluged golf course but acceptable given the splattering rainfall. What, nothing in a coal black Burberry? It was left by a departed guest at the middlebrow establishment that Lamont had recommended, the Inn of the Missouri. In sunny San Diego, Kevin had just about forgotten the existence of rain. O'Donnell realized that he would not leave the item behind if he stowed it in the lobby closet; according to the local TV newscast as he dressed that morning, heavy rain would continue without respite for another day at least. He sat on the end of the firm bed as he pulled up his dress socks, in front of the television set, trying not to annoy Mercedes. He had the volume placed low. Into her pillow she had mumbled hello but wanted to sleep another hour. He doubted that she realized that she had awakened in Missouri. Kevin had mismanaged the adjustment of the color tinting on the television screen; the announcer in the studio peered out over a vivacious purple tie and under a lime green tinge in his blonde hair. Three persistent inches of rain had fallen in the last forty-eight hours over Buchanan County. And similar torrents had covered Kansas City, Missouri just to the south. Thunderstorm percussion, plus tubas and viola, had raked across the interstate highway as they drove from the Kansas City airport the previous day. The thunder crack so violent it decided to bypass Kevin's eardrums and plunge straight to his heart. The rented car seemed to sway from the shock waves. Or it might have been a momentary hydroplaning. Mercedes was driving, pinning the speedometer at five miles above the limit despite the storm, laughing when splashes from livestock trailers and oil trucks drenched the windshield like a car wash. A number of small streams beneath low steel bridges had the look of flowing cocoa from soil runoff. Local farmers were largely displeased with the precipitation, the slicker-clad TV field reporter had declared, against an indifferent audience of young alfalfa, given the moist springtime that year in northwestern Missouri.

With time to use and no particular agenda to consider, Kevin migrated to the oil portraits of the founders. Tall palms in forest green planters lifted long reedy fingers, ready if requested to fan the venerable paintings. Tubular lightbulbs in brass hoods attached to the frame feebly lit the faces of Art and Alex Gierson. A serious countenance on each fellow. Old oil portraits to Kevin were often interchangeable except as to sex. These examples were better finished. They each possessed eyes with a strong blue color; one fellow's hair was silver and thick all around while the brother showed only thin gray strands in lonely clusters near his ears. There was a familiar grainy character in the narrow faces of the Gierson brothers. Their cheeks resembled wooden slats facing north and south, with the foreheads perpendicular in orientation. A look not so much hard as durable. 'Gunstock Oak' he thought, the color of the hardwood planks his father helped to install in the Victorian vestibule at his home. (It had been on a humid September afternoon, the Saturday after the fall semester began. Kevin's usefulness was compromised by his enjoyment of the moment: working on his first house with his Dad. Kevin kept parceling out the oak boards with the bevel on the wrong side for insertion into the previous one. When his father deftly tapped one into place with a claw hammer a delicious echo in the high ceiling vestibule accompanied it. Every time the old house creaked from the wind he was reminded of it). Even at a few paces distant he determined the paintings' composition was by the same artist. The artist's signature was indecipherable, just a series of angular strokes. Resembling the craggy Rocky Mountain terrain beneath them as they had flown from San Diego. At least the dating of the portraits was clear: 1924. The subjects looked to be in their sixties, but Kevin labeled this as an inexact estimate. His general view was that driven, accomplished individuals often appeared older than their contemporaries.

There was a bright brass plate attached to the wall beneath each portrait. The lighting in that area dropped from recessed ceiling fixtures. Kevin moved close to read a plate, anticipating the artist's name and identification of the particular Gierson brother. Instead it simply read 'On loan from Kilmartin Museum, St. Joseph, Missouri.' Kevin was surprised to read that notice. However he was quickly distracted by a series of black-and-white photographs to the right of the Gierson portraits. Handwritten on two photos was the date 6/1/79. These were family portraits of 'sodbuster' farming families, probably in the Missouri or Kansas prairie in 1879. The picture on top displayed an impossibly handsome young father in a full beard, unpressed overalls and a flannel shirt. Arranged across the foreground of the block-like house were also his wife in a faded dress. She was sitting on a straight chair with an infant on her lap. The husband flashed a smile that matched modern-day vacationers poking heads through cardboard figures of cowboys at an amusement park stand—ha, ha. He didn't really have to live like this. His bride's expression suggested the occasional wave of despair that woke up with her some frigid February mornings. Beckoned to consciousness by the lingering call of Bobtail quail competing for territory with the heavy air. A son of about five years of age held the father's hand; immediately beside the father, seemingly equal in status to the family, stood a self-confident mule in a thin leather harness.

The other dated photograph was also a family portrait. It was a different group of parents and children sitting in front of a simple rectangular structure. Its flat roof appeared to be layered with surviving sod. The walls of the farmhouse were formed from dried sod blocks—all the panache of piled sandbags. A door of braced wooden planks angled inward to a shadowy interior. An earthen mound—perhaps an ancient Indian burial mound—was flush against the back of the home. The perspective was hillless otherwise. There was no mule lined up with the folks in front, but a cow was perched on the roof—a goddam cow— its mouth buried in the thick sod that grew there. Beneath both photos was replicated the brass plate indicating a loan from the Kilmartin Museum.

"Aren't they the most unusual pictures, Kevin?" The commanding voice of Lester Lamont, all the more so because he was striding the home turf of the Gierson reception area. His suit was blue pinstripe and his thick necktie a red and blue check. As Les swiveled to scan the photography collection, Kevin noticed that wide blue suspenders were straining against his white shirt.

Kevin and Lester proceeded through a pair of shaded glass doors that were embossed with one-foot high letters stating 'GGC.' A labyrinth of hallways with gray tiled floors and white walls emerged into a series of conference rooms on the main floor of the headquarters building. At one doorway Lester had to punch a number of silver keys to release the security lock; Kevin noted a pair of white signs flanking the door with crimson block letters reminding the tardy to sign up for the immanent Glee club contest. Lamont strode the corridors in quick, aggressive steps, as if he were dribbling a soccer ball the entire time They swept by Gierson products displayed in occasional photo exhibits and enclosures resembling a jeweler's merchandise case. Kevin was glad that he had bothered his friend Bob Goodall to contact some engineering professors back at the University to define gaskets and related products. Worthwhile because Kevin assumed that the products were mostly metal when in fact they were largely rubber-made. No use sounding off on Gierson's troubles with only a half-assed notion as to what they manufactured.

Lester Lamont's next in command greeted them just before they reached the designated conference room. Another tall fellow, with eyeglasses and a crew cut, clutching a large coffee mug. Kevin recognized him as Les's colleague who had checked on the speakers' list back at the San Diego breakfast meeting. "Kev-an" the fellow said. "I'm Ted Mower. I saw your terrific work out there at the El Dorado in California. Saved our sinking ship. This presentation should be a little less bizarre."

Presentation? Earlier on the telephone Lamont had casually mentioned that a few other managers would visit with them during the day. One, two, three people at a time, Kevin imagined. With him quiet mostly, taking a ton of notes in his inscrutable handwriting on the yellow legal tablets. And nodding authoritatively at decent intervals. How much trouble could he get in doing that? Kevin joined their short procession into a conference room; a large table, oval in shape and of highly polished oak-veneer was two-thirds surrounded by six other Gierson people. Five men and one woman. A floor-to-ceiling window flanked one end of the room; vertical plastic slats were angled to reveal the rain-beaded window and to tease in subdued light. Kevin propped his umbrella against a chair near the wall. Then he sat down between Lamont and Mr. Mower. The swivel chair with velvet fabric on the arms sank lower that he anticipated. It was like a ballyhooed stage performer making an ever-deeper genuflection. On the wall behind the two gentlemen directly across from Kevin was hung a rectangular framed mirror. It had golden leafless tree limbs painted along its length, just below the black frame.

Ted Mower also had a set of fat manila files with him and he opened the one on top and called the group to attention. He quickly announced names of the attendees for his benefit but Mower was half way through the list before Kevin realized that he had not recorded a single one. Luckily, business cards from the unfamiliar Gierson people started flipping across the slick surface of the table towards O'Donnell. And with something like the speed of blackjack cards being snapped out of the dealer's card shoe. It had not occurred to Kevin before this instant that he should be prepared to reciprocate with his own card. He did not have one.

"Folks, for Dr. O'Donnell's benefit I'll very briefly recount some of the history that has lead us to this juncture," Ted continued. Ted tapped the stack of file folders with a knuckle, the stack climbing a solid four inches above the table. "These short executive summaries will start to give him more of the critical detail that he's going to want."

"Kevin, image problems cropped up for Gierson Gasket Company when we strayed from our classic roots of delivering solid, long lasting product at a good price to the more 'elevated' posture of bragging, downright bragging about the superior position of our gaskets and related items. For a while in the trade journals, places like *Gasketry Monthly* and *Gaskets Today* and *The American Journal of Gasketry*, we got talked into running ads like this." Ted pulled an eight by eleven-and-a-half inch advertisement from one of the middle folders, displaying four-color brilliance. The picture on it captured a fireman in heavy rescue gear, a big black-and-yellow helmet streamlining over his head like a Martian invader. Crooking in his arm an axe to make a Viking proud, he stood amid the steaming rubble of an explosion-torn building. Fine dust hung like a white aura over the scene. The cinderblock wall behind him was punctured with a cavity, roughly the shape and size of a ceremonial portal in a Chinese palace. A mandarin with now-shattered eardrums might be convalescing nearby, focusing on the moment nonetheless. The caption to the advertisement said, "The expensive machinery did not survive the blast, but the old Gierson gaskets did. So what else is new?"

For a moment, the eyeballs on Mower and Lamont swung upward like the automated machine gun turrets on an embattled warship. Over the years Kevin had twice watched every episode of *Victory at Sea*. "Ouch, that hurts," Mower said. "Gierson's earlier ads were quiet, plain vanilla messages. Never got us in trouble when we used St. Joseph, Missouri advertising firms, people like Wesner Meirs. Apparently one of the attorneys at our outside counsel in Kansas City, down there at McCarthy, Foley, O'Shea, McKenna, Tucker, Keller and Kallenbach had recommended that we live a little and engage the services of a high flying advertising outfit in New York City. The advertising firm of Stanella, Galante and Perri—it seems they had just picked up the Gucci account. We've since switched back to Wesner Meirs—but the damage was already done."

After a brief silence Kevin noticed that everyone was looking at him. Expecting some kind of a response, undoubtedly. He did not breathe for a few seconds as he got sucked up in a mild panic, shocked for being speechless for perhaps the first time in his life. It had not occurred to him to question Les Lamont on what the Gierson managers expected today or at the expiring moments of the project a month down the road. So Kevin pretended for a moment he was thrust in the middle of a senior seminar back at the University: catch your breath and thoughts by moving the focus back to the other participants. He was always fairly dangerous with the flippers on a pin-ball machine.

"Is this reading of the situation one that everyone here can agree upon?" Kevin wondered. "Perhaps it was time for a dramatic shift in how Gierson presented itself to the world. Not be apologetic about it in the least." Kevin had taken a stance a mite more aggressive than he had intended. Now he was swirling around words in his mind like he was juggling a bowl of fruit salad. Perhaps soften his comment just a bit by plucking out from the juice the right slippery sections of pulp and skin.

"I'm with you, Dr. O'Donnell. At least I'm part way there." This was said by Marlene Zekel, the lone woman in the room. To link the business cards with the appropriate person Kevin had arranged the cards in a semi-circle, reflecting the table's shape. There was an engineer there and other cards listed the human resources and marketing departments. With a quick movement of his vision he could catch a name and then catch the glance of the card's originator. It was like bouncing a soundless tennis ball off of the table. Marlene Zekel was a thin woman, perhaps mid-forties, with long elegant fingers that were matched somehow by her straight blonde hair. Perfect white teeth flashed as she spoke. She had a gold brooch the shape of a swan on her left lapel, emerald beads for its eyes. In her hand was a thick silver tube that encased a fountain pen. He had not seen her standing but Kevin thought her to be tall. But with the low chair that he was sitting in, it occurred to him that everyone at the table seemed taller than him. "By that I mean a fresh approach in our marketing is called for," Marlene said. Marlene was an associate director of marketing, her card revealed. "We may rightly criticize that marketing campaign as too aggressive, but some break with the past is still okay in my book."

Kevin was delighted with Marlene's support, qualified as it might be. It was like the gift of a Liebfraumilch, wine too sweet for him to ever drink. But he might serve it to other guests. He wished that he had sketched out the particulars of the meeting in greater detail with Lester Lamont prior to this moment. While it did not serve his immediate purpose, Kevin could not refrain from visualizing a swirl of crinkly confetti and paper streamers, of deep blues, orange tints, and red and white hovering around them. Entwining the nine people in the conference room, much like the front rows of basketball fans when the first basket is scored. Confetti and streamers because the thread of this early conversation was so insubstantial and potentially jumbled. Here he was in the castle keep of a major industrial enterprise. With metal bearings moving hard objects nearby, and aluminum pipes ushering steam power to clanking machinery, nimble material carts with hushed electric motors gliding crated goods toward the loading docks, toward the interstate highway and railroad junctions, to a world market for tough Gierson gaskets. And the substance Kevin was serving up so far, in spite of his vibrant tone, barely had the essence of dust coating the inside of an aspirin bottle

"I'm afraid this line will get us off track," Les Lamont said. He leaned forward as he spoke, resembling the position of a three-point stance in football. His neck with enough girth that Kevin figured Les had lettered as an offensive guard somewhere in the Big Ten in college. Suddenly shout out "hut, hut" and he might send the table flying. "We already know that Gierson's received a wave of criticism for our aggressive advertising campaign," Les continued. No need to revisit that argument now. What we as a committee have been charged with is nothing less than recapturing for Gierson Gasket Company the goodwill of our buyers, the public and our employees. The long term consequences of that are major for this company, for its stockholders and St. Joseph, Missouri itself. Not a responsibility to be taken lightly."

Kevin realized that he was avid for another cup of coffee. He was annoyed that none was provided in this conference room. In the movies there was usually a tray over on a credenza, perhaps a silver coffee service on it, the coffee urn poised on four stout legs. With Danishes and succulent grapes surrounding it. From a distance the food treats looking like slabs of stone and smooth boulders at the base of a gleaming tower. Groucho Marx would be indulging himself, and

Chico Marx would be stuffing infinite interior pockets for the meager days ahead—just before they get thrown out. The trip from the West Coast was tiring and he awoke early in the unfamiliar hotel bed. It had surprised him that Mercedes was hot for him after her shower late at night; he was more than accommodating to her desires. And the dreary wet day did not totally revive him, despite the pressures of this gathering.

As he scanned the room he noticed for the first time his image in the long mirror on the opposite wall. In the modest lighting people were faintly nondescript, with resemblance to faceless characters in a dream. Beads of rainwater scurried, then rested on the tall window, adding an opaque effect to the light. His stupid low chair situated his head in the mirror as if he were Lamont or Mower's young son. In visiting Dad for the day. His eyes were roughly at the level of their shoulders. A toy Corvette or ice cream truck might be dangling from his soft juvenile hand, ready to traverse the tabletop on plastic wheels. Kevin inspected the mirror image the way he examined any group photograph: hoping that he did not look stupid. In a department store the tall mirrors on support column always caught him offguard, with hair a bit disheveled from trying on sweaters or a shirt not tucked in quite right. Funny how you never look quite what you figure the other people are seeing.

"Let me pose this question, then," Kevin said. "How would this group characterize the three or four main factors about Gierson Gasket that this team should emphasize in order to recapture the right spirit about the company?"

"Have you seen our mission statement?" a gentleman across from Kevin asked. His card identified him as an engineer. The fellow was a little hefty around his stomach. His tie coiled a bit at the bottom as it rested on his belly. "It points out characteristics of this firm such as exquisite precision in engineering, and, a balanced approach to problem solving and our lives. Plus traditional values, and an optimistic attitude in all our endeavors. That's a lot to capture if you ask me."

"And I did ask you," Kevin said excitedly. "You have given me a great idea. Now I am not a marketing person and my idea will need fleshing out from people with those skills. What you have described for me is the classic American glee club. And what were those signs I saw big as life in the corridor as Les and I came in from the lobby? Time to sign up for the Gierson Gasket Company glee club contest!"

Kevin O'Donnell had little or no control over where this might go or if it would latch on to anything productive. Not dissimilar to the rare times he fished from the shoreline with his brother at a New Jersey beach. Cool surf pulling at his sockless ankles, he would wheel the unfamiliar rod in the ocean's direction. Gritty moist sand lapped against his heels as gravity excavated his footprints. He knew nothing about fishing but he enjoyed dealing with its paraphernalia. Slicing strips of frozen whitefish for bait and managing to poke it through the hook with unpunctured fingers. He cut the bait with a scaling implement that rivaled the size and shape of a Bowie knife. Then a rubber grip in his left hand and the other on the fiberglass pole. The metallic whirl of the reel releasing string mimicked a serpent's hiss. Once the line was launched, the persistent breeze took over as guidance system. Where the hook and sinker would splash down was better calculated by the odd flounder or blue fish ambling by than by his own skeptical mind.

"What an extraordinary angle," Les Lamont said. "Your observation, Kevin, might seem simple but it holds a lot of truth in it concerning this company. I have a bias here that I must admit to. See, I sang barbershop quartet and did a number of roles in musicals at the University of Wisconsin. In Madison. Judd Frey in *Oklahoma* was my best work. I was an economics and music major, if the truth be known. And Glee club stuff might seem so square but it is so heartland, so Missouri and all that. If we could run advertisements using actual Gierson employees singing their hearts out…its too much. It's great."

"Maybe the annual contest we already have could be used to pick the winning team or teams," Marlene suggested. "And we could place the singing teams in attractive setting all over the country—or even the world—to show us bringing the Mid-West with us wherever we do business."

The Gierson employees present other than Lamont and Mower broke into two chattering groups, as if on signal. Jumping up and breaking out into competing show tunes might happen at any moment. Perhaps like the Rodgers having the Hammersteins over for brunch, the atmosphere a tad brittle from arguments over the next act. Apparently they were energized by his cockeyed idea; Ted Mower had plucked a flyer from the depths of his cache of files. Lester Lamont started placing ballpoint blue X marks on it, likely noting sections of text that could be modified to include Kevin's suggestion. Mower was muttering that the suction cup engineering task force in Wichita had vowed to take first place for the third year in a row...

"Les, can I offer an action item?" Marlene asked. "I'm on the St. Joseph Community Arts Council and we have our monthly dinner this evening over at the Kilmartin Museum. I'm a board member there as well. Perhaps you and Ted Mower and Dr. O'Donnell can join us and we can solicit support for the Glee club idea, see how it floats with the Board of Trustees crowd. See, my rationale is that there are lots of community movers and shakers there usually. In fact Truscott Edwards of St. Joseph Power and Light is being inducted on to the board this evening. Cocktails are at 6:30 and dinner happens about an hour later. Coc au vin tonight. I know I can get you on the agenda."

"Super,"Les responded. "I've got to run to some other meetings now anyway. Ted can get the particulars about getting there for Kevin. I can start circulating Dr. O'Donnell's concepts informally this afternoon with the guys upstairs. Up in the 'Tower of Terror.'"

Out in the corridor now, Kevin had collected his umbrella and was clutching the wooden handle like a fencing foil across his legs. Everyone except Ted Mower had started to drift down the corridor. Then, Marlene and two of the other meeting attendees backtracked to the doorway area. Their gait seemed sheepish to Kevin. Finally Marlene's eyes brightened and she quickly said, "Dr. O'Donnell. 176-

22-4874. My Social Security Number." The two other people followed suit. With a deadpanned expression Kevin responded to Marlene. "Why, 353-00-1234," and similarly mangled the other numbers.

"Oh, that is so funny," Kevin heard Marlene say as her group maneuvered toward a set of gleaming glass doors, "As if *he* would get a few Social Security numbers mixed up."

CHAPTER NINE

Ted Mower had hand designed a detailed map to guide Kevin O'Donnell to the Kilmartin Museum but Kevin went astray anyway. In his busy but organized office Ted laid out a 12 by 18 inch sheet of graph paper. He draped it over a small drafting table by a window; a high intensity lamp on a spindle arm provided hot illumination for Ted's cartography. Rain continued to pelt the windowglass. It was even more driven than earlier in the day. Just outside Ted's office, well-trimmed forsythia bushes continually quivered in the storm. Keep this up and they may turn into giant green tumbleweeds bounding down the lawn. Perhaps it was the weather, but the tilted drafting table reminded Kevin of the sturdy, angled English basement doors that hugged the foundations of brick houses on Spruce Street and Pine Street back home. They are often in bright colors, similar to this blue table. Tracing in silence, Mower's writing implement vaguely produced the sound of light traffic at a distance. He drew in roads and route numbers, exit ramps and landmarks and marked with inked arrows the sections that were not to scale. The Episcopal Church earned a steep spire to note it and a McDonald's Restaurant at a key intersection merited off-color arches from Ted's black pen. From a telephone directory pulled from a tall bookcase, situated beside a studio photograph of Ted, a brunette-haired women and two teenaged children, he checked the name of the furniture store located a short way from the museum. Yes, exactly. "Cosco's," without a "K." Kevin's directional problem lay not with the map. The problem was that street flooding had created several emergency detours. At an underpass close to the Inn of the Missouri, three cars were abandoned in a surging reservoir of backed-up water. The minor flooding stretched muscles by lapping at axles and lower door panels. The stranded automobiles were oriented at odd angles to the roadway. They were like empty bumper cars awaiting the next round of frenzied drivers. The detours threw a curve at Ted's crisp map, abruptly channeling Kevin south at one point when he needed to go west.

At Kevin's request Mercedes was instantly joined to the guest list for the dinner meeting. Kevin had explained to Ted Mower that she was spending the day with other Gierson managers. She was searching for data for her doctoral dissertation. Items such as sales trends and changes in market share compared to advertising budgets. The percentage of business generated offshore. The night before, Mercedes said that she would carry a bright lantern to illuminate dusty file drawers and remote storage closets. In search of honest data. Likely she had called a taxicab to get to Gierson that day. Or perhaps she had scrounged a lift from the busy airport van sponsored by the hotel. But she would find little interesting to do in the small unfamiliar city at night. Now in effect tacking to the Kilmartin, rolling like a two-cushion billiard ball to the target, Mercedes served as navigator. She was holding Ted's large map close by the windshield. To capture more light most likely.

Kevin owned a Christmas carolers figurine set that looked much the same. Mercedes' brown hair not tucked behind her left ear softly caressed the graph paper directions. Without elevating her sight from the map, Mercedes would point with a hitchhiker's thumb to direct the next turn. The windshield wipers, fixed on regular speed, gave a definite snap every second as they reached their right-side perimeter. For the last day, Kevin and Mercedes has been virtually mesmerized by the sweeping fan on the windshield. He flicked the wipers off a few times. Within moments rain spread like a curving gray ameba on the glass. Again the rubber blades needed to tirelessly rake the surface clear. "Damn rain's a royal pain in the ass," Mercedes said. "Don't we have a real map with this car?"

"Yes, but the detail's a little sketchy on St. Joseph itself. I don't think the mapmakers ever quite got to visit here. Actually, maybe that was them floating facedown near the cars in that flooded underpass we saw. I might have stopped to check out the drivers, but, hey, dinner and everything. It's so rude to be late. So, you were saying earlier that they were pretty helpful to you over at Gierson today?"

"I was kind of shocked at how helpful they were. Shocked and delighted. They offered me a lot more data than I would have gotten by writing to them. You got an ugly umbrella from the hotel. I'll need to get a tractor-trailer from them to get my data loot home. So this is working out okay for me—not that I would like to spend a ton of time here—but what is it doing for you, if I can be so blunt?"

"First things first," Kevin O'Donnell said. "As to borrowing the tractor-trailer, absolutely. A big-rig driver ran off with a lonely reservations clerk there just last week. Left his truck behind. If you'll make a stop at Food Giant and Sears Roebuck for them, you're home free. And what's this trip doing for me? I've wondered about that. I'm happy to get the consulting experience. And the money. I could use a remodeled kitchen, as you've pointed out. It's a little scary seeing how these big companies operate, but they'd say the same about my lectures. In a way I feel sidetracked from my search for Uncle Philip's photos. That has sort of a life of its own with me. Like it is pulling me along. And very patiently. I'm not pushing the process right now. I'll get back to doing that soon enough. But as long as I hang in there, even in a sort of nonattached way, I don't know, I think it's all right."

The Kilmartin Museum was cut into the top of a small hill. It issued a long straight asphalt driveway running perpendicular to the street. The landscaping was sparse; however, grass thick as a plush carpet appeared almost black in the soggy evening. The sole break on the front lawn was a gnarled tree stump, of indistinct species, about four foot across, and partially covered by an ivy blanket as if tossed like a hastily thrown tablecloth. The museum building looked small when they first pulled off the roadway. It was a brick structure with a substantial covered veranda. White columns stretching from floor to ceiling quartered the veranda's length. Like two braids of watery hair, runoff from the rainstorm gurgled down the gully on either side of the driveway. A small plateau extended behind the museum. It was here that cars parked on a crushed stone surface, advancing beyond the now-curving paving. Kevin could not see any parked automobiles until he crested the hill; twenty cars or more were there already. From high, square-cut wooden posts on opposite corners of the parking area, flood lighting penetrated the diaphanous atmosphere. The spacious bulbs were housed in hoods that in a pinch would have served as helmets for Joan of Arc's soldiers. Despite the brilliant wattage, in the dampness the fine cars seem herded into a dilapidated used car lot. Under the canopy of the bobbing umbrella the couple had to step nimbly to avoid soaking their shoes. Water had pooled a bit around the tires of the parked Oldsmobiles and Dodge vans. This gave the unlikely impression of having seeped up though the packed chunks of stone. It was a little after 6:30 p.m. and he and Mercedes were probably among the latecomers. Everyone else, Kevin figured, knew how to get to the museum and how to avoid the wettest streets and the slowest clusters of traffic.

Kevin silently acknowledged his sometime habit of anticipating places and events in exhaustive detail and with no basis whatsoever. Seats at a sports stadium. A rental cabin at the Pocono Mountains. An interview for a research grant and a patio for a barbecue at his sister's neighbor. Emerging from a platform escalator at a major train terminus, Kevin would point out to friends how the station's tiled ceiling was burnished with gold tint and was not black from cigarette smoke. Or somehow clouded from ancient locomotive steam. His companions' look was uncomprehending; apparently they had not thought about the building in advance. An advertising banner trailing a puttering monoplane at the beach was twice the length that he expected. And Happy Hour rocks for two hours, not one. Consistent, if not logical. Triggering this acknowledgement was the jewel of a museum residing behind the gray veranda and the matching oaken medieval doors and the splash of stain glass in a semi-circle just above.

"This place is exquisite," Mercedes said, immediately inside the Kilmartin Museum. Kevin nodded his head vigorously, in silence. High overhead were chandeliers glowing softly. Cut crystal pinwheels radiated out from them in a dozen directions. Lights recessed in the ceiling and attached to various oil paintings created inviting subdivisions in short corridors. The flooring was polished hardwood, narrow planks that angled away from cloth-lined walls. The floor gleamed so brightly that one could glimpse art works in it, suspended upside down. Founding Fathers and snow-crested Mt. Rainier standing on their heads. From the perspective of the entrance the design appeared to be a rectangular figure-eight. A main corridor lay straight ahead. A longer intersecting hallway paralleled the outside walls of the building. The top of a interior staircase, with slate steps and brick sides, was visible on the far right front of the museum. It's descending metal railing curved abruptly, as if drilling into the basement below.

Kevin could quickly recognize several artists represented near the entrance. Thomas Hart Benton with a western setting. A Charles Wilson Peale portrait, perhaps of the abolitionist Anthony Benezet. Then, a small Titian with dark brown towers, heavily draped and anguished human figures and the turquoise corner of a lagoon or lake. In the center hallway, just ahead of Kevin and Mercedes, a group of meeting attendees gathered around a white-haired woman in a silver wheelchair. They listened with interest to a tall gentleman standing near what looked like an original Edward Hicks' *Peaceable Kingdom*. Given the spotlight-driven shadows of the museum, the speaker's silhouette hovered and floated about the small party. Vaguely ghostly yet surprisingly familiar. The shadow darting among his audience was that of Gierson's Ted Mower. He was gesturing energetically with his right arm. He might have been tossing fat softballs to a crowd of teammates lined up to take fielding practice.

Ted had not yet noticed Kevin and Mercedes' presence as he addressed the group. He was saying, "Les Lamont has known Truscott Edwards for years, I understand. Each had a child in high school in the same class. And Truscott called Les this afternoon after one of the power company's transformers got struck with lightning. It knocked it flat out. There was a small explosion even. A technician declared that it created a fat black mushroom cloud over the immediate area. No one was hurt, thank God. They are okay with power so far but they are watching out for brownouts in the St. Joseph area. Oh, hi, Kevin. I've been telling folks that Mr. Edwards will not be attending the dinner meeting tonight due to possible power emergencies. You may remember that he was going to join the arts council board tonight. But that's not all of the problem. There's a notice out now that the Missouri River may overflow its banks in the next day. That threatens Gierson's docking and rail loading facility right on the river. We move a lot of product through there. It could be seriously threatened. And this must be Mercedes, I guess?"

Ted excused himself from his group and slowly walked Kevin and
Mercedes around the first floor of the Kilmartin Museum. Mower was
not quite acting like a guide since he had apparently visited the place
only once before. There was a lighthearted tingle in the air with the
prospect of natural disaster at least brushing up against the City of
St. Joseph. Ted's warning was being passed like a magic baton from
person to person throughout the museum; Kevin saw a woman wearing
a blazer and a name tag emerge through a brown door marked 'Private'
to scoop up the latest reports. Any possibility of a formal tone for
this gathering had evaporated. One of the great holidays from routine
had reared its exciting head, Kevin observed. Like a grade school
blizzard closing, the days off are twice as sweet being unexpected.
Neighbors who never speak almost compressing their spines pushing
each others Chevrolets onto the plowed street. Mismatched woolen
gloves wrap around the sticky cold rear bumper. Exhaust smoke of
a straining engine envelopes straining vapors of human breath. Pairs
of rubber boots skittish as insect feet on compacted ice. Great to see
you, no problem. Sleds packed two and three screaming kids deep
careening down the playground hill and slamming into snow drifts
as big as sand dunes. Not that many years before Kevin and his
friends had been evacuated out of Ocean City, New Jersey to escape
Hurricane Belle. The tension around town had been simply delicious.
At a bakery on Wesley Avenue, a block from the beach, customers
gobbling sticky buns scanned faded sea charts. These hung beside
framed shots of the 1917 *Sindia* grounding disaster. In November
shadows, the battered freighter was perched on the beach at Eighteen

Street. It lay parallel to the triumphant water's edge. Local bystanders, now in a ghostly realm, featureless in drab winter clothes in the black and white pictures, were already distant immobile ghosts. Dark statues in groups of two and three. Everyone in Ocean City suspected something major was bound to pummel that barrier island someday. Kevin's friends roared and laughed with wisecracks the entire way back to Philadelphia. The opposing traffic lanes on the Atlantic City Expressway had been reversed to allow twice as many lanes for westward escape. Automotive momentum from that convoy might have sucked the skinny pine trees on the median along with it. For the hell of it they drove the reversed section of the expressway. All grown men essentially being sixteen-year olds, Kevin figured. Inland about ten miles, traffic congestion eased; every vehicle was hurtling at least ten miles per hour over the legal limit. Cars hitting pockets of water propelled sheets of spray over the highway shoulder. Near dark green thickets, here and there clusters of motionless young deer materialized roadside, with uncomprehending eyes. They were like speckled lawn decorations. It was equally distracting to see the parked state police in yellow slickers motioning with red emergency lanterns for traffic to keep barreling. At no point was there an opening in the clouds as big as a beach towel. This gray canopy flattened the sky's perspective quite a bit. Hurricane Belle sailed due north, substantially missing New Jersey, Kevin remembered. It pushed with casual violence into Long Island, its turbulence expended before it reached the Sound. He thought that it may have killed a motorist with a breakaway tree limb. In all of the commotion, the wrong town was evacuated. One never knows about such things. Kevin's crowd returned to their vacation house the following day, leisurely, under whispering winds and pastel blue skies

Ted had now steered Kevin and Mercedes about two-thirds around the outside corridor. The home stretch was populated with a Jackson Pollack, perhaps a Kandinsky down the end, and two small Reuseaus in baroque brown frames. As arts council board members, other visitors to the museum likely had little new to observe in the collection. They spoke quietly and with animated fingers. Perhaps describing river dikes and flood stages of the powerful Missouri. One fellow patiently interlocked the open fingers of both hands, then meshed closed fist against fist, like the knuckling teeth on a gear. Presently, a series of bird sculptures arose nearby on glass shelves. Green wrought iron supports curled out from the corduroy wall covering. The shelves were set at different heights. The fowl resembled a flock of Canadian geese caught at the ecstatic moments of liftoff from a lake. Kevin had paused to examine them when he heard a crisp set of high heels negotiate the corner behind them. A snap on the hardwood as commanding as castanets. It was Marlene Zekel. She stopped abruptly, like a tap dancer. Her eyes were bright as her smile; she had one of those long, soft raincoats draped over her shoulders, cape-like. It was a yellow coat, reminding Kevin of fashionable gunslingers in a Clint Eastwood cowboy movie. Where do they buy those clothes? With their address in the saddle, could they use mail order? But he did not figure she was preparing to whip out a revolver to shoot them. At least not him. Kevin and Mercedes and other people there were in business attire. Beneath her unbuttoned coat Kevin saw that Mercedes was sporting a jaunty blue cocktail dress.

"I heard about Truscott not being here and the power problems and the flooding prospect," Marlene said in excitement. She must have hurried in from her car to dodge the wretched weather. She was breathing deeply still. A thick strand of white pearls expanded lightly at her neck. Bubbles of moisture arrayed like rhinestones on her patent leather clutch. "But we can still hold our dinner and the rest of the meeting. And we have another guest," she said looking at Mercedes. Marlene softly clasped Kevin's left wrist, thereby gracefully rotating the four of them toward a meeting room in the rear of the museum. As she walked, her raincoat billowed out at the hem like a curtain in a mild breeze. A thumb and two fingers of hers held his arm for three slow strides.

Lester Lamont had arrived for the dinner meeting. Kevin saw his wide shoulders and muscular arms push the woman in the wheelchair into the small banquet and meeting room at the back of the Kilmartin. At every wheel revolution the chair emitted a barely audible click. The woman's hair was a gorgeous white. The color well matched with the silver aluminum chair wheels. She presented herself rigidly upright in her seat, while wearing a light burgundy suit. Many a ponderous blocking sled at football practice up at Wisconsin had likely resisted Lester's strength. Les pounced on an unoccupied round table. With one hand he quietly lifted away from the table a now unneeded chair and then motioned for Kevin's coterie to join him.

In a way that happens in dreams or in distant, perhaps juvenile memories, with unknown people moving around a location for ambiguous purposes, arts council members never totally settled down that evening. One cause for exiting the banquet room from time to time was clear: the offer by the museum administrator to use an office telephone. To check in with family about the storm and possible flood. More than one attendee got a busy signal at home; telephone lines within a thirty-mile radius of St. Joseph must have been crackling. So repeated attempts were warranted. But within a half-hour family connections were largely fulfilled. Restlessness seemed to remain, however. It came in eddies, like the variations and interludes of the rainstorm outside, motivating two or three people at a time to repair to the corridor beyond the banquet room for greater privacy for conversation. Several people volunteered to visit the front veranda to scout the weather. The banquet room had a row of stout casement windows. However they were lodged at a second floor height and partially obscured with linen curtains. One fellow commented that he forgot a file from his car that he wanted to retrieve. Reports ebbing back to the dinner tables were unfolded in straightforward terms. The arts council members moved from table to table, reminding Kevin of a bridal couple at the reception. But they reported with the steady tone of nearly-fossilized war veterans describing enemy entrenchments. Nothing much more than rain and wind gusts and reasonable speculation so far. There was thunder far off to the south, the rumble penetrating into the Kilmartin Museum, but a cannonade not particularly threatening. The sole exception to the calm was the gentleman in search of the file from his car. To Kevin the man looked annoyed when he went out. However he had borrowed a fisherman's rainhat from a secretary in the administrator's office. Its slick yellow surface gleamed under fluorescent lights. That seemed to reverse his mood. He came back to the dinner with the vinyl hat still guarding his head. Raindrops in the shape of inkblots had scattered about the knot of his pale blue tie. There was now a look of a gargoyle on a mission about him. Water had pooled in the curled-up brim and on the pushed-in crest of the hat. He was an irrepressible archbishop of mirth as he dipped his hand into the moisture and sprinkled it like holy water at several tables, surprising friends, getting huge laughs. He skipped Kevin's table, however.

Early during the dinner Marlene Zekel leaned toward Kevin and whispered, "That's Eleanor Gierson Todd, you should know." While Marlene had complained about still feeling chilled, her yellow raincoat now rested inside out on the shoulders of her chair. With her eyes and arched blonde eyebrows Marlene indicated the older woman whose wheelchair Lamont had navigated into the room. "A real power around this town and she is just turned eighty-five years old. You want to get to know her. It's always very helpful."

Equally quiet, Kevin responded, "Related to the Gierson family, so it sounds?"

"Daughter of Alexander Gierson. He was one of the two founders of Gierson Gasket. Eleanor Gierson Todd may have been the highest-ranking woman in a large American business back in the 1950's, the

1960's. She wasn't content to be a large stockholder. She did real work. And very effectively, no doubt, from what I've seen on this arts council over the years."

"Dr. O'Donnell," Eleanor Gierson Todd said suddenly. "Les Lamont has been telling me about your new project for Gierson and the interesting advertising idea on the glee club that you've cooked up already. I'm a frustrated thespian myself—husband, children, working career—kept me away from all that. So I a sucker for artistic endeavors. And you've mixed in a little commercial angle, pretty sharp stuff. I know we will get along just fine."

Kevin felt like the high magistrate of the solemn tribunal had entered the courtroom and immediately lavished on him a radiant smile. Acquittal, or even exoneration, had arrived from her chambers. She had the kind of refined voice captured on documentary tapes of English duchesses who endured the London blitz. And who then refer to the bombardment and appalling destruction as "all that unpleasantness." Another feeling presented itself just as fast. Mrs. Todd came across to him like the vibrant kindergarten teacher of thirty years ago. And you discover to your delight that she has nourished just as big a crush on you.

"Well I'm not sure how it will all play out," Kevin responded. "I mean, I haven't actually heard these people *sing* yet."

Mrs. Todd was amused and Les Lamont beamed a smile toward the entire table. Ted Mower sang a few off-key bars, a line from the not played enough *Chapel of Love*. Which just cracked up Mercedes sitting immediately to his left. Ted and Mercedes had been speaking intently for a quarter-hour. Kevin noticed that Eleanor 's cheeks were delicately brushed with rouge and her eyes had a shade of blue so soft that it mildly embarrassed him to look directly at her.

Eleanor picked up the conversation again. "I'm hearing too from Lester that you have a very interesting history project, I'll call it, about looking for original photographs from your ancestor. Your uncle or grandfather or whatever. Are you still pursing that?"

"Interrupted for the moment but that's temporary. Photographs taken in 1906 of San Francisco a few days before the earthquake and fire leveled the town. And my Uncle Philip had other subjects in the old west that are intriguing. American Indian photographs particularly. But I have concentrated on finding the San Francisco material first. The plates might be in a storage locker on a U. S. navy destroyer accidentally sunk off of San Diego back during the Korean War. From what I've seen he deserves some attention for his work. It's not just family pride."

"Well I have a suggestion that perhaps Marlene can chime in on," Mrs. Todd said. "I think that the Kilmartin Museum might be able to help fund your research if we can get consideration of doing periodic exhibits of your uncle's work right here at the Kilmartin. Assuming, of course, that we all agree that it's quality work."

Marlene asked, "Would that conflict with university funding of your research?"

"No," Kevin said. "Given the family connection they are reluctant to provide monetary support for my efforts. So there's no conflict there. This is some interest in my search by a book publisher but that is not firmed up yet. I am more than ready to hear about your offer."

Kevin quickly thought that the word 'offer' might have sounded better as 'idea' or 'concept.' And in fact he had never allowed the significant cost issue of retrieving the photographs (assuming they were on board the *U.S. Fiddler*) full and fair play in his mind. Lying something like one hundred feet below sea level off of California. While he could be reasonably focused on financial things, he had let this problem exist out there on its own, unmolested and unsolved. Sort of like the sunken ship. If the Navy had no interest on its part to compel the government to fund a salvage operation of the ship's contents, those ancient photographic plates might as well be resting on the Sea of the Clouds on the earth's moon. The electric lights in the banquet room blinked off and then on for a few moments. This repeated several times. Storm interruption undoubtedly. Until the electric voltage reconnected, the room was startlingly silent. Kevin then noticed a series of suspended light fixtures above the crowded and again buzzing tables. The lights grasped by slender aluminum poles descending from the high plaster ceiling. The fixtures were circular with a metal center like a gray bulls eye. Mother-of-pearl colored glass surrounded the center, a halo hovering strangely when illuminated, similar to a planet's aura under infrared photography. At the end of the room from Kevin's current perspective another series of light fixtures were much different. Each was tethered to the ceiling with a thin chain. The bulbs were muted by off-white cloth shades of a quilted pattern that resembled ancient hot air balloons. Minus, that is, the pilots' straw basket. And seeming to float at an identical altitude. The set of four lights triggered in O'Donnell an image of Paris Commune balloons of 1870 gliding to freedom from the stifling Prussian siege. The thunder drummed again in the City of St. Joseph and across drenched Buchanan County; angry artillery unable to disturb this peaceful flying squadron. "In all my years coming to the museum," Eleanor Todd said, "I've never seen the lights go out from a storm. We often have a lot of food stored in our freezers for meetings and parties. I hope that is the last of any power outages that we might have."

"I would think that you have some emergency power generation here," Les Lamont suggested. "Maybe it is required by municipal law or something."

Marlene Zekel said, "Actually that's not the case, about the law, but we have some lighting backup power that *is* required. But the museums freezers are on their own if the power is out. A short outage is no big deal. A few hours could be dicey."

Kevin O'Donnell recognized something that moment that had been escaping him since Marlene arrived for the dinner meeting. At first he thought it was her dress with a little too much cleavage showing for this kind of gathering. Not it. What was the most striking difference was her demeanor and attitude since the morning meeting back at Gierson Gasket Company. Rattling off the resources of the Kilmartin Museum to fund aesthetic research and to withstand the rigors of summer weather ratcheted up her position versus the Gierson managers, Lamont and Mower. Her blonde hair was unleashed around her neck a bit, more flowing than at the earlier part of the day. She was not demur or recalcitrant back at the office in Kevin's experience. But she sort of shined here. The tall, pretty, polite women who comes out of the grandstands to pinch hit a grand slam at the company softball game.

Word had circulated among the tables that the business meeting would be postponed due to weather concerns. And because of the unnerving prospect of power failures in the vicinity. The recording secretary may have written: meeting called due to possible electrocution and/ or drowning. Marlene then suggested that she show their guests the exhibit room on the basement floor. It was decorated with the current display of ceremonial masks from the South Pacific. Mrs. Todd had mentioned that any display of Philip O'Donnell's photography would be stationed there. Ted and Mercedes had resumed their conversation and said that they would pass at the idea. Les Lamont needed to follow up with Mrs. Todd on the glee club idea for Gierson advertising. That left Kevin and Marlene to make their way through the elegant corridors, past a petite Brancusi sculpture that he had not noticed earlier and a renaissance tapestry suspended from a wooden dowel, as they gravitated toward the staircase with the dramatically spiraled iron banister. Marlene's high heels did not tap against the wooden floor quite as loudly as before.

The staircase to the lower level of the Kilmartin Museum laid out steps with the widest portion on the left side and a fairly narrow platform closer to the right. The shape resembled pizza slices. But ones that never terminated at a center point. Given her high heels, Marlene Zekel selected the left side and carefully placed her footing step by step as they maneuvered on the black slate surface. It seemed a few degrees cooler just half way down to the basement.

"I'll let you in on something," Marlene said softly when they exited the staircase. "You can really help me out a bit if you can participate in Eleanor Todd's idea. About some funding for your project." She stopped, as if to check to see they were not within anyone's hearing. There was no one nearby. "It was my push to get external foundation funding to support rotating artistic exhibits. Part of the idea was to bring new and even unusual presentations to St. Joseph and the museum. I made a big deal of using some of my contacts with the Hertz foundation and some research on the Kahn foundation, the Mudge foundation and a couple of others. Now two of the future exhibits have run into problems and we had to scrap them from coming here. So I'll be embarrassed if I don't line up some others really fast."

Kevin had not responded as they reached a set of open doors at the end of a wide corridor. He could observe colorful masks lining two rows of shelving and a long credenza against one wall. Mostly the masks were brown, perhaps of palm tree origin. Some reflected gold paint and others were strewn with ribbons and furs like a mink stole or had genuine shark teeth attached. Fat frozen grins alternating with doomsday scowls. He disliked masks of this kind as a general rule. Disliked them because commentators always found in them some enormous profundity about the human condition. As if wielding a machete to chop coconut shells into grotesquely shaped ears brought a finer audit of the beating heart. Likely they were developed just for fun. Perhaps to hustle an extra buck or two. Or to deflect a face for whom even a mother has disappointed second thoughts. Nevertheless, Kevin stood for a moment beside Marlene Zekek, seemingly absorbed as her, as she indicated the exhibit's sign at the entrance: 'Courtesy of Kilmartin Museum and a Consortium of the Kahn, Hertz, Mudge, Moore, Wertz Foundations.'

"Even if a publisher wants my material on my uncle, that shouldn't interfere with doing some exhibits here at the museum, Kevin said finally. He wondered if, at this point, he should raise the indelicate question of how much money might come his way from the museum. He did not have a good estimate yet of what was needed to fund a salvage operation of the ship's contents. Divers would not plunge into the cold, murky San Diego Bay depths in leaky, rusty scuba gear to promote his hopes and dreams. And beyond the slippery reach of an aquarium's trained seals. It required a first-class operation. Probably some cost basis that grows exponentially for every ten meters of recovery depth. Kevin envisioned the burgeoning cost leaping ever leftward across the desk calculator's display face. But any amount of subsidy would help; would give him leverage with other potential revenue sources. Keep him in more control of the project versus having one giant benefactor. Granting sources could be foreboding entities if you screw up the assignment. 'Dr. O'Donnell, we were wondering about the somewhat flimsy data content on this report…'

A rumble that could have emanated from tables being pushed over a roughly grooved floor was just detectable in the display room. The deep bass sound was repeated. Kevin knew it was thunder, seemingly closer than earlier that evening. This dislodged his mental argument over the costs of the salvage expedition. He could not get that all resolved now anyway. There was a sensation, too, that got his attention, a feeling analogous to static electricity from a woolen sweater being pulled over bare skin. Dissipated lightning charges, hovering ghost-like in the atmosphere? Kevin had yet to decipher this when he noticed that Marlene was straightening out masks that were already in excellent alignment. Picking up a mask and resettling it right where is was on a bouncy bamboo tripod. As she leaned upward to grasp a small grinning mask from the topmost shelf she raised one foot behind her for balance, like an aloof figure skater. The action stretched the clingy blue fabric of her cocktail dress against her long legs. It was then that she asked, "Kevin, who exactly is Mercedes?"

"My girlfriend," Kevin said. "She's a graduate student, but not in my university, She's in the business school doctoral program over there."

Mercedes did not acknowledge that she heard his answer. "There's more thunder," she said. "I just put in new carpets in my house and

I hope that I don't get water damage. I got a small place after I split from my husband and I didn't even consider things like flooding at a time like that." Kevin was looking at a framed Japanese rice paper watercolor that was obviously not part of the mask collection. Would he find too little production by Uncle Philip to fill even this modest room? Would this print of purple mountains, half-moon shaped boats and birds immobilized on blazing cherry trees accompany his own exhibit in this space? Marlene Zekel was beside him, scrunching her shoulders against the cool air, nearly touching his right shoulder. The thin string of pearls delved deeper down her chest. "Hard to believe it's June," she said. "It's so cold." In a seamless fraction of his life, Kevin experienced another loss of electrical power in the Kilmartin Museum and linked with it was Marlene at his face. She was kissing him on the lips while holding the back of his head with one hand. There was not pitch black darkness from the power failure. With one unobscured eye he could see that the exit sign in the room now shined in Christmas-time red. Out in the corridor an emergency light provided some soft whiteness, only about as demonstrative as a flashlight held stationary. The craggy and indented coastline on the Japanese artwork had vanished behind the eclipse created by Marlene's face and hair. Reviewing it a little later Kevin believed that he had not reacted physically at all. Neither kissing back nor pushing her away. Finally Marlene stepped away and said, "I sure hope you find those photos and then need to come back here real soon."

Marlene twirled away from Kevin almost like a partner in a ballroom dance. She left the room without another comment. Kevin followed a few paces behind. The normal flow of electricity to the building was still absent. The single emergency light in the corridor protruded from a red metal box fixed near the ceiling. There was a clanking of multiple sets of shoes rushing down the spiral staircase; presently the figures of Mercedes and Ted Mower burst into the lighted area. As if late for their juggling act. "Kevin," Ted called out before reaching him or Marlene. "Me and Les Lamont need to hurry over to our docking facility, over by the river. The Army Corps of Engineers is predicting that heavy flooding will pummel that spot within four or five hours. The flood level has gotten dangerous. You and Mercedes are welcome to join us. In fact we can use all the help we can get."

Marlene Zekel was the first to respond, saying that she needed to go home to change her clothes. She would head down to the river after that. Kevin and Mercedes agreed that they needed more suitable gear and decided to return first to their hotel.

"I'll follow you to your hotel and take you to the river after you get changed," Ted told them. "You don't want to be driving at night near an unfamiliar flood zone anyway."

Marlene Zekel had already vanished when this plan was getting worked out with Ted. When Kevin and Mercedes followed him through the front door of the Kilmartin, out on to the soaked veranda, the parking lot was down to a handful of hunkering automobiles. As they made through the windy rain to their car, Kevin could just glimpse the glistening tail lights of several vehicles moving in close convoy down the steep museum driveway.

CHAPTER TEN

*"Isn't this exciting?" (Philadelphia Phillies pitcher Tug McGraw
speaking to catcher Bob Boone, pitcher's mound conference, 1980
World Series vs. Kansas City Royals)*

Standing in soft rain on soft grass ten feet from the embankment,
Kevin O'Donnell absorbed the river's intention. The message from
the Missouri River was clearly intelligible. To any observer, and in
any dialect: This Flood is Not a Joke. Thirty yards east of the Gierson
Gasket Company distribution center, positioned at the river's edge,
Kevin, Mercedes, and Ted Mower had just arrived and were getting
oriented. Minimal had been said since they exited Ted's car. When
roaring in from the highway in his vehicle, fishtailing slightly like a
chase scene, Ted's fine Oldsmobile—so low-mileage it carried a new-
car fragrance—had pounded over several sets of train tracks. The car
had traversed a small railroad marshalling yard. This was just inside
the Gierson property line. The Oldsmobile illuminated a set of boxcars
painted in bright yellow, and blue, and orange, like giant Lionel toys.
But no action occurred here; the freight cars were deserted and their
open doors exposed a hollow interior. Immediately they had passed a
dozen tractor trailers backed into a long loading dock. Light blazed

down on the mammoth trucks. This was from a row of mercury lamps attached to the back wall of the distribution building. On the side of the structure opposite from the churning river. The rain provided a cool mist to temper the lamps' ferocity. Fork-lift trucks wove about the workers scurrying near the yawning doors of the trailers, evacuating as much Gierson product as possible. Three additional delivery trucks waited a turn at the packed loading platform. Seemingly impatient to play their role, the motors idled on these vehicles. Bobbing metal taps, capping their vertical mufflers, beat a soundless staccato at the whim of the hot exhaust.

But this was just backstage. No place for Kevin to richly experience the flood's immanent collision. It was glued to the river bank that he could feel the tension produce by the gathering high water. As though a rampart of water would deluge them like a Pacific Ocean tsunami. (Earthquakes could propel tidal wave energy from Chile's dangling coastline to Japan's rocky beaches, Kevin knew, shock waves gliding silently as sharks beneath the endless ocean surface, but roiling the American Mid-West would be a stretch). Artificial lighting was less plentiful here versus the business side of the building, where trucks lined up like suckling young animals. It was likely that little activity took place riverside during nighttime hours, accounting for the dismal lighting. Several portable lamps had been set up already to counter the darkness. Including the type that burns beside the Interstate roadbed for midnight repair work. Their glare triggered mild spatial disorientation that Kevin's cerebellum took several seconds to correct. Other lights and strobes were being hastily unpacked from several contractor vans. In the whirl of activity and the yelling back and forth, with odd illuminated structures coalescing in the dark, it would be no surprise to see a Ferris wheel emerge. Here to help, nevertheless Kevin was satisfied to avoid snapping together electrical components in this dampness. The electrical power ran through strands of cables the color of black licorice and the diameter of a racquet ball. The cables raced toward the Gierson building and leaped headlong through an open window.

Visibility away from the Gierson property was uneven. As best as he could discern from this prospect, the landscape was less developed on the opposite side of the Missouri River, the Kansas anchor. Scattered lights were haphazardly distributed on a gently rising slope, like first stars in the early evening. There was an absence of headlights' glow. Perhaps that pristine stretch was roadless. Or motorists there had the good sense to seek drier ground. A thin screen of evergreen trees paralleled a section of that bank, where, swaying in the weather, wobbly branches induced lights behind them to blink. North and south of the Gierson location, back in Missouri terrain, a hodge-podge of commercial properties abutted the river. Few clues emerged to indicate what type of enterprises these might contain. Corrugated roofs angled over one and two-story structures, none very monumental in scale. It appeared that the Gierson facility housed triple the square footage of its neighbors. Building lots of various configurations, work-a-day Monopoly sites, touched the river edge. There were stacks of wooden pallets in a rough pyramid shape and piles of loose material in three-foot cones that could be gravel, crushed ore, damp wood chips. Several piles were more rounded; scale models of treeless mountain ranges. Refuse dumpsters the size and color of elephants passively waited by garage-style doors, near stained cinderblock walls and dripping exhaust vents. Similar to the Gierson distribution facility, narrow docks on the northern perimeter ran perpendicular to the embankment. These were unlike pleasure boat walkways with broad quays of maple or cedar planks. Instead, venturing out about forty yards into the Missouri River, there stood a black metal superstructure braced above the waterline. And slightly wider than a catwalk, the type sometimes attached to petroleum storage tanks. Nearby there were two of these docks. Odd clusters of piping that were a mystery to Kevin poked up at regular intervals along the docks. No watercraft herded at the Gierson location. However, at a different property about one hundred yards to the north, a barge riding low in the water was tethered to a dock siding. The barge's shape reminded Kevin of an infantry landing craft; like a large cake pan with no decks visible above the four flat sides. *What a party-crasher such a vessel could be: down whomps the exit ramp and the soldiers' grease guns race out firing...*

"Ted, is it safe to park your new car so close to the river," Mercedes asked. "Do we have any real idea of what might happen tonight?"

"Not that I am aware of," Ted said. "I guess I was thinking I could jump in the car at any point if the flooding reached much over these banks and move it away. But I figure now that I could even forget or be preoccupied if it is a worse-case flooding situation. I'll go move it now. When I've done that, I'll find out what the three of us can do that's useful. Les Lamont is in what they are calling the Command Post, inside the distribution building."

The quivering electrical storms that had mesmerized dinner time had vanished. The rain now enveloped Kevin and Mercedes more like a light fog. He felt surprisingly comfortable and dry in a windbreaker loaned by Ted Mower. Fortuitously, out of the cavernous trunk of his car, like a calculating flea market maven, Ted had produced jackets for him and Mercedes. The Gierson logo in cherry letters curved sensuously across the white cloth. Ted was coaching softball that spring; apparently the team got a break in the price by buying in bulk. Kevin had a Gierson baseball hat and Mercedes wore her San Diego Padres cap. This appeared considerably more lived in versus their sailing venture. She had exchanged her contact lenses for glasses back at the hotel. He rarely saw eyeglasses resting on her fine nose. But they had conventional running shoes on their feet. It was likely that clammy moisture would penetrate his soles soon enough.

"Team Alpha? Team Bravo? Team Alpha or Team Bravo?" A short fellow armed with a huge flashlight and a clipboard, wielded almost like a Roman slashing sword and a legionnaire's shield, approached the pair with impatient strides. He was not familiar to Kevin, who was able to spy his round face and fleshy eye sockets under a hooded coat. "Got to stick with your team," the guy continued, cheeks already ruddy with exertion. Friar Tuck doing his rounds? "If you are not already assigned I'll put you on Team Bravo. That group needs the most manpower." Then he flipped a plastic cover over the clipboard and briskly recorded their names, like two for dinner, non-smoking.

While the man inscribed this information, for an instant Kevin wondered if Zekel, Marlene was also recorded there. But he was as quickly distracted when their enroller supplied them with work gloves from under his puffy and glistening coat.

No reason to wait for Ted Mower. Crisply evading the lighting specialists, the two recruits hustled with their guide to their post, smack in front of the central glass doors of the distribution building. This perhaps sixty feet from the frothing Missouri River. Two first downs to defend from the Missouri River. At a glance Kevin noticed a long tree trunk plowing through the water, just out beyond a metal dock, a stubby branch angling up like a periscope. Maybe a camouflaged and joyriding bullfrog perched there, Gulf of Mexico or Bust. Scads more storm debris was likely to be sluicing down the pulsing river. Snakes, too, and clear plastic six-pack carriers.

"There's quite a turnout of help tonight," said the fellow without looking back at them. "Red Cross, and some National Guard folks. City emergency workers. They wear those crimson vests with the yellow sashes. A couple of Army Corps of Engineer staff are assigned to the Command Post. And lots of Gierson employees. But some Gierson employees are Red Cross volunteers or Guardsmen, too. One is a Guardsman who volunteers at times for Red Cross. So it's complicated categorizing everyone." "Outside agitators, that's us," Kevin responded, bringing the fellow to a fast stop. Who said, "We expect everyone to do his duty," and indicated with the beam of his blazing flashlight Kevin and Mercedes' work team.

More precisely a spectator team for a short period as the plan of action slowly emerged. Twenty-five or so people were standing in small groups, men mostly but there were four or five women included. Then, snorting ominously, puncturing the night with strong headlights set nearly at eye level—blocking Kevin's sight of the operator—a tractor pushed a narrow plow parallel with the building. It was curling up a shallow trench, four fingers deep and three feet across. There was a white concrete walkway leading from the pair of glass doors to the river bank; as though the headlights had perception, the tractor did not try to penetrate the hardened surface. The neatly sculpted trench ran more or less in a straight line, staying a reasonably constant two yards from the building's extremity. As Kevin marveled at the solemn care taken with this process, someone yelled for them to grab the nearby plastic tarpaulins to line the trench. Always an inspiring vision, Mercedes' long legs in blue jeans stretched taut as she and Kevin fitted the thick plastic tarps like seedling covers across sections of the torn earth. Newly homeless earthworms were bound to be wriggling through the wet clay. The tarpaulins were new and not particularly supple. It took effort to conform them with the rectangle of the trench. He wondered aloud if this mild construction could somehow channel flood water from its destructive intent. That did not seem plausible. Their little ditch resembled a welcoming bed for a mass of red begonias. They had not exactly replicated the Panama Canal.

"It's a liner for our sandbag wall, Kevin." Ted Mower had returned and summarily joined Team Bravo. And where might that sandbag wall be? "I heard that we'll have to start filling sandbags now to build our moat for our castle," Ted said. "God, I hope this works."

In stereophonic waves, loud truck horns caught Kevin's attention. Two bulky dump trucks were patiently backing up toward Team Bravo's position from either end of the building. Mechanized bookends. The large distribution facility stretched a good eighty yards fronting the river. The entire Gierson property collared twice that much yardage along the Missouri. He wondered why the drivers chose to back in to their location. Then Kevin realized that if the intent was to unload from the rear of the vehicles in this confined space, the trucks would be trapped by not backing in. As he had deduced, the vehicles stopped long before they would have collided or squashed the work team. A grinding and whining sound accompanied the slow upward tilt of the matching dump truck beds; up, up, inching toward a fifty degree angle. Rocket launcher position. Suddenly, deep red gates slung open within moments of each other and sand and dirt-like material plunged out pell-mell, causing the gates to swing like massive wind chimes now waving goodbye. Immediately a young woman in a motorized buggy the size of a golf cart appeared out of the moist haze behind one of the unburdened trucks. The sight reminded Kevin of golfing tournaments with his talented brother-in-law. Where refreshment carts, driven always by lovely young ladies, at random times bounced up to the sunny tee or green, laden with bottled water and juice and chilled cans of beer. A snow white golf visor on her blonde hair and a yellow polo shirt to coordinate with her shorts. Then galloping away like a Civil

War cavalry raider. The service kindly eased the sweating purgatory of the poor golfer matched with a scratch player. But this was a City emergency worker, it seemed, given the bright red coat and yellow stripes like a crossing guard. A heap of woven material that Kevin surmised to be empty sandbags rose behind the driver, almost level to the top of her head of luxurious auburn hair. Stacked that way, must have been static electricity holding the bags on board. Right after the cart rolled to a halt, people started grabbing fat armfuls of flattened sandbags. Could have been the hopeful-for-parole crowd working the laundry in a prison movie. A fellow plunked down a pile near Ted Mower. Ted held up one bag to demonstrate the procedure for Kevin and Mercedes. Three foot or more in length, narrower than Kevin expected, and more tubular than a pillowcase, Ted touched the open end to the brim of his soaked baseball cap.

"Fill it about two-thirds, no more than that," he explained. "It's crucial that you don't fill to the top. It doesn't get sown shut. Fold the open flap in against the bag, like you're securing a turkey's neck folds against the stuffing falling out. We can only build a wall about two feet high. Four filled bags on top of the trench liner, then three more on that base. And two sandbags on top. Snug as you can make it. Do your best. I'll go check on how other people are making out."

Rome would not yet be officially opened if Kevin had directed construction. Some delay with the occupancy permits. Nevertheless, in he plunged. Shovels both long and short had been stacked like muskets against the wall of the building, handle end aiming at the clouds. Kevin selected a short spade and lugged it back to Mercedes on his shoulder like a baseball bat. His Louisville Slugger proved to be a good choice. A plastic grip at the end like a thick stirrup made it easy enough to manhandle in his white cotton work gloves. A debutante in the construction business. Somewhere Tony Connelli and Vic Kesson were howling about this. The blade's surface dimension was barely the equal of a notebook page, but he got a fast rhythm together to fill the bag that Mercedes was supporting. (Mercedes was working without the gloves, whose fingers hung out like roots from her jacket's left pocket. As he had noticed at more intimate moments, she had shapely and powerful wrists). Kevin pulled from a commissary of pure sand. A pleasant sharp ring ensued with each shovel full as he sliced into the mass of silicon, like coins rustling in a sack. Somehow, digging out sugar for ten thousand cups of tea and coffee had been practice for this, in miniature. He anticipated the weight of a functioning sandbag fairly accurately: thirty to thirty-five pounds. Like an unconsumed case of Ortlieb Beer bottles, sixteen ounce returnable type, or thereabout. Mercedes painstakingly directed the first few sandbags into the trench like they were paving a patio. And with non-standardized huge Belgian blocks since no two bags were filled with an equivalent volume of sand. But, veterans of several stuffed bags laid down, they began dropping them in quickly, like jumbo hotdogs tightly packed in a cellophane wrapper.

The burgeoning sandbag parapet was being erected in sections along the entire Gierson property. Occasionally, when two sections came together, the connecting bags had to be partially emptied to secure a proper fit. Ah, Promontory Summit, Utah, Kevin would say to no in particular. Kevin found himself noticing the efficiency of other sandbag partners; he tried to be a half-shovel faster than they were. "Pace yourself," Mercedes said a few times. But Kevin had nearly hypnotized himself and was unconscious of much strain. The muscles in his upper back felt strong and fluid as he progressed through the semi-circular shoveling motion. Similar to changing screens on a slide exhibition, he was enjoying different themes alighting in his mind. Within fifteen minutes of getting the bag routine in line, it seemed that he had worked this all of his days. The sound of the sandbags hitting the tarpaulin liner was sharper than that of the upper layers. Easier to lift a bag to reposition it than to drag it across its resisting brothers. What is brand new is familiar in the next quarter hour. Reminded Kevin of his first trip to Europe, back in college. Just beyond the immigration control in Charles de Gualle Airport, passport not yet tucked securely in his backpack (which he toted along with blossoming jetlag), Kevin already heard his buddies casually refer to "the States."

While he had no basis for a benchmark, Kevin felt that the team was making reasonable progress on extending the sandbag barrier. Perhaps three-quarters of the complete Gierson property confronting the Missouri River had a line of bags stacked two feet high. Team Bravo had grown considerably. The volunteers were shoveling fill and pounding down sandbags relentlessly. Red points of smoky cigarettes waved like mosquito punks as workers attended to their tasks. He was so into his work motions and his thoughts that Kevin had not measured the flood's progress for a time. He saw that it extended over the embankment. Roughly one-half of the grassy territory between the sandbag wall and the river bank was claimed by the flood. The remaining lawn was battered, too, by the workers' hauling and their boot heels, as though invisible steeplechase horses had trampled through there. Startled at the flood's progress, he stepped back quickly and nearly tumbled over the low sandbag wall. Earlier, a nearby metal dock platform cleared the water by several feet; presently it seemed to float on the river's vibrating skin. Clusters of long twigs and strips of cloth and white plastic bottles bunched up briefly against the side of the dock before slipping under the structure. Only now did it occur to Kevin that flooding would not be gentlemanly, wait for their side to be lined up for kickoff. If it so pleased, the river could barge right into the locker room during Coach Mower's eight-point pep talk.

With renewed determination Kevin resumed his efforts to help complete the barrier. Mercedes desired to work the spade and sand for a while, so he held the bags open like an earnest trick-or-treater. Within a few minutes he picked up again with his reverie. Odd, he thought, that he and Mercedes would find themselves on the soaked edge of a major waterway playing with shovels and sand with dozens of busy strangers. For the two of them it was like a crazy beach contest that a local radio station might stage. Hey, screw the sandbags. Let's just sculpt the sand into a giant dinosaur. With raised armored scales on the tail the shape of family heralds and mammoth lidded eyes leering at the river. But folks right around them might lose a Winnebago camper or a job or even a house from this disaster. His biggest concern was blisters; Mercedes had pulled on the work gloves by then, too. Kevin was forced to acknowledge fatigue by now; he propped the expanding bag against his shins, moved his right foot back a little for more balance. But even a tired state can be pleasant, as soothing as a deep-muscle massage. On the rarest of instances in his life, moments transitory as a breeze, Kevin felt that he was pushing at the door of a secret chamber, ready to contact his deepest center and be totally unfettered by care. If not a door, at minimum a crystal clear window into that tender space. Never certain to him so far if he would actually penetrate that realm. Sometimes the sensation was triggered by days of wrenching hard work. A melancholy Indian summer afternoon could launch it, with the dreamy muffled sound of small airplanes at the horizon. Or the quietude of Christmas Day, with every commercial storefront shuttered. The simplest gesture in this state would make the hair stand out on his neck. The way that Mercedes flicked the last clingy grains of sand off of the shovel into the bag. Three or four specks might tip the balance tonight. Or the Red Cross worker who visited them, offering black coffee out of a battered green thermos bottle. An older guy with a gray, vibrant mustache, wearing an ancient hat of a railroad engineer, and with the cap angled in a manner that declared that it was authentic. It tickled Kevin when the fellow commented that his Norwegian-born mother used to gorgeously label this kind of Missouri night as 'rainweather.' With one hand still awkwardly clutching open a sandbag, Kevin sipped the hot drink out of a Styrofoam cup. When finished, he crumpled the cup, the fragments feeling in his gloved palm like a handful of popcorn, and then he flung the remnants riverward.

"Look at that boat," Mercedes said loudly. "What in the name of God is it looking for?"

"Is that it over on the other bank," Kevin asked. "I guess those are searchlights we see. I can't see any of the people on the boat, though." Prior to this moment, Kevin had not registered that there had been no boats moving that evening on the Missouri River. Now he saw the outline of a craft a short distance upstream, three-quarters of the way or so over to the Kansas side of the river. An eerie, slowly moving light show. Red running lights outlined the front and back of the boat, perhaps forty feet apart. A mobile central porthole hung brightly, as if strung on a reeling clothesline. The vessel emerged into view as slightly disembodied given that all of its parts were not visible. The two searchlight beams pouring off of the boat crossed in an X and subsequently formed a capital V against the opposite shore. Then, as the boat gently veered toward the Missouri embankment, roughly in the direction of the Gierson Gasket Company enterprise, the searchlights angled to the water every which way, like radiant swizzle sticks.

"I guess the boat's checking on damage from the flood," Kevin said. "I wonder whose boat it is?"

"Are you crazy—don't answer that," Mercedes responded. "They wouldn't check on flood damage in the middle of the flood. They must be looking for someone missing in that river."

They continued to watch the moving lights bobbing on the Missouri for seconds more when Les Lamont appeared for the first time since their arrival with Ted Mower. Les being the only individual on the immediate riverfront without raingear and still wearing his tie and suit from dinner at the Kilmartin Museum. Ted stepped up beside Mr. Lamont just moments later. "What's with this boat out there," Mercedes said as a greeting to Lester.

"There might be some teenagers missing. Swept downstream from a park a few miles upstream. But we just got a message in the Command Post that calls it a false alarm. The rescue folks on the boat are just being extra careful about that. But we have another problem that I'd like you three to handle for us. You see those metal docks with the weird pipes and things. They are called slow mobile docks. You can actually release them from their current position—heading straight out into the river—and swing them in parallel with the river bank. There's some advantage to them that I don't follow. But those babies are expensive to build and it's less likely they would be ruined by storm debris if we can swing them in forty-five degrees, like a huge gate, to press up against the shoreline."

"What in the name of God can the three of us do about them?" Ted Mower wondered. Kevin had never served in the military but Ted resembled for him a resolute second lieutenant that he might have served with there. Taught skin at his temples tight to his skull, fiercely even short hair moving up the side of his head until it merged crisply with his cap. Could drop to do thirty push-ups to pass the time...

"Well the problem," Les resumed, "is that the three fellows who know how to operate the dock's releasing mechanism are not here. One retired a month ago and moved to South Carolina. One man is in St. Joseph General Hospital with a severe kidney infection. The last one is on vacation fly fishing in Montana. Luckily we got hold of him by telephone at his cousin's house. He actually called in when he heard about the flood on television." Suddenly Kevin realized that his sweat socks were wet. He was contemplating this unfortunate development when he discovered that Les Lamont had big plans for him concerning the metal docks and their releasing mechanism. In for a penny, in for a pound, and all that and he was soon following Les through the glass doors of the distribution building. Immediately inside, a woman was holding a receiver to a wall telephone. Armstrong Spring Creek, Montana holding on the line: the fly-fishing employee who knew how to manipulate the docks.

"I can't give easily written instructions," the guy said to Kevin. "You have to sort of feel your way through the process. Visualize that you are troubleshooting on your car's engine. And Mr. Lamont said you have a superior memory."

Kevin had faith that there was some relationship between the inscrutable metal and rubber parts stashed under an automobile's hood and the car's ability to move on the roadway. Last time that he shopped for a new car he did not even pretend to check out the engine visually. Not that it was a complete enigma to him. For example, the fan near the radiator was for cooling the power plant, not for propulsion like an airplane propeller. The heavy black battery doesn't help the vehicle to move exactly, yet it will not even start if the battery is dead. (Batteries speed his godson's toy cars fairly well; must be some scale issue that Kevin would have to reflect upon later). Strangely enough, the gasoline that funnels into an opening near the *back* of a vehicle plays a role in this locomotion. Pressing down on the accelerator must pump the gas up to the front somehow. Funny, come to think of it, how you can hold the pedal pressure absolutely steady and the pumping still works. Not like a bicycle tire pump. Not feasible to drain a keg of Rolling Rock Beer that way. Must be that those vacuum tubes are involved. Kevin did little or no troubleshooting on anyone's car engine. At least no one he liked. The fellow on the telephone was going on about three dials similar to a safe's combination locks and a big handle just to the side, out there on the docks apparently. *Calibrating a car's timing belt would be a helpful analogy, he told Kevin in closing. Oh, goodie.*

Kevin swept his vision left and then right as they left the building and headed for the nearest Gierson dock. The Great Sandbag Wall of Missouri must be near completion now. The workers fell back into groups of a half-dozen or so individuals, nearly motionless, placed like human pylons on either side of the low barrier. Les Lamont dropped off and Mercedes and Ted Mower formed his escort toward the barely visible walkway. Shoes and socks already wet were strangely more comfortable once he waded through the cold wash on the embankment and gingerly made his way onto the grated flooring of the structure. Mercedes and Ted tramped close behind him. It reminded Kevin of the metal roadway on the Tacony-Palmyra Bridge back home, crossing the

Delaware River into New Jersey. Heading over to Vallari's Restaurant to get a good dinner. In the rain he hated driving his Camaro over the slick steel joining section of the aging drawbridge, some hell for leather motorist tailgating him. Only fair if they still only charged a nickel to cross it. Ted kept motioning with a flashlight for Kevin to keep sloshing outbound along the dock; apparently the releasing mechanism was at the far end of the gangway. The lighting on the structure itself was abysmal. The illumination from the haphazard light array thronging a section of the riverbank was more helpful.

In adulthood, and as a homeowner, Kevin had learned that he was not afraid of climbing. So immediately he started up the metal steps drilled like giant staples into a black tube about fifteen feet high. It would have been dangerous to crowd his hand with a flashlight. Therefore Ted played stagehand and patiently tracked his climb from the slightly rocking walkway, where railings provided good handholds for Mercedes and Mr. Mower. Two-thirds up the pole, Kevin saw for the first instance that the sandbag wall did stretch the entire length of the Gierson property, with offshoots angling back some distance like arteries toward the rear of the distribution facility. Such a beautiful palisade of piled sandbags, he felt greedy in a way that he had the best panoramic view of their creation. He thought, too, that awareness of his immediate mission must have grown among the fatigued sandbag crews. Now fifty or so people had abandoned the more remote northern and southern stretches of the completed wall and began congregating at the surging embankment near the foot of the dock

For the first time Kevin looked at the array of dials and levers that decorated the releasing mechanism for the mobile dock. He had perched on a platform about as spacious as the in-box on his desk back at the university. At least this was devoid of a slippery mound of unread journals. The fellow on the telephone from Montana had assured him that this was a mechanical process, not an electrical device. Lightning could still fry him but not this contraption. Nothing of that fellow's advice had stuck with Dr. O'Donnell. On one small panel, slightly embossed from the blue box at the top of the pole, Kevin could ascertain three dials. Might mean something. There was a thick handle with a black rubber grip, maybe the dimension of a slot machine handle, but this was to the left side, not his strongest leverage. Kevin was about to gingerly test one of the dials, planning a series of careful preliminary tests, slowly weaving his way into the psyche of the device, virtually coaxing it into cooperation when Ted Mower abruptly swerved the flashlight beam away from the box.

"Holy Jesus," Ted yelled, but apparently not as a devotional gesture. But it served as a signal for Kevin to gaze out into the river, where he saw a sight that scared the total hell out of him. Looming nearly at mid-river, but drifting noticeably in the direction of their end of the dock, a floating one-car garage slowly heaved with the pulse of the stormy Missouri, all the while carrying a small brown dog on its peaked roof. It was like a ride that did not quite pass muster at Disneyland. Sorry, but have you fellows tried Allentown's Dorney Park? Mixed breed the dog could charitably be labeled. But a trace of class that Kevin could detect in a flash. Once it sensed the notice of the humans on the dock and on shore, the mutt held its narrow head regally, as if to say, "I planned to be on the roof of this garage. It will transport me to safety. I'll read your obituary over recuperative Milk-Bone in the *St. Louis Dispatch*." Equally compelling was the garage: Kevin owned virtually the same model garage back on Walnut Lane, at home. Ordered it last summer out of a catalog to replace the decrepit lean-to on the side of his house. Talk about a soft sell. Bullet points extolled the oaken joists, the three side windows with decorative shutters, a vapor barrier beneath the garage floor—but not a hint about its flotational capability. Shouts from the folks on the shore called for rescue of the buoyant dog. Kevin saw several exercised people rushed out a few yards onto the dock, adding to its increasing shakiness.

Ted's hefty flashlight was trained on Kevin again. Mercedes shouted, "Kevin, have you figured it out yet? Let's get going."

You got it. No need to answer. Kevin O'Donnell leaned into the wet pole like he was trying to force a door and grasped hard on the side lever with his left hand. His right work glove was missing; now he pulled the left off by the middle finger and sailed it into the night. The handle would not respond initially. But cousin to a recalcitrant jar lid, it snapped down suddenly, and Kevin could feel through his soaked running shoes the disengagement of the dock from whatever held it in check. Prior to this juncture Kevin was unsure what power source swung the dock in to the bank. The flow of the river apparently. He scrambled to the bottom of that pole so quickly that he must have missed a few steps descending it.

A clap on the back or two, some subdued cheers as Kevin raced with Mercedes and Ted Mower to the second and last Gierson mobile dock. Their footfalls drove out thick marbles of floodwater. Must have looked like speeded up video tape as he about bolted up the same type of steps on the pole holding the control box. He was exhausted. Only when Kevin mounted the miniature platform at the top did it occur to him that he did not remember how the dials were set on the preceding control mechanism. He called down, "I'll sing *Wichita Linesman* to amuse myself if you get someone to check how the dials were set on the first one." Already the first dock was nearly parallel with the riverbank. Both Mercedes and Ted set off on this new mission.

The releasing lever on the side tempted Kevin like that last slot machine quarter. However, he figured that he would not be so lucky as with the first contraption. So he looked out at the river instead. The garage with the dog had vanished. But the rescue boat was hovering about, as if keeping an eye on this spectacle, the way that a helicopter reporting on traffic hovers stationary near trouble spots. Shouting from people along the bank started to increase noticeably; what's the big deal and where did they get the energy?

The mist from earlier had just ratcheted up to palpable rain. This made it a little difficult at first for Kevin to pinpoint the source of this new excitement. Ted and Mercedes were up by the other dock, then they were twenty yards beyond it, arms pumping in a determined run. The fat barge from the property just beyond the Gierson boundary had broken its mooring and was loose on the river. Its hull was presently bumping in against the embankment but moving due south in the direction of Kevin's current location. What might have been one hundred twenty yards of separation earlier was reduce almost in half. No need for a second long look: down he went to the dock's grated flooring, submerged six inches under the greedy Missouri, swinging down more than climbing off of the pole. It was dreamlike like for him to run through the water covering the dock, attempting to generate any speed for getting back to firm land. To collect himself he switched to a jog when he hit the narrow strip of grass still visible before the sandbag wall. Kevin thought that Mercedes and Ted had not looked back to ascertain his current location as they approached the ponderous barge. When it surged right up to the bank, the pair scampered aboard it and disappeared from Kevin's view.

His racing thoughts were the converse of his tired muscles. Kevin figured that Ted and Mercedes took him to be high up on the pole on the dock, oblivious and in harms way from this barge. "It's a barge from the porcelain factory," a voice called to him as he came within twenty yards of its side. "It is filled with bathtubs and kitchen sinks." He was in luck. While the vessel still moved southward, it was close to the embankment. He was up to his shins in the cold river water, still supported by the river bank, moving like a slow-motion football replay, when he spied Mercedes and Ted clambering over wooden crates toward the rear of the barge. Did they hope to find a rudder back there? Severe injury could accompany a shift of that cargo. Now the barge was surging up and crashing down right in front of him. He planned to board it and got his left hand on a curved metal flange on the barge's side when the laden craft suddenly fishtailed like Ted's car had earlier. Instead of hitting the deck of the barge, Kevin splashed in a flailing belly flop into the Missouri River.

Kevin was facing the embankment and the Gierson distribution building when his head surfaced. Ploddingly, and then more desperately he reached out his hands to swim back to the riverbank. It seemed that the barge was lurching away from him. It would crush him if it reversed course. Storm current was in control and he stayed parallel to the land as he was swept southward. At this moment he was perhaps ten yards below where he first plunged into the river. An image of a tree trunk crashing into his head instantly haunted him—anything might be trapped in this flood—prompting Kevin to reach out his left arm to ward off invisible obstacles. Quickly a hand grabbed that arm, swinging him around a half turn. A slender forearm was projecting from the side of a boat, a thin wrist that might have been a woman's. Then a voice that he recognized, "Hello, John the Baptist, want a lift?" and he clearly saw the fragile strands of blonde hair and brilliant smile of Marlene Zekel. Marlene and some stout guy in a life vest hauled him into the boat. They let Kevin collapse on a pile of ropes coiled on the deck, where he shook at first with cold. Hey, Marlene, give it a rest, he thought when he realized that it was the adventurous brown dog, former occupant of the floating garage, who was licking his clenched hand.

CHAPTER ELEVEN

The broadcast studio housed a variety of lighted dials and controls. The instruments were not packed in exactly. One could comfortably place three fingers between the bass and treble indicators, or between the more prominent tape deck buttons. The studio was more like an airplane cockpit stretched by an expanding universe. Kevin O'Donnell sat there quietly in a leather swivel chair. He felt nervous. He knew that a lot was at stake. A cornucopia to be lost or gained depending on how he prevailed on the airwaves. A half-hour before show time, Kevin had paced the drab corridor of the radio station. Unobtrusively he had positioned his scuffed docksiders between the dingy lines of the azure floor tiles. Thirsty, dusty leaves of a lonely palm plant repeatedly brushed an alternating shoulder as he paraded like an impassive palace guard. He restrained himself from kicking out a straight leg, like a corporal marching in a greatcoat at Lenin's Tomb. With little effort he might have memorized the haphazard notices on the corridor's bulletin board where a calendar ran six months late: a glorious Christmas wreath radiated on a weathered New Hampshire barn door. Kevin had to endure the thirty minutes until the afternoon music program would finish. Through a window panel on the door to the studio he could see the elegant black hand sweep the seconds of the wall clock.

Past the thirty-second mark the hand progressed like a measured golf swing. However the minutes did not seem to advance. Kevin had been tempted to retreat to the parking lot, to momentarily revel in the vibrant southern California sunshine. Where yard high crimson salvia and a bank of yellow geranium flanked his rental car. And where an infinite dome of powder blue sky suspended a few harmless puffs of clouds. Concentration won out, however. Now he used another relaxation trick taught by his old fencing coach: to maintain your equilibrium, glue your mind to a few small but significant details that could affect your performance. Right down to the tying of the laces of your fencing shoes. Acknowledging this as he waited in the studio, he bounced his finger along the five silver switches shaped like boxwood leaves under the five open telephone lines. Then he reversed the cap on a blue ballpoint pen to ready it for business. At forearm's length, he delicately twirled the circular volume controls; the 'pots' as the controls were known in the trade, but not actually changing them from their original position. On his left side were two empty record turntables. The hard-plastic concentric circles molded on their surface were at rest. Seen peripherally the turntables were like models of helipads on a hospital roof. He disregarded them for now. Deliberately he ignored the engineer in the other room—he was an annoying person anyway—treating the huge single-pane window between them as though it was sheet rock. And acting like his fat headphones were only earmuffs that were not responsive to the engineer's voice. In obvious exasperation the engineer finally tapped a soft fist on the glass. He held up a sign hand-drawn on tattered construction paper: '15 Seconds To Airtime.' At the last of those seconds Kevin turned and smiled excitedly at the engineer, and firmly announced into his open microphone, "Hello, America, from Station WXIT in rain free San Diego, California. *Call in, America* is on the air!"

Immediately they launched into two minutes of advertisements that Kevin recorded in the 'traffic' log. One minute of promotion for his new show and sixty seconds divided between a Chula Vista car dealer and Sea World. The advertising traffic log. The ancient jargon of the radio trade that so quickly resurfaced for him. It was two years since Kevin had last filled a temporary stint at a radio station. His college roommate had lured him into this media almost twenty years before; they had shared the early morning disc jockey duties on the university radio station for a month each year. They arranged it during the off-season from his fencing team schedule. Clock radios around campus jarred students awake with Jimmy Hendrix and the Chambers Brothers. *"The time has come again..."* A secret thrill that his voice was welcome in so many coeds' darkened bedrooms. A quick radio play to launch the show most mornings. Their *Exalted Theater of the Air* was the *piece d'resistance*. They created and recorded it evenings before with their maniac friends; it slipped past the censors at the six a.m. hour into collegiate radio infamy. It was whispered that the shadowing of a listeners' cult attached to their *Buzz Korbett—Space Kadet* skits. To this day Kevin was confused as to what that 'festoon' joke really meant. What incalculable blackmail potential from just one of those eight-track tapes. Every few years, during graduate school and college teaching summers, O'Donnell had grabbed a broadcasting job somewhere. With short-term assignments Kevin was not particular as to location: St. Cloud, Minnesota; Roswell, Georgia; even Munich, Germany with *Radio Free Europe*. Staying away from the technical side of the business, he never needed a license and avoided untold chaos for unseen millions. Mostly rock music DJ work for him; a little interview programming; a touch of commentary presentation. Kevin took it as it came, enjoying it like multi-layered gelatin with whipped cream.

"We are back live," said Kevin O'Donnell to his radio audience, "and you heard the toll-free telephone number that you can use to contact us. I'll be on the air for the next three hours, until 8:00 p.m. Pacific Time, to talk with you. I'll toss in a little news reporting and maybe the odd song or two along the way. But mostly it *is* talk and it is up to you to select the topics for our discussion. It's only fair to warn you that I will likely be running this show just for a few weeks or maybe a month at most. So if you want to get your hands around me, so to speak, there is no time like the present.

"I mentioned that I might mix in a little news occasionally on this program, *Call in America*. In fact I have a newspaper story of a particular incident from the mid-west last week. Perhaps you heard about the terrible flooding that hit northwest Missouri and parts of Kansas. And St. Joseph, Missouri, just north of Kansas City, got pummeled along its waterfront on the Missouri River. I happened to be there with a friend on an assignment with nothing to do with broadcasting. Without planning it I had front row seats to the pounding action. One of my St. Joseph contacts alerted me to a report in the *New York Times* that I want to read for you."

Kevin smoothed out a long column of newsprint on his desk. There were two cutout newspaper photographs that he laid adjacent to the writing. Previously he had used a yellow highlighter to remind himself of the sections to share with the audience. "Did you know that before the advent of the printing press it was standard practice to read all writing aloud? Anyway, the report goes like this."

This *New York Times* travel writer had the rare opportunity to see an unleashed force of nature—the Missouri River at flood stage—as it dramatically collided with hardworking Missourians trying to protect their property and livelihood. Since I have been producing travel articles about Kansas City and other large mid-western cities, I don't know St. Joseph, Missouri very well. I was asked to pitch in with a report and agreed to give it a try. Chance took me to a section of the industrial waterfront just north of downtown St. Joe, where I was poking my car in and out of various business properties to see what was up. Some older buildings looked vacant and their gates were wrapped in chains clasped by padlocks but a number of others were throbbing with activity and energy. Big tractor trailers coming and going were splashing through puddles. Police cars and fire official sedans were racing in and out of different properties. I explored a couple of places and made my decision where to investigate more fully.

One large compound had quite an array of vehicles and equipment such as strobe lights spread around. The Gierson place. They manufacture gaskets there. However their main objective seemed to be to construct a long line of sandbags to protect the one main structure. Luckily, there was something a lot more interesting unfolding just one property up the river, at the Republic Porcelain Factory. A huge barge packed with their products was roiling on the flooding river, pulling at its mooring lines with tremendous force. The standard methods of securing the barge to its black metal dock were clearly being tested to the limits of their endurance. Twisting like linguini cooked al dente, the thickly braided mooring ropes reminded me of boat anchorages in Venice and Capri. Conditions were much too threatening to attempt unloading the high-quality bathtubs and kitchen sinks from that vessel. The main concern of Republic officials was that the eight ton gross weight barge might tear loose and damage one of the few main bridges over the river downstream.

This temporary reporter accepted the kind offer of the Republic managers to use one of their office telephones. To alert my Kansas City colleagues of the possible catastrophe in the offing. (Impossible not to appreciate the masculine appeal of the richly grained wood paneling in the executive suite. Where a gleaming brass Stiffel lamp directed illumination on to my note pad). To call about the hefty packed barge that might be launched like a battering ram toward one of the City of St. Joseph bridges over the Missouri. Might even make it passed the bridges and later rip into Kansas City property. Events moved quickly that evening. By the time I finished my call and returned to the riverfront at the Republic Porcelain Factory, the barge indeed had broken free and was threatening to take out a dock at the adjacent property downstream. The one with the long, low sandbag phalanx facing off the flood. I was informed that someone's dog had gotten loose in the river, too, and a Gierson Gasket Company employee had unwisely plunged into the water to save the canine. Obviously he was unaware of the looming Republic company barge. Two other Gierson people were then motivated to scramble right onto the barge in an attempt to steer it away—somehow—from the fellow floundering with the dog. Luck was with them to some extent; the barge swerved passed the man and dog but unfortunately it totally crushed the dock immediately below. No injuries to anyone—man or beast—but that dock will have to be dismantled and hauled away for junk.

Kevin then held up the two black-and-white photographs that he had scissored from the same news account. Given that it was nighttime and set in a soggy atmosphere, the clarity of both photographs was admirable. White reflections had the intensity of exposed light bulbs and the black surfaces were a strain of India ink. The travel writer from the *New York Times* was credited for the pictures. An occupation that apparently demands a variety of skills. One shot must have been positioned from the very edge of the embankment, near the hot emergency lighting. Since the river did not recede for half a day, as if savoring its adventure, igniting the next cigarette from the last, the photographer had to be standing calf muscle deep in water. The shot captured the barge entangled with the pretzelled remains of the second Gierson mobile dock. Steel poles were crumpled like lacquered plywood. The dock stretched like a vast net sacrificed to capture a ponderous leviathan. Kevin had been still recovering his strength and equanimity when the rescue boat had embarked a totally exhausted Mercedes and Ted Mower. There was no photograph of the embrace that the three long shared on the boat's slippery deck. But there was one taken back on shore of Kevin with the panting young dog that was reproduced in the newspaper. His Gierson hat had departed, perhaps in search of that garage, but Kevin was still wearing the cherry and white jacket supplied by Ted Mower. Given the oddity of the names, Kevin had gladly helped the reporter with the spelling for the caption: "Spunky Lewis'n'Clark catches his puppy breath along with would-be Gierson Gasket Company rescuer, Andre Bijou."

"Wouldn't be in the newspaper if it wasn't true," Kevin continued. "That's pretty much how I remember it." The engineer in the other room still offered a quizzical look since no listener was yet motivated to respond to the show. A wrong number would be welcome at this juncture. Lets see. Is there an Isabel here? What does this Isabel look for in a man? Anything, you know, unusual about this Isabel? "Of course, believe one-half of what you see and none of what you hear is also sage advice," Kevin suggested aloud. Finally the engineer showed some affability and arched his eyebrows as he informed Kevin through the headphones that a caller from Philadelphia who knew him was on the line. It was Bob Goodall's patrician voice that broke the silence. The very Bob Goodall who thought that racket ball was the national pastime. Mostly because the Devon Horse Show did not travel well and lacked trendy promotional items. Bikers emblazoned in Horse Show dungaree vests—not a chance. Before Kevin aired his comments, Bob said that he needed to speak with Kevin privately about his search for Uncle Philip's work. Something big was up. Something very big. That would have to wait. Enormously intrigued, but needing to remain professional, Kevin threw the silver switch to place Bob Goodall on the air.

"Hello, Kevin," Goodall began, acting as though he did not know him. Would you mind if I performed two songs over your airwaves to welcome you to our lives? They are a couple of popular country and western songs performed as best as possible in the style of Luciano Pavaroti." Right away he plunged in with:

"My sad heart cried out 'Arrivederci,'
As Jo Dee packed up her red Jeep Cherokee."

Fortunately Goodall only remember a few short verses of the song. He told Kevin then that he had saved the most melodious piece for last, a certain hoedown song so fashionable of late. At least in some circles. In his best Italian tenor voice he belted out the tune.

"Too much class to put a ho' down
On the twangy streets of Nashville.
Had been there; he knew the lowdown,
Of whether or not she would…

At an instant, the red indicator lights of all five telephones shot out an impulse at O'Donnell's retinas. Their fierce spherical glow had almost a physical presence. Bob Goodall's voice had quickly vanished. Thank you, Mr. Marconi, for this enjoyable wireless mystery, he thought. It had forever astounded him that ghostly radio waves could actually be employed. More astounding than the fat airplane fuselage that soars through the air because at least the airplane is visible. Sleek sheets of tangible aluminum forming the wings fastened by wide bolts in exact rows. The jetliner's shadow chasing across verdant barley fields and skimming noiselessly over hilltops like shady ground fog. Kevin never directed a talk show before this. But he felt that the surge of telephone calls was an indication of some reasonable level of acceptance by the tuned-in public. Yet only a momentary reprieve if he could not sustain and even enlarge listeners' interest and involvement. For good luck, Kevin envisioned the gigantic cabbage heads and boulder-sized gourds displayed with such pride at state fairs. Concerned as he was that those 4-H Club participants would eventually migrate to growing red ants the size of sheep dogs. (Beneath his contempt was Professor Goodall's conspiracy theory that the photographed pumpkins were actually normal size and the scale issue lay with Old McDonald's cardboard brethen). He pressed the purple button that channeled his voice solely to the sound engineer and said, "Anything interesting on these callers that you've just screened? Death threats? Marriage proposals? Wait, is there a difference? And is that President Reagan trying to get ahold of me?"

"Not quite," the engineer. said. "But it is a fairly impressive assembly of individuals for this early in the program. I'm not going to tell you who they are before I put them through to you. That'll teach you to ignore my pre-show instructions."

Kevin reminded the audience one more time that this show was about them and their lives. In effect it was directed by the listeners, their concerns and comments. With a flick of his thumb resembling a coin-toss, he opened the first telephone connections for all to hear.

"Kevin? Am I on? It's Mike Schmidt of the Philadelphia Phillies. Good evening to you." Kevin thought that he had muttered hello, but he knew that he froze for an instant at the trigger of the All-Star third baseman's voice before pulling in another telephone call. Schmidt was destined to be in the Hall of Fame, all observers said. Probably the greatest third-baseman in history. On television and radio interviews he had heard Mike Schmidt's voice many times. But never directed at him. Kevin was definitely disconcerted. He was expected to converse with and then dispose with the first caller before proceeding to the second. "Move them out of there like shiny Fords rolling off of an assembly line," the station manager had informed him at the interview. "And we don't do service after the sale." Already he had screwed up by having two lines open simultaneously. Rather than admit that publicly, he queried the engineer through his private line if he would comment on the next prospect. Might as well shovel all of them in at once, one burgeoning compost heap of conversation. A gentleman by the name of Waterfront—nothing familiar in that to O'Donnell. Safe enough: Kevin threw the slender silver button to bring the caller onboard. "Professor," Kevin heard in a familiar booming tone, one that instantly filled the radio studio with an echo of caroming electrons. It was Tony Connelli. "I'm Chester Waterfront," Tony went on to say, "but you can call me 'Chet' if you prefer."

"Would you happen to have a friend there by the name of Marcus Hook, by some chance?" Kevin asked. Some in-joke that he did not explain. "You're pretty quick. Marc is right here," came the answer from Tony. "And he sends his warmest regards."

Without the screening advice of the sound engineer, Kevin ventured on to the third caller. A person he also knew, Stephen O'Hanlon, Ph.D., M.D., MBA, MA. Steve did not teach in the American Civilization Department at Kevin's university. Instead O'Hanlon was tenured in biophysics, the field of his doctorate. A rare joint appointment with the medical school if Kevin remembered correctly. 'Dr. O'Hanlon, Doctor' Bob Goodall had greeted him at Provost Feeney's retirement luncheon at the faculty club. A little taller than Kevin and about seven to ten years his senior, O'Hanlon's hair was the light reddish kind that resists going gray. Even among a crowd of snobbish academics O'Hanlon's extraordinary brilliance was acknowledged. Kevin always found him unassuming, almost naively so; rumors had it that Dr.

O'Hanlon once made it to the final three candidates for the Cleveland Philharmonic's conductor post—his master's degree was in music. A courtesy interview he labeled it ever since. In fact, Steve liked to brag about his identical twin brother, some obscure basketball player or other from the Philadelphia area.

"Dr. O'Hanlon," Kevin said. "I have the privilege of introducing you to a man named Chet Waterfront and also Mike Schmidt of the Philadelphia Phillies. Not every day you talk to fellows of this caliber."

"No, you don't," O'Hanlon responded. "But I know Mike Schmidt rather well. The Phillies hired me as an off-season batting coach for Mike after his rookie year."

Two glowing red dots for the last two unopened telephone calls. The miniature bulbs must be roasting by now. No retreating at this juncture; metal treadles would puncture his reversing tires. Kevin would have to add the callers to the conversation or look foolish. The three fellows already onboard were being patient but Kevin needed to pounce quickly. He flipped the fourth switch for his fourth inquisitor and immediately heard a soothing female voice. "Kevin O'Donnell. Well I'll be." The timbre of the southern accent rose and dropped like a piston on an oil well, the kind shaped something like a giant caterpillar. "Thought I'd tumble out of my porch chair when I heard your voice on this station. You were all of eleven years old when you last knew me. Do you remember Sister Katherine in the sixth grade? That's me. Except I left the convent and my religious order quite a long time ago. Now I'm Teresa Palowich of Belmont, North Carolina. Married and with two daughters and one son. They run the full range of teenage years. Has your handwriting gotten any better, by the way? That has worried me for a long time."

Kevin remembered. Tall, lean and pretty, severely so thanks to the black and white headpiece of her nun's habit that completely encased her hair. Like a supper club band leader, formal dress every shift. A silver crucifix anchored a long rosary of brown wooden beads. The beads had multiple facets like a diamond's crown. Leaning a bit over a student's desk to check work in progress, she pressed the rosary against her mid-section to keep it from becoming an annoying pendulum. Sister Katherine taught every subject for his sixth grade class. From his permanent second row desk Kevin had endless time to observe her. Deep eyes of the softest blue he recalled, a tinge of a pastel shade. As she sought for a positive element in a student's incomprehensible fractions, she pursed her lower lip. A pianist's hands of long pink fingers, wearing a single plain ring. Her hands reached out from black sleeves that carried a light quarter-moon of chalk dust at the close of a busy blackboard day. Sister Katherine wrote right-handed. She erased the slate board with wide energetic swings of her left. In February's slanting afternoon light, soft clouds of the off-white dust hovered like incense near the blackboard, eventually dissipating near the fluorescent ceiling lights. Strong hands, too; might fire a smokin' knuckle ball past a hapless eleven-year old batter. Only now did O'Donnell realize how young she had been the year she taught him—early twenties at most. Many possible routes for her feet to track after that.

"Teresa, hello," Kevin said with mental hesitation that he pressed to keep out of his tone. Strange to speak with her so informally. Treated as an equal, no less. "I have to ask you to wait as I bring in our fifth and last telephone guest." The last red telephone light resembled the flash indicator that warns the subject on newer cameras. An exchange of momentary cataracts for capture of your smiling mug. No time to plead for screening advice from the engineer. "This is Kevin O'Donnell. Whom do we have on the line, please?"

"Mr. O'Donnell. My name is Sarah Breedlove. I'm proud to say I am a Navaho Indian. I live in New Mexico. I may have some information of value to you about Indian Ghost Dance photographs. The one's that your grandfather—I'm sorry—your uncle took many decades ago."

Where in God's name did this come from? Kevin had heard of the Ghost Dance, an exotic Indian religion he thought. However he knew nothing about Philip O'Donnell photographs of the ceremony. If that is what it was called. Uncle Philip had written to family about a lot of his adventures. Kevin knew this from pouring over the letter cache lent to him by his cousin Maeve Ward in Donegal. But Ghost Dance material? Limited comments from his uncle on that apparently. But there was some information that he recalled on the topic on the trifolded lined stationery with his uncle's angular script. The writing with the line so straight across a capital 'g' you could rest a cluster of knick-knacks there. Kevin felt like shouting out to Sarah Breedlove, "What? What? Tell me about it." Time, though, to maneuver back to the other participants and create somekind of theme for this impromptu conference call.

Kevin confirmed that all five callers could hear each other clearly. "Remember the rule," Kevin said then. "The telephone callers can't listen to the radio as we speak because that will distract them." There was a seven-second broadcast delay that the radio station used to protect against unacceptable language on an unrehearsed talk show program. The minute and hour hands of the large wall clock in the studio were deftly aligned to that principle. Kevin had long felt that these precious few moments were time that was somehow unaccounted for on the very seam of the universe. Insurance, too, that the world could not evaporate suddenly with earnest language and deep sentiments hovering for delivery to the public. Working in this profession fulltime might instill in one a judicious hesitation about what one said—if not what one truly thought. But he needed to shepherd this flock along tonight…

"Mike Schmidt," Kevin said, the Phillies look like a threat this year. Maybe you'll be back in the World Series like three years ago. And the Philadelphia Seventy-Sixers just beat Los Angeles last week to win the NBA championship. It's a great time for Philadelphia sports teams."

"It was terrific for the Sixers. Terrific. And we are pleased with the way our season is progressing. Still early though. But the reason I called is to talk with you about that article you wrote in *Baseball Monthly* last year. The one on the players' strike in 1981. Was that the same Kevin O'Donnell as you? A lot of us were pretty steamed about that article. It didn't seem that you did your homework in order it write it more accurately."

Kevin answered, "I put something together for it, yes. That was my piece. I was just trying to contrast a strike of financially comfortable baseball players with a more typical walkout by production workers. Or by modestly-paid service workers. I wasn't trying to do an in-depth economic analysis because economics is not my specialty."

"You are entitled to an opinion," Mike Schmidt continued. "But you didn't seem to know anything about the battle for free agency rights by ballplayers. Our desire to sell our skills to the highest bidder, same as any other trade or profession can. People take a big risk in pursuing a career in professional sports. Few people make it to the major leagues—even American Legion level ball has good athletes. And lots of guys who reach the major league make modest livings at best and for just a few years too. For the privileged of getting fat round bullets fired past your head. And spiked shoes using you for a dart board. This is a lot more complex than you portrayed it in your material. I didn't get the impression that you interviewed a single ballplayer before doing that article."

Kevin had not even thought about interviewing professional baseball players before dashing off his short piece for *Baseball Monthly* magazine. He was not paid for the article—it was an opportunity for some exposure in a venue that he would not normally consider. His neighbor's cousin worked for the magazine. Over a few beers he had discussed the idea with the neighbor during a Fourth of July block party. Evening was spreading a comfortable grasp over Germantown and East Falls, while the sky revealed faint stars at a leisurely holiday pace. Kevin pictured his white shorts and gray New Balance running shoes stretched out before him. For comfort he had pulled his entangled key chain from his pocket and rested it on his thigh. He had sprawled on a venerable chaise lounge that was on the verge of collapse and spoke animatedly with Mrs. Whitney about her suggestion. She was a silver-haired neighborhood activist who organized this annual event. He could almost smell again the lighter fluid from the just-started charcoal grills in her driveway. Golden flames flashed nine inches above the heaped coals. With a long plastic spatula as a fly swatter, Mr. Lawrence Whitney cast a scrupulous watch to shoo away curious children, his giggling granddaughters included. Police sawhorse barricades were staggered in a line projecting out from the Whitney property. They stretched across McClane Street, blocking automobile access from Walnut Lane. The temporary police barrier was like a rough-hewn split-rail fence slightly zigzagged from an earth tremor. Cherry bombs and firecrackers exploded at times in a shadowy grove across the way, near the Walnut Lane Golf Course. Young kids would tear over there to investigate on fat-wheeled Huffy bicycles. Their shirt tails puffing a bit from a combination of a cooling breeze and their momentum. Recent freedom from school seemed to inject adrenaline into their leg muscles. The cyclists' excited shouts pierced to the top black fringe of the highest maple trees and beyond. Never thought that such an idyllic scene on the other side of the continent would bring him to this awkward radio discussion. Of course it had been a wet, threatening January morning when he mailed that article off to *Baseball Monthly* magazine. He had slipped his manuscript into a cold mailbox just down from the Whitney's corner home. The paintless metal handle on the mailbox more chilled by several degrees than the Heineken Beer cans at their Independence Day gathering.

"Kevin, if I could jump in here I would like to," Steve O'Hanlon said. "I am not familiar with that baseball article that Mike spoke about. But it does remind me of a situation that involved you and me a couple of years ago. Do you remember how I mentioned one time that I was involved in writing a grant proposal to study eye color being related to personality traits and perhaps even as an indicator of truthfulness? The proposal was directed to the National Institutes of Health."

"Oh, absolutely, "Kevin said with enthusiasm. "And I wasn't trying to hook up with that project by any means. But it struck me that the research could be of enormous value in situations involving critical negotiations. Negotiations of national or even global importance. And situations where different cultures come into contact for the first time. The Native Indians' initial confrontation with Spanish Conquistadors. Any time people sit down face-to-face to work out a peace treaty or an armistice. Could have put this to beneficial use at Panmuynjam in Korea, during the Korean War. Steve, if I remember correctly, I pulled together some materials and typed you a brief memo on my thoughts. I found the idea that fascinating."

"I was positively startled," Dr. O'Hanlon said "at how much of our concept that you picked up from a short, off-hand conversation over a Cobb salad lunch. And your friend Goodall had even distracted me then with a quiz on state capitals—the ones in Australia. A lot of what you volunteered to send over to me was quite perceptive. Although we had pretty much hit on the same ideas ourselves. But my issue tonight is how you let your quality thinking go off course. You didn't follow through on a good start. I mean when you came up with a suggested study population for the research—focused exclusively on blonde, blue-eyed females between the ages of twenty-five and twenty-nine. That hurt the credibility of what you produced for me quite a lot."

Mercedes was likely to be listening tonight and at this exact moment to his first radio show from San Diego. She was back in Philadelphia, having driven there in a rental car with the runaway dog, Lewis'n'Clark. Half of a spacious trunk was crammed with the data gathered at the Geirson Gasket Company. Something of a border war had erupted between Missouri and Kansas authorities over the origin of that dog. It wore a slender collar decorated with cheap rhinestones but lacked a registration tag. No owner stepped forward to acknowledge the failing of exposing that harmless puppy to the flood's cold, pummeling force. The once in a half-century phenomenon that attracted insurance adjustors like a siren call. One morning state representatives got into the act, arguing in sonorous legislative chambers that no self-respecting Kansas—or Missouri—dog-owner would have let that fine dog slip away. Mercedes was babysitting Lewis'n'Clark at Kevin's house; her apartment lease strictly forbad pets larger than a cat. Presently she could be listening in on the Pioneer receiver in his living room, maybe watching the volume indicator surge and blink crazily. She liked to stretch out on the leather couch, on its plush taupe fullness, her calves and feet swinging lightly from the fulcrum of her knees. He experienced this vision as if she were sitting by his side in the broadcast studio and looking sharp-eyed at his suggested research approach. To Stephen O'Hanlon he quickly responded, "Well, I guess I was without a girlfriend at that time. Maybe it was on my mind a little bit. But don't some women say, 'It's as easy to fall in love with a rich man as a poor man?' Would it be so bad to focus the initial research on a nice bunch of women?"

Kevin pushed the switch that privately connected him to the screening engineer, noticing as he did so that the engineer sitting over in the next room had his face obscured by a newspaper. Hopefully scouring the Help Wanted section in the Singapore *Daily News*. More likely that he was devouring the section in the *San Diego Bulletin* on emergency room patients discovered to have torn underwear. As he observed him through the large window Kevin was reminded of prison visiting-room images in old movies. He always found them so depressing, including the ones produced in color. The convict speaking through the thick glass screen on a heavy black telephone to a listless girlfriend or wife, begging her to try to get access the Governor one last time. And he just knows that the milkman or his brother is being so 'attentive' to her in these dark days: instead of the gawky waitress uniform of the last visit, now it is a sharp coatdress from the Marshall Fields' catalogue. And that auburn touch-up—downtown hair salon, not drugstore quality. "Is it time for the next advertisements," Kevin asked the engineer rather plaintively. "I am getting cooked right here."

"Not for another eight minutes," the engineer said. "Ad revenue for this program was a little thin, apparently. Not really the kind of format that I think will succeed in this market."

It was suddenly clear to Kevin that he might fare better by switching the conversation line over to someone who knew him better than Mike Schmidt and Dr. O'Hanlon. Not to worry, he said inwardly, about a rough start to a new radio talk show. It was just getting the puck in play, so to speak, mixing it up with worthy competitors, and a ragged initiation could produce sound dividends as the evening evolved. He almost said 'Sister Katherine' but reined that comment in and said "Teresa, can you tell us how you moved from teaching as a nun in a Catholic grade school to being a wife and mother in North Carolina? Must be some tale behind that."

"Not really," Teresa responded. "I won't bore your audience with that. So you won't mind, I'm sure, if I pick up on the theme that Dr. O'Hanlon, I believe it is, has introduced in follow-up to Mr. Schmidt's thoughts. Indulge me, Kevin, if you will."

After a slow deep breath Kevin said, "Be my guest. Remember that *Call in, America* is all about you folks."

"I am reminded of the report that you wrote for a combined history and geography project that you had in my sixth-grade class. It was my idea that you should get credit for both subject areas. Do you remember what I am referring to"?

Kevin was uncertain if he could remember anything correctly right now. But he responded "Yes, Teresa, it was on an event in Germany I think. But you will have to refresh that picture for me and share it with the listening audience."

"Oh, marvelous," Teresa said. "It was a report on the building of the Berlin Wall by the Russians in 1960. You did some reading, some research, actually, and put together a report that I gave a ninety-eight score to. You had your own text and pictures out of *Life Magazine*, and lots of maps. Maps of Berlin and East and West Germany. Even one that showed the distance between Philadelphia and Berlin. Making an effort to show the relevance of this event to our lives in the United States. I was amazed how much World War II history that you knew. More than most high school kids did, then or now. You even predicted that the Berlin Wall would be demolished soon. But of course in nearly a quarter-century that hasn't happened."

"I enjoyed doing that project," Kevin said. Now he clearly remembered the encyclopedias voluminous as medieval bibles dominating the table at the public library. The local library but with twenty-foot high ceilings and climbing windows that might dress a parliament building. Probably late-April: on the trees, sea foam-green miniature leaves rippled like paper. Watchtowers of creaky history books flanked his elbows. The gold capital letters on the spine resembled narrow castle windows. Two cute classmates in plaid uniform skirts and white blouses snickered as they strolled by his work area. Staying resolute as an Irish monk, Kevin trawled through the endless texts. And he could see the news magazines opened like rolling waves on the dining room tablecloth at home. A decent analogy he thought because then-Sister Katherine had launched him toward the luminous shores of higher education through that assignment. He continued, "My mother was somewhat mad that I sliced up that *Life Magazine* issue before my father could finish reading it."

"You had a very steady report going for eighty percent of the total product," Teresa said. "But the last one-fifth was truncated, too many ideas packed into too short a space. It seemed like you knew that you had an excellent grade in the bag and kind of pulled the plug on your effort. I didn't comment on that at the time. It was among the best that I had received. And you sort of had me boxed in because it was my idea to begin with. You did well against most other students on that project but not your best against yourself."

Kevin waited for a moment, hoping that a terrific response from him would pop up like a Kleenex. And he had shown such persistence over the years on so many tasks. Was that for nothing? Had not the sweat of his brow nurtured something of treasure, at least of an intellectual sort. But at the moment he chose not to fight back and to hear everyone out fully. "Teresa I'll get back to that, but I want to invite Sarah Breedlove of New Mexico to weight in now."

"I had learned about you through your friend and co-worker, Dr. Goodall," Sarah said. "I have written the draft of a book on the Anasazi Indians and my agent sent it to the firm of Lee and Winslow. The editor there happened to mention your name and said where you teach. I called there and the secretary at the university directed my call to Dr. Goodall since you were away."

"How can I be of help," Kevin asked.

"My family has had copies of pictures of our Ghost Dance ritual taken by a traveling photographer. I think that it was your uncle. My immediate family and tribe are mostly in New Mexico. The pictures were taken about 1896 or 1898, even though the Ghost Dance phase had supposedly died out among Indians a few years before that. We know for a fact that it had not died out. Some of my oldest relatives remember hearing as children that the photographer was Irish. But his real name was lost to us. On reservations the Ghost Dance was banned by the Indian agents and after the Wounded Knee massacre it had lost much of its support from Indians. Given that the dance or the special shirts Indians wore did not protect them against soldiers' bullets."

Dr. Stephen O'Hanlon responded to Sarah before Kevin could. "One of the things that has always fascinated me about the Ghost Dance religion was the influence or mixing of Christian belief with the native beliefs of the Indian tribes. How the claim was widely made that Christ had returned as an Indian, or at least a messiah had come to promise redemption of what the Indians had lost. It gives me the chills to read the accounts of Indian emissaries who visited with the prophet Waukova in Nevada, and how they claimed that they met Indians returned to life, people who had been dead for thirty or forty years.

And based on what I know about the Ghost Dance religion, it would have been unusual to have allowed a white man to see and photograph the ceremonies. Particularly after Wounded Knee and suppression of it on the reservation. How would you know if they are authentic pictures, actual Ghost Dance ceremonies?"

"Oh, they are real, alright,' Sarah answered. "The results were very accurate. A patch of trodden, grassless earth about the size of a circus ring. No fire set in the middle but some small fires were built off to the sides, curling up smoke. Several warriors in long Ghost Dance shirts, and the participants standing in a rough circle, a few with arms outstretched. The photographer is said to have participated in the ceremonies at times. It is something of a legend now that the photographer—he had nicknames from the tribe like 'Forty Shades' and 'White Blonde'—actually fell into a trance on a few occasions after hours of nighttime dancing with the Navaho. My people say that he came to believe that the Ghost Dance religion could help the Irish people in their battles with the English. The English controlled Ireland in his day. Pretty much the same concept as the Indians had in retaking their lands from the white man. Getting the buffalo herds back, and flocks of wild turkeys, and our freedom to roam mountains and the verdant plains again. I understand, Dr. O'Donnell, that you are looking to recapture the reputation or build the reputation of your uncle. Dr. Goodall told me that and so did the editor at the book publisher. The earthquake calamity was important, certainly. But the interests of my people continue to reverberate to this very day. The archived material that we have should not be ignored in your quest concerning your uncle Philip. My grandmother had saved it in a cedar chest, wrapped in linen like a mummy, away from sight and light. Ha. Kind of a little King Tut's tomb for your family's history. Your friend Goodall has my telephone number."

Kevin was ready to jump in quickly when he noticed that Sarah Breedlove's telephone connection was dropped. A momentary quietude from all directions but to Kevin it resembled cymbals of danger clanging. The most horrifying sound to a broadcaster: prolonged silence. Dead air. The sound engineer had ditched the newspaper, looking through the broad window at him with an anxious scowl, his forehead wrinkling. No movement from him, though, toward an advertisement or news break. Kevin deluded himself for a handful of seconds that he was like a jazz maestro, playing the sounds between the notes. Lightly clearing his dry throat Kevin said, "Mr. Waterford—Mr. Chester Waterfront I mean—have we lost you after all this?"

"Not at all. I've been fascinated," Tony Connelli said. "My friend and business partner Marcus Hook here is a little confused, but that is to be expected. Since I happen to know you, Professor, I know that you have been committed to finding old San Francisco pictures this uncle of yours took back in 1906. A lot of activity has been set in motion to make that happen. Some people have gone out of their way to make that happen. So the picture of old San Francisco can't be forgotten. You will recall our recent boat trip on the San Diego Bay where you were piloting the boat for much of the morning. Things got a little zany at one point, with a Naval submarine tender bearing down on us. My dear buddy Marc has commented that maybe you hadn't really learned enough about boating to want to control the sailboat under those conditions. See, we had both owned boats over the years and had a lot more experience than you did, and in a lot of different settings for boating. You might be surprised to know that Marcus can be very focused when he wants to. For example, every time we play golf together—been doing it for years—he always tries to get a hole-in-one on the par-three holes. And last year at Riverton Golf Club he did it on our last hole when our score was tied and we were playing for money. His tee shot landed past the pin, but rolled back and went in. Like it had eyes. I was shocked—and out fifty bucks."

"Must have been a miracle," Kevin said.

"Oh, that's an exaggeration," Tony answered. "But in all candor, I heard that the hole-in-one was mentioned in passing in the Vatican during Bishop Neumann's beatification hearings. But I am with you, buddy, don't you worry. Give me a call."

"I think I should say something in my defense and so I shall," Kevin said. "I always get involved in the game, well prepared or not. In part we learn by doing. Maybe as a child you watched some adult drive a car with a stick shift transmission. I don't care if you viewed that a thousand times, the first time you drove such a vehicle you stalled the car in very short order or ground the gears in a terrible shriek. Two years ago I worked in August for *Radio Free Europe* in Munich, Germany. It is a quiet time in Europe, vacation time for much of that continent. I was assisting the program director and she was interested in trying out some new ideas. She believed that she'd have a freer programming hand during the month of August. *Radio Free Europe,* as you may know, broadcasts information on democracy and freedom and capitalism into Eastern Europe and the Soviet Union. Like any other station they want to grow their listening audience. Their programs had gotten a little stale. Inspiration seized me and I called back to Philadelphia and telephoned a radio personality, an absolute legend, named Hy Lit.

"I had spoken with Hy once before and he remember me. And if you know Hy, he don't lie. Hy Lit gave me a great suggestion. Run a contest over *Radio Free Europe,* let people in Prague, and Budapest and the Soviet Georgia win a colorful tee shirt. They would do so by answering their telephone, 'I listen to *Radio Free Europe.*' Had to say that right off to win. You couldn't say 'hello' or identify the caller in any way. A simple but terrific format. We set up the contest just that way and it was a fantastic hit. We were mailing out a van load of tee shirts per day within two weeks to the contest winners. Soviet authorities were frantic. We learned later that the Soviet secret police—the KGB—decided to make a sweeping round of arrests of listeners, right in Moscow. Crush this outbreak of freedom-loving in the very heart of the beast. Fate had it that on the assigned day of the raids, the chief of the KGB was home with a miserable case of food poisoning. Dozens of secret police vehicles were idling along the street, along one of the huge walls beside the Kremlin. Big black cars, some Mercedes Benz and unknown Czech vehicles, like a funeral directors' auto rally. Picture their operatives in padded business suits and wide fedoras ready to roll—kind of like a gangster theme in that police agency. As a courtesy before the raid ensued, a telephone call was placed to the home-bound police chief. Right on the speaker phone in the Kremlin they heard the telephone in the chief's house answered 'Ya slushaya Radio Svobodnaya Evropa.' It was the police chief's wife Marina, and anyone in the world would have recognized her crisp Ukrainian accent. Give me a break. "I listen to Radio Free Europe" she said and they knew that communism's gig was up in old Russia and the Soviet Union. One by one the motors on the police cars were silenced, the dejected secret policemen lighting Turkish cigarettes here and there on the sidewalk, watching through the smoke that they exhaled the brilliant dawn rising over Red Square. Maybe that Berlin Wall still stands, but I say our radio contest played its role in chipping away at that ugly barrier.

"Oh, I see that my sound engineer is setting up advertisements that we'd like you to listen to. There is an ad for Aqua Dale spring water— only sold through retail outlets, now, no home delivery anymore. But believe me, you'll be a whole lot healthier for making the trip to the store yourself. I am new here and I apologize for forgetting the engineer's name, but we'll be right back...Lot's more fun on tap here at *Call in, America*—the program that is all about you."

CHAPTER TWELVE

In Denver, Colorado, there was a flight delay for over two hours. Unwitnessed thunderstorms, like threatening phantoms of the night in the vast Sierra Mountains, delayed arrival of the aircraft that would continue Kevin's itinerary. No flights went directly to New Mexico from San Diego. This included Sante Fe, Kevin's ultimate goal for the long day. O'Donnell arrived in Albuquerque, New Mexico after ten o'clock at night and Sarah Breedlove was not available to collect him at the airport. It was too long a journey for an airport pickup even by New Mexico standards. Sarah and her husband, Eduardo Hernandez, had a family party to attend, an obligation long standing on their calendar. This left Kevin to his own resources for getting to Sante Fe. Broad aluminum gates now shielded the handful of closed airport merchants from customers as well as itinerant shoplifters. Pulled down from the ceiling were the kind of gates that stretch along shopping mall corridors at night, like endless prison cell blocks. Red and white magazine covers and wooden Indian Kachina dolls and tiered sweatshirts huddled beyond reach. The frosty welcome for late night airplanes everywhere. Made Kevin feel a little out of sync; local folk suggesting that there were superior places to be seen around town. There was some mix up about the van ride from Albuquerque to Sante Fe, unclear to Kevin if a late evening run was still available. Several airplanes besides Kevin's had disembarked passengers at the Albuquerque airport within the same quarter-hour; dozens of traveling parties at an airport curb described a ragged line to await scarce taxicabs. Belatedly Kevin got the sense to join them. Baggage carts were dispersed along the small crowd like broken down cars; these needed to be unenthusiastically pushed every few minutes as taxicabs gathered passengers. Lugging a hard plastic suitcase and a small canvas bag that were strangely heavier than departure in San Diego, Kevin repeatedly counted the dwindling number of taxi hounds in front of him. He was exhausted and unwilling to rent a car in that condition. His radio talk show, *Call in, America*, had been shifted to a midnight to four a.m. slot by the exasperated station manager. Aqua Dale Spring Water had cancelled its advertisements and there had been other less explicit complaints. At least he finagled a few days off to bolt to New Mexico. Finally, Luis was the taxi driver at the airport who wearily slung Kevin's luggage into the trunk of the stalwart yellow vehicle.

During the seventy-mile ride to Sante Fe, safely keeping each other awake, Luis and Kevin talked in spurts on literature and anthropology and housing conditions in New Mexico. Three score and ten miles in the expanse of New Mexico was a roller skate in the park compared to back home. The good road passed under them effortlessly. During the silences Kevin noticed that white stars pierced a cloudless black sky, and he savored the cool air that tempered the June night. Glorious high desert weather. At modest intervals road signs announced the presence of San Felipe Pueblo and San Ildefonso Pueblo and the cutoff for the road to Farmington. All of this was unfamiliar to Kevin. He had been to the southwest but never to New Mexico. Nothing visible locally from the backseat beyond the laboring swath of the taxi's headlights. These earthly places were lost in shadow while galaxies a billion miles away were quite distinct. Eventually, from a dozen miles distance, after cresting a hill on the interstate highway, a grounded constellation of lights outlined Sante Fe at midnight. It resembled a nebula in the night, inviting him to connect the shimmering dots. Kevin was still tired and so enamored with the adobe buildings that sprang up like monoliths on the outskirts of Sante Fe that he forgot his cheap baseball hat on the seat in the taxicab. The preliminary sight of the thick, earth-colored walls and deeply recessed windows was as foreign to him as a Donegal village portal. However the taxi ride and companionship were quite enjoyable. He hoped that driver Luis saw fit to wear the new black cap as an extra tip.

A latenight greeting at their doorstep from people whom he had never met previously. Sarah Breedlove and her husband, Eduardo, were difficult for Kevin to discern at first due to the bright hallway light that poured out from behind the couple. The light flowed into a small overhang and dispersed into the front yard. Perhaps even his retinas were sleepy. Standing so close, the couple might have been glued at the hip, and stepping on each other's toes as they greeted him. Her hair was dark, black and long over a round, soft face. Eduardo's curly hair was blonde, perhaps from the sun and the grip of his handshake betrayed his profession as an auto mechanic. Sinewy tan arms emerged from a fresh aqua tee shirt. The logo on the shirt ran 'Hernandez Auto

Service' above the decal of a hot rod. Up the stairs to the second floor Eduardo went with Kevin's luggage without a mention about it. Three track lights were directed down from the second story landing. With every few steps that he ascended, Eduardo's shadow grew exponentially. Kevin saw that their house was of adobe construction. Sarah walked him arm-in-arm through the hallway on pine flooring into the first floor living room. A little over five feet, Kevin estimated, given where her soft hip occasionally brushed his thigh, Sarah carried some extra pounds but was shy of being heavy; she was formidable to him in the way that she possessed her personal space. He figured that it was a new home for the family and he saw that it was filed with spanking new furnishings for the most part. The walls were painted soft mustard yellow. Over the fireplace, a long slate mantelpiece pushed eight inches into the room and offered a secure platform for carved wooden candlesticks and clusters of miniature Native America jugs. There were pouring jars with elongated necks and an intricate flower pattern that reminded Kevin of Moroccan design. Mountain vistas in watercolor were wrapped in gold colored frames. A pair of them hung like staggered windows on the wall opposite the compact fireplace. A rug as large as the men's golf tee anchored the room. It incorporated Mexican burgundy and cobalt threads with floating reproductions of Anasazi Indian petrogliths. At the center of the rug, stick figures of a man holding a cactus plant and his frenetic hound were endlessly jumping toward a radiant sun.

Kevin had never asked Sarah on the telephone if she had children. He had guessed from her choice of words and the sound of her voice that she was thirty or thirty-five years old. The latter seemed about right. Her husband might be a few years her senior. However, he observed a collapsed playpen and an Indian-figure doll that leaned haphazardly against a dining room wall. A child's wooden blocks, painted with bright capital letters, were stacked like an architect's pueblo model, square room upon square room. Stuff probably moved there after the baby was put to bed, creating more space in the living room to host their guest.

"I can't believe that I have arrived at such an ungodly late hour at a house with a baby," Kevin said. "Why, my mother would kill me for having done that. And I have a small gift for you folks that is in the suitcase that Eduardo carried upstairs."

"Oh, our April sleeps like a little bear at night and she will be delighted to see you in the morning," Sarah said. "She is tired because we were at a graduation party for Eduado's nephew this evening. Rafael graduated high school recently. He starts working for Eduardo in the service station as an assistant mechanic next week."

"Assistant mechanic means pumping gasoline and cleaning antifreeze off of the service bay floor," Eduardo said.

"Kind of like being an assistant professor," Kevin said. Then he added, more abruptly than he had intended, "What are we doing to see those Ghost Dance pictures?" Sarah had said flat out to him on the telephone that she did not have those treasures in her possession—or control access to them.

Sarah said, "We can meet some of Eduardo's people at the festival in Sante Fe tomorrow. Right on the plaza downtown. Perhaps later in the day we can visit the pueblo out of town where some of my people live. We have to take it as it comes. Let my uncle and my cousin's get comfortable with you and what you are about. But I am convinced that everything will work out."

"Sarah's cousins can be damn prickly when they want to be," Eduardo said. He had been sitting on a mauve leather chair, resting his legs in blue jeans on a matching ottoman, but he straightened as he spoke as if to more adamantly make his point. On his right forearm, deeply purple dye from a hawk-shaped tattoo rotated, as if hovering, as he gestured repeatedly toward Kevin. A soothing New Mexico accent delivering a forthright message. "Now I admit that I am a bit prejudiced at them because they disliked that Sarah married a Hispanic guy rather than some kind of Navajo fellow. Although our having the baby has softened them somewhat. But your challenge is cut out with those two. But they respect a stand-up guy all the same. So be contrary with them."

By eleven o'clock in the morning the next day Kevin was walking the perimeter of the plaza in Sante Fe. There was a blue panel covering the baby stroller that he directed carefully through the leisurely crowd. Lavender rose bushes in robust half-barrel planters blocked automobile traffic from accessing the plaza area. It was as safe for pedestrians to walk on the street as on the sidewalks in the immediate plaza quarter. Guiding the instantly responsive wheels of the stroller, he maneuvered April Hernandez ever so deftly from point to point. The panel shielded the baby from the penetrating sunshine at eight thousand feet above sea level and it could deflect any occasional rain shower. April would wave her soft arms at the least provocation and repeatedly she twisted her head over the side of the stroller to spy on Kevin. Beneath a yellow and white hat, her black curls would sway into view as she did so. Baby teeth peeked through a half-smile. Curious deep brown eyes examined him. Back at her house, as they headed for her mother's Dodge van, April had reacted joyously at the smell of honeysuckle blossoms trailing in the side yard. Her powerful grip tugged at the trailing vine and loosened several yellow petals. Kevin got to carry her since she was not yet walking. Her mother had taken two days off from her job, for Thursday and Friday, to assist his mission. Sarah Breedlove was an assistant curator in a Native American museum located a block off of the plaza. On the telephone she had described her recent work: cataloguing a collection of waterproof woven baskets discovered at Bandelier National Monument, near Sante Fe. The baskets were estimated at six hundred years old. For all that he teased Mercedes about her high school atlas, Kevin was the indefatigable map fanatic. Over the desk at the radio station he had stretched the brown and yellow folding map, the map of New Mexico as expansive as an oversize desk blotter. Autumn colors for a beginning-of-summer trip. Each corner of the map presented a cutout of the principal cities in the state. All downtown Sante Fe streets were designated. Already he could anticipate the major sites camped out for a hundred years or even a few dramatic centuries on the outskirts of the Sante Fe plaza. Two major buildings plus two obelisks in stone. The Palace of the Governors and the Cathedral of St. Francis were the most venerable structures. The Cathedral was a full block distant from the plaza, up a barely perceptible gradient, framed from behind by a serious western mountain range. As an Eastern flatlander he was knocked out by the sheer volume of the western mountains. The scale of the violence that had muscled those intimidating peaks and cutting rock into place. Like a protestant church in an Irish village, the Roman Catholic cathedral was the highest manmade item in Kevin's sightline. Anchoring the church at the front façade were two stout towers, like a shoulder at each corner, each tower with a roofed portico at the top; the edifice was largely of tan stone, in a Romanesque design, a fashion noticeably unexpected given the adobe ascendancy of the region. French-born Bishop Lamy had inspired and overseen the construction of the St. Francis a hundred years before. Only upon reflection did Kevin notice that a layer of muddy brown stone ran in a band around the middle of the building's walls. The tints were off kilter, but the walls resembled sandwiched sandstone deposits in desert environments. Mid-day light and a clear sky pulled out the rose hues and blood reds and a touch of hunter green of the pinwheel-shaped stained-glass window. This hovered over monumental leather-clad front doors. The Pope's Swiss Guards might march through them at any moment, hefty halberds of oak grasped tight to their sides, gleaming steel points above their caps. High cast iron light fixtures, on black stanchions, each holding a set of three globes resembling a pawnbroker's symbol, patrolled the northern side of the Cathedral. These were found in a miniature commons apropos Paris. Blanketed in the shadow of a mature pine tree, Bishop Lamy rested in peace behind a low gate and an undulating black iron fence.

After they had visited the Palace of the Governors museum on the north side of the plaza Sarah, Kevin and April made for the Ore House Restaurant to have lunch. In the back of the stroller O'Donnell had stored the museum brochures and a soft cover book on the Anasazi Indians bought in the brightly-lit gift shop. He imagined curling up on Eduardo's leather chair, over a nice glass of chilling Scotch, after the family had retreated to bed, as he delved into the vanished ancient tribes of New Mexico and Arizona and Colorado. Wrapping the slick covers of the Anasazi book was a striking photograph: the White House ruin at the Canyon de Chelly, in sepia and gold tints and almost purple shadows. These items contributed to the weight of the stroller as he quietly wrestled it up the staircase at the Ore House Restaurant—no sherpa guide stock in him. No stockroom assistant stock in him, for that matter. Sarah had proceeded with the baby in her arms, resting her safely on her left hip. Only at the top of his climb did he recall that the stroller was collapsible and thereby easy to handle; they stored it in the hollow in the back of the hostess' podium. The restaurant balcony on the southwestern corner of the plaza had just one table unoccupied. Squeezing past the busboy hefting a jingling tray of dishes, Kevin and Sarah and the baby slipped into it. Immediately April commenced fidgeting on her mother's lap, waving a teaspoon like a conductor's baton. Latin music from the plaza bandstand might have loosely followed her direction. Blazing trumpets that in Spain might announce a bullfight plus the vibrant contribution of an electric guitar. He thought that he also discerned an electric keyboard and a tambourine. However, when April managed to insert the tip of the spoon into her mouth for closer, more direct examination the band managed to carry on without a hitch.

"Oldest public building in continuous use in the United States," Sarah said about the Palace of the Governors. "The original structure dates from 1610. One-time governor and former general Lew Wallace finished writing *Ben-Hur* while living in that building. The Palace of the Governors was partially destroyed in the Indian uprising of 1680. For twelve years in Sante Fe, and about twenty years up in Taos, New Mexico, the Indians threw off the Spanish government and re-established Indian rule. It was a bloody and destructive confrontation. This was the only region in the entire United States where Indians recaptured control for any sustained period. The native people used the Palace of the Governors for their own administrative needs during that time. When the area was taken back by the Spanish they called that the Reconquest."

Snatches of this information Kevin had gathered during their cursory walk through the Governors' Palace Museum. Nevertheless, Kevin listened closely as he worked through the light food in front of him. He had ordered a green salad with mandarin orange pieces and roasted chicken strips dredged with sesame seeds. With every succulent bite he was downing long gulps of spring water. It was not uncomfortably warm, despite the steady sunshine of the day, given the constantly low humidity of the region. The restaurant balcony was open to Lincoln Avenue by the plaza's western extremity. An overhang gave all of the tables benevolent shade. He had read enough about the threat of altitude adjustment sickness to take precautions. The city was a remarkable mile and one-half above sea level, the benchmark that Kevin had just vacated in San Diego. Moderate exertions for the first day; easy on alcohol; drink scads of water. The Ore House Restaurant carried San Pellegrino spring water, his number one choice. Kevin could not determine if his mild vertigo as he had transported young April Hernandez to the van that morning was the unaccustomed altitude. By the time Sarah had backed out of the driveway on to Canyon Road his dizzy spell had subsided completely. His late-night radio schedule and the potent honeysuckle fragrance and his excitement about a whole new category of Uncle Philip's photographs were equally suspect. And any new setting was vaguely unreal to him for twenty-four hours. Even the aromas, the scents of the place had to be worked through and catalogued in his mind. He would slip in a funny face to amuse the baby and then scan the plaza as Sarah spoke. From their initial foray he had calculated that the rectangular plaza would have fit snugly into a football field, particularly on its two narrower sides. The length of the plaza would not quite pave the playing surface from goal line to goal line. (It would have required a calculator to compare it with that more cumbersome unit of measure, the State of Rhode Island). The bandstand was on the northern edge across from the unimposing entrance to the Palace of the Governors. Clusters of mature oaks and cottonwood trees delivered shady spaces roughly at each corner of the plaza. Earlier they had stopped at the basalt marker connoting the terminus of the Sante Fe Trail. The monument was only of the scale of a petrified tree stump, and was placed by a women's historical group in 1910. The other monument in the plaza was a pockmarked white marble column, pointed like the Washington Monument at its summit, and reaching about twenty feet high. It aimed toward the stratosphere from the center of the plaza. Late nineteenth century inscriptions on a square base extolled the heroism of Federal Civil War soldiers in their two battles with the Confederates in 1862. One engraving memorialized the bravery of the Anglo settlers who had defeated the Indians of New Mexico. The descriptor 'wild' or 'savage' for the native people apparently having been officially eradicated from the message at some undisclosed time.

"Sarah, let me ask you a question," Kevin said. "Why are you willing to go to this trouble for me—and I appreciate it totally—when you hardly know me at all. Even taking two vacation days from work?"

Sarah smoothed April's black curls for a moment, as though surprised by the question, and needing to fashion her response. On Sarah's brown fingers were lodged a diamond wedding ring and a small turquoise stone ring. The turquoise ring was closely matched with a turquoise pendant suspended from a leather string around her neck. Sitting quietly now on her mother's lap, devouring the fluffy inside of crusty bread, April was totally absorbed in her own activity. Perfect miniature fingers relentlessly excavated the white center of the bread. Several pea-sized cotton balls of bread fell like uncooked croutons on her mother's salad. Round green sunglasses sat angled back on Sarah Breedlove's dark hair. As she moved her head Kevin caught fleeting glints and shadows of their surroundings in the curving plastic eyeglasses. Sarah said, "I read something in the last year that may have been a motivator of sorts in all this. A part of it at least. It was a review of a book on Carl Jung, the psychologist from the 1930's and 1940's. A famous name but I knew nothing about Jung. What was he, German, Austrian? A spiritual guy, I guess, and that appeals to me. But the book review was discussing his writing concerning how a person's perspective in life changes as early as your mid-thirties. I am thirty-six, now. I was fairly old to be a first-time mother. April is thirteen months old, exactly yesterday. We have been married for five years. And I am very healthy and energetic. So here I was, starting out on the new adventure of child rearing and diaper-changing as I had already hit the classic mid-point of life. Your children are supposed to be your legacy. Now that's fine, I guess, but it feels partial or incomplete in a way because it was a personal goal to have kids but there is still the other parts of my life to consider. I was raised to be part of a bigger family, a community. I was brought up in San Paco Pueblo about seven miles north of town. Live and breathe around here as a Navajo Indian and you have a sense of struggle and history. Some adobe homes on the pueblos are a thousand years old. When Christopher Columbus was cruising the Atlantic Ocean the buildings had already existed for five hundred years. Although they get resurfaced every year, I like to run my fingers over the walls for inspiration. The fresh surface is gritty and bits of straw stick out here and there. It thrilled me that April rubbed the same walls recently—imitating me of course—as Eduardo held her up. And those ancestors had their own children. That did not stop them from accomplishments, like the group of Indians that drove off the Spanish in 1680. What risks they took rather than just going along with the sad state of things around Sante Fe. Ha, and no disposable diapers to help them out."

"But I don't quite catch the connection with you helping me out like this," Kevin said. He was playfully squinting his eyes at April as if to hypnotize her. Then he sent two fingers walking across the table at her like a miniature hopscotch player. "Does it have anything to do with the specific kinds of photographs that my uncle took, or is that irrelevant? And what is the connection with Carl Jung's writing on people growing older?"

Sarah answered, "No, the pictures are not irrelevant in the least, but they are not the sole source of my motivation to help you. Please don't underestimate the importance of the Ghost Dance experience to the people in my background. The photography's existence has created a connection between you and us that needs to be better defined. You should see the photographs in their original state and hold them with your fingertips and examine them. And I don't know what you will do about them; you'll have to figure that part out yourself. Assuming my cousins would let go of them. Maybe you should give them to the pastor in the Cathedral over there, display them at your university, there are endless possibilities. But I felt a need to bring you here to get that process started. As to the age issue, I realized this was the best time to link up with you to let you know of the photos' existence. It's like the Pueblo revolt in 1680—one day they just got the whole show rolling."

Kevin glanced at the St. Francis Cathedral, up two substantial blocks on San Francisco Street, and its intersection with Cathedral Place. His vision ran directly over a temporary carousel at the far run of the plaza, about half the distance to the church. A crowded festival attraction, it seemed. Baby strollers were parked in a row just away from the revolving wooden horses and the whirling arms that were waving to the various youngsters' entourage. Its musical accompaniment was drowned out by the music from the bandstand. Like the pattern of life, the make-believe mounts rose and fell in reciprocal harmony. The merry-go-round's yellow and white striped awning was a fair match to April's sun suit. Again he was struck how the Cathedral managed to be the crux of attention while standing at the end of the street a block from the plaza. From his second story perspective on the balcony, the street leading to the St. Francis was like a lane in a bowling alley— impossible to resist looking down it. And what friendly people in Sante Fe, a woman was vigorously waving at them from the street corner just below. Then Sarah announced, "Oh, there is Eduardo's mother."

With lunch finished, they descended the two flights of stairs from the Ore House Restaurant, intending to regain the street and meet Sarah's mother-in-law. Encased in great concentration as he marched the steps, Kevin was the porter for the baby this time. Ten or twelve degrees of added heat were waiting on Lincoln Avenue. With no baseball hat to scatter the sunlight, Kevin squinted for real for a moment as they encountered April's grandmother. The little girl and her grandmother seemed equally enthralled by the miracle of meeting once again. Sarah mentioned earlier that Mrs. Hernandez babysat April three days a week while she was working at the Native American museum. It was the woman's fourth grandchild, but Sarah declared that she maintained the indelible enthusiasm of a first-timer.

"Mama," Sarah said to Eduardo's mother, "This is Dr. O'Donnell. Although he insists that we call him Kevin. And Kevin, this is Gabriella Hernandez. Oh, Mama, you should see him play with April. He is funnier than those professional clowns they get to entertain at children's birthdays. I see Aunt Clarita didn't come with you. Well, if you two don't mind for a little while, I'll take April over to ride on the merry-go-round. She will be crazy for days if I don't do that. While I do that, Mama, can you take Kevin over to see the Indian market? And we didn't get to see those shops over on Palace Avenue that you like so much. I will find you later."

Gabriella Hernandez was taller than Sarah and with white hair that swept back from her forehead and her gold chain necklace against tan skin, she moved with an elegant slow stride. Gabriella and Kevin moved diagonally across the plaza. She wore deep blue slacks and a light blue blouse and held against her side a large straw pocketbook. "I am a famous customer over here on Palace Avenue and at the Indian market," Mrs. Hernandez said. The voice similar to Eduardo's: rolled at you like a gentle wave and flowed steadily past your position. Then she gestured with her right arm, like the maestro directing applause to the soloist. "Why I almost expect for the merchants to run out on the street and cheer as I arrive."

They were walking almost directly toward the bandstand across from the Palace of the Governors entrance. Music, however, became fainter as they progressed; the band had shifted from throbbing merengue to a poignant ballad. Kevin did not know the purpose of the fiesta that brought mostly cheerful cliques of people of every age to the Sante Fe Plaza. A knot of scruffy teenagers and disheveled backpackers by the central memorial got a look of scorn from Gabriella. There were festooned stands advocating water conservation, and petitioning for world peace, and one exhibit solicited donations for a school trip to Vancouver. Hot steam dissipated in an oak tree canopy from a cooking demonstration; the chefs were promoting chili-based grilling marinades. Beef medallions, bursting cherry tomatoes and yellow sweet pepper slices sizzled on a new black cooking grill. A pungent smell lingered longer than the smoke. Perhaps the aroma reminded Kevin of a question that he sometimes posed to himself: what is the best and happiest setting in life? A festival in an unfamiliar scene had frequently come to mind. Horse races in crowded medieval plazas, Tuscan jockeys in vibrant colors that represent locale or family lineage, hooves kicking up sand and mud in a thunderous sweat. He imagined steel drum music pinging his ears on a sultry Caribbean evening while aqua waves caressed a white beach. Or night carnivals in satin and feather costumes with a new and breathless lover in Rio de Janeiro. He had scant experience with such gatherings. And Kevin and Sarah Breedlove had not discussed this interaction with her mother-in-law. Therefore, if his premise was correct, this festival of unknown origin had sufficient intrigue for now.

They walked passed the bandstand and Gabriella stopped their motion. This was just across the street from the central door to the Palace of the Governors. A half-dozen young dancers in frilly dresses rehearsed in the street. This section was also safe for foot traffic. The girls were warming up for their performance on the bandstand stage. Like football players prior to game time, the youngsters ran through brief and intense drills. Deeply concentrated eyes and the flawless complexions of ten-year olds. Black patent leather shoes clicked lightly on the asphalt, tapping one two three (stop); one two three (stop). Gabriella did not want to disturb them apparently. "Palace" to Kevin was an odd name for the building across from them, given that the structure was only one story in height and lacked striking adornment along its walls. There was a covered walkway known as the Governor's Portal that stretched the length of the building along Palace Avenue. During Sarah and Kevin's lunch at the Ore House, about thirty Indian craft and jewelry merchants had set up shop under the full reach of the block-long portal. Two or three people manned each exhibit. Merchandise was displayed on the pavement, resting on faded rugs or plastic sheets and the proprietors of each station sat on overturned delivery boxes or low beach chairs. A few squatted effortlessly as they rearranged their wares. Their bracelets and their letter openers and small pottery pieces. The array of rugs and plastic sheets in solid colors formed a kind of quilt as it stretched down the block under the overhang. Indian merchants at the very gates of the Palace, Kevin thought, seemingly patient in their sweatshirts and old windbreakers, drinking coffee out of thermos cups. Outside the Palace of the Governors, with its now unseen museum exhibits of a stagecoach and a Conestoga wagon and rooms devoted to the history of the 1680 pueblo revolt, it was easy to forget the battle lust that had raged literally where Kevin and Gabriella now stood. Five minutes before the first Indian assault in 1680, warriors may have silently traversed the ground that lay between here and the site of the present-day Ore House Restaurant. Where the young ladies twirled on the Palace Avenue roadway, in the vicinity of Kevin and Gabriella, with calf-length skirt pleats opening and rejoining like oriental fans, Navajos may have clustered to launch their unanticipated attack. At that ancient moment, immediately inside the Palace of the Governors, a daydreaming guard clutching a heavy musket may have hummed the very ballad Kevin recently heard from the bandstand. And possibly giving thanks to God for the endless fine weather of old Sante Fe.

Gabriella and Kevin succeeded in crossing Palace Avenue and, as they reached the shadow of the Governor's Portal overhang, Gabriella said, "Are you married, Kevin, or have a girlfriend? This is a great chance to catch a bargain on women's jewelry. Particular silver or turquoise items. A lot of times they are worked together. Now that tourists are so overrunning Sante Fe, many of the old-time store merchants have gotten pushed out of the plaza by high rents. Least that's what my girlfriend who has a store says. Tourists bring big money with them but we get more riff-raff now, too. But the Indian market still has bargains. They have got to sell items they make themselves or have made by the immediate family. It's been the rule for fifty years."

Mrs. Hernandez might have been reading his mind. Kevin had planned to call Mercedes that morning in Philadelphia before she drove to the library to work on her dissertation. Mercedes had picked up a part-time job for the summer in a dress shop near Rittenhouse Square. Her temporary employment was due to begin any day. Anyway, he missed connecting with her when he finally tried to telephone after breakfast. Wolfhound aspirant Lewis'n'Clark was unreliable for taking phone messages. Young April Hernandez had been showing off during breakfast, holding on to kitchen chairs as she tried to walk in stocking feet, grasping the chair edge with the intensity of a rock climber, her mouth and cheeks puffing with exertion. The hubbub had distracted Kevin. Mercedes was not big on having Kevin buy her gifts, but she had exhibited a taste for quality jewelry on occasion. An aunt had willed her several prized heirlooms: a Majorca pearl necklace and a dusky silver necklace that repeated a pattern of delicate mollusk shells. The exquisite seashell necklace had been a bridesmaid gift to her aunt from Mercedes' mother. She would check them out by swiveling the rearview mirror in his Camaro in her direction. He guessed that she would been unfamiliar with anything in turquoise; better advantage sticking with silver or gold pieces or even a western leather belt or bracelet. Mrs. Hernandez shared a greeting with several of the Indian merchants as they strolled down the block, first exploring the eastern half and then reversing to see the western section. "Her bracelets are particularly distinctive," she would say or "I bought cufflinks for my son Eduardo's wedding from this fellow," but then she would clam up, as if she were just another casual shopper at the market. Kevin quickly decided on a silver and turquoise money clip for himself. That set him back as little as three dollars. Next he bought a narrow, light bookmarker in silver, with engravings than might have been hieroglyphic, and a turquoise stone at the end that was the size of a middle fingernail. The silver strip was barely the thickness of four sheets of paper. Unusual as it was, the merchant sold this for two dollar and fifty cents. He took a second bookmarker, with a simpler design, for Bob Goodall. While completing these minor purchases, Kevin was more focused on the silver bracelets that a number of exhibitors sold. He did not want to compete with Mercedes' good necklaces and she would get more wear out of a bracelet. She had hinted about wanting a Hamilton tank watch but that was unavailable here. Better as a Christmas gift anyway if they were still a couple six months hence. Back and forth Kevin went from two merchants on the western side of the block, examining a very slender piece and a thicker bracelet in plain silver that was at least one inch in width. The slender bracelet had an intricate zigzag etched its full length. The wider one had slightly raised edges and gleamed even in the shadow of the portal. Gabriella was the stoic jewelry manikin as he compared the features of each bracelet. The heavier piece was five dollars more but he ignored that factor. The two women selling it looked with admiration as it lay on Mrs. Hernandez' wrist, as if they had never glimpsed it before. The Indian women were opposites in build—tall and short—but their eyes and cheekbones suggested that they were sisters, probably in their thirties. The gentleman with the competing item was sixty or so, with leathery brown skin, wearing a navy-blue sweatshirt fresh from a store shelf. His rumpled cap displayed the University of New Mexico logo. The fellow said that his son specialized in etched silver bracelets. The competitors were equally low key in their approach. No need to hurry the decision and besides, decent jewelry needs the right home. Kevin, moreover, was silently exulting in the truly unique setting of the Indian Market. Its sense of place was palpable. He wanted to take the market home with him, physically and mentally. While making his decision, he endeavored to emulate the plum tree in a neighbor's yard back home: from a drenching rain the shimmering and now heavy branches bow almost to the lawn, with the water absorbed straight through the capillaries of the small burgundy leaves, satisfying intensely the tree's need of sustenance.

"I'll buy this smooth silver one," Kevin said suddenly. To aid his decision, Gabriella Hernandez had been slowly twirling the larger plain bracelet on her strong wrist in a graceful movement. That closely mimicked the warming up exercise of a fencer with the epee or foil. A motion that Kevin had executed thousands of times. The bracelet did not have a clasp. It formed the shape of a 'C' around the wrist and could be gently molded for any desired tightness. "I have two ten-dollar bills right here," he told the taller of the sisters handling the merchandise. The shorter sister quickly polished his present for Mercedes, then bundled all of his purchases from the Indian Market into a white plastic bag with a convenient cord handle and set them along their way on Palace Avenue. Customers of every merchant seemed to get that bag with multiple purchases. They walked in an easterly direction through the growing crowd of market patrons, walked across Washington Avenue beyond the plaza where auto traffic was encountered for the first time in two hours. The pleasant afternoon weather continued with bright but unoppressive sunlight. Spiky yucca plants grew out of terra cotta containers on the sidewalk, green reeds climbing as high as Kevin's head, but this did not block off cars and trucks. This stretch was still Palace Avenue; there were enclosed shops along here that Gabriella examined intently, peering though dwelling-size decorated windows. Quietly, she would stand entranced at each window, holding up her eyeglasses to view the closest items. A candle shop with cranberry tapers suspended in pairs, a shop of antique dolls, a store selling aging musical scores and some pre-owned wind instruments. From store signs not yet arrive at along the promenade, Kevin made out one for a haberdashery and one for a year-round Christmas shop. A confectioner's was conveniently located adjacent to that.

"Oh, you are a history professor, aren't you Kevin," Gabriella asked when they were strolling again. Since few had ever heard of the specialty of American Civilization he nodded that that was close enough. "Then you might find interest in this plaque on the wall", she said. He dutifully noted the dull brass plaque of about eight by ten inches that reported:

This Building was Partially Wrecked in
the Pueblo Indians' Uprising of 1680.

Mrs. Hernandez said nothing more about it. She moved away into a modest courtyard immediately next to the building with the plaque, into a space that served as an outdoor display room for a secondhand furniture dealer. While the notice that he had read was of minor import, Kevin was reminded of the small memorials that he had seen on buildings scattered across Paris. Plaques that had abruptly moved him. They marked the event where French Resistance fighters had died at the hands of the Gestapo and Nazi soldiers, often a day or two before Free French and American armor had liberated the city.

Presently he followed Gabriella into the courtyard, where there was a mix of shadows from high eves and strong sunlight in the center. With approximately the floor space of a two-car garage, the courtyard resembled a box canyon, with the single open side fronting Palace Avenue, and with cloudless sky drifting overhead. A pair of wooden doors for sale, with peeling green paint and rusted hardware, rested at a sharp angle against one bright adobe wall. On the doors, an underlying color like the crimson section of peach skin baked in the sun. In the very heart of the courtyard a small decaying wagon had shoots of weeds pricking through its rotting gray slats. There was a narrow bench in arguably better condition spanning both the bright space and the shade, the bench also gray and suffering from exposure, and from the walls hung wire birdcages and wreathes woven from twigs and brass-framed mirrors that were largely devoid of quicksilver backing. A set of rickety ladder-back chairs, varnished the color of uncooked popcorn, were stacked with the nonchalance of unemployed lobster traps. The word 'knick-knack' could have been invented for this ramshackle emporium. Gabriella was at it again, pointing to a larger plaque this time. She had been browsing by a doorway that lead into the core of the building. Ducking under a suspended rusting lantern Kevin read:

Every Major Figure Associated with the Building of
the Atomic Bomb at Los Alamos, New Mexico
—A Major Scientific Achievement in World History—
Walked Through This Sante Fe Portal For
Planning Meetings in 1942.

Kevin took a breath that sucked down to his toes to avert a dizzy feeling that had suddenly moved through his head and chest. "Altitude sickness," he said to Mrs. Hernandez. She happened to have a small plastic bottle of spring water in her cavernous straw pocketbook, emergency supply for young April undoubtedly, and he drank this voraciously while sitting on the questionable bench, leaning into the shaded portion of the courtyard, and tapping his right foot on the sandy ground, tapping one two three (stop); one two three (stop).

CHAPTER THIRTEEN

Out the back door of her house, Sarah Breedlove carried a silver tray and a glass pitcher brimming with iced tea. Her legs slowly propelled her through the secluded patio, a cool grotto where privacy was created by five-foot stockade fencing. The hovering drink mixture included bright wedges of lemon bobbing with clusters of translucent ice. She came into view projecting a wide smile, pink lipstick and good teeth, the harbinger of liquid restoration for his equilibrium, but she transported the tray as carefully as a container of unstable nitroglycerine. A wavelet of tea crested the top of the pitcher nonetheless. A tablespoon or so made a run for it down the outside glass wall. Overturned plastic tumblers were situated around the pitcher like identical satellites. Except, that is, for the single upright one—about one-half the dimension of the others—which was likely filled with fruit juice for April's benefit. A baby moon perhaps. April was sitting on Kevin's lap and her soft fist curled along his little finger. In place of green lawn, the backyard wore a thin layer of colored pebbles, mostly white but with blue ones and black ones interspersed like a lottery game. The pebbles rocked gently, resembling marbles, when he shifted his feet. This surface must have added to Sarah's challenge in carrying the iced tea treat. A lone leafy tree in the yard provided more expansive shade than that of the table's umbrella. O'Donnell rested comfortably on a well-cushioned patio chair; he strained, however, to hear Eduardo's conversation on the kitchen telephone. It was a business call apparently; Eduardo may have said a few times, "Well it *could* be a good idea. I'll have to think about it. No promises, though." It was the same 'business voice' that Kevin's father used at the office at times. Attentive. Precise. Noncommittal. Eduardo had arrived home early from his service station to watch April, and to allow Sarah to take Kevin to San Paco Pueblo that late afternoon or evening. A Ford pickup truck, with a long flatbed and oversized mirrors and freshly washed sides, cooled ticking in the driveway when Sarah's van returned from town. Beads of water were spread across the side panels like those dots of hard candy fixed to strips of white paper. "Da, Da," April had announced upon sighting the truck. "Ta-da," Kevin had said in response. But Kevin hoped that his visit had not diverted Eduardo from his business at an inconvenient juncture. He had built up the enterprise from all but nothing, according to Sarah Breedlove. Bought the dilapidated garage operation over time on a handshake deal with the former owner as he worked there. Seventy-five dollars in payment a week for fifteen years. Difficult money to squeeze out of his budget at the time. Now the place purred like a motor that Eduardo had fine-tuned. And this Ghost Dance photography chase was Sarah's doing after all…

"Kevin," said Sarah, "I fixed this iced tea the way we like it. Spilled a little along the way, too. We like those new decaffeinated tea bags and put sugar in it while it is still hot. Of course, lemon, too. I hope you can drink it this way. Ha, I didn't even ask you about that. It will do you good, anyway."

"I will help you set that down by grabbing April's glass first," Kevin said. "And don't worry about me. I was back to myself by the time I finished the water that Gabriella gave to me. She has one of those pocketbooks where women have *everything*. She would have saved Moses twenty years of his trek in the desert. Maps...compass...Swiss Army Knife to slice the manna. Made sure that I didn't leave my purchases behind on the rickety bench, too. She was also a great help in shopping around there."

"Well, we Sante Feans are used to how high up in the sky we are," Sarah said. "And you have a lot on your mind. Gabriella can be funny. She talks about all the shopping she does over that way on Palace Avenue. It's more like browsing most of the time. It is just fascinating to her. She doesn't have a lot of money. Her husband died over eleven years ago, I think. I just love her, though."

Eduardo Hernandez had terminated his telephone call and was now swinging open the back screen door with a lot of energy. He was in clean clothes and he must have had time to shower before the three day-trippers got back. Eduardo had his own package, tucked like a football in his right arm. A United Parcel Service package, maybe five inches square. Kevin figured it might be an automotive part, such as a starter or one of those never seen brake pieces. Not likely Eduardo would order a can of motor oil via UPS. Given time he might get of hang of this car part thing...

"I am about to kill that nephew of mine," Eduardo said. He sat diagonally across the table from Kevin and took the glass of iced tea from his wife with a nod. The UPS box was placed on the table without comment. "Rafael. He has a lot of gall, that young man. Does he know everything. Not even on my payroll until next week and he is hell bent on changing the shop already. Sarah, you know Johnny Rigo. The guy who rebuilds engines for some of my customers over in his own place. That's Rigo on the phone just now. He is very talented— Kevin, I will put it in terms you will understand: Rigo could connect a Thermalite temperature gauge to a '71 Mercury's heating core with his bare feet at midnight. In the pitch dark. You know what I mean. So he runs into Rafael at that restaurant, Jack's Still Here. Rafael tells him that he is going to suggest that Hernandez Auto Service gets into doing van conversions. Van conversions. Adding better seats and carpet and sound systems. Customized decals. Big money in that, supposedly. But it takes investment and expertise, too. Now Rigo is lit up like a rocket and wants to do a partnership with me to develop a van conversion business."

Sarah stepped over to Kevin and said, "Can I borrow my daughter?" She plucked up the baby and carried her over to Eduardo's lap and grasp. April's dark eyes reflected this exchange as fascinating and her black curls bounced like light springs with her mother's strides. "Eduardo," Sarah said quietly, but above a whisper, "You have been a little bored with the way things are going at the garage. Just adding another service bay or whatever won't change things much. Yes I know Rafael is precocious in a way, too assertive maybe, but he has your best interests at heart. Remember how he figured out that wiring problem for Mr. Tilman last summer. He helped you to keep a good old customer that time."

"Now, that," Eduardo responded, "was an outright miracle. Twenty engineers from the automobile factory wouldn't have found that problem. Beginner's luck. A part of that electrical system was put in backwards, it seems like. He figured it out because he didn't know what to expect like the rest of us did."

"Rafael is kind-hearted, Kevin, I should tell you," Sarah said. "He really has a gentle nature. He's the one who introduced us to those decaffeinated teabags. He brought them over a few months ago when he came over to baby sit April one afternoon. He said they would be soothing and healthier for us to drink."

"Now this whole thing is not something that our guest should have to worry about," Eduardo said. "And it has me thrown off kilter a bit. Kevin, I even forgot to give you this UPS package. It was sitting on the doorstep for you when I got home this afternoon."

Eduardo gently pushed the package across the table's glass surface, thrusting his arm out its full length in slow motion, causing the box to spin quietly as it found its way to O'Donnell's reach. It was like an excruciating shot in table shuffleboard that is positioned on the glossy playing surface just so. The type of shot that Kevin had rarely executed. He never recognized the author of handwriting other than his own. However Kevin knew that the typing on this package was from the department secretary back at the university. Her typewriter was a borderline relic; easy to imagine it reposed in cobwebs in the attic of an aging notary public's office. He teased her not to take the first offer that the Smithsonian Institution makes on it, hold out for a larger premium. The vowels that it typed were increasingly faint and 'm' and 'n' were nearly indistinguishable. Professor Bob Goodall's name was typed on the label as the sender.

"Do you want to bring that with you, Kevin," Sarah wondered. "We should really get going to the pueblo if you feel okay."

Kevin O'Donnell decided to leave the package behind, unopened. Since it had originated from Goodall, might just be a jack-in-the-box. Plus he was excited about the visit to the pueblo and he might have trouble concentrating on more serious content. For safekeeping, he placed it on the heavy slate mantelpiece in the living room, after stepping carefully around a child's large puzzle on the floor. The puzzle was about half assembled. It partially blocked the hieroglyphic reproduction at the center of the living room rug. You could still see the skinny dog vaulting at the sun but the leaping skeletal fellow holding the cactus plant was mostly obscured. He recalled that April and her dad had worked on the puzzle in the early morning for a while. Immediately Kevin was out the front door and seated in Sarah's gray van. She deftly backed out onto Canyon Road and directed the vehicle with a little more speed than the rides with April on board. Motoring north toward Sante Fe as she had in the morning, Sarah diverted them around the city on a bypass unfamiliar to Kevin. This road lead to a different interstate highway than the connection with Albuquerque and Luis' lumbering taxicab.

As the outskirts of Sante Fe dropped off by degrees, Kevin finally got an unobstructed view of the vast New Mexico countryside. The sight was drenched in late afternoon sun. Several narrow strips of clouds, arranged like rotated Venetian blinds, failed to impede the sunlight. The clouds reminded Kevin of sterile medicinal gauze stretched like fresh taffy. Parched and brooding mountains lay off at a great distance. Rolling there in melodic waves were hills paved with yellow and white sand and isolated juniper trees and sage bushes green almost to black. There were fewer cacti than he expected to find. The plant life reminded him of a Christmas tree farm where each fat tree is methodically spaced to allow easy customer surveillance. But here covering endless acre upon acre and with thousands of tannebaum to browse. For a five-or-ten mile vista fanning north, no buildings were in evidence. The smooth highway and its white painted lines might have been a natural occurrence and Kevin and Sarah its first human interlopers. Sculpting down the nearest hills were rock and gravel-laced gullies. In some instances gravity and flash floods had arranged the rocks in a roughly triangular pattern at the bottom of the cutout. Stones the size of beer barrels, apparently having cascaded earlier to the base of the gully, served like cornerstones to support the smaller loose rocks that followed. At a good clip the van roared past dry creek beds. These resembled abandoned sunken roads. The creek beds ran straight for maybe sixty yards before curving abruptly out of view.

Labyrinths with sandy walls and footpaths. Bursting rainstorms were likely to revive them to their intended fluid state, at least for a few hours. The only water in evidence was a section of sand and rock moistened by a spring. A quick glint of light reflected off of a shallow pool as they drove by it. Perhaps the escaping water was as exhilarated by the setting as he was and had forgotten to evaporate into the dry air.

"Whom do we bring with us when we are in a strikingly new place," Kevin asked, mostly to himself, but vocal enough for Sarah to hear. He was watching the extremity of a strip of cloud, now bending like an elbow in a puffy sleeve, reaching behind a nameless mountain, scratching its shoulder. "Maybe you feel these things differently than me, but I usually am so much more aware of myself in an unusual and new place. Like right now in New Mexico. Or crossing Park Avenue in October or standing directly under the Eiffel Tower, feeling that its girders could suck you up like a magnet. Or hiking through a natural arch in Utah. The feeling for me does not last much beyond the immediate experience but at the moment it is so damn transcendent. All your problems are petty while gazing at a Van Gogh self-portrait. There is a painting of a medieval cardinal or a pope in the Tate Museum in London. In fact, it might be by Raphael, like your nephew's name. It knocks me out. They have a mahogany bench and I can sit there a half-hour devouring it. It's an oil painting on a wooden panel, about four hundred years old, and you'd swear that the artist is just now scrubbing his brushes clean with turpentine, the paint looks that fresh and bright. You are watching yourself as the dazzling thing unfolds before and all around you. But exactly *who* is watching with you? And is it someone old or someone new? Maybe there is no time connected to it at all."

"Look at this setting around us without using words in your mind," Sarah said. Her voice was matter of fact, as if she had had this type of conversation previously. "Direct your consciousness to look at it without thinking and just see it. It is possible to do that for a while, if only for a minute. Answers will come to you without asking endless questions. My uncle, Big Mike, taught us how to do that. You will meet him this evening at the pueblo."

For the love of God, how do I get into these conversations with Sarah, Kevin wondered. The van was off of the interstate highway now, about a half-dozen miles north of Sante Fe, moving much slower along a tree-lined, two-lane asphalt road. What is with all these trees? Willows and broad oaks and adolescent cottonwoods. Much less than a forest or even a sturdy woods, but consistent flanking of the road for about two miles. They had passed a sign for San Paco Pueblo and Kevin realized that a decent and reliable stream had to run along here, the ancient lifeline for the pueblo. Lifeline for the trees, also. Probably steered Spanish explorer Cortez like a map to reach the village in the 1500's. Kevin could imagine the deathly quiet astonishment all around as Cortez and friends had tramped into view...even the pueblo dogs were plunged into puzzled silence but the hounds might be the first residents to tentatively advance toward the lightly armored knot of visitors...

The curving road that led into the heart of the San Paco Pueblo began to attract scattered clusters of low adobe buildings. These offered brown walls and gently sloping roofs, and then what was likely the most significant concentration of pueblo structures, including a red brick church that could appropriately anchor the leafy square of a prosperous Vermont town. A nearly life size marble statue of the Virgin Mary, set on a pedestal among flowering rose bushes in the church garden, perpetually rail thin in her ivory robe, with her right arm raised in patient benediction, waved motionlessly to Kevin as Sarah angled her van into a parking area adjacent to a village graveyard. There was an unpaved surface resting on the parking lot. Tan dust clouds, no more energetic than a foot in height, gently raised behind the rear wheels. Kevin and Sarah emerged into the early evening light. Already he was accustomed to the pleasant trailing warmth of the late June day. Sarah had donned blue jeans in place of her flowery skirt from their visit to Sante Fe and sneakers instead of low-heeled flats; a lavender purse on a long strap angled to her left hip from her right shoulder as she stepped briskly past the church and the darkened Pueblo council headquarters. They were walking on the crest of a low hill, at the edge of a smooth asphalt road, by a building under construction with a wooden sign that read 'Tribal Artists' Cooperative Center.' On their left appeared the post office for San Paco Pueblo. A sizeable valley dropped off from their right, leading gradually to a mountain peak framed between tall western pine trees and the edge of a rectory or similar church property. "Over this way," Sarah said abstractedly, pointing quickly toward a collection of buildings at the base of the hill. It gave the impression of a schoolyard with a basketball court contained within structures on two sides and largely open on the others. Cars were tightly parked on the grass by a low cyclone fence and perhaps a hundred people or more were gathered around the cement basketball court. A series of lofty trees provided shade for the onlookers, trees with trunks as muscular as smokestacks and likely centuries old. "Just wait to you see this," Sarah told Kevin as he walked fast to match her stride. "These children are just terrific."

Kevin did not know that a schoolkids' basketball game was on the agenda. Must be the championship game because the fans were armed with a number of still cameras and at least two people were aiming video cameras at the court, probably getting their visual bearings through the viewfinder. Before he could question her about the game, Sarah stopped and hugged a tall man in a flannel shirt and blue jeans and black boots. This was at one corner of the playing area; now Kevin could see that a weathered cement grandstand, like a miniature of Palmer Stadium at Princeton University, addressed one side of the court. It was humming with onlookers, mostly adults, some with babies on their knees, with people particularly favoring the highest row of seats. Kevin waited for Sarah to direct him to his own perch. Now she was speaking animatedly with another man, much younger than the gray-haired fellow whom she had hugged, and a woman close to her own age.

"Kevin, this is my uncle Mike and my cousins, Martin and Alison. After we watch the kids here we will get a chance to talk. You see best from the side over here. We can help ourselves to those seats right in front."

There were handshakes exchanged and then Sarah and Kevin sat in a couple of lawn chairs near the mid-court area. This was on the side opposite the cement grandstand. Surrounding them were people on lawn chairs and a few people rested on bright blankets like a picnic. Several men hung back at the cyclone fence, leaning there on one elbow, exhaling cigarette smoke. There did not seem to be any benches for the basketball players or coaches nor was there a scoreboard in evidence. Both basketball teams must be in the locker room because the court was vacant; not even a single brown ball rolling around in anticipation of the contest. A voice came over a loudspeaker and Kevin noticed a small elevated stage near a building. The stage held an Native American in a bright red shirt and a white cowboy hat, a microphone in front of him on an aluminum stand. He was chanting in an Indian language; beside the fellow was a man with a small leather drum that was held in one hand and banged with a wooden stick. A teenage girl carefully turned the dials of a silver and gray tape recorder that rested on a table. This let barely audible background music out of the two loudspeakers. Suddenly, immediately to the right of the stage, heavy metal doors swung open from what looked like a grade school building. Three lines of children raced out to center court, dressed from moccasins to headdress in ceremonial Indian clothes. The children stood absolutely still. The music and the drumming and the chanting stopped, and momentarily Kevin could hear only the sound of an inquisitive bird, perhaps a willow flycatcher, from above and behind him.

Kevin came within a nanosecond—which he knew was some infinitesmal measure of time—of commenting to Sarah about how fabulous was this team of cheerleaders. Why his university could not field such a brilliant troupe. Sarah virtually interrupted him with her remarks. "Ha," whispered Sarah, "these aren't the cheerleaders, that's for sure. This is no ballgame. It's the grade school dance team, redoing a performance that they did last fall. It is hard to keep them practicing over the summer so be sure to enjoy the performance."

There were thirteen dancers, as Kevin counted, but it seemed like a greater number given the size of some of the boys' headdress and the fullness and bright colors of everyone's costume. Like the handful of climbing rows of the grandstand opposite, the height of the children reflected the impact of each year of age. He figured they ran from six or seven to about thirteen years old. There was just one more girl than boy in the dance group. Probably several sisters and brothers dispersed among the team. Silence was dissolved by the light tapping of the drum from the stage, then heavier drumming, at about four or five beats before a split second hesitation. Chanting resumed, more undulating in pitch than before but with a steady, firm volume. It seemed to beckon the dancers to awaken, to initiate the dance, but the children refrained as of yet. He marveled at the uniform calmness of the kids' faces. They might have been looking out into empty sky on a carefree, windless day, in the thrall of daydreams or longing. Then one of the taller girls swung her left arm out, then her right, stretching open her fingers and arching her shoulders slightly, and rotated a sharp quarter turn to her left. The dozen other dancers followed suite. They moved forward, toward the stage and the source of the music, with the swath of colors in their outfits looking like the migration of butterflies, bigger than life. Every dancer's basic garb was white cotton or white linen but with blue and black geometric designs on the girls' skirts and the boys' armbands and belts. No two outfits seemed identical; however, there were patterns evident, particularly for some of the girls. Near their dress hems were four small triangles, all red or all blue or vibrant green, balanced upside down like a swaying stack of crockery. Several of the boys had vests fashioned from animal hides. The long hair of the beautiful brown pelt was smoothed down like flattened grass and the animal tail swung like a subtle pendulum. One fellow had a broad yellow arrow outlined in black that streaked down his short tunic as if pointing at his dancing feet. But Kevin was mistaken about that. He saw more clearly as the dancers maneuvered to his left—away from the singer and drummer and the young woman orchestrating the tape recorder—that several boys carried a stringless archery bow pointed at both ends. This was painted in bright orange, plus red and black. When they carried the bow closely to their side, the colors melded with the white background of their clothes.

The first dance was completed. Fervent clapping from the audience followed. The children moved to new positions on the court, forming two rows. They did not openly acknowledge the applause. Their motions and facial expressions were more labile than earlier as they prepared for the second exhibition. Kevin thought that they may need to align the rows with outstretched arms, or glances with phony smiles, the way some cheerleaders might, but this was not the case. Quickly they went into a modest crouch just as the chanting was resumed. The dancers advanced toward Sarah and Kevin before turning a half circle to face the grandstand. It was the position of a hunter's crouch that the youngsters' had assumed. Stalking deer or buffalo or absentminded pheasants. Drumming moved to an intense crescendo, having started out modestly like the foothills, then building into a peak of noise, finally causing the kids to leap forward in unison with a shout. Thirteen late-day and gradually lengthening shadows in immediate pursuit. The two rows of dancers swerved around once more, in serviceable but not exact precision, again facing Kevin and Sarah. Kevin noticed the detail of the large headdress on the four biggest boys. It was as if headless big horn sheep had climbed on each boys' head and shoulder; two of the skins with brown hair and two in an off-white tone. But the black horns that rose out of the animal pelts like a pair of thick parentheses or powder horns were probably from bison rather than sheep. The thick covering ran from mid-forehead, over the dancer's head, and reached down their back almost to the waist. Like a monk's cowl the faces of the boys were largely obscured, particularly with the white fur pieces. The furs were not necessarily heavy, but the boys bore them as though they had weighty significance—even in a crouch their shoulders staying parallel to the ground. As they moved closer across the width of the basketball court he got a better sense of the patient detail that was crafted into all thirteen outfits…the late night fabric cutting and sewing by the mothers and grandmothers who were undoubtedly his neighbors for this performance. Kevin figured the footwear might be everyday sneakers but all of the dancers had elaborate Indian boots or moccasins. Out of the thicker boots showed tufts of fur insulation. The girls had ribbons in their hair and several had long russet feathers attached to their belts on the left side. The two youngest boys—perhaps seven and eight years old—had smaller headgear than the older fellows. Covering them was a beaver or racoon skin cap, wound almost like a flattened turban, which was one deviation removed from a Davy Crocket hat in a Walt Disney production. One of these young fellows projected a smile intense enough to pressure his jaw. Observing this, Kevin thought, "One thousand years of San Paco Pueblo's life and death, with its messenger at the fulfillment of that millennium a seven year old boy, in a haute couture wardrobe, smiling and dancing to break your heart, having fun…"

This dance ended with the two rows re-aligning into a square, followed by the children slipping down to one knee. They abruptly flung their arms out in front of them. The spectators were roused to waves of warm applause and Kevin clapped furiously. He even tried to whistle but he never could do that effectively. A light bird sound at most emerged from his lips. The dancers were back to their beautifully clad feet; the somewhat ragged square now emerged as two concentric circles, three performers surrounded by ten others, colorful backs to the audience. The dancers stood motionlessly while the chanting and drumming ceased, perhaps with eyes angling up, recalling their next routine. Two of the inner circle were girls, maybe the oldest and youngest on the court. A middle-age woman approached the dancers from the stage area. She slipped two long-stem roses, one red and one yellow, through the outer ring of dancers to the two girls in the center. Crumpled aluminum foil was wrapped around the stem bottom as a sheath for the thorns. Each girl grasped the rose at the protected end similar to the way that Kevin would have clasped a foil prior to NCAA fencing competition.

The sound of the background music, the leather drum, and the chanting in an Native American dialect resumed for the next performance. Sarah had informed Kevin that this was the last set of the day. The concentric circles of dancers began to revolve energetically and in opposite directions to each other. Several dancers on the outside ring jumped away from the rest and then looped back to regain a spot on the bigger circle. A few other dancers then imitated the maneuver. This had a kaleidoscopic effect that induced Kevin O'Donnell to hold his breath momentarily. It was like some elaborate astronomical model of planets and stars and comets agitating beyond and around an invisible sun. But the dancing shadows splashed against the concrete surface were the sun's local representatives and not so easily ignored. The dancers on the outside circle were roughly arranged by alternating heights, so that the shadow cast by one was shorter or longer than its immediate neighbor's. Then the younger set of children stepped out from or into the circle, depending on their location. Kevin saw how the peak of each shadow merged with that of its nearest partners. Eventually the two girls holding the roses broke free from the center and moved to the side of the court closest to Kevin and Sarah. Behind them, the other performers collapsed the big circle. In close formation, they hurriedly formed a crescent, off slightly to Kevin's left side, while dancing vigorously in place. The massed shadow of the crescent group built a wobbling apex on the concrete surface. This resembled a mountaintop rumbling from an earthquake tremor. The girls clutching the red and yellow flowers started tapping the rose blossoms lightly against the ground, in and out repeatedly from the gray shadow to the powerful sunlight. The crescent dancers converged ever more densely, while slowly moving the shaded image toward Kevin. In and out of the sunlight went the rose petals like the rapid points of thin swords. Finally the two girls flung up their arms, colliding the roses above their heads. The eleven dancers in the crescent suddenly fell to one knee and carefully rolled down to their backs, while the rose-bearing girls twirled the stems overhead. Utter quiet from the spectators… Matching the motionless children on the ground. With amazement Kevin watched as both standing girls seemed to float over to them, with the older dancer handing a rose to Sarah. The younger child gracefully depositing the red rose into his right hand.

****

"Don't be disappointed that Big Mike was not around after the show," Sarah said. She was handing a cold drink to Kevin. But this time a frosty pilsner of beer as he sat in her living room back on Canyon Road. They had bought dinner at the San Paco Pueblo—spicy barbequed chicken and French fries and garden salad—in support of the parents' group collecting money for the elementary school library. For desert he ate a cube of strawberry gelatin with a shot of whipped cream on top. Tossed on the Hernandez' dining room table were two tee shirts that Kevin purchased for the same fundraising endeavor. One with endangered animals peering from atop a green and blue globe, graceful cheetahs transporting turtles and frogs. And a black tee shirt with two-year old touring dates for the Grateful Dead rock band. The 1981 concert tour dates printed in white letters. "The grade school dance program had virtually collapsed over the years," Sarah said, "But Big Mike got it revived not long ago. He has a huge influence at the pueblo. And you were the most rapt spectator I ever saw. Ha, you actually tried to whistle—you've got to work on that part. Big Mike knows genuine enthusiasm. My cousin Martin said before the show that they would be available to see you tomorrow afternoon or evening. I may not be able to take you. But we will lend you a car."

Sarah excused herself to go to bed, leaving Kevin alone. As they wakened early in the morning, Eduardo and April were likely sleeping when Sarah and Kevin had returned home. It was much too late to telephone Mercedes on the east coast, two time zones distant. Kevin moved to the mantelpiece and the UPS box from Bob Goodall. In stepping there he noticed that the child's puzzle on the floor had vanished. Eduardo, it appeared, had left big scissors on the mantel to assist Kevin in opening his mail. Scissors with a plastic handle as bright yellow as a rain slicker. Standing by the empty fireplace, Kevin hacked at the edges of the package while trying not to damage its nearly weightless contents. He was impressed by the care taken in preparing this mailing; cousin Maeve's packaged from Ireland had been re-packed inside the UPS box. It was likely that his department secretary was responsible.

Kevin discovered a packet of letters wrapped by rubber bands and on top was a separate letter from Maeve Ward. Maeve lived in Ardara, on the hilly Donegal coast in northwest Ireland. Six miles from Genties. She taught secondary school in Ardara. With a smile he recalled standing in her front garden, overlooking a windswept plummeting cliff, sheer wet rock dropped as a bulwark against the ocean. He stood looking for the faintest trace of America across the inky-blue Atlantic Ocean. Preoccupied seagulls labored through the breeze, honoring some northward rendezvous. Would he ever get back home from such a wild place? Back from where the sea-gusts might yet carry the echo of the fearsome druid's call? Maeve's letter to Kevin was dated in late May, about three weeks before it arrived in Sante Fe through Bob Goodall's efforts. O'Donnell returned to his chair beside the beer glass to examine his new treasures. He started with Maeve's typed note:

Dear Cousin Kevin: I have been meaning to send photo-copies of these letters—easy to do now with the lovely new equipment that we have at school—letters that apparently were written in the summer of 1903 by local people in Glenties and intended to be sent to Uncle Phillip O'Donnell in America. I reckon that would be three years before the San Francisco earthquake took place. Imagine that: eighty-year old correspondence. I would question if they were ever sent since the authors would have had to make hand-written copies at the time. (My, how science and technology marches on for our benefit today!). Since Uncle Philip had traveled so much in the States his friends in Ireland might not know where they could send return mail. The letter here by Paddy Breslin, probably a great uncle of yours, may be the most interesting for you. And Kevin when are you going to come see us in Donegal. It's been five years at least since we last set loving eyes on you.

One of the rubber bands broke and snapped, as though surprised, as Kevin pulled open the group of photocopied letters. Time to relax, he thought; he did not think that Sarah or Eduardo would mind if he grabbed a reserve beer from the kitchen. The lamp by his chair—the lamp rested on bent wooden legs that curled like deer antlers—offered a three-way bulb that Kevin clicked to increase illumination. Kevin found the Breslin letter that Maeve recommended for close inspection. He spent a half-minute familiarizing himself with the handwriting, respectful that the source of it was a long-dead relative. Finally he let himself delve into it.

Dear Philip, You may laugh to your eyes tear up at the good crack that we had in following your instructions about performing the Indians' Ghost Dance here in Glenties. The wake for old McManus had broken up that night. Charlie McManus who was ninety-one years of age it was calculated, and a stodgy wake it was, too. Of course his granddaughter Agnes lost a baby to the grippe last winter. RIP. Tempting it was during the rosary to call out 'Holy Mary Mother of God, pray for the poor man in the bog,' but we kept it proper instead. Disputes have already arisen about the notorious event. The Ghost Dance that we did later that night, that is. Notions about it are as varied and individual as the lads involved in the performance. Wise to advise you not to blame the potcheen or any legal brew for our strange visions and sightings and feelings that night. Not a half-bottle of Jameson Whiskey on hand. Unfortunately good strong tea was all we had, and pots if it. Cups too many perhaps. And the drumming and fife playing by the Givens brothers had no unearthly aspect to it, saints preserve us. Not any more than when they play at the church hall for the monthly marketday dance. Quite a few lads said that it sounded like American Indians were creating their infernal music in our Donegal glen, not the Given lads, when we don't even fathom how such foreign music sounds. Philip, you will remember how your letter to me last year described your feelings when you joined your Indian friends in a Ghost Dance. The lightheadedness, the surge of power that seemed to lift up your arms without you willing it. A wee bit of that happened to us, I must admit. It was a full moon, too, that night. More likely the moon was the cause rather than the Indian dance for young Jamie Boyle to go screaming and tearing off into the bog land behind Widow Bonner's place—I could see that coming for a while from the queer way that the boy twitched his cheek coming down from a communion rail. God be praised. Jamie is expected back from hospital in Donegal Town within the fortnight.

So maybe you could move on to that tropical Hawaii place right soon and by 'n by we'll be cavorting a fine hula dance down the Mulantyboyle Road near Glenties. Near our old cemetery with the ancient stone slabs carved with the gyrating suns and the wee birds with the giant eyeballs that seem to follow you as you serve as solemn pallbearer at some more recent interment. And, Philip, I do hope to see you once again in Donegal my friend.

Kevin often fell asleep in a chair at home and he could sleep on a long train ride or nighttime airplane flight. He was dozing when his delayed flight had descended into Albuquerque the night before. There was the beer, too. The second bottle half-consumed when he finished his review of the Irish letters. There was not so much as a ticking cuckoo clock or a prowling cat or dog to disturb the air and create noise. Kevin's old house in Philadelphia was eternally settling and softly groaning in the mid-night hour. Letting himself relax, he squeezed his eyes not quite closed. At his feet the rug's woven figures of the skinny man and his prickly cactus and the jumping dog seemed to be moving, but he gathered that was only his wavering eyelids, or his emerging imagination, as sleep began to circulate through him. At night Kevin often dreamed of being able to soar without wings; he loved that feeling when he defied all boundaries and logic and let his body float just beneath the ceiling. He was in that mode again. In his blissful dreaming state he joined the stickman's entourage, sailing out beyond the earth just behind the leaping dog, bathed in the sunlight but not yet feeling the full force of the burning solar globe.

CHAPTER FOURTEEN

Where am I, Kevin wondered. The window at the head of his bed had shifted ninety degrees from its normal setting. The lined chintz window treatment was replaced with light chiffon curtains. The curtains were a shade of pumpkin that he would not have selected. Pumpkin was his favorite pie but not his favorite color. Odd, too, because his triceps muscles remembered at some deep layer the strain of hanging those heavy curtains in his house. His mother had helped him measure the correct height before he drilled the screw holes for the brackets. She slipped two strong fingers through his belt loop at his back. This was to steady Kevin on the stepladder. The old plaster would crumble if he had to re-bore due to careless measurement. Kevin had placed a pencil mark on the wall resembling the crosshairs on a riflescope. Maps for buried Spanish doubloons might be sketched with greater nonchalance. Then he had tentatively squeezed the trigger of the electric drill. The slowly rotating drill bit resembled a DNA double helix. And the motor section of the drill offered the heft of bowling ball material. But this was not his house. That was it; it was Sante Fe, New Mexico and the bedroom window was sitting right where Sarah and Eduardo had placed it by design. An east facing window and the growing dawn light had wakened him early this morning. Gazing over the neighboring yards, the muted landscape remained a soundless witness to the evolving day. A capital idea: a guest room where the light of dawn is likely to rouse your visitor. Oh, up and about so early, are you? Help yourself to hot coffee from the kitchen. Time yet to catch Mercedes on the telephone before she went to work, or to the library, back home. Mercedes was still house sitting for him, taking care of Lewis'n'Clark. Kevin would get her to call him back right away, to avoid clobbering his hosts with the long distance charges.

There was a telephone in the living room, on the end table. Kevin recognized the precise color that dressed the walls as he waited for Mercedes to return his call. The paint was an exact copy of a pothos leaf that had recently succumbed to drying soil. Kevin was a haphazard in-home gardener. As the leaf faded to its crumbled brown decay, it passed through an early stage when a soft mustard yellow gave it a delicious satin appearance. Only one leaf in a hundred was affected. More attractive for a half-week than the still thriving green leaves that reached out of the flowerpot. The living room wall color was precisely at that rich blonde juncture. Funny how he never noticed the leaf until it was too late for water to resuscitate it. Of course he raked up a quarter-million autumn leaves in his front yard and spied maybe a dozen at most while they plummeted silently to earth.

"Kevin, is that you," Mercedes asked on the telephone. "How are you, love. I wasn't sure if I copied the number right. I am drying my hair and wrote it down with my right hand. Have you spoken with Bob Goodall in the last few days?"

"No," Kevin said. "But I got a package of old letters from Ireland that my cousin Maeve sent to the office. They were written in 1903. Bob forwarded them to me. I read them last night. They were wonderful."

"Reason that I asked is that Commander Lapworth from the navy had called here and I told Bob about it. Commander Lapworth said that they would let you send a team of scuba divers to visit that sunken destroyer off San Diego. To see if any of Uncle Philip's photographs of San Francisco were on board. But you would have to pay for the divers. And you have to move fast—within a few weeks at most. There is so much going on for you. I am just an old shoe compared with you. Did you see the Ghost Dance pictures yet?"

No old shoe by a long shot, Kevin thought. He imagined Mercedes sitting on his taupe colored sofa that she admired. Drying her hair in resolute sweeps, the brush pushing waves of brown hair in slow motion. Dressed in a bathrobe open on top like an evening gown, with Lewis'n'Clark getting an eyeful of curving skin. "I haven't seen the Ghost Dance pictures yet," Kevin answered. She had laughed when he had said that he would ban the dog from sleeping in their bedroom. "Tonight I think that I will see the photos. And you know how to scuba dive, don't you. Maybe you can help me with that. I could spring for one more airline ticket for you. I have already gotten a nice check from the Gierson Gasket Company."

"Oh, Kevin. You'll need professional divers. It could be dangerous," Mercedes said. "I just took a basic course and had four or five dives at most. What are you trying to do, drown me? Have you fallen for a Sante Fe cutie already?"

Kevin said, "What I meant was that you could help me supervise whom I might hire, how many divers. What it should cost. And I want to see you, too. And to touch you. You know that's true. But I must admit I have fallen for a New Mexico sweetheart. She is one year old or so. She is squealing right now in the kitchen while she attempts to walk on her own for the first time."

"I am being a witch." Mercedes said and then laughed. "I can work extra hours at the dress shop for a week or so. Then they would probably let me take off for a few days. I am going there today so I'll find out about that. I still need income this summer."

Kevin said, "I'll be back in San Diego in two days to do the radio show. They are stuck and have kept me. We are so derelict, taking off time from part time jobs. But I will start investigating what needs to be done to mount this expedition to the deep blue sea."

Kevin had the run of Sarah and Eduardo's kitchen and he made breakfast for himself. First he rooted through the walk-in pantry and its broad ladder of papered shelves. Glass bottles of chili peppers, with caps like red or green turbans, were interspersed with soup cans, extra virgin olive oil and unopened salsa containers. High-necked bottles of rice wine and balsamic vinegar, and a Worcestershire sauce bottle in paper wrapping, clustered like the business district in a city mockup.

An architecture of mismatched structures that defied the flimsiest zoning laws. In his opinion some disorder in a kitchen pantry was a sign of good mental health. Then scrambled eggs and thick sausages and tortilla corn chips. As he ate breakfast the kitchen was pleasantly wrapped in the smell of fresh coffee beans. Since Eduardo's Aunt Clarita was ill Sarah had decided to accompany Gabriella and Clarita for a trip to the doctor. Kevin was satisfied to be transported into town late in the morning. He occupied the daytime with visits to shops and museums and to the cool and silent interior of the St. Francis Cathedral. He admired the baptismal font that was wrapped in veined marble and set like a shallow wading pool in the center aisle of the church. One shop west of the plaza sold giant flower urns from a sidewalk display. The urns were tall enough that he would be challenged to dunk a basketball in them. A hotel or mansion owner might buy a pair to flank a majestic lobby or ballroom door. Kevin bought the *New Mexican* daily newspaper. Lingering over two cups of coffee he soaked up its articles on real estate, and its advertisements for horse saddles and rabbit traps. Sarah collected him at five o'clock as Kevin loafed in the caressing sunshine. She pulled to a quick stop on San Francisco Street. All the while April Hernandez looked on quizzical as a state trooper from her anchored car seat.

Sarah Breedlove wrote directions for Kevin to remind him how to return to the San Paco Pueblo. He was driving there on his own. Sarah used a green felt tip pen on white typing paper. She underlined the instructions for turnoffs with two or three thick stokes. He may have been capable of retracing the route without her assistance. However, he thought it rude not to tuck the directions into a front blue jeans pocket. The folded paper went in beside the new money clip that he had bought at the Indian Market by the Sante Fe plaza. The clip of turquoise and silver helped him to organize his usually disheveled pack of dollar bills. Even more considerate was the vehicle provided for his use: Eduardo's white Ford pickup truck. Apparently one of the Hernandez Auto Service mechanics had driven Eduardo to work that morning. They were rearranging the storage room and Eduardo was not expected home by dinnertime. Kevin viewed the loan of this large truck as a special honor; he maneuvered it into the street in hesitant stages. Might look like a sixteen-year old with a driver's permit backing out of the driveway. While Kevin adored the stick shift in his Camaro, he was pleased that the muscular truck had an automatic transmission. Once he straightened it out on Canyon Road, and adjusted the expansive mirrors to his liking, Kevin felt quite secure, confident even to punch in the tape deck player to hear what was on tap. Perhaps something with a Spanish sound. Something like the tunes that enjoyed in a Sante Fe bookshop that afternoon. Not quite certain of the first song bounding out of the Ford's tape deck, but then Kevin recognized Eric Clapton's guitar work as the track progressed.

Kevin had succeeded during the day in ignoring the implications of this evening's meeting at the San Paco Pueblo. Something told him not to try to control or dominate its outcome. The look on Big Mike's face most of all. Sarah Breedlove's uncle had a don't-screw-with-me countenance that augured dismal consequences if Kevin adopted a hard stance. The guy had larger than average brown eyes and a large nose and sensuous lips. When Big Mike smiled at Kevin the previous evening, the man's mouth pulled back as if to launch a grimace. Kevin suspected that Big Mike would give little thought to tonight's conversation and perhaps had forgotten why they were getting together. O'Donnell comforted himself briefly that there were the San Francisco photographs of Uncle Philip awaiting recovery. Kevin had two baited crab traps dangling from his research boat. Quickly he recognized that this was a dangerous mental diversion; both traps could he hauled aboard dripping, but empty, save for tangled, knotty seaweed. Then another picture came to Kevin and he gradually labored through it. As a fencer, Uncle Mike could not successfully thrust a saber, it was as awkward to wield an eight-foot knight's sword. Or a Saracen's curving scimitar, like the Grim Reaper's whistling tool. But Kevin O'Donnell had persevered in the past with the light and mobile fencing epee, and his springing footwork, and he resolved to survive this contest also.

For perhaps the first time in his life Kevin O"Donnell had forgotten about dinner. In his stomach were tingling butterflies that might not embrace the addition of food. It was beyond seven o'clock as he slowed down for the quarter-mile leading into the heart of the San Paco Pueblo. With little effort he had retraced the journey there. The hand-drawn directions remained undisturbed in his pants pocket. Signage along the way was good. Plus he had effortlessly memorized the route while Sarah had driven there twenty-four hours earlier. Daylight seemed inexhaustible on this late June date. Of course, it is June twenty-first: longest day of the year. If he had a hand free, he would smack himself in the forehead. Normally his sister would call him to remind him not to miss that day. Following Daisy Buchanan's admonition in *The Great Gatsby* to be alert for it. A token of how busy he had been to forget the date of the summer solstice. He directed Eduardo's truck into the same parking lot that Sarah had used. It was almost deserted. Parked there was an aging green truck with a sagging load of hay suspending on worn dusty tires. There was a visitors' office over the low adobe wall from the parking area; Sarah had anticipated that it would be closed at that hour. Following her instructions, Kevin stepped over to the church rectory by the red brick church. There he spoke through the screen door with the housekeeper. He needed to do little more than introduce himself when the diminutive woman placed a telephone call from the rectory vestibule. Quietly the housekeeper spoke an Indian language into the instrument. Before using the telephone she flicked on a pair of lamps attached to high-backed wooden secretary. Soft light fell on envelopes in maple pigeonholes and stacks of pamphlets regulated by tan and green paper. She had not invited him inside; Kevin waited for his hosts on a wooden blue rocking chair on the front porch. A slate gray Persian cat bounced up to the small porch and curled beneath the matching chair. An altar boy in his time, O'Donnell was comfortable with the formal and unhurried etiquette that hovered around a priest's residence. Kevin was reminded that as a youngster he had had to visit his local rectory in order to join the altar boy corps, to demonstrate his fluency in Latin. Or at least the minimum requirement to recite it from memory. At age eleven, the latter capability was closer to the truth. As a spoken language the old lingo of the mass was as incomprehensible to him as the Indian dialect used by the rectory housekeeper. It was Sister Catherine who trained his cohort of prospective altar boys. A dozen impatient guys staying after school two days a week. At the nun's insistence, the liturgical training days precisely alternated with the basketball team schedule.

Sarah Breedlove's cousin Alison arrived moments later. She drove a restored Volkswagon sedan. The vehicle was banana yellow with a blue horizontal stripe along the frame. "Follow me, please, Kevin," Alison called from the car. "We'll go over to Big Mike's house." Without a comment Kevin returned to the pickup truck. Three minutes later he was the tail of the two-vehicle caravan winding through the pueblo. Immediately they passed the grade school and the basketball court. This was down the hill on their left. A lone teenager there was bouncing a ball against a smooth brick wall, sending it caroming over his head like some orange cannon shot. Driving beyond that location Kevin found that automobile traffic on the pueblo road was scarce. Given the color and shape of her car, like one-half of a yellow ball, it would have been easy to follow Alison on a crowded interstate highway. The asphalt road dipped and climbed through a series of low hills that were topped with houses. Most of the homes were one-story in height but a handful had two floors. Perhaps a third were wooden construction with adobe predominating. In one driveway was a silver Chevrolet Impala so new that the sales sticker was displayed in a side window. The neighbor's yard had a panel truck that likely was on its second rebuilt engine. Kevin could see the bluish flicker of television sets through a few living room windows. The national evening news programs would be over. Perhaps game shows were broadcasting, or major league baseball. Who would you cheer for in New Mexico?

"Can't live in a place like New Mexico," Bob Goodall had intoned. "No major newspaper and no professional sports." Could it be that the Phillies' Mike Schmidt was trotting the base paths of the baseball diamond, having crushed a home run in some Texas or California stadium? The biggest house in his view had three stories of adobe and a garden wall built from knee-high hedge. It was here that Alison abruptly steered her yellow car into a gravel driveway. Kevin followed a little too quickly. He stomped the brake pedal hard to avoid smacking the Volkswagon. This was successful amid a spray of gravel pellets that noisily leapt for cover in his rear wheel wells.

Big Mike's house reminded Kevin of an old frontier garrison. It was confident and solid as a block of black walnut tree. From the front and side yard its outline loomed over him and Alison like a perfect cube. However there were large apertures on the top floor where twin porches grasped white railings. The sculpted railing balusters resembled wagon wheel spokes. Wooden rainspouts that were characteristic of Sante Fe reached out narrow tongues at the lofty corners of the building. Must take a quarter-century to rot a wooden spout in the high desert. An off-beat joke on unsuspecting New Mexican termite colonies. Mere fifteen inches of annual rain in the region versus thirty-six back home. Through the dusty, sandy yard they walked to the rear of the home. Kevin saw an open porch attached to the second story. Topping the unroofed porch were a series of thick vigas. These were the logs that provided structural support to many adobe buildings, often protruding a few feet beyond a wall. Early Spanish explorers must have envisioned them as protruding cannon. Like the primed weapons on a brisling man-of-war. At Big Mike's house the vigas had the girth of boardwalk pilings and were two feet long overhead. They were spaced about one meter apart. Daylight was finally diminishing as Kevin and Alison clanked up the external plank staircase. With Alison ascending in front of him, slim in her dungarees and gray and white top, Kevin noticed that her heels left a light patina of sand on the first handful of steps. On the porch, several torches in bamboo frames had been lighted. Enough daylight remained that their effect was minimal for now. Amber glass containers that might hold flickering citronella candles were stationed like nervous sentries on the three open sides. There was a round table on the porch, covered by a blue and white vinyl cloth; Big Mike and Sarah's cousin Martin sat there at twelve o'clock and three o'clock from Kevin's perspective when he gained the height of the structure. From a white ceramic ashtray in front of Martin, a strand of cigarette smoke plumed upward. Given the still air of the gathering evening, there was just a minimum of quiver at the top of this narrow smoky column. Cake plates dotted with chocolate crumbs, and half-filled coffee mugs, reminded Kevin of the dinner that he had skipped that evening.

"Wallace was mad enough that he said he would be a candidate for tribal council," Martin was saying to Big Mike. "You know that he has two kids in the grade school. He says that their schoolbooks were shabby by Christmas time, let alone the second semester of the year. Half the history and geography of the world might have been torn out of those books, he said. They won't know Austria from Australia. Not that he ever gave much energy to his own education, from what I hear.

Of course people do that. What they won't do for themselves they fiercely want for their children."

Big Mike and Martin had scarcely acknowledged the arrival of Kevin and Alison. "I've never cared much for Mr. Wallace," Big Mike said to Martin. "He can be a canker sore on your ass." Sarah Breedlove's uncle had a deep voice, just a shade lighter than Lester Lamont's baritone. "Wallace borders on being a hothead. But there still might be something to his criticism. He might be right. Good to keep in mind an old saying I heard, oh, ages ago: 'Your enemies are more valuable to you than your friends.'"

"If I have come at a bad time we can reschedule," Kevin said. With Alison he stood behind the two vacant chairs. As he spoke, he waved his left hand in short circles, similar to Eduardo in his living room the previous evening. "Seems like we are breaking up a meeting or something."

"Not at all," Big Mike said quickly. He stood up, a good three inches taller than Kevin O'Donnell. "Martin and I are being rude. And hello, Alison, dear." He nearly lifted her off of her feet with a hug, as if to permit her to dance on his boots. "I presume you don't want dinner. Cake is available and coffee, too. My housekeeper can handle that for you. Maybe I'll produce a Coor's beer or two after we talk."

As Kevin and Alison took the open seats Big Mike went to the door accessing the house and said something in an Indian dialect to a person inside. "So that I am not confused," Martin said then, "Go over again how Dr. O'Donnell contacted Sarah. Was it through her book publisher?"

"Yes," Alison said. "But it was sort of indirect. And *she* contacted Kevin. After hearing about him from her publisher, she spoke with his colleague at his school and found out about this radio show that he was hosting. Kevin had informed his friend about that. I think that she called him on the very first night of the show. So Sarah's voice was on national radio. Eduardo and Gabriella were so excited about that. Give me a break."

Big Mike had returned to his seat beside Kevin, trailed by the housekeeper who was sporting a tray with coffee paraphernalia. The woman also delivered two more ashtrays. These were also circular white ceramic dishes; the type that Kevin had seen perched on sidewalk café tables in Paris. Without comment she dropped them like oversized coasters in front of Alison and Big Mike. "Do you know much about the Ghost Dance," Big Mike asked Kevin.

"It wasn't much when Sarah called my radio show," Kevin said. But I have a Ph.D. and I'm a professor and research is a big part of me. I trooped over to the library at the University of California at San Diego. This was the day after I first spoke with Sarah Breedlove. They had some material on the Ghost Dance at the Geisel Library. I was able to read it while I visited there. I would not call myself an expert on such a short course of study."

"Just a crazy cult would you call the Ghost Dance," Big Mike asked. "Something that should be suppressed by the authorities?" He did not smile as he talked but Kevin suspected that Mike was curbing a grin.

"Well, Christianity was a cult, too, for about three hundred years in the old Roman empire," Kevin responded. "I guess it is the old 'whose religion is being gored' that places it the cult category or the mainstream religion."

"Jesus, yes," Big Mike said loudly, backing it up with a laugh. So demonstratively that, for a moment, he leaned back and balanced his wrought iron chair on its rear legs. Then Alison said, "We are certainly not going to answer Mike's question for you." Having lit a cigarette, she was tapping it soundlessly to release a terminal cluster of gray ash into the white ashtray. The ashtray that with black letters advertised 'Pernod" along its side. Already there was a pink ring from her lipstick attached to the cigarette's filter. An unintentional smoke ring wafted up from her cigarette as it struck the ashtray. Kevin watched the smoke float tenuously skyward, leading him to notice the distant mountain range over Martin's shoulder, the mountain in the descending night a close match to the brown color of a Capuchin monk's robe.

"Did you pick up on the events surrounding the dancing performances or the theology of it all," Big Mike asked Kevin.

"Some of each," Kevin answered. "The reports of the dead coming back to life, the reputed return of Christ to the earth in support of the Indians. The hope by some tribes that natural upheavals like earthquakes and storms would overpower the white man and return the Indians to control of the western lands. And the prophet Waukova's letter to the Indian tribes. He implored them to avoid telling the whites that Christ walked the earth again. It was the letter instructing them to dance for four or five days straight to bring this revival, this salvation of the Indians, to fruition. Some of the reports and the songs of the period seemed to say Indian's and whites could co-exist peacefully. Others seemed to claim that the white man would be overthrown and buried under the earth. Destroyed by a gigantic cataclysm."

Martin said, "There was a mixed kind of message at that time, the late 1800s, say about 1890, on the possible effect of the Ghost Dance. It wasn't clear if Waukova was Christ reincarnate or a prophet for Christ. I think he claimed to be only a prophet." Martin wore thick black-framed eyeglasses and he had a full beard of black hair, speckled lightly with silver streaks near his chin. The silver strands became nearly parallel when he puffed on his Winston cigarette. He was about forty-five years old, and likely twenty years younger than Big Mike. Martin's demeanor struck Kevin as that of a faithful lieutenant to Mike, who was Martin's uncle according to Sarah Breedlove. Kevin looked for any physical resemblance between Martin and Alison, who were siblings. He could not see any but the illumination on the porch was diminishing gradually as the minutes went past. At least Kevin felt more certain of himself as the conversation progressed. Climbing the stairs to the porch, Kevin's calf muscles had twinged a bit like a burdened customer on a store escalator.

"I have a question that is very important to me," Kevin said. "How do you know the photographer that Sarah told me about is my uncle, Philip O'Donnell."

"Take it from me that it was him," Big Mike said. "It was remembered by some of our pueblo elders years ago that the man—an Irishman— was planning to go on to California, specifically to San Francisco as his ultimate goal. I don't think that you have to burden yourself with too many questions about his identity."

Big Mike reached behind his chair, almost to the railing of the porch, and produced a hefty Coleman lantern. Kevin was amazed at the size of Mike's hands: like the bronze cast of Franz Listz' far-reaching hands that are displayed in the Orpheus Club clubhouse in Philadelphia. Listz must have depressed a dozen piano keys with one hand. Big Mike lit the lantern after raising its glass chimney and moved it to the center of the table. He was wearing an olive drab western vest; from an inside pocket he produced a cigar case. This looked like a pair of attached miniature torpedo tubes wrapped in black leather. Each tube was capped at one end with a brass fitting that had to be unscrewed to free the cigar. Big Mike did that and sliced off the end of a large Ashton cigar with cutting implement that appeared out of another vest pocket. He started lighting his smoke with a Zippo lighter. This created a controlled conflagration at the tip of the stogie, like a Bunsen burner clearing its throat. Without a comment Alison had entered the house and returned bearing a cedar chest about two and one-half feet long. Alison rested it unopened on the porch table. Beneath the vinyl cover, the table was heard to shift quietly from the weight. Meanwhile Kevin stirred the sugar in his coffee five or six full revolutions, thereby generating a fierce muddy whirlpool in the mug.

Kevin observed that the cedar chest was constructed of seven pieces of rose-tinged wood. It was in pristine condition. A single piece formed the bottom and two matching doors would swing open from the centerline of the top. Single sections of wood formed the long sides and the two ends of the box. With the doors on top closed, the chest stretched about twelve inches high. It possessed the dimensions of a model of an enclosed river barge or a small coffin. Kevin had imagined this tabernacle would resemble his square-shaped reproduction bible box back home. The one he had purchased at the Kutztown Folk Festival and relied upon to store important documents. His passport...airline tickets...receipts for Christmas presents. However the cedar chest on Big Mike's porch presented the shape that it had—nothing else. And brightly it rested in the Coleman lantern's glow. However that was increasingly offset by the lazy haze of two burning cigarettes and one potent and simmering cigar. His eyes developed a mild stinging sensation from the lingering nicotine cloud.

"Show the man what we have here," Big Mike said to Alison. This moved her to swing open the two doors at the top of the cedar chest. Kevin could not suppress the desire to get the best look possible and he swept to his feet and leaned over the open chest. There was a roll of white paper that Alison removed and placed on the table beside Martin. Kevin could see the sides of about twenty glass plates, with the plates stacked against each other like narrow volumes askew on a bookshelf. Alison started pulling glass plates out of the chest and handing them to Big Mike. Mike immediately began to arrange the plates in three rows in front of him. The uniform plate size was 6 by 8 inches. The light from the Coleman lantern burned so brightly that Kevin had trouble focusing for a while on the content of any single photograph. He walked around and stood behind Mike's chair where the cigarette and cigar smoke were also less intrusive to his vision. His estimate of the number of photographic plates was highly accurate. With his finger wagging in front of him as though to plink piano keys, Kevin counted the twenty-one plates that Big Mike had arranged in a mosaic of three tight rows.

"Countless times over the last eighty or so years our pueblo people have examined these photographs," Said Big Mike. "Why they were left with us by the photographer is unknown. If there are others that you uncle took of the Ghost Dance is also unknown. Only twenty years ago—in 1963—did someone notice something very unusual and unexplainable about this series of shots. Help yourself to a good close look. Feel free to pick them up."

Kevin leaned forward and systematically ran his sight across the three rows of photographs. The scenes were apparently in the late afternoon or early evening. There was enough light to see crisp details of faces and clothes, and reasonable documentation of solitary leafless trees and sharply rising mountains in the background. Dancers formed a large circle in several pictures and one had a small cluster of Indians in the circle's center. They were like basketball teammates clasping hands before the first jump ball. *'Our Lady of Victory, pray for us'* his schoolmates used to say. There was a square formed by alternating men and women in two consecutive photographs. There were Indians as spectators in two shots, resting on the ground on blankets with giant zigzag designs, and staring in the same direction with intense composure at an unseen attraction. Three close-up exposures focused on different men standing rigidly, yet with knees bent and coiled with energy, with arms and hands raised as if to grasp a parallel bar in a gymnasium. After he viewed all twenty-one photos Kevin reminded himself to breathe. He wondered if Uncle Philip had managed to join one of his own pictures. Perhaps in Indian garb and with his back to the camera.

Martin said, "It appears to us that three different variations of the Ghost Dance were performed on the same day, judging from the numbers of people and the consistency of their clothes. A long, fringed Ghost Dance shirt is identifiable in two of the dances. What someone noticed to be unusual twenty years ago is that the mountains in the background for all of the shots are not the mountains local to us here at the San Paco Pueblo. We had always assumed the ceremony was performed at the village here, to limit knowledge of it in the outside world. It is amazing that had not been noticed earlier. But it is true: these are not our mountains in the pictures."

Quickly Kevin picked up one of the glass plates and held its image close to his face. The plates were an eight of an inch thick and weighed about one pound. In his hands was a photograph of a circle of dancers around a smaller cluster of participants. He could discern smoke from a campfire drifting up at an angle on the right corner of the shot. Beyond the rising smoke stood a steeply climbing cliff, perhaps two hundred yards distant from the Ghost Dancers. Near the crest of the cliff, at about its central point, rested a darker concentration of shadow, perhaps from a gully or protruding ridge of rock. This semicircular marking was a sharp contrast even in the black-and-white photography of the work.

Kevin said, "Moving this many people out of the area for the Ghost Dance would seem peculiar, as Martin said. Some of the people are older folks and there are a couple of babies and children in the crowd. There were no automobiles or buses available that long ago to move people around. So, there is no idea as to the precise location?"

Alison responded, "The youngest children in the photographs might still be alive. They would be in their late eighties now. However they would not have any memory of it. The rest are probably all dead now. But let me show you something else."

Alison took the white roll of paper that had been in the cedar chest and pulled apart four sheets that she flattened on the table near the glass plates. She handled the paper very gingerly. She handled it as though it might be tissue paper from a lingerie shop. Kevin could see a single undulating line in red ink crawl across each sheet. The paper looked like white shelf paper that could come in a long roll and seemed quite durable. "One of the women in our pueblo worked for a short while for a cleaning service that worked at the Los Alamos nuclear research center. That is about fifty-five miles from here. It was 1963. Twenty years ago. The ride was too much and she had an old battered Plymouth car and she quit after a few weeks. She was familiar with these photos and she had learned how the background mountains are unfamiliar to us. She wasn't the most reliable of people but she was okay. She claimed that one stretch of the mountains near Los Alamos seemed familiar and she even sketched it one morning before she quit the job. It reminded her a lot of what she had seen on these pictures. She had worked as a housekeeper for Mike at one point. Supposedly she got out of her car and did a reproduction, panoramic style, on these four sheets of paper. She clamed she tried to capture a view of 360 degrees. She had the roll of paper in her car because the cleaning service issued it to her. It actually matches pretty well, at least to parts of the mountains in the photos. However, she could have made up the story or even copied off of the photos when she worked for Mike. So we don't know."

"Could there be a double exposure involved in the pictures?" Kevin asked.

"Even if it was," Big Mike said, "it still doesn't explain why the photographer would have gone to the trouble to use a different background than around here. And for twenty-one glass plates? You can clearly see the faces of the Indians and they could have been identified at that time."

"Has anyone every made copies of these photos", Kevin asked.

"Definitely not", Martin answered. "We have had a strict rule against that for eighty some years now."

Kevin looked upward as he pursued his next thought. The cloud of smoke puffed out by his companions gently migrated like incense through the openings between the cylindrical vigas that crowned the porch. First stars of the night had grabbed good seats for this performance. Kevin breathed deeply and exhaled deliberately. The cigar and cigarette smoke launched pirouettes and somersaults in playful response. As successfully as possible Kevin tried to let any contrived thoughts seep out of his mind and float like weightless particles, whirring silent neutrons and electrons, in the gray deluge of smoke over their heads. To resist the lure of obscuring his real feelings behind fancy verbal wallpaper. "I want to have the photographs," Kevin said then. "I want to take them with me."

"Do you want to study them, professor," Big Mike asked. "Take them back to your university?"

"I didn't say that," Kevin Said. "I want to take possession of the photo plates. And keep them or use them or dispose of them as I see fit. Make copies of them if I want to."

"That's pretty much why we are here," said Big Mike. "Just so you know, Martin, Alison and I have discussed this in advance. And we have been entrusted by this village and tribe on the future handling of the photographs. They are yours to take. For no easily communicable reasons we believe that they should be entrusted in your care now. Maybe it was how you came west looking for your uncle's work and your heritage. Even more important, and no offense, was your uncle's apparent support of the pueblo in trying times many years ago. Dangerous times, no less. Our tribe has gathered all the meaning that it needs from the pictures. Please take the cedar chest also. It has preserved them rather well over the years. And let me give you something else. To help you celebrate this big evening of yours."

Mike took the cigar case and unscrewed the second brass cap. Out slid the remaining Ashton cigar. Reappearing was the small cutting implement that could unsheath one end of the cigar. Two steel blades that open and shut like paired resisting guillotines to rend the tobacco sheaf and the crunchy contents of the quality smoke. Mike lopped off the end with an authoritative click and handed the cigar to Kevin O'Donnell. Not a smoker but for a handful of years in his twenties, Kevin slipped the gift into the pocket of his shirt. Alison and Martin had already repacked the wooden chest with all of the Ghost Dance photographs and the paper holding the former housekeeper's rendering of mountain ridges drawn in thin red ink. With deep ceremony he shook hands with his hosts. Then Kevin retraced his way down the staircase. He lugged the cedar chest through the yard now lighted with broad moonlight and a string of dull footlights set haphazardly along the base of the house.

****

The loaded chest was heavy. It pulled at his forearm muscles like a stout bundle of oak firewood that might reach to his chin. Pushing thirty pounds for the container and its treasures. However he did not want to reveal that fact since Alison had traipsed it across the porch with little apparent effort. Perhaps she had been silently cursing the strain as she maneuvered the chest to the table. The cab on Eduardo's F-250 Ford truck was spacious and its size enabled Kevin to position the cedar box on the rider side floor. He rested the chest on the floor mat as though it were an infant being cradled in a bassinet. The night air was cooling so Kevin donned his windbreaker before he hauled himself into the driver's seat and fired up the V-8 engine. He was wearing one of the tee shirts that he bought at the pueblo the previous evening and a long sleeve print shirt. Yet he zipped the polyester jacket to the top to maximize his comfort. For seconds as he cruised the truck through the pueblo he was troubled by an intense ticking and knocking sound from the back of the borrowed vehicle. Kevin hated to loan his car to anyone. Eduardo deserved to get the truck back in working order. Then he realized that pebbles from Big Mike's driveway were tumbling in the truck's wheel wells. They were dropping off onto the road like the frantic whirling plastic balls on a televised state lottery.

Where to go and what to do? He would not rush the answers. More beneficial to allow the responses to come to him as Kevin steered the truck through the gently curving road exiting the heart of San Paco Pueblo. He was returning to the interstate road that would connect with Sante Fe and the Breedlove-Hernandez household. On his left side, visible only in moonlit glimpses through narrow breaks in the trees, was the humming chill stream working back to the pueblo. That might do it. Let his mind emulate a stream in a mountainous terrain; no guarantee or requisite of a specific terminus but confident that it would find its way as it twists and plunges and shimmers through the eroding embankments. Without any reckoning from his wristwatch Kevin knew it was closing on ten o'clock. Sarah and Eduardo would be tucking in the house for the night. But Kevin was in no hurry.

There was one source of counsel that he considered accessing. It struck him as he guided the truck onto the interstate highway, bound for Sante Fe. He had observed the previous day with Sarah that solitary public telephone booths were positioned under bright lamps by the side of the road at some indeterminate interval. There might be a picnic table and a dented trash barrel provided in the same pull-off. No luck on a restroom, however. Kevin was thinking about calling Mercedes. It would already be midnight back home. He could call anyway and call collect. One of the telephone booths appeared a few minutes into the ride. It was near a curve and he was vigilant as he slowed the truck into the sandy parking area aside the phone booth. Its glass accordion door was absent and indecipherable graffiti splashed across a side window but the telephone looked serviceable. Mercedes would provide him with topnotch advice, anxious not to push him too far on his different alternatives. But this was unfair. He had to take this from his feelings and his gut and not from her sensible and supportive logic over the telephone wire. Kevin would be catching her after a long workday. And a day he spent moping around the tranquil back streets of Sante Fe. Tapping fingers on the steering wheel, Kevin watched tan moths flit around the telephone booth light fixture. Then he cautiously maneuvered the truck to face the highway again.

There was a lever by his knees that read '4 x 4'; Kevin engaged the four-wheel drive by yanking the handle back toward the seat. This helped him safely tear out of the unpaved parking area in the event that a car rounded the curve at high speed. Even the regular headlamps of the truck were powerful. They helped him to recognize that sand-lined exits from the highway cropped up frequently, providing unofficial access to the desert around him. He was looking for a spot with low hills. He wanted it to be close to this roadway. Something resembling the terrain of a craggy golf course, minus the vibrant green cover. He pulled the turn signal indicator toward him, igniting the potent high beams across the flawless black highway. No other vehicular lights were in sight. Outcroppings the height of a two-story building rose on his left, prompting Kevin to swiftly cross the flat medial strip to the northbound lanes and then off the interstate into the dark New Mexican desert.

Kevin was searching for a location where headlights would not be observed. Where he would not attract the suspicion of the state police or the local cops. He could not safely drive pell-mell in the direction of the distant mountains. Kevin had no intention of catapulting like a maniac into some invisible ravine. With his rib bones and Uncle Philip's glass plates shattered in a thousand shards in a flaming wreck. There was an emerging feeling that his chosen spot should not be so remote that people might never traverse it. Kevin also figured that he wanted to find a location that he could rediscover it if he was lucky or particularly diligent. And that might be five years or twenty-five years from the present. The truck churned the little rocks and sand beneath the powerful tires, one time creating a low thud against the undercarriage. At about one hundred yards off the highway he swung the truck to his left. Behind a twenty-foot wall of sandstone he stopped the truck and pulled on the emergency brake. It would be difficult to spy him from moving traffic on the interstate. As that saying goes, a galloping horse would not notice him.

From the time that he had departed Sarah's house that evening, Kevin was aware that Eduardo had left several shovels on the flatbed of the truck. They were not tied down and they would slide clunking across the plastic ridged surface as he made more severe turns. One of these tools might be useful to him this evening. The gas tank was three-quarters full. Kevin left the motor running. The high beams continued to glow and illuminate a comfortable space in front of him. While it was not a particularly scary site, Kevin wanted to ward off snakes and coyotes and wild mustang horses and the odd tyrannosaurus rex—or similarly curious desert brethren—as he considered his next steps.

The moon that June night was close to full. At least to his untutored eye. The concept that nighttime light was much brighter away from a city was in evidence as he stood behind the truck and selected a long handle spade. He felt spoiled enough to search for cotton or rubber gloves but none could be detected. Rarely had Kevin dug in soil except for gardens that had previously been worked. The soil in the gardens would be like an earthy cushion, where he could amuse himself by mounting a work shoe on the sinking spade, treating it as a pogo stick. This arid, compacted surface might be a much greater challenge in excavation. Plus he wanted to avoid a spot where rainwater might collect, rare as that might be near Sante Fe. He commanded something within arm-waving distance of a sacred trust and he was planning for the long term.

Kevin started digging and then abandoned two places because the ground was so tough and resistant to his efforts. On his feet were sneakers with moderately thick soles. He could feel the cutting top of the spade push back at his foot, pressuring the arch in his right foot in his attempts to create a trench. Concerned, rather than despairing, he poked the desert floor like a maintenance worker spearing paper along a roadway. The compacted soil bounced the shovel in his fingers, like concrete under ice...twang. Maybe thirty feet beyond his initial scrapings Kevin found a softer patch of sand and dirt. From the first determined penetration he could see that this might work just fine. All that he required was a stretch of the planet in which to securely bury the cedar chest and the twenty-one ancient photographic plates of Indians celebrating the Ghost Dance.

Kevin found it comforting to face the truck's headlights as he dug the sand and soil beneath his feet. The high beams were blinding so he reduced the lights to the regular setting. The artificial illumination reduced the pleasant moon and starlight considerably but he wanted to create a grotto for the cedar chest with enormous precision. As though driving in a thunderstorm or ferocious traffic, he thought it wiser to keep the truck's tape deck silent. Kevin was no type of soil engineer. Does it make sense to pour sand and earth lightly around the chest or tamp it down densely? It was moisture that was his greatest concern. Even hungry animals would not find much to attract them to this excavation. Once Kevin had assisted Lawrence Whitney back on McClain Street near Walnut Lane in burying the Whitney's collie in their backyard. Not legal, perhaps, but it was the interment that his neighbors desired. By the next spring the dog's grave was unnoticeable among the reviving azalea bushes. Wait, would it be different in this arid clime? He would be wise to smooth it over when he was finished, disguising his tracks with a debris juniper branch.

Digging and plugging he unearthed some rocks the size of footballs. He would heave then underhand against the sandstone wall to his right. The grit of sand on the rocks felt like sugar grains to his ungloved fingertips. O'Donnell decided to soldier on until at least one-half of the cavity was completed. Time for a break then, to consider his progress and his decision. He returned to the truck and carefully removed the chest, carrying it to a level spot in front of the vehicle where the lights were not so overpowering. The twin doors secured the top of the chest handsomely. Their borders extended a full inch around the opening of the chest. He swung them open, leaving them angled like wings over the container. Instantly Kevin realized that he should take the paper drawings with him. Have something tangible from this experience. He placed them behind the passenger's seat of the truck. He held up one of the photographic plates. It was a shot taken of a large crowd with their backs to the camera. Silently he said, 'Uncle Philip, if you are enmeshed right in this crowd of people, forgive me for not publicizing these pictures right now. That is such a small part of what you have accomplished. And who knows what San Diego will bring. Your day will come. If it has to be a thousand years don't fret the time or the wait." As he went to return the photo Kevin for the first time noticed a linen cloth lying under the twenty-one plates. Gingerly as pulling a bandage off of a fresh wound, Kevin extracted the cloth and maneuvered it over the tops and sides of the glass. Some more protection perhaps from water. Then he closed the chest doors and returned to the hole near the upright shovel.

The deeper he went, the more resistant the solid ground became. He could not worry about that. By poking in at odd angles the soil eventually gave way. A mound of pebbles and dirt and sand grew by degrees half a spade-length from the hole. So absorbed was Kevin in the effort that, only when he had reached an acceptable depth and width, did he view his watch to learn it was a quarter-hour past midnight.

Kevin O'Donnell heaved up the chest and walked it over to the hole. His steps were as deliberate as a toddler climbing stairs. Grasping the two narrow ends, he lowered the chest with the photographs into the excavation. His wrists scraped the earth on the sides of the hole. Using his hands rather than the spade, Kevin started pushing loose soil around the sides of the chest. Then he needed to use the shovel to bring more material from the mound that he had created. The space around the sides was filled in tightly and completely when he suddenly stopped. He pulled the doors open and rested them against the wall of his little trench. Kevin stood up and zipped open the windbreaker jacket and pulled it off quickly. The he undid his shirt buttons and removed the long-sleeve shirt and dropped it on top of the jacket on the ground. He was wearing only the Grateful Dead tee shirt on his chest. No surprise to him that the desert night air was quite chill. The tee shirt came off his back and went over his head and then he scanned the printed touring dates from 1981. There it was. Providence, Rhode Island on July 15th, his birthday. His girlfriend at the time had treated him tickets to the Grateful Dead concert. For six weeks that summer he had fulfilled a disk jockey job in Providence. Immediately before the sojourn to Munich for *Radio Free Europe*. Kevin placed the tee shirt with caressing fingers over the linen cloth that already covered the plates, completely within the enclosure of the box. This should provide even more protection from the patient and potentially destructive elements. A bit clumsily he replaced the long-sleeve shirt and the windbreaker over his exposed skin. Down went the covering twin doors of the cedar chest and he filled in the remaining open spaces, packing in the earth until his buried treasure was completely out of sight. Since there was no desert vegetation handy, Kevin smoothed over the digging site with his sneakers. Thus leaving a series of curving parallel lines and circles of varying size imprinted in the dust and sand from the soles of the footwear.

Kevin could feel the cigar in his shirt pocket as he tucked in the shirttail with a little more diligence. His Dad's brother Brian used to smoke the Ashton brand. Kevin recalled the festive O'Donnell soirees, wedding receptions and funeral luncheons where Uncle Brian's smoldering cigar provided a source of constancy in the whirlwind of family milestones. Unusually appropriate to possess such a cigar on such a night as this. Kevin reached through the driver side window and pressed in the electric cigarette lighter on the dashboard. With extra stretching he also grabbed a cassette tape from a battered cardboard box between the front seats. Without checking the performer's name Kevin switched the tape in the audio player with this replacement and hit the rewind button. The lighter popped back, ready to fire the cigar; Kevin held the plastic handle gingerly, with fingertips lightly blistered from the dig, and managed to start a glow at the Aston's wide tip. Puffing, puffing furiously to get it stabilized. Kevin stood with his back against the truck, coughing in spurts from the unaccustomed smoke and tried to focus on the brilliant night sky. The wisdom of experiencing the cigar was questionable, Kevin thought. It might leave him sick to his stomach or even a bit wacky. He was feeling hungry from his skipped dinner and the physical demands of burying the chest of photographs. Might just try to curl up and sleep though his discomfort, right through until morning.

Presently a deep male voice, maybe two feet behind Kevin, said emphatically, "Hello—I'm Johnny Cash."

So startled was Kevin O'Donnell that the cigar flew out of his hand, tracing a parabola as it flew to earth like a film of a NASA rocket run backwards. The cigarette lighter remained tightly clutched in his left hand, instinctively held away from his body. Kevin was not certain if he yelled from astonishment at the intruder; he did realize within seconds that he was now hearing the record album, *Johnny Cash at Folsum Prison*. 'The Man in Black' as Johnny Cash was frequently called, rocking a high security prison auditorium with his country music trio. The song *Fulsom Prison Blues* was ripping out of the good speakers in the interior of Eduardo's truck. He remembered how Bob Goodall had played the album for him at a dinner party about a year before. The unusual concert at a California penitentiary was a 1968 event according to the album cover. Fifteen years ago now. The guitars in the band were electric, the screaming crowd of convicts more so. Kevin replaced the lighter in the dashboard. The cigar was easy to locate. Still glowing hot red at one end. Sign of a good cigar, Uncle Brian used to claim, when it stays lit with little attention given it.

Composure re-established, Kevin figured that there was a reason he was hearing this album. He knew that he was still hesitant to leave the chest of photographs buried in the New Mexico desert. It would be a snap to grab the shovel and exhume the cedar box and its unique contents. A professor would not see himself coming and going carrying nearly two-dozen Philip O'Donnell Ghost Dance pictures. They could be the darling of the academic research season. A standing–room crowd at the major conference presentations. The Kilmartin Museum in St. Joseph, Missouri would deliver all of the big guns for opening night of his exhibit—Missouri River be damned. The editors of the *Journal of American Civilization Studies* on the line? Again? I'll get back to them. Mr. Johnny Cash understood turmoil and the criticism of an off-beat style, yet he became a country music superstar nonetheless. Something of a rebel in Cash's ways Goodall had reported. Just what would Johnny Cash advise concerning the photographs if he were standing beside Eduardo's big truck right now?

"Well, you are being a fool, young fellow, not publicizing the Ghost Dance pictures," Johnny Cash would say. "Chance of a lifetime to hit it big in your profession. And that has to be pretty boring to begin with, so you need to liven things way up. Let me magically transport you to the top of that mountain peak. There we go, watch your footing. Now we can see the lights of Sante Fe. At least the suburbs of town, with its glittering streetlights and fluorescent all-night gas stations. (Johnny would be rolling his black-sleeved arm in the general direction of the city. His rough-hewn face would blend in without comment at the San Paco Pueblo). Imagine that that circle of lights cradles a world of professors, and people who love Indian traditions, and people enmeshed in Irish heritage. You could buy every lovely Navaho carpet for sale in New Mexico. And babes love a celebrity—might not get mentioned at the colloquiums that you attend. You can grab that shovel yonder and capture all of these buried riches in a blink of an eye."

"But that is not what you have done in the music world," Kevin would say. He was hoping that Goodall's banter held water for once. "You paid a price for not going along with mainstream Nashville, you and that Willy Nelson fellow. Having second thoughts, are we, Johnny?"

"Well, so *I'm* the one's whose life work is under the microscope here," Mr. Cash retorts. Got an extra one of them seegars, there? Never mind. Keep in touch because I am out of here."

Once Johnny Cash had vanished Kevin snuffed the cigar on the ground, climbed into the truck and stopped the tape player. Exhaustion wrapped him like the blanket he did not have as he crawled awkwardly to the passenger side and curled up hoping to find a sleeping position. It was cool enough that he slid the control button into the red zone on the dashboard to pump heat into the cab of the truck. Then he flicked the ignition key to stop the motor. Kevin was concerned that he might run out of gas if it ran all night. He reached almost to the other window to disengage the headlight switch. A moon approaching fullness dropped soft light on the black dashboard and the wrinkled knees of his trousers as Kevin let sleep descend.

Much like a red-eye airplane flight, Kevin O'Donnell survived the slumber in the truck's big seat. The moon had gone off duty and let the sun attend to its shift. He got out of the truck to walk around the vehicle when sunrise arrived. He looked over briefly at the site of last night's excavation and silent said 'Let it be." The truck's engine sounded angry in the silent desert morning. Kevin backed out beyond the rock wall on his left. It was surprising how he had avoided some gullies the previous night when he had entered the desert. Carefully he maneuvered the truck to the edge of the interstate highway. It was a cloudless sky that rose above the distant mountains. A series of ridges there reminded him of an ocean wave formation on a windy day. That was helpful. Kevin reached into his pocket and pulled out the sheet of typing paper that Sarah had employed to give him directions to San Paco Pueblo. Previously he had noted that dusty pens and pencils crammed into a shelf below the glove compartment. He selected a blue pen and carefully drew the mountain view in his un-painterly hand, on the reverse side of the paper. Kevin allowed a few cars and a convoy of parcel delivery trucks to rip by him before he crossed over to the southbound lanes and rolled toward Sante Fe. He made a mental record of the first mile marker on the route. Together with his crude mountain drawing he should have some chance to find the location of the buried photographs in the future. The truck would be deposited in time for Eduardo to leave for work at his regular early departure.

Few vehicles were in motion as Kevin gained the block where Sarah and Eduardo lived. Hopefully one of them was available to let him into the house. He had not anticipated that the front door would be unlocked but that was the case. Stealthily as a burglar he swung the brown door into the entryway. Shrieks of laughter were charging at him from the living room. There was loud clapping, likely from Eduardo. Young April's squeals mixed with it also. "Just wait until Gabriella sees her," Sarah announced excitedly. With peripheral vision Sarah spied Kevin and waved him into the living room. "Kevin, come quick," she said. "Ha. So, you're not dead. Look at the baby. She walked on her own today. For the first time." In pretty sky-blue pajamas April Hernandez was standing on bare feet with her hands in the soft grasp of her father. "Show Kevin how you can walk," Eduardo gently instructed his daughter. Suddenly Kevin felt shy about being in the room. Like a burglar of the household's intimate joys. He stood motionless and said nothing. Then he saw the triumphant face of April with her flawless skin and her bounding black curls as she swept away from her father and raced the four feet to her mother's outstretched arms. Kevin had missed seeing April's very first steps and he was immensely glad for that. And perhaps he saw step one-hundred, and step one-hundred-and-one, and one-hundred-and-two that she took across the plush rug, across her kingdom of New Mexico, her Land of Enchantment.

CHAPTER FIFTEEN

Return to Folsum Prison: Now, Two Men in Black

Hello, I'm Johnny Cash...and Hello, I'm Luciano Pavarotti.
Immediately the great tenor in the gorgeous black tuxedo
commences with:

'My bills were all due,
The bambini need shoes
And I'm busted.

'Cotton is down
To 500 lire a pound,
And I'm busted.'

Wild shrieking applause nearly masks Johnny's soft harmonica...

Several steps away from Kevin O'Donnell, supported by the plank floor of an unfamiliar fifty-foot boat, clustered alien life forms. As large as adult humans, they stood upright on cumbersome web feet. Observing them, Kevin sensed chills like those that coursed through him in trigonomic waves in New Mexico a few weeks earlier. A portion of this new experience was cemented in dread. However a lighter excitement floated above, weightless as a meringue. Kevin had always clowned around when they studied Morse code back in Boy Scouts—would it be an SOS that he desired to communicate, or BYOB, Bring Your Own Bottle? With concentration he watched as one of these argonauts awkwardly tramped eight feet to confront him directly. Its figure was packed tightly into a clammy black skin. Grotesque yellow metal tanks grew from its back. In place of a pair of eyes and a nose this creature offered a single oval snout. It was black on the sides and frighteningly transparent in front—the front could be mistaken for plastic. The snout was substantial enough to pot a two-year old bonsai plant or a delicate tea rose. The inhabitants of the distant planet Lugar, with their bobbing antennae and teeth tinted in lavender, possessed a less threatening prospect. A limb reached up to the head of the alien now invading his personal space. It abruptly yanked off the cycloptic contraption at its face. Mercedes was then looking at Kevin from beneath a scuba-diving wetsuit. Her brown hair was totally concealed by the wet suit's tight-fitting hood. Mercedes shuffled her left foot with its blue rubber flipper, to adjust her weight and balance to the ocean swell that caressed the diving boat. The *California Gold Rush* lay offshore from San Diego. His girlfriend's eyes squinted as she asked him, "Kevin, are you alright? Are you ready for this dive? You look a little green around the edges."

Kevin was wearing scuba gear but he had not yet slipped on the hood or the diving mask. His hair was open to the breeze that swooped about the boat. The breeze was like air powered by the wings of invisible swallows. He could imagine that the sunlight was playing tricks with his image. Sunlight reflected off of the green ocean and the bright plank floor of the boat. It reflected off of aluminum generators and hefty yellow plastic bags with giant zippers designed to haul diving equipment. It was an hour shy of high noon; the sun was silently escalating to its maximum allowable power on a partly cloudy morning. The center strip of the San Diego sky was open. On the perimeter were flat thin clouds the color of faded khaki. They reached into view like a retractable canvas roof over an immense swimming pool. Kevin thought that it was reasonable that he felt apprehension coupled with excitement as they prepared to dive to search for Uncle Philip O'Donnell's San Francisco photographs. They might be on the *USS Fidler*, a hundred feet below the surface. The warship now resting on its side immediately beneath the lightly heaving *California Gold Rush*. Kevin always believed that his face had the transparent quality of an essentially honest person. And a touch of sallow color on his cheekbones, given the situation, would bring convergent testament to that.

"Maybe it's a mild case of seasickness," Kevin answered Mercedes. "It is a choppier ocean today than I've experienced before."

"Okay," Mercedes said. "But you have to do us a favor. We have to keep Zachary and Melissa happy this morning so that they will do their best looking for the photographs on that destroyer. I heard them grumbling this morning about how you buried the Indian pictures back in the desert. I wish that you hadn't told them about that. A couple of times they have asked me if you will keep what we might find safe and secure. Given the risks they may be taking down below. Not a bad question. I have wondered about that myself."

"No, anything that we find will be carefully guarded," Kevin said. "San Francisco pictures would be different because I have had several years to think about them. Even though they may ultimately be more important, the Ghost Dance pictures are mysterious to me. And that strange letter that one of my relatives wrote to Philip O'Donnell from Donegal in 1903. Can you imagine. Irishmen dancing a Ghost Dance in Donegal, the very same night as a solemn wake. I want to study the Indian material with a long slow sweep, when the time is right. And if not me, then someone else someday."

Zachary and Melissa were business partners. With financial assistance from the Kilmartin Museum in St. Joseph, Missouri, they had been chosen by Kevin to lead the dive to the sunken destroyer to search for a locker of Captain Bulwer. A locker filed with photographic plates ostensibly made by Philip O'Donnell in 1906 and earlier. The Captain may have brought that with him on the ship's last venture into the Pacific Ocean in October, 1952. A brief and disastrous Korean War-era tour with Petty Officers, Second Class, Anthony Connelli and Victor Kesson on board. Kevin was certain as to the hired divers' last names and he had startled their assistants back at their shop when he specifically said goodbye to Cliff, Darla, and Jose on his initial visit to their establishment. The diving and fishing tackle shop rested on long-weathered pilings a little over a mile north of West Harbor Island Marina and the San Diego Bay. The shop was the first structure lining a busy inlet that fed into the ocean. Neighbors included other fishing supply stores and an outboard motor repair business and a venerable shack that appeared to serve as a convenience store and cheap souvenir outlet. Small trucks, and cars, fancy and near derelict, were wedged into a parking area covered with crushed shells at Zack and Melissa's place. A pleasant ocean smell would be stirred up with each crunch of Kevin's footwear on the half-inch layer of shells. The pink or ivory-colored crustacean pieces were uniformly ground to the size of a dime. At the doorstop, he had to scrape off pieces that were wedged into the ridges on the soles of his sneakers. So exuberant were his efforts that he did not immediately notice two anglers, beer company pins fixed to floppy golf hats, who looked at him like a recent arrival from Pluto. On his first visit to the shop Kevin had observed that, in addition to diving instructions and diving tours, the business apparently thrived by selling vast quantities of bait.

Kevin had located this business by a review of the San Diego telephone directory. He fancied their advertisement, a full quarter of the yellow page, which mentioned the willingness to help the novice diver or fisherman. Having initiated the glee club campaign for the Gierson Gasket Company, Kevin felt a bond with a sharp marketing concept. There was also a pen-and-ink rendering in the directory of the tackle shop hovering above the inlet. Zack and Melissa were authorized scuba diving instructors. At a junior high school swimming pool, the musty air of which suggested equal molecules of chlorine and oxygen, Kevin took the two-week class to get licensed to scuba dive in the ocean. The midnight-to-four a.m. radio work was advantageous for this venture since classes were provided in the afternoon. The imperfections of the swimming pool were quite perfect for simulating diving conditions in certain ways. Light was diffused by high, glass-block windows that punctured one wall; unintentionally this mimicked the atmosphere that he expected to find ascending from a deep dive. Echoes in the tiled pool house brought a brief hissing sound to his ears as his head broke the surface. It reminded him of the sound of waves while swimming in the ocean. He felt sufficient disorientation sometimes when he emerged from the deep end of the pool that he would rip off his mask. This resulted in the strap stinging his ears, like a puppy being teased by a child. The last session of the training course was the most challenging: it finally plunged them into the cold Pacific Ocean. He did this together with three other straining students. For a moment the vastness and quiet of the ocean seemed to drain his breath. A feeling not unlike a bizarre dream, where phantoms of human beings or sea life float at the periphery of your vision. Actually, in the grip of his concentration, he had forgotten to suck on his mouthpiece. The instructors limited the neophytes to a descent of fifty feet. Repeatedly they were warned against a too rapid ascent to the surface and the devastating danger of the bends.

Kevin's adventures this day would be an even more compelling challenge, a sharper risk than the diving course finale. In a few minutes Melissa, Zachary and Mercedes would plunge through the ocean canyon of 100 feet to the captain's cabin on the *USS Fidler.*

Thirty-one years earlier, U.S. Navy frogmen had rigged an entrance hatch as they had excavated the munitions and other official valuables from the ship. To protect the naval vessel from Soviet Union spies, and treasure hunters, and generally curious divers, all other hatches and large portholes were welded and bolted shut. A padlock the circumference of a bread plate secured access to the ship's interior. To counteract corrosion, the padlock was replaced at an unrevealed interval over the years. Through Commander Lapworth's intercession, Kevin obtained the padlock combination numbers that the diving crew needed to enter the ship through the hatch. Not at all reluctantly did Kevin agree to serve as the gopher for the recovery effort. Like some underwater bumble bee, he would hover by the fifty-foot depth marker on a white nylon line that would be directed to the destroyer by the other divers, the line ultimately lashed to a rusting bulkhead. Through amateur hand signals flashed from Mercedes or Zachary or Melissa, Kevin would discover what extra tools or phosphorous lamps or rigging was needed to complete the salvage of Captain Bulwer's trunk. A motorized winch on the *California Gold Rush* could be engaged to raise the locker if needed. Intense games of charade played below sea level, gloved fingers undulating like black or yellow octopi tenacles. Back to the *California Gold Rush* he would cautiously climb to assist his teammates, to fetch the missing equipment. The amount of time spent submerged was a critical safety factor; he could save precious minutes for the others through this arrangement. It would be anathema to him to remain onboard and completely uninvolved in the salvage operation. His half a loaf of involvement would be discernibly better than none—not a starring role but quality minutes off of the bench.

"Isn't that Zachary a real hunk," Mercedes asked Kevin. "Those powerful shoulders and arms. I watched him carry those big duffel bags on board. They were filled with heavy air tanks but he hoisted them like they were filled with marshmallows. 'Get Zack in the sack' is a big motto around the marinas in San Diego, I hear. Boy, all that unclean living is doing him good. Uhm, um."

"Shame how muscle bound he is, though" Kevin said. "Not that he isn't smart, or anything Back in his office I noticed that his desk was just swamped with well-thumbed copies of *Scuba Diving Today* and *Scuba Diving Monthly* and the *American Journal of Scuba-Divery.* Better know in the trade as 'scuby-duby-do.' But on the other hand, Melissa does nothing for me. Tanned, toned, her red hair flipped softly just on to her shoulders, right where those single-strap tops hang from. Probably was a runway model or something and that is why she is so stuck up. Dime a dozen in these parts. I hate it when she insists on helping me get into my wet suit. The damn thing always gets caught right around my butt, somehow. Disgraceful, I tell you. Disgraceful."

"All right, you love birds. Time to get together to review the dive rules one more time." This was called over to Kevin and Mercedes by Zack. The dive co-director was wearing his full complement of diving gear. He had his mask propped on his head, just above his wide blue eyes at his forehead, the mask like an animal's thick horn that had not yet fully matured. He was a powerfully built man, abundantly filling every section of his black wetsuit. Even his chronometer was more of a small clock strapped to his granite wrist than a standard-size diving timepiece. From Zack's size-eleven feet emerged blue rubber flippers that were so worn and stained from emersion in salt water that Kevin's diving getup was a first communion suit in comparison. As Kevin trekked with Mercedes to Zachary and Melissa's position he thought that he heard his heart thump powerfully in his skull. Was he that excited? No, it was a pump or generator somewhere below deck, radiating a metallic tone that mixed in some alluring way with the tension that clung to this enterprise.

Kevin appeared to be listening intensely to Zachary. However, he was zoning into and out of attention to Zack's instructions, as important as they were to the operation's well-being. Kevin had been an avid student of diving in recent weeks. He had memorized virtually all of the training manuals' diagrams, imagining maneuvers and safety techniques in his mind as he showered each morning, and he felt that a measure of this pre-dive meeting was officious clap-trap. And like everyone else, as a child he had absorbed at least fifty television episodes of Lloyd Bridges in *Sea Hunt*. Kevin shot glances at other boats at a distance from the *California Gold Rush*. A pair of power craft ran closely together like ducks, about 200 hundreds yards off, but he could identify nothing about them. He was wondering if the Gierson Gasket Company executives might have put to sea also. At eight-thirty the night before he had spoken by telephone with Lester Lamont and Ted Mower. ("Kev-in," Ted had exclaimed over the phone to the reconnected prodigal consultant). The fellows were staying at the Hotel Eldorado in San Diego, in town for a few days to film a commercial based on his glee club concept. Three Gierson teams had been selected through internal competition to perform on film. The Waterloo Special Gasket task force had rocketed to the top with a competent delivery of *"Oh. Susanna.'* This was according to Les Lamont. But Lamont's St. Joseph team had landed a spot in the television advertisements fair and square, even pushing the glee club envelop with *"Yackety, Yack, Don't Talk Back."* Prior to the competition, O'Donnell had asked Les if songs like that fit the genre, a gentle tease that Les, to his ultimate advantage, had apparently not recognized. Lester invited Kevin to view the filming of his group; the visiting video producers were searching for striking locations around the harbor and the San Diego seacoast that would give the ads visual impact. Tied down by his salvage expedition, Kevin had to deflect this invitation from the Gierson Gasket Company.

"We have two of these new diving computers," Zachary said then. "As you might remember the purpose of it is to assist the diver in how fast he can ascend safely. You don't want to get your blood filled with air bubbles—get the bends—now do you? That could cripple or kill you. Melissa will operate one computer and Kevin you can have the second one. That's because we will be working at two different depths in the water. As we demonstrated for you in the training class, the diver has to swim toward the surface with the light staying green. If you are ascending through the water too fast, the light blinks red, very rapidly red."

Kevin heard all of these instructions. The computer was fitted into a small oblong box, gray as a parking meter with white dials and amber display screens, and it was attached now to his belt by a black braided cord. Zachary adjusted the dials to reflect the depth that Kevin would reach while Melissa worked on her device. He was more conscious however of the scent that emanated from the ocean—a smell that he always forgot about until he was within calling distance of the water's crest. With a home in Philadelphia he lived only seventy miles from the Atlantic Ocean. Funny how he forgot about its impact on his nostrils until he was well within to its salty proximity. He looked past Zachary to the port side of the boat. Their employee Jose was present, checking equipment that might assist the salvage dive. The two strips of clouds had closed noticeably, resembling lines of awnings stretching across an alley, reducing the direct sunlight about fifty percent. The khaki color of the clouds had transformed into a medium gray, a herald of potential rain showers. But Jose labored in sunglasses black as onyx nonetheless. Tan skin on his lithe arms had the color of mahogany. Over the side he flung a lead weight that propelled the nylon depth line on a rapid descent beneath the boat. The line's plastic holding reel, spinning rapidly, gave a high-pitched whirring sound, like an excited bird. An aluminum ladder shaped roughly like an inverted fishhook swooped over the side of the boat and lead to a narrow platform just above the ocean's plane: a diving platform. Small waves took turns nipping at it. A kind of precipice was the platform, Kevin thought. Less threatening than the edge of a cliff, but a step into danger nonetheless. He observed that there were white seagulls above the boat, traveling as an amiable pair in the diminishing sunlight, swaying and looping in the breeze, searching for their next fishy meal and apparently oblivious to any threat to their existence from the Pacific Ocean.

Handshakes were exchanged through the nylon gloves of the four divers: the intuitive signal that it was time to proceed. First to the diving platform were Melissa and Zack; they were standing upright facing the ocean, momentarily still as school kids awaiting the teacher's direction, when Zack vehemently flipped himself into the choppy water. He made a full summersault. His maneuver reminded Kevin of a dismount from a balance beam that he would see in a college gymnasium. Melissa followed suit before the ripples from Zack's plunge could dissipate against the *California Gold Rush*. Due to Kevin's gloves the aluminum ladder professed to be neither warm nor cold; while he preferred to appear nonchalant, he positioned his flippers with exacting care on each textured step of the ladder. The steps were quite rigid. However his mind flashed an image of a tenuous rope ladder that twisted and shook on the climb to a trapeze artist's platform. Or perhaps the dangling rescue apparatus quivering in the wash of a Coast Guard Chinook helicopter. Mercedes filled his vision with the image of a cavorting seal or a Sea World dolphin as she tossed her body into the green ocean. The water was transparent for about eight feet if you stared directly at it. Yet Mercedes quickly disappeared from view. She had been swallowed whole by the sea. It remained unclear to O'Donnell why this acrobatic method was the preferred way to dive from the boat. Passably well he did the same as he suddenly tumbled forward into the ocean, in his active mind even shouting out, "Geronimo."

He reached out broad butterfly strokes when he became oriented to his position in the water. Down into an increasingly forest-green netherworld, Kevin pumped his arm muscles and kicked his legs with the supple flippers. The sucking of oxygen through his hard rubber mouthpiece resounded in his head. A quivering school of yellowfin tuna scattered in infinite directions as he cut through. Probably regrouping as planned off the Baja Peninsula. So different from the training run in the Pacific Ocean the previous week. On that late afternoon the focus was on him and the other few students. Now Zachary and Melissa, with Mercedes in their flow, had rocketed down to the naval destroyer and the job for the day. He had been dropped off at the first day of kindergarten, so to speak, and it was time to manage his own affairs. He could not locate the depth line initially. When he found it he gave it a fierce and comforting tug. Twenty-feet of depth already. Black numbers were embedded in the nylon stands at five-foot chunks. Thirty more feet until he stopped and took his assigned position. Kevin reasoned that the other three divers would be guiding the white line to the ship and he soon noticed clusters of air bubbles wafting up along the line like watery incense. This helped him focus his sight on the three shadowy outlines of the rest of the dive team. Perhaps they were forty feet more deeply submerged than he and they continued to move away from him. By his size alone he could identify Zachary; however, in their enveloping jet black wetsuits and identical orange air tanks, Mercedes and Melissa were indistinguishable right now. Immediately Kevin could recognize the gray superstructure of the *USS Fidler.* For moments it reminded Kevin of the furtive shadows sketched by the weathered rock formations in the early dawn in the New Mexico desert. The ship's profile became more distinct the deeper he swam. Gun turrets, shattered funnels, a fractured crane, varying level of decks whose names and functions he did not know. The front quarter of the *USS Fiddler* had a lengthy, narrow fissure. This was in the immediate vicinity to the forward eight-inch gun, rendering the vessel worthless to raise and salvage. Commander Lapworth had pointed out that most of the damaged Pearl Harbor fleet was resuscitated and returned to service. The one cruiser that avoided damage was sunk in the 1982 Falkland Island war between Britain and Argentina. Now he could more clearly see as Zachary and one of the women twisted the depth line in a giant knot around a metal pipe that protruded from the ship's deck. A big extravagant knot like the bows on fake packages in a Christmas display. Worthy of a John Wanamaker's holiday window. The nylon line stretched with a keener tautness between the destroyer and the endlessly bobbing *California Gold Rush* .

Mercedes and the two others huddled around a section of the ship about one-third of the distance from its uppermost deck. Their air bubbles, while emerging at different rhythms from their respirators, managed to coalesce above their heads into shimmering clouds that gracefully migrated toward the surface. There were as many as seven distinct layers in the deepest areas of the ocean he had read, and even here he began to observe two or perhaps three gradations in the particle density and color of the water. Schools of fish were also partial to certain ocean levels off of San Diego, something like orchestra patrons selecting the mezzanine or the swankier main floor. He had heard talk of albacore and rockfish and sculpin in these waters but he could recognize not a one of them without a fish market label. Kevin figured that Zachary was rotating the tumblers on the thick navy padlock. A bit clumsily with the gloves, perhaps, but the cold depth was hostile to bare fingers. Particularly touching metal surfaces. Part of Kevin's role was to watch for uninvited divers. He was charged with scattering them like the tuna just above. With no spear gun in tow, aggressive hand signals would have to suffice. Float like a butterfly and sting like a bee, the heavy weight champion Mohammed Ali used to say. Carried to a new extreme in these circumstances. Kevin nearly made himself laugh—a dangerous practice fifty feet under the sea.

Mercedes and the two hired divers had just disappeared from his view by swinging open the access door and entering the *USS Fidler*. It was unimaginable to Kevin how devoid of light it would be within the ship. The two women had lighted halogen lanterns before slipping inside. It was an ethereal light that momentarily trembled with their arm motions as they penetrated the interior. It was disconcerting for Kevin to watch this action and for seconds he wished that he had not involved Mercedes in the dive. Should he charge down there to see if she was alright? Better to hold his position and prepare for action if called upon. Kevin had insisted that they were not to open Captain Bulwer's locker down below since salt water might quickly corrode the glass photographic images. So it could be a worthless unopened box of knick-knacks that gets lugged back to the salvage boat. Other than this derelict destroyer Kevin had no clue as to the whereabouts of the San Francisco pictures. This was a one-shot option. The photos better be there or forget it.

As parts of seconds crawled he felt emotional pressure mounting inside his chest, and he needed a diversion pronto. He was able to calm down somewhat by reviewing in his mind the research that was bedrock to this quest. Bob Goodall had howled when he discovered that O'Donnell did not own an operating camera and only occasionally took amateurish pictures for his class presentations. For example, the picture of the golden roof atop the New York Life Insurance building, a towering creation with a pyramid-shaped roof, located at Madison Square in New York City. Kevin took this exposure from a street corner virtually in the shadow of the Flatiron Building. Radiant lemon sunshine bounced off of the precious sheathing on the Kodak slide. And a "Tow Away Zone" sign blocked a quarter of the shot. But by faithfully trudging to the library on the most alluring April mornings and on stinging January days Kevin had diligently research photographic history. He could competently reconstruct the state-of-the-art when Uncle Philip was active in the field. Paper film had existed for thirty years already but glass negative plates provided much sharper quality at the turn of the twentieth century. From 1839, glass had been the preferred negative surface for clarity and distinct detail. Photographs taken by the Daguerreotype glass plate process by 1860, if not before, matched the black-and-white film clarity of the 1980's. A difference in the earlier decades was that paper film created reproducible pictures, even if they had a brown or yellow tint and a soft focus. The Daguerreotype made unique images. No two quite alike. Commercial pressure had doomed the Daguerreotypes. Newspapers and magazines and even family albums would covet easily reproducible photos and a convenient paper form. By the time that Uncle Philip was working, the glass plate processes had at least reduced the amount of time needed for an exposure. He had been able to capture the Ghost Dancers with unblemished accuracy. The very earliest Daguerreotypes could take eight or ten minutes before an exposure could be fixed on the silver-coated glass. Therefore, a famous daytime picture of the Boulevard du Temple in Paris, an early street scene by Daguerre, taken from a high window in 1839, shows no pedestrians or carriage traffic in a populous and bustling commercial district. An estimated one hundred people there were not represented on the exposure. Except for a bootblack and his top-hatted customer who were stationary due to the exacting shoe polishing procedure. Yet building details, down to paper taped over a single broken windowpane, were captured in the picture in unerring detail. The photo gave Kevin a ghostly feeling—the masonry and brick structures have permanence but hustling human life is lost or invisible. Scuba diving fifty feet down in the Pacific Ocean, waiting for Mercedes and Zachary and Melissa to emerge from the *USS Fidler*, there was a spicy eeriness to his remembrance of the Daguerre photo. But there were lighter memories, too, from his research on early photography. There was an original Daguerreotype in his library at home, a fine portrait of Matt and Arnold Wexler, owners of a photography studio in Philadelphia just before the American Civil War. The immigrants from Dusseldorf, Germany ran the most exclusive studio in town. The business catered to successful merchants and civic leaders and such. Appointments were required for a sitting and every subject wore this or her finest garments. Sea captains and army generals sported epaulets and gleaming brass or silver buttons below their staunch beards. However, for reasons unrevealed to this day, the Wexler partnership collapsed in spiteful sibling rivalry. The original toney downtown shop was abruptly abandoned; some reserved sessions for prominent people were not honored. The brothers then hastily set up competing studios. In the classroom Kevin argued that their new marketing approach created retailing shock waves, a force field that reverberates in Philadelphia to this very day. An approach likely concocted in the heat of 2:00 a.m. anger and disappointment. And the unsheathed sword of a wounded spouse. Instead of 'Wexlers Fine Daguerreotype—by Appointment Only,' solid citizens and the hoi-polloi discovered at the corner at 3rd and Locust Streets a huge, ugly storefront sign that blazed 'King of Daguerreotype' and dead on cattycorner from that a garish orange and black sign for the estranged brother's 'Daguerreotype-City.'

Kevin needed to stifle a guffaw but he was not totally successful. Calm down, he thought, calm down. He tried to focus on his breathing but that was worthless. That was where a belly laugh resides and battling it only makes it more ferocious. More infectious. Makes more of a bubbly, tickling creature that gets what it wants. Hu, ha. Ha, ha, ha, ha. Breathe very slowly, that might help, he cautioned himself. Ha, Ha. Haa…There is air still in this tank, there must be, but Kevin released his right hand from the depth line and could not resist the urge to flail his arms and start to claw his way to the general brightness above him. Where above the waterline the oxygen was infinite and ready to bring him back under control. Where the first gasps of air would triumphantly lift his shoulders out of the water. Buoyant as an empty soda can in the choppy waves. The quicker to get there the better, that would be the way. And it was more than fresh air that awaited him: there was suddenly a fiercely bright light that drew him, white illumination penetrating as a searchlight. This new light was not immediately above him. It was off to one side and increasingly more compelling and alluring by the millisecond. He did not want to risk shooting straight up and missing the light. He tried to move at an angle to get to that precious, luminous place. Oh, this is startling but not exactly painful, Kevin realized. What exhilaration this brought him. So preposterous that fear so weights down our lives, he thought. Upward at a 45-degree angle he pushed his body. Repeatedly kicking his legs, kicking his limbs like an ecstatic frog.

In a way this resembled flying over a national border or momentous frontier on a coal black night. You traverse the official boundary with no conscious sense of the moment of crossing. No declaration over the crackling loudspeaker from the airline co-pilot: "Dr. Kevin O'Donnell, You Are Now Dead." Anticlimactic in some ways. Already you have jettisoned past concerns and to-do lists. You have readjusted your mind to the new conditions lapping at you. So many times he had read about the track of these celestial events: the dearly departed are the first to greet you after you have passed to the next world. Beloved Aunt Beatrice with a radiant smile, and miraculously, all of her original teeth. And yet, harsh judgment for a life improperly lived may still await you. Quite like meeting the capable and affable defense attorney in the marble lobby of the courthouse, morning of the trial. Accept that comfort while you can. Consciousness of this new existence, this new realm, was not particularly expanded for Kevin so far and that surprised him. Maybe that alteration comes in stages, like the gradual and caressing effect of anesthesia before surgery. With the patient zinging her best jokes up to lights out.

It was through modest schools of languid silver fish that Kevin channeled with his determined strokes. No human forms recognizable in them. Perhaps less initiated heavenly hosts play masquerade to shatter the routine. There it was, in drenching sunshine: a vast stadium coddling the saved, the amphitheater a million times the Roman Coliseum in stature and capacity. Monumental stone archways, frosted in gold shavings, vaulted ever upward, as though chasing a bounding Slinky toy in perpetual motion. Kevin's sister had imagined it that way and she was right. Although she did fear an element of boredom among the eternal rewards: the endless singing of laboring hymns from heavy prayer books. In that she was completely wrong. The energy and ambiance was outdoor rock concert with a tinge of deserved smugness. Attendees paid some major levies to get here. Every joyous soul resplendid in their glowing spirit and apparition. No motivation to smoke weed and no one asking, "Do I look fat in this robe?" If they so desired, they probably knew if the Philadelphia Phillies would gain the World Series that autumn. He'd have to remember to ask. And find out how one gathers such knowledge.

No Heavenly Being was yet in his vision but Kevin was patient. Something akin to visiting a sports palace while out of town. You don't know the local traditions all that well. Better to maintain a low profile initially. Leave your Eagles sweatshirt on the hotel room credenza and see how friendly the natives might be. His deceased forebears were equally reticent it seemed. No grandparents or great aunts or uncles or second cousins had emerged from the crowd to meet him so far. Kevin had the feeling that there was the equivalent of a "Will Call Window" that he would have to locate to get himself properly seated. He decided to search for that and scan his vision over the assembled multitude at the same time. While no one was interacting with him, Kevin could at least move at will around the stadium as he search for his Will Call location.

There appeared to be some VIP sections in heaven, scattered throughout the ascending levels of the gigantic stone building. Likely these were for saints canonized officially by the church. Some clusters held celebrity rather than officially venerable souls. Abe Lincoln with his signature top hat; George Washington equally tall at the shoulder blades as the Great Emancipator—make decent power forwards, those two. Probably would play for the Boston Celtics. Nearby congregated Martin Luther King, Jr. and Albert Einstein. It was not ascertainable if FDR was allowed his martini. However well-deserved confidence flowed from his devilishly grinning face. Joshua Lawrence Chamberlain, the Maine lieutenant and later governor who saved the Union cause at Gettysburg's Little Round Top, presented a faraway expression behind the lush mustache. Perhaps he was not fully removed from the prospect of flanking gunfire. World War II diplomat Raull Wallenberg may have had gunfire echoing yet in his cochlea. However he lounged serenely to Chamberlain's left. Kevin had seen but one badly executed photograph of the writer Flannery O'Connor.

There she sat, straight black hair and lupus-free, while holding court for an amused William Shakespeare with her thick Georgian draw.

As he flitted from section to section and level to countless level, Kevin began to spy a few individuals whom he knew personally. No one particularly close to him. This orientation to the afterlife was such a gradual process. Undoubtedly his emotions were still confused. These feelings experienced in his previous life would have appropriately been labeled *uncomfortable*. There was a measure of relief when he saw his best high school history teacher, sitting at attention at the terminus of a balcony. The main textbook that he had selected for their class was worthy of a college course. Then appeared an older gentleman who had for years worked at the local recreation center. The fellow had managed the summer basketball leagues and sometimes honored Kevin by choosing him as assistant scorekeeper. Close by were the two never-married sisters who had lived up the street from his childhood home. In his earliest memory their hair was identically gray and they were as tall as his father. In a lean-to greenhouse extension to their house they nurtured orchids. Out in the back garden they planted gorgeous dahlias and pink hydrangeas. Their wisteria clung to a brown trellis and eased over the perimeter of the kitchen roof. The ladies had kept to themselves generally. However, adorned in their own ghoulish black and silver costumes, for ten years they produced the best neighborhood haunted house for Halloween visitors. Delighted kids and parents had trooped from blocks away to partake in the fun. Glowering carved pumpkins flanked the porch entrance. Electric orange candles blazed in the curtained windows on two stories. Kevin recollected that he had later served as one of the altar boys at their funeral masses. The elderly women had died only seven months apart. Some relative of the deceased had given the young servers five dollars after each funeral. This was a reward usually reserved for wedding ceremonies. *"Dies irae, dies ila,"* warned the small church choir. Day of judgment, day of wrath. This was sung early in the funeral service, just after the priest had blessed the closed coffin. Beads of holy water clung as if magnetized to the smooth metal casket. A mist of the water grazed Kevin's unflinching hands. Something like superstition always barred him from reading the nameplate fastened to the coffin. In his black cassock and white surplice, clutching a white candle easily half his own height, Kevin tried to make his thirteen-year old face look solemn as a bishop's. Meanwhile the severe hymn boomed off of the stain-glass windows. The *day of judgment, the day of wrath* had worked out quite satisfactorily for the women. In addition to the Halloween candy bars, Kevin remembered that a cut glass dish in the haunted house's vestibule held a fortune in quarter-dollars. Before the excited trick-or-treaters could repair to the street to continue their rounds, one of the sisters would raid the dish to add even more ballast to the children's goodies bag.

Kevin was getting closer to the penetrating white light. The vision of the heavenly stadium was rapidly obscured. Despite the powerful illumination, his mind had drifted to the thought that he had not yet heard choral signing or liturgical music. *Nearer my God to Thee* was of the protestant persuasion and not one whose words he knew. It would not be his favorite choice. He did not believe that any particular religion, or even the need for religion, was a prerequisite for heavenly acceptance. But a stanza or two from his own Roman Catholic background would be reassuring in his continuing state of confusion. Nothing from the mournful dirges that they sang during the unending stations-of-the-cross during Lent. An overheated church and wearing a late-season overcoat, the Friday benediction service seemed interminable. Christmas music was too particular; too rooted to the scenery and scents of December. What would cheer him was the one hymn that he looked forward to belting out each March 17th. The practice session for it was the only one when even the most sacrilegious of the guys readily participated. *Great and Glorious Saint Patrick.* And to think that the famous Irish evangelist would be on stage here for the rapturous performance. Hanging loose with his favorite saintly buddies and archangels. Perhaps Michael and Gabriel and Raphael. Do they take requests here? A weight seemed to be lifted from his head and shoulders just as Kevin gleaned the first chords to a stirring song. Another shock to his reeling consciousness.

> Shenandoah
> I long to hear you,
> Away, you rolling river.
> Oh, Shenandoah
> I long to hear you,
> Away, I'm bound,
> Across the wide Missouri.

Was Kevin gazing on heaven through a glass darkly? This was his immediate impression but he was light years off on that. Gradually he realized that he had surfaced from a dive and that he had reentered his normal atmosphere. Stinging salt water jabbed at his nose. A saline odor quickly penetrated the avenues to his sinuses. His vision was partially obscured, but the impediment was a heavily fogged set of diving goggles. He pulled them off with one hand, catching his right ear, managing to sting that, too. Quickly he yanked out his respirator's mouthpiece and started sucking gulps of air. In front of him at a distance of forty feet was a powerboat with three figures standing in a line on the rear deck. They must have been standing on a platform because he could see them from the knees upward. Behind them was another boat. It was projecting an array of commanding spotlights across the people on the first craft. Thrashing his body in a half turn, Kevin found that the *California Gold Rush* was stationary roughly eighty yards away. The choppiness of the waves had subsided considerably. However there was still a gentle swell that raised and lowered him like a set of bobbing shoulders as the ocean moved beneath him. As he looked back at the pair of unidentified boats he heard a strong solo voice and light background music:

> Oh, Shenandoah,
> I love your daughter,
> Away you rolling river,
> Oh, Shenandoah,
> I'll come to claim her.
> Away, I'm bound away,
> Across the wide Missouri.

"That's a wrap," was yelled through a battery-powered megaphone. Then followed a flurry of clapping and shouting from a half dozen people. The three folks on the boat closest to Kevin clasped their hands in dramatic triumph. Wait a second. Kevin's eyes were clear now, and better focused, and he realized what he was encountering as he bobbed lightly as a cork in the Pacific Ocean off of San Diego. The group of performers on the nearest vessel all wore white yachting pants and polo shirts in a deep cherry hue. Two men and one blonde-haired woman. The more hefty of the two men called over to the boat with the spotlights and with what Kevin now realized was professional video equipment. "Let's do the song for our holiday party now," the man said. "We are ready to rock 'm and sock m?'"

It was Lester Lamont of the Geirson Gasket Company who strode one step in front of Ted Mower and Marlene Zekel. All of them with their backs to Kevin. The Gierson people were addressing the video cameras on the companion boat. Silence for a while from all parties, then rock'n'roll music boomed smoothly out of speakers obscured from Kevin's sea level view. O'Donnell recognized the type of music. However he could not place the name of the song since it had never been recorded. Les Lamont stretched out his arms and began to sing nearly identically to Barry White.

> Sail away with me on a sea of love
> Blessing pouring down from heaven above
> Cling we will in any stormy sea
> Days of total bliss
> And nights of extasy

Like a pair of hovering palace guards, Marlene Zekel and Ted Mower stood close behind Les, sweeping out their right hand and then the left in time to the music. Their dance steps were nearly like running in place, effortless and very sensual. Then they came together in a pair, remaining behind Lester, to his right side. Hands clasped, they switched to what seemed to Kevin to be a Latin style of dancing. He was not sure that it matched the rhythm of the soul music particularly well. Yet the steps were performed with great precision. The gentle wash of a passing ship bounced Kevin for a moment; nonetheless he kept his eyes beamed on Ted and Marlene. He watched their knees and counted in his head. Ted had mentioned once that his new daughter-in-law was Hispanic and that she had taught the Mower family a few samba movements. That must be it. Les Lamont's backup dancers moved as fluidly as salt marsh reeds during the draining of the tide. And Kevin would have sworn in a court of law that Ted and Marlene's routine sharply tapped out one, two, three (stop); one, two, three (stop).

CHAPTER SIXTEEN

A few stalks of wheat
By the cold metal railing –
Sunshine and shadows

Michael Van Horn
Bensalem, PA
Born 1964

For seven years Kevin had neglected to send a note to Saul Bellow. Seven years, the reign of a typical untroubled marriage. The time required for the human body to replace every cell, a trillion here and a trillion there. Mr. Bellow had won the Nobel Prize for literature in 1976. Kevin O'Donnell had read his novel *Herzog* a minimum of three times. *You have to fight for your life*, as that book exclaims, had motivated Kevin in many crises. Upon hearing the announcement Kevin had immediately considered writing some of his thoughts to the author. However, desiring to get the words just right, he procrastinated inexcusably. A plague of locusts could run the full cycle of rebirth, crop devastation, abrupt retreat and reappearance since Kevin's initial pledged to correspond with the novelist. In his defense, O'Donnell argued that the rash of immediate responses and congratulatory notes are often self-serving. And insincere. A scurry of activity after the announcement from Stockholm; the countless stuffy invitations and persistent reporters on the telephone. A cunning graduate student looking for a reference and the like. It oddly mirrors the neophyte widow: exhausted from the family's descent on her home for the funeral, with the diner-like meal requirements, now standing motionless as a console table in her vestibule as the cars pull away. Perhaps a pendulum clock there ticks loudly. How to manage her first steps into the lost sanctuary of the house? Some human contact in the following hollow months constitutes a treasure to her. Undoubtedly Saul Bellow would appreciate his unsolicited letter from an unknown reader in a similar vein. Or fold it as a coaster to insulate polished wood from a cold glass, a privilege for Kevin nonetheless.

It was a mid-December Sunday morning at Kevin's house. The temperature was just above freezing and there was strong sunshine. The sunlight highlighted a few high kitchen window-panes in need of washing. Sharing the generous light on the windowsill were red carnations in a tall cylindrical vase. Flowers that Mercedes had grabbed at the supermarket. Mercedes had stayed over on Saturday night; early on Sunday she had left for the airport for a flight to Pittsburgh and a family reunion before Christmas. On December 22nd, she would return to Philadelphia. A recent and positive report from her Ph.D. dissertation committee had her virtually airborne already. Data from the Gierson Gasket Company was extensive and on point. As her trailing shopping cart he had watched her nearly vacuum merchandise off of store shelves. Terrycloth bedroom slippers and bright flannel shirts and one-size-fits-all gloves. Constrained by the parameters of a graduate student's budget, yet Mercedes would distribute holiday gifts to every second cousin. A late season away-game for the Philadelphia Eagles; no need for Kevin to organize sweatshirts and a green jacket and a wool knit hat to head to Veteran Stadium. Endless Sunday newspaper sections and hot food. Dishes and a skillet from his pancake breakfast lay like a tableau of tectonic plates in the stainless-steel sink. When his last coffee mug was empty he would attend to that clutter. His parents were coming for dinner and he must shake the house into order by mid-afternoon. While never discussed with them, he felt a need at times to demonstrate his domestic competency as a not-yet remarried fellow. O'Donnell was in the small library off of the dining room. This was an interior room of the house, where a cheap FM radio that always got muddled reception was whispering classical music. With some effort to drill through a plaster wall, his father might connect a speaker line to the library from the living room stereo. As he sat on a swivel chair he thought that, since it was seven years since the promised letter to Saul Bellow was conceived, getting ideas in perfect order was worth consideration yet.

He figured that he would initiate the letter by recalling the exact time and place when he had first heard of Bellow's Nobel Prize. The genesis and history of every phenomenon, good or bad, was fascinating to Kevin. It was on the East River Drive in Philadelphia as Kevin drove his former laboring Mercury Cougar to his then apartment in suburban Plymouth Meeting. Several of the aging cylinders of his two hundred horsepower motor were firing as weakly as cigarette lighters. Yet he could just keep pace. Late afternoon. Automobiles drawn like magnets toward the declining sun, with growing traffic swerving vigorously and dangerously up the curving park road. The road was obediently attuned to the shape of the meandering Schuylkill River. The Cougar moved at a velocity that diverted even an art connoisseur from appreciating Edward Remington's famous *Cowboy* sculpture. Lincoln Drive, which the road fed into directly, threw even more outlandish curves at you. Lanes more narrow by a quarter, but drivers also consumed these like getaway vehicles. Their private *Wide World Of Sports* venue where the agony of defeat means death. It is the fiercely twisting Wissahickon Creek that Lincoln Drive parallels on the left that creates this challenge. Must have been the all-news station on the car radio that reported on the award. Was it solely coincidence that, not two or three days prior, he had reread Bellow's *Dangling Man*? It was November when he had learned the Nobel Prize news, but he continued to use the rusty charcoal grill on his patio late into the autumn. Kevin had his appetite already set on picking up a salmon filet and a bottle of white wine for dinner. Perhaps a half-dozen forest green asparagus spears to blanch in boiling water. Green vegetable dye, the color of a lime rickey drink, would seep across the bubbling pan. He recalled how he intended to sketch out his letter to Saul Bellow that very evening. Knowing that he may need to keep half a mind on the pinot grigio absorbing a fast chill in the freezer.

No small responsibility this letter, even seven years overdue. It was good that he was still keeping his approach fluid. He would be able to restructure the sections once he had a better compass on the letter's direction. There was a quality Oliveti electric typewriter attending him. The typewriter rested a hand's length away. He pressed the switch to turn it on, maneuvering the sleek quarter-moon shaped button like a miniature see-saw. Prior to this tranquil morning he had noticed how the motor's sound was subtly uneven, prone to tiny accelerations, and there was a discernable variance to its modest volume. But its printing was precise and superb. The classical music station began producing static in short bursts, like Mozart on an electric organ or leftover code for the French Resistance. In abrupt annoyance Kevin shut off the radio. Following immediately was the most recently acquired sound for the house—the padded feet of Lewis'n'Clark. A rapid four-count flamenco beat. From around the edge of a half-open French door the dog's lithe frame appeared. Kevin had slight canine experience for judging, but at times the dog had a mechanical aspect to his gait and movements. Lewis'n'Clark would move his head in a nearly programmed sequence: right turn, leftward sweep, look straight ahead. Exaggerated yawn. Repeat the cycle. But a master of timing in spite of any minor flaws or annoying personality traits. His appearance was a clear signal to Kevin to transport his thinking to the present tense, not get bogged down completely in the delicious sinkholes and sugary caverns of history. Dogs, Kevin had heard, had a viable memory of eight weeks at most. To Lewis'n'Clark the dawn of recorded time was the beginning of last month. Supporting evidence would be the sliding halt the dog makes during a wild ball chase to grab a cluster of dry cereal. Although there was that one recent instance when his pet stared at Kevin's new garage with...what...longing? The letter to Mr. Bellow would likely benefit from assuming an equally current perspective.

Well, I have had a smashing good year, Mr. Bellow, and how is it with you? More accurate to say that, at a minimum, these have been 'interesting times' for me. I am in an end-of-year stocktaking mood that visits my consciousness about December 15th. Shut down for business until the winter solstice. Taking emotional inventory. But what a ridiculous start to the correspondence that would be. Since the gentleman has no knowledge of his existence, precious attention from Mr. Bellow should not be exhausted on chattering details of his life. This was like a slush pile resume or a section of unsolicited marketing material. Flickering moments at most to detain the interest of the reader. The initial two pages of a book are the hardest to compose, he had heard Saul Bellow say on a television interview. A diluted form of comfort to Kevin now, but that does not propel the letter for as little as one paragraph. Must still bait a hook with some intriguing and wriggling morsel.

How, Mr. Bellow, can we reconcile the American adoration of luxury and wealth and comfort with the tenacity and sacrificial spirit demanded of a great power? If the price of freedom is eternal vigilance, can we maintain that posture from a Barcalounger? Kevin had recently learned that an American easy chair firm had contracted with the Department of Defense to provide seats for Abram's and M-60 tanks. Solid lumbar support as American armor faces the Russian hordes across lush German meadows and farmland. Was it not a much fiercer spirit in the Nazi U-boat crews in their unheated, weakly ventilated and Spartan submarines? The gray tubes struggled to plow at ten knots through cold and black Atlantic Ocean waves. One of the two narrow lavatories on board was typically commandeered to store valuable potatoes. The human miasma that reeked from the subs upon return to port in Bremen would sicken dockworkers for days. But then again, the German side lost, and almost all of their U-boat *kriegsmarine* were killed. And during World War II, Japanese officials mocked the idea that American sailors could withstand equatorial Pacific heat on long submarine tours. Who would ever know? In air-conditioned relief, the U.S. Navy subs patrolled for endless months and systematically demolished the Japanese merchant marine.

This would not suffice. Back to the personal approach for the letter. However something more intriguing than earlier. Kevin retreated from the library chair and strolled to the living room of his house. This room was in minor disarray but it was consoling to him nonetheless. Leaning against the taupe sofa and two matching chairs were four poster-size photographs of San Francisco. Kevin had angled them to remain shaded from the sunlight, to preclude fading of the images. This hewed to the advice of the camera shop owner where he had the enlarged pictures mounted on poster board. The professional results were destined for exhibition at the Kilmartin Museum, in St. Joseph, immediately after the New Year. To provide haphazard pedestals, three or four volumes of the 1960 *Encyclopedia Britannica* elevated each photograph above the hardwood floor. The bindings of the encyclopedias were leather and shaded in deep burgundy. They were adorned with gold lettering slightly cracked from wear. The pictures were black-and-white shots from early April, 1906. The view was from the San Francisco Bay. Stretched to a size of three by five feet, there was a suggestion of graininess in the photos. However, it was not severe enough to diminish enjoyment of the content: a harbor with boats under sail and vessels with smokeless steam funnels, and buildings constructed with trim brick or with elegant granite blocks, some structures climbing eight stories in height. Lacking was the slightest hint that the earth would violently shudder and fracture the buildings like walnuts two days hence. Ships' cargo awaited stevedores on the deserted docks and the narrow piers. The commerce of the globe endlessly commuting through the Golden Gate. Steinway pianos and Disston commercial saws exchanged for coffee beans and delicate porcelain crockery. Behind the dockyards, streets climbed substantial hills until they disappeared as faint lines into the intermediate distance. Streetlamps were housed in containers resembling giant water jars. They reminded Kevin of a Parisian cityscape. The exposures represented four of six shots that would create a panorama of the city from the perspective of the bay. Missing were the second panel from the left and the sixth panel, intended for the far right. Despite the absent elements, the panorama held together convincingly. The blown-up shots were reproductions of the glass plates hauled to the surface by Mercedes and her two companion divers. This was accomplished with great care and effort and in nerve stretching danger back in June. Uncle Philip's glass plates were stacked out of order in Captain Bulwer's trunk. Salt water had thoroughly corroded the images of the bottom two plates that Bulwer had stored in his sea-going container. Only a palimpsest of scattered and indecipherable etched lines had survived on those glass sheets. The other four plates were rescued in near-perfect condition.

How to react to this treasure trove with the two vanished photographic siblings? In effect, two of the children had been sacrificed. Fed inexorably to the eroding sea so that the other four would survive. Dr. Kevin O'Donnell playing the academic game without a full deck of cards, some of his less praiseworthy colleagues might intone. "It's just like the Roman Coliseum," thundered Dr. Bob Goodall in Kevin's cramped office back at the university. Bob was given to doffing non-regulation summer clothes when he did not have a summer class. He was wearing a pith helmet and a tee shirt and safari short pants, looking scarecrow tall in Kevin's narrow office. "More precious from what is stripped away," Bob declared. "You have to use your imagination." Kevin had returned to Philadelphia in thick July heat. On his lap on the airplane he had cradled the photographs wrapped in chamois cloth and resilient packing material. During the monotonous flight, only the children passengers received equally fervent attention as his historic pictures. He waved off any refreshment and he hid the plates under a cotton airline blanket against his excited stomach during the landing. Kevin had arranged the glass plates in his office on the back of a cleared bookshelf. He leaned the plates cautiously against a previously dusty blue wall, angled like a model of a lean-to greenhouse. Despite the heat and the inoperative air conditioning system, Kevin had squeezed the sole office window nearly closed. He did so as though to thwart a violent squall from Tahiti or a mindless Kansas tornado from crashing in to destroy his artifacts.

Goodall's exclamations had a strong impact on Kevin's feelings. Touching in the lack of jealousy, assuming there was research value in this O'Donnell family hoard. Bob Goodall's critique was one that he could incorporate into the letter to Saul Bellow. His friend passionately argued that the Coliseum of ancient Rome is more spectacular because one can observe it very guts, the layers of brick walls that raised the stands for the 55,000 howling spectators. The formidable exterior stone wall of the Coliseum dominates the travel brochures and picturesque calendars. However, it is the labyrinth of interior brick walls and supports, varying in color and texture and pattern, and the patchwork of marble blocks and white cement filling that takes away the breath of the reverent visitor. It is as though the building process is frozen two-thirds of the way through the ancient construction project. Emerging from the cool shadows of the massive travertine archways, the entering tourist is instantly awed by the soaring levels of brick walls and facades. The walls are cloaked in different colors like layers of geologic sediment, the edifice now reflecting the warmth of the noontime sun. Vanished is the almond-shaded rock surface that was employed to conceal the brick construction. Three-quarters of the amphitheater floor is also removed, revealing the subterranean corridors where a scourge of malevolence may forever stalk. Open to close view from walkways is the underground, fetid warren of cages for wild animals and cells for gladiators and public enemies. The equally aged Roman Pantheon, said Goodall, is an incomparable jewel despite the building's colossal strength. The lowest supporting walls are twenty feet thick. Its marble flooring is as indestructible as diamond material while its colors are precious gold strands and floating lavender fields. However it is so perfectly preserved in its role as a historic Catholic church that it is less recognizably human.

Kevin had invited Professor Goodall to join an early Christmas season dinner party at Tony Connelli's house the previous weekend. Goodall was apparently dumbstruck at the shenanigans around the extended dining room table—present also were Vic Kesson and Maxine and Mercedes—although Bob was tightlipped about this in the intervening seven days. Kevin surmised that Gloria was living with Tony, given her intimate feel for the location of linen napkins in a cherry wood lowboy and her ease in preparing the best Caesar salad on earth. How could you make such a divine dish as a guest? She flitted in and out of the refrigerator and the pantry a dozen times. What was that ingredient that made it so special, so delicious? He wanted to prepare the identical salad for his parents. In his mind—triggered by Goodall's interaction with Tony and Vic—Kevin played with a vignette that he might share in the letter with Mr. Bellow.

It seems that the prime contractor on the Roman Coliseum brickwork back in A.D. 79 was Antoni Connellius. The job estimator was his faithful Germanic slave, Victorius Kessonium. They were called 'Toni" and 'Vic" to their faces by the movers and shakers in the Tiber River Contractors' Association. Behind their backs they were given the same nicknames by their allegedly ramshackle workforce. Bushy, veteran eyebrows were raised when Toni and Victorius breezed in late to the mandatory pre-bid conference conducted in an antechamber in the Forum. A problem with a façade on an aqueduct repair they had vehemently blamed on faulty specifications. It was in an earthquake zone moreover. It attached a taint to their fledgling firm nonetheless. Contemptuous the competitors might have been at the meeting, but

Toni's firm won the mammoth contract for the brick work on the Roman Coliseum. Victorious Kessonium's acquired Latin was quite fluent. However he was hung over from red wine from a Bacchus festival and he had inadvertently inserted the builder's guarantee as twenty *centuries* rather than twenty years in their proposal. Now that is the spirit of an endlessly expanding Roman Empire. His mistake clinched the deal for the Connelius company. Toni was furious at his slave. Mighty H. Jove, he exclaimed in his domineering voice. What morons would believe that this playground boondoggle would be anything more than forgotten dust in 2,000 years? Then the first bags of denarii were deposited into his bank account by the Roman senate. Perhaps he was being a *tad* hasty. Probably could be a little more conscientious on this project after all. Not easy to translate this concept to his bricklayers most likely. The officious building inspector looked askance at every step of the interior construction of the Roman Coliseum. Toni's horde of workmen arrived daily looking unwashed and disheveled. They carried a lunch of goat cheese and hard bread in soiled burlap sacks. They tossed apple cores into unsightly piles at their feet and they were known to place banana peels on the top of marble staircases. At the noontime meal break they played childish games of brick tag and kill-the-man-with-the-brick. With torn togas and leather straps ripped from their sandals the workers would return to their tasks, still hurling raucous insults at each other. On a continual basis Toni observed the bricklaying progress. His employees' work was excellent and creative in resolving unimaginable problems and he could not have improved upon it, despite the occasional chaos that he endured during the day. Under pressure to meet the 80 A.D. deadline,

Antoni was required to hire as a subcontractor the outfit of Alveti the Younger. Each dawn Alveti's disciplined employees marched the three leagues from Chestoronia on the Appian Way, moving in precise formation, establishing a sort of Praetorian Guard for that firm's spotless reputation. Alveti the Younger managed his small crew from neat daily ledgers written on crisp scrolls that were to Toni absolutely prissy. Luckily, Toni was able to assign them to a scattering of minor projects on the Coliseum. One morning the building inspector said to Toni, "I am shocked at the patterns that the Connellius workers are playing out on the growing amphitheater walls. Their results are positively whimsical, I tell you. Whimsical in the swirls and imitation of cumulous clouds or tossing heads of wheat on a sunny day in the country. Radiant sunbursts of joy shout from the crowns of brick archways throughout the building site. And terra cotta rain gutters reach out like fingers to tickle the patrons as they would head for their seat to watch gladiators fight to an agonizing death. This levity must stop immediately. The Emperor will not tolerate such frivolity and insolence." Up to his gizzard with these kinds of puny complaints, Toni Connellius finally grabbed his tormentor by the tunic, thumped him repeatedly on the chest and said, "Listen, Pasqualebus. Let me tell you how this works. You pay your money. You get your brick walls. You don't ask a lot of questions."

Probably not the most auspicious way to launch his letter. He would keep this material as background for the moment. Kevin was now standing in the small pantry off of his kitchen. The walk-in closet was colder than the rest of the house. He held his coffee mug against his polo shirt as though that might warm him. Impossible to maintain an older home in a uniform condition. On narrow shelves his spice collection was clustered rather than organized; he was searching through the bottles and jars for a clue. Just what did Gloria use in her Caesar salad that made it different and better than his usual recipe? It wasn't coriander or cinnamon or rosemary or ground garlic. Every homemade Caesar salad uses fresh garlic. He already was familiar with Worcester sauce and extra virgin olive oil. Soy sauce or balsamic vinegar would be much too salty or bitter. He watched her coddle an egg but that was a standard ingredient. Gloria had trimmed her blonde hair since the summer, and she had minimized the curls, giving her what Kevin thought was a more chic appearance. While she moved swiftly around the space, Gloria exhibited a lot of grace in a kitchen run by another woman just a few years earlier. How different were so many things since Kevin first met Gloria. Perhaps that was what distracted him from completely remembering her salad recipe. But he had also rotated in and out of Tony Connelli's kitchen. Mercedes and Bob Goodall were his invitees and it was impolite to leave them unattended.

Kevin decided to finish the half-cup of coffee that remained in the pot. He had to get to work. However he milked a continuing coffee break as a timeout from the real world. The house needed straightening before he launched dinner preparations. Out in his new, still-uncluttered garage lay shopping bags of holly branches drenched in shiny red berries, and lengths of pine roping coiled like snakes in green fringe. Soaking moisture in a plastic bucket, and resting upright against intersecting walls was a sumptuous, fresh Christmas tree. If the water in the bucket had frozen around the stump he would use a claw hammer to crack it loose. Kevin went ten dollars over his budget when he bought the tree. Secretly proud of his high living room ceiling, Kevin picked a Norwegian spruce that would dramatize the height. Maybe not a good day to place it on a stand and trim it since he might need extra lights and ornaments, the tree was that zaftig. He wanted to delight Mercedes with his Christmas décor and create a uniquely festive atmosphere for his home. She was planning to spend the Christmas weekend at his house. They would be heading into their sophomore year in a relationship so to speak. Kevin felt a need to rekindle the excitement that had stirred him when they first met nearly one year before.

This was a topic that might interest Saul Bellow. Kevin was deeply satisfied with the relationship so far but he was not certain if it was true love. If such a condition exists. Whom do you ask? What is the supporting evidence? Is true love even necessary? Mercedes remained perplexed by his snap decision to bury the Ghost Dance pictures in the desert north of Sante Fe, New Mexico. Kevin valued it as the wisest and least selfish action of his life, professional and otherwise. It resembled Ulysses commanding himself strapped to the galley's mast while he listened to the transcendental joy of the Lorelei singing. Like the Greek hero, Kevin had momentarily experienced the sweetness and the otherworldly electricity without cascading destruction all around him. Mercedes shook her head for a while at his inept scuba diving during the rescue of Captain Bulwer's trunk. Luckily for him the attractive lights of the Gierson Gasket Company video shoot had slowed his ascent and prevented him suffering the deadly bends. The best way to share the truth about that incident still eluded him. However, when the old San Francisco photos were revealed, Mercedes said that his persistence was admirable and that she was pleased to be part of the salvage operation. Undoubtedly they were adjusting to the possibility of a long-term commitment and that brings critical thinking to bear. Not all possible prenuptial agreements or considerations get reduced to writing. As though weighing the evidence in an important trial, Kevin still wrestled with the appropriateness of buying the Hamilton tank watch for Mercedes. It was not the money; the classic watches are a fantastic value. She was very independent about money and he strongly supported that. And nothing had changed on how quick they were to slip each other's clothes off when the opportunities emerged.

What concept of time did Mr. Bellow embrace? That might be a worthy opening gambit for the Bellow letter. Can we live only in the moment? Or perhaps time is something that must be appreciated by reflection as Marcel Proust had written. Kevin essentially accepted the argument that a focus on the moment brings great personal rewards. The reduction of self-consciousness and the melting away of anxiety, like chunks of dreary ice tumbling from a pitched roof. But he was not willing to forgo the past. Many events in his life appeared more preposterous or meaningful or enjoyable across a chasm of time. He could not be like Lewis'n'Clark, mister no-time-like-the present, scrounging in his bowl for crouton-shaped cereal, while a black racquetball ricocheted between his white paws. Kevin's house on Walnut Lane had candelabra on end tables and bookshelves, curving lead crystal pieces that are laden with red or emerald holiday candles. When he extinguished the tapers the waxy smell of the smoke plume would make him twelve years old again. As a Boy Scout, he always made Christmas lanterns from empty tuna cans that he covered with crimson felt. In each can he placed a short green candle and a cheap glass chimney bought at Woolworths. His aunts would pay four dollars a pop for them, a lovingly absurd markup. And while we are absorbed so fully in the moment, phenomena not of our making are striding on gigantic legs, intent on delivering us good or ill. The Eagles quarterback focused on his streaking receivers is a half-moment away from a blindside tackle. As an acquaintance in the university's astronomy department liked to say—the woman was perennially ranked in the top echelon of Halley's Comet experts—"What goes around, comes around."

The dining room in his house was essentially under control. The kitchen and living room would need the lion share of his attention this afternoon. On the dining room table were information sheets from Monahan's Reality in Ocean City, New Jersey. Light blue and peach colored sheets outlined the facilities of the rental homes. You learned the realtor's shorthand for air conditioning and the dishwasher and the number of whole and partial bathrooms. Mercedes and Kevin were considering renting a house in Ocean City for a week or more the following July. Two or three bedrooms and at a minimum of two baths. Guests are a high probability. Customer traffic requires that one visit the town in November or December to scope out and hook the best deals. Kevin was prepared to pay at least two-thirds of the rent. He was partial to the Golden Mile area. Something near 28th Street, and close to the ocean. On the Saturday after Thanksgiving they drove down in his Camaro, riding loosely bundled in winter parkas. With a large envelope filled with tagged house keys obtained from the realtor, they cruised around to inspect the properties. Except for curbside puddles from Friday's rainstorm—water did not drain well in the barrier island town—they could roll to a parking place anywhere Kevin desired. There would be scores of cars fighting for the parking near the beach eight months later. On most of the long blocks even the substantial brick homes were deserted for the cold season. There was a deliciously forlorn feeling to the buildings under winter wraps. A plump seagull stands at the apex of a peaked roof on one of the dwindling number of small cottages in Ocean City. Mammoth single homes with countless balconies, and garages for three cars, and duplexes, and four-unit residential properties were demolishing the quaint buildings. A sentimental watchman then is the bird, arrayed in his natural uniform of gray and white. A residue of rainwater clings to the weathered brown shingles of the roof, forming a faint outline like a map of a nameless Asian landmass. Cool air surprises the prospective renter upon pushing open the tight front door of the units. Kevin and Mercedes had shrieked with laughter at each other's incompetence with the unfamiliar keys. Doorknobs for bedrooms and metal cabinets handles are cool to the touch. While the homes and duplexes have heating equipment, the visitor checking properties is not permitted to adjust the low-set thermostat. On sea-facing decks, particularly on the second floor, a bracing wind caresses Kevin's exposed ears. The chill compels him to retreat inside through the sticky glass doors, abandoning each deck within five minutes of arrival.

He felt that he was getting some traction finally. Kevin would be able to leap into the letter at any moment. The classic O'Donnell tactic of circling his target. Then strike, strike hard. Ocean City, New Jersey was one of the centers of the universe for him. As a child in the 1950's he had vacationed there with his parents and grandparents. In the 1960's he spent high school Senior Week with his closest friends in the shore town, inventing fun. Chased by the over-vigilant cops along the speeding boardwalk for God knows what. Impossible now to walk a bare-foot half-mile on the shoreline on a summer afternoon, marking his position vis-a- vis soaked stone jetties and angular fishing piers, without accosting someone he knew. And what he called 'near connections' with people were beyond account: the people who vacationed there before you made their acquaintance. So close in time and proximity and yet you did not intersect personally. Kevin realized that so much surrounds a person that will never be recognized. On several occasions Kevin witnessed the annual Night in Venice boat parade along the inland waterway that parallels Ocean City. Vic Kesson had once described to Kevin how he and Tony Connelli officially entered the parade one sultry July. Their application claimed that their theme was the Mystery of the Adriatic Sea. Victor owned a powered sailboat so that was an excellent stage. They had persuaded a few friends and some of Vic's nephews to act as galley slaves. The follows had stripped to the waist and were allotted with genuine lifeguard oars and black cardboard chains, while Victor beat a huge drum for timing and Tony flailed a thick leather belt for motivation. Jealousy alone must have deprived them of a prize; Vic reported that he was certain that the partying spectators ate up their hilarious performance.

Nearly time to start the letter to the novelist Saul Bellow. O'Donnell lacked an address for the author. However he viewed that as a detail to be resolved upon the correspondence's completion. Someone in the English Department at the university would assist him. The Ocean City contribution would be beneficial, help him get started and assuage his mind from the frustration of remembering the missing Caesar salad ingredient. Some pungent cheese other than Romano? He did not think so. Anyway, Kevin had a personal and professional fascination with the battle of Gettysburg of the American Civil War. In early June of each year he would recollect how the Confederate Army of Northern Virginia had initiated its slow drive in June, 1863 from Culpepper, Virginia to Gettysburg, Pennsylvania. The campaign started a month before the battle. The southerners' best chance for total victory was in the balance. Cavalry general and cavalier Jeb Stuart had barely hung on at Brandy Station versus Union cavalry a few days earlier. A patent indication that it was time to completely dishearten the Federals. Otherwise evolving and thunderous northern might would ultimately prevail. At least 64,000 Confederate troops moved north with General Robert E. Lee. This equates to the attendance at a packed Eagles game at Veterans Stadium in Philadelphia. During a quieter moment at a home game, Kevin sometimes thought of this analogy as he scanned the vast stands from his seat high up in Section 723. This entire boisterous crowd migrating toward blood and battle to settle the issues and the fate of a continent. Odd the secret things that he so cherished in his mind. During a timeout in the game his seatmate and friend Hugh Kirsterini would be asking about getting some food or a couple more beers. But Kevin was in Commander-mode and was thinking about how he would swing the entire lower deck attendance as infantry up the left side of the Potomac River, feinting at Washington, D.C. and frightening the populace, while the 30,000 upper deck crazies like himself would proceed undetected northward through the pastoral Shenandoah Valley. They would shepherd the slow-moving wagon trains and the field artillery, obscuring the chocking dust of mules and horses on dirt roads behind the misty peaks of the Blue Ridge Mountains. The two columns might converge like powerful rivers before Harrisburg, the Pennsylvania state capitol. The Confederate army maximizing political as well as military advantage. Responding to an uncharacteristically demonstrative General Lee, the butternut and gray-clad host could cheer, "Give me a C...O...N...F...E...D." Then he realized that Hugh was waiting for an answer; he asked him to grab some crackerjack or a bag of shelled peanuts.

Every visit to the Gettysburg battlefield gave him profound chills. Ice of glacial strength swept through his tendons and muscles, nourishing flushed skin down his shoulders and on to his quadriceps. Culp's Hill, the Wheatfield, Seminary Ridge. The Devil's Den. Big Roundtop and Little Roundtop. Kevin imagined seeing acres of field hospital tents. A low moan hovered around the canvas shelters like foul ground fog. Over 50,000 casualties in three days' fighting. Half expecting ghosts to tap him on the shoulder, trying to shag a light, dour couriers in black chesterfields commissioned by Abraham Lincoln. On a walk along Cemetery Ridge, the target of Pickett's Charge, more accurately called Longstreet's Assault, Kevin was moved to count his strides across the assault's target: the ground immediately flanking the Copse of Trees. A healthy stride over the glistening lush turf was roughly a yard in length. By his walking measurement, it was less than a quarter of a mile that defined the critical southern objective. What is labeled the High Water Mark of the Confederacy was reached on the ground that he measured. And thrown brutally back on itself in horrific carnage. On a breezy summer day, Kevin observed that his top destination when he was a young fellow in Ocean City was a strip of boardwalk running a quarter-mile in length. Pretending to be lost in thought, Kevin monitored his steps to survey this distance, silently counting his steps exactly as he had in Gettysburg. He started at 9th and the Boardwalk, where the old music hall jutted due seaward on stout pilings. The building might have floated in from an English coastal town. Disappointed tourists in Bristol, riveted to the strand and scratching their heads saying, What the Heck? Except for that structure, the beach side of the boards was devoid of buildings for a hazy mile or more. Across the way was Kohr Brothers Soft Ice Cream and along the stretch going south were Mack and Manco's Pizza and Shriver's Salt Water Taffy and Morrow's Nut House and near the end of his four hundred forty yard stroll, the genteel Moorlyn movie theater. He had seen the movie *Johnny Tremaine* there when he was seven years old, a major thrill. A ghost of Kevin would forever walk this section of the beach town. If only he had a wayback machine and could travel to Gettysburg on the eve of the decisive Civil War conflict. He might have persuade both combatants to switch their target, shift 150 miles to the east, to the quarter-mile of space anchored at 9th and the Boardwalk in Ocean City. Bring the bride, bring the kids, hog out on thin crust pizza and foaming birch beer. Leave strawberry Popsicle sticks glistening with sand crystals in their wake rather than shattered limbs and congealed blood. Ocean City, New Jersey did not exist in 1863. The town was founded in the 1880s by Methodist ministers. Nevertheless, the throng of blue and gray troops could have cooked out with bleached driftwood on the unincorporated sand dunes, and among the clusters of struggling pine trees, and then gently serenaded each other with *Tenting on the Old Camp Ground Tonight*.

Everything that Kevin was floating for the letter to Saul Bellow revolved around questions. That was a mark of respect. The author would educate him on one or more potentially weighty topics. The nature of the topic may lack significance; there was no hierarchy establishing the questions' value. It was the *process* of asking that mattered. So here goes: Mr. Bellow, what is your recipe for Caesar salad? Have you ever consumed an exceptional meal in a restaurant and the management dances around the question of the ingredients used? A phalanx of smiles guarding proprietary recipes. So frustrating for the customer. Kevin did not have Gloria's telephone number and it seemed foolish to call Tony Connelli about this dilemma. Sometimes it is the minor key that is most haunting to the listener. Without that one missing ingredient he would not tackle Caesar salad again. An example of how he felt impacted his beliefs concerning the space odyssey that he had lectured about in April. The time capsule space shot. Professor Bob Goodall had provided consulting support to NASA for that enterprise. Goodall had suggested the use of Beethoven's Ninth Symphony for the golden music disk. Advancing technology—science does march on—had reduced the physical space required to capture the four movements of the classical piece. There was an opportunity to add some short work to the disk, something needing little playing time. NASA refused to waste any useable space for its time capsule. Bob pursued Kevin's advice. 'Pack every rift with ore,' the poet Keats had demanded, spurring Kevin into prompt action. Even a minor composition could be important. A worthy contrast to Beethoven would be rock and roll. On the telephone Kevin sought the wisdom of the radio disk jockey, Hy Lit. This was the first ever conversation between them. After a half-minute of consideration, Hy said decisively to Kevin, "Add Jackie Wilson's 'Your Love is Lifting Me Higher' to the time capsule. It brings a nice Philadelphia connection and it is about the best song even conceived in the genre." Jackie Wilson's smash hit was added to the outermost groves of the disk, immediately after Beethoven's symphony, and was thereby launched into space. Kevin harbored the optimism that the song would be amplified at the correct speed, and that the Lugar Ruling Council would revoke the life-long exile imposed on musical critic Lugnut. Allow their Dante to return to Florence. Perhaps the upbeat Wilson song would become an unofficial political or spiritual anthem on the distant planet. A more positive emotion, a gentle force to nudge the course of history toward fellowship, and love, in that oftentimes cruel world.

Kevin had flicked on the television set that due to a miracle of engineering and luck conveniently fit under a kitchen cabinet. The pre-game shows for the National Football League had just started. The Eagles were eliminated from playoff contention but he maintained interest in their game today, and in many others around the league.

So much less excitement than he experienced in January 1981, almost three years ago, when he had driven to Philadelphia's Veteran Stadium for the playoff game between the Eagles and the Dallas Cowboys. The winner of the contest would move to the penultimate championship game, the Superbowl. That would be staged in New Orleans. His friend Hugh Kirsterini already had his airplane tickets for the trip. Traffic from the crowd going to the Eagles-Cowboys playoff game had flooded the streets around the stadium by late morning. In fits and starts, and a million shifts of the new Camaro's gears, Kevin had inched his way to his favorite parking lot on Broad Street, across from the stadium. Overhead, birds in deep black feathers were aligned on telephone wires like the formation for an offensive play. On the telephone lines the birds telegraphed an obvious aerial attack: no running backs behind the quarterback, wide receivers split. The late December and the January playoff games were conducted in biting, raw cold in Philadelphia. Kevin and Hugh wore layers of protection and hooded parkas. Kevin carried a small thermos of tea—best drink to keep him warm—which he smuggled passed the security guards. It was impermissible to sneak in hard objects that might become missiles if the game turned ugly. Section 723 sat on the upper deck, past the endfield on the western side of the ballpark. The Eagles won the game rather convincingly; Kevin felt comfortable about the outcome going into the second half of the contest. There was one gorgeous run by halfback Wilbert Montgomery charging around the right side that Kevin would visualize forever. Wilbert's feet prancing at enormous speed along the sideline, just staying in fair territory by Kevin's eyesight, ripping a dagger wound into the Cowboys with a thirty yard gain. Late in the game occurred something that rarely happened to Kevin—he regretted *not* doing something. Was this a phenomenon that should be brought into the still unwritten letter to Saul Bellow? No. Avoid negative emotions. The Eagles were well in command of the game when this had happened; victory was nearly assured. A surprising stretch of quiet had blanketed the crowd for a few minutes, just a mellow hum from all directions. It was probably a long timeout for television advertisements. A single voice in the crowd suddenly rang out against the muted background. "Super—Bowl," shouted the deep voice of one perceptive fan, getting everyone's attention. At that invitation, 64,000 tender, tender hearts, nourished with Eagles-green blood, jumped up and rocked the building with echoes upon echoes of "Super—Bowl." I wished that I had been the initiator of that fabulous moment, Kevin often thought, rather than a jubilant member of the chorus.

This recollection, however, brought him one useful item. It reminded Kevin of the hotdogs that Hugh had bought at halftime. Steamed hotdogs covered in mustard. Spicy Dijon mustard, that was the last ingredient that he was in search of from Gloria's Caesar salad. Terrific. Well, so much to do: straighten the house; dig in the refrigerator for the spicy mustard; check on a clean shirt for dinner. Move the San Francisco photos to make comfortable space available for his parents in the living room. And the Saul Bellow letter. Kevin just about skipped to the study and slid into the chair by the typewriter. The electric power was on and he twirled in a quality piece of white stationary. He finally knew everything that he should say to the author. In one blast of typing he actually set it down in the Oliveti's beautiful print, taking no time at all: 'Dear Mr. Bellow,' Kevin wrote, 'Congratulations. Congratulations!'

Epilogue

I will never forget for as long as I live and breathe, Victor Kesson told a friend in the construction business, of the time that Tony Connelli and I saw the Eagles play Dallas to get to the Superbowl, back in '81. Our Eagles were winning in the third quarter and the fans were unusually quiet for about two minutes. Suddenly, Tony leaps up, and in that famous bellow of his, shouts out "Super—Bowl." It absolutely brought down the house.

Made in the USA
Middletown, DE
29 November 2022

16056974R00215